I0636429

THE SULTAN'S
HAREM
MYSTERIES

THE SULTAN'S HAREM MYSTERIES

DRINK THE GREEN WATER

THE MILKMAID'S MILLIONS

Hugh Austin

COACHWHIP PUBLICATIONS

Greenville, Ohio

The Sultan's Harem Mysteries, by Hugh Austin
© 2022 Coachwhip Publications edition

Drink the Green Water published 1948
The Milkmaid's Millions published 1948
Hugh Austin Evans, 1903-1964
CoachwhipBooks.com

ISBN 1-61646-524-7
ISBN-13 978-1-61646-524-7

DRINK THE GREEN WATER

or,

Young Caldwell's Toe

1

Life & Letters. A Senior Partner and a Surviving Partner. A Proper Employee and an Improper Secretary. Significant Reminiscences. Young Caldwell's Toe. A File Clerk Delivers Fatal Letters. The Sad Death of a Barrister.

Since he could have a chat about the dead and those who were soon to die, Mr. Henry Harrison Perdue had decided that it would be both gracious and enjoyable for him to answer the inquiry of Young Sultan's Boy in person. "In compiling the Life & Letters of my uncle, the late Horace Seneca Sultan," Young Sultan's Boy had written to him, "I find in his papers the copies of a series of letters to you, and certain replies from you, beginning the 21st. inst. of July, 1888. . . ." And he had not been unflattered to learn that Horace Seneca Sultan had preserved, and so presumably had treasured, his letters for a matter of fifty-eight years until his death, or fifty-nine years to the current date of the 21st inst. of July, 1947.

He had been particularly flattered in view of the fact that their friendship, as friendships sometimes do, had petered out a quarter of a century gone. Indeed, upon reflection, he had recalled that it had ended abruptly in the fall of '22, when Horace, at the dangerous age no doubt,

had gone quite mad and voted Democratic, against Hard-
ing. But, as the flattering preservation of his letters had
induced a sentimental mood, Henry Harrison Perdue had
dismissed that painful memory with the decision that since
Horace was now dead he might be forgiven, and with that
charitable thought he had continued on his way around
the corner from the entrance of the building housing the
law offices of Debrosses, Perdue & Party to the entrance
of the building housing the law offices of Sultan, Sultan
& Sultan.

He had then, as abruptly as had been the breaking of
his friendship with Horace Seneca Sultan, come to a stop
on the sidewalk in that old sector of the financial district.
A fastidiously and stiffly dressed wisp of a man of eighty,
he had stood there surrounded by an aura of such impeccable but charming dignity that he might have remained
even through the rush hour without having been jostled by
even the most hurrying New Yorker.

It had suddenly occurred to him that his erring friend,
the *uncle* of Young Sultan's Boy, had been Young Sultan.
To a man whose pride it was that he carried in his memory
a forest of family trees, if at least three-fourths deadwood
as is peculiar to that variety of timber, it had been disconcerting to wonder if he had grafted a twig on the wrong
branch. The answer, as in his long life he had found it to
be to so many problems, was time.

Chronologically, he need go back no further than that
contemporary of his own father's, *Mr.* Sultan, the survivor
of Sultan & Sewell, who had founded the firm of Sultan &
Sultan with his son, Horace Seneca Sultan, and Horace—
dear old boy! dear old boy! even if he had voted—had been
known as Young Sultan. *Then,* and that would be some fifteen years later, his younger brother—fifteen years younger,
they had women in those days! Women, ah, women. . . .
Oh, yes—the younger brother on had been taken into the

firm and its name had been expanded to Sultan, Sultan &
Sultan, comprising in order, *Mr.* Sultan, Young Sultan &
Young Sultan's Brother. *Then,* and that would be in the
fall of '15, *Mr.* Sultan had gone to his fathers, a fine old
gentleman and particularly sound on codicils, and in the
course of time Young Sultan had become known as *Mr.*
Sultan, and his younger brother, Juvenal—Juvenal—Juvenal *Cato* Sultan, had in his turn become known as Young
Sultan. And *he* was the one who had had the Boy! And so,
after all, Young Sultan's Boy *was* the son of Young Sultan,
the second brother in point of time to be known by that
name and the first to die. Indeed, he had departed this life
with his wife, via an automobile accident, when so very
young, under forty, that he, Henry Perdue, had scarcely
known the lad.

This reflection had brought Mr. Henry Harrison Perdue to another pause in the very doorway of the building
that was the address of Sultan, Sultan & Sultan. After having anticipated a pleasant half hour of reminiscences of
the dear and long departed, it had been something of a jolt
to realize that Young Sultan's Boy was in cold sober truth
not only very young, possibly even not more than thirty-
five, but also had been born into a generation without
either dignity of its own or respect for that of its elders.
True, true, for the senior partner of Debrosses, Perdue &
Party to call upon the surviving partner of Sultan, Sultan
& Sultan was entirely fitting and proper and could entail
no loss of dignity on his part provided the house of Sultan, Sultan & Sultan had not lost *its* traditional dignity.
In this day and age, however, he had feared that he might
be in for some unpleasant surprises.

He had found some encouragement in the thought that
at least Young Sultan's Boy had not *moved the offices*. Mr.
Henry Harrison Perdue classed *moving the offices* with
moving one's father's grave just for the sport of it. Yet he

had known it to be done. He had actually known the third
or fourth generation, soulless young whippersnappers, to
move the offices to some modern building in some more
modern part of the town, in one horrible case even to
Radio City. He had learned what that portended. He had
learned what he would find were he injudicious enough to
enter such an office. He would *not* find dignified counselors with dry coughs, decorously attending to the whereases
of the estates of deceased testators. No. He would find
brisk young attorneys grasping for *new* clients. One might
as well enter a lair of advertising men. But the offices of
Sultan, Sultan & Sultan remained in the building where
they had been born well over a half-century before, and it
was a building of which Mr. Henry Harrison Perdue heartily approved, since it was as like the building in which
had been born the offices of Debrosses, Perdue & Party as
were two mass-production houses in a suburban real-estate
development.

He had found comfort in the familiar pink marble pilas-
ters in the lobby, in the groaning and unsteady rise of the
elevator in its open shaft of grillwork, a rise slightly faster
than that of a pan of yeast dough, and as he had walked
down a wide, quiet corridor he had found reassurance in
the mahogany doors with their gold-deaf names, *Wickerworker, Bradley & Broome, Counselors at Law,* and then
below in smaller letters, for the guidance of the uninitiat-
ed, *The Annette Kripper Estate, The Peabody Pitkins Trustees.* A fine firm, Wickerworker, Bradley & Broome, not a
member under seventy in it. . . . *Jessup, James, Jordan &
Dounce, Counselors at Law,* an equally fine firm, though
Young Jessup, only fifty-five, must be something of a trial
to seasoned men like James, Jordan and Dounce. . . . *Sultan, Sultan & Sultan, Counselors at Law.* . . . Mr. Henry
Harrison Perdue had taken a deep breath and had opened
the door.

II

He was met by silence, a deep untroubled silence like the tomb, and he gratefully expelled his breath, confident that everything was as it should be, that he was to be confronted by no modern innovations or youthful indignities in the offices of Sultan, Sultan & Sultan. Everything, at least in the reception office, was exactly as it had been on his last visit twenty-five years before, before Horace had voted. When one entered the reception office one entered the office designed for one's reception, for the reception of gentlemen or, perhaps, a widowed lady, and one was not stopped short by fences, bars, or ropes as if one were a peddler. No. One opened the heavy mahogany door and then, when the door was closed behind one, one gave a genteel cough.

Mr. Henry Harrison Perdue gave a genteel cough and waited. He was not, of course, actually kept waiting. His cough was answered within seven seconds. It was not answered by some one peeking at him through a window, peephole or other narrow and guarded aperture as if he were a wild and dangerous animal. No. It was answered by an employee of the firm appearing in the open doorway of an adjoining office.

The employee smiled courteously and said diffidently, "Good morning, sir. Is there anything I may do for you?"

Mr. Henry Harrison Perdue was for an instant disconcerted by the appearance of the employee. She was a tall, blond and tanned employee who would have looked more at home on a tennis court. She also had facial features and a physical figure. It was not strictly traditional for such an employee to have either features or a figure, and in the offices of Debrosses, Perdue & Party, in the offices of Wickerworker, Bradley & Broome, in the offices of Jessup, James, Jordan & Dounce, such an employee had gray hair instead of blond. However, upon a second look Mr. Henry

Harrison Perdue decided that there was such a thing as carrying tradition too far and that it was even possible that in this particular instance Young Sultan's Boy had made a departure that might well be copied, at least in the offices of Debrosses, Perdue & Party. Particularly since the manner and tone of the employee had the subdued, desiccated quality that was the essence of the tradition.

He said, "Thank you," almost added, "my dear," and gave her his card. "Mr. Sultan," he said, "if it's quite convenient."

The employee said, "Won't you please be seated, Mr. Perdue, until I can let him know that you are here?"

Mr. Perdue said, "Thank you, my dear," and, benignantly smiling, sat his frail body upon a leather sofa that was as mellow and as lustrous as old wine.

The employee returned to her adjoining office and sat in her chair that swiveled between a typewriter desk and a small desk switchboard and she sat facing, grimly, the switchboard and she put a plug in the switchboard and flipped a switch that rang a muted bell in the private office that was the sanctum of the surviving partner, Wm Sultan, Young Sultan's Boy. The telephone was answered by the secretary of Young Sultan's Boy.

"Yes, Roberts?" her voice inquired.

In her office adjoining the reception room, Roberts said, "One mummy coming up." Her bitter voice did not carry beyond the door. "Life & Letters," she added.

The muted ring of the telephone had decorously interrupted the quiet voice of Wm Sultan in the dictation of a letter to his secretary.

"'My dear Counselor,'" he was dictating. "'I deeply appreciate your invitation for me to be your associate in the defense of the Crondyke Codicil, but I fear I must decline—'"

He raised a dignified eyebrow at the stenographic note-book which his secretary had slapped down on the corner of his desk.

"I beg," he said, "your pardon?"

"It's going to be a sensational case!" his secretary protested. "It'll end up in the criminal courts!"

"Precisely," said Wm Sultan in a tone of distaste.

His secretary held her temper. "It will be exciting!" she pleaded. "It'll bring some life into this damned tomb!"

Wm Sultan's ears winced at the improper word. They were large ears and somewhat more expressive than is common to that usually merely receptive organ. When they heard that improper word, for example, they shrank a little closer to his head and there was a slight but indubitable curling around the edges. To be more exact, while both ears shrank a little closer to his head, as though to withdraw from the offending sound, it was only his right ear that curled around the edge. It was not that his left ear had a coarser temperament or was of a more vulgar nature, and so was not equally offended by the impropriety of a profane word when uttered by a female voice. It would have been equally unresponsive to a Bach sonata. It was, in short, a mite deaf.

He turned this unresponsive ear to his secretary and inquired, "Where were we?"

The secretary glared at the ear. Outwardly it was indistinguishable from his other ear. They were equally robust ears. Had they been sculptured ears an art critic would have spoken of them as being vigorous in execution. The secretary would go no farther than to say that on him they looked good. To an unprejudiced eye they were, perhaps, not unappropriate to his head, which was large, to his face, which was bony, and to his nose, which was also at least vigorous in execution. Above his ears there was hair, and the secretary's indignant inspection observed, and not for the first time, that there was no touch of gray in its sandy color. He looked like a young man and he did not look younger than his years. Oh, yes, he looked like a young man, and living. That's the way he looked.

She said, savagely, "'But I fear I must decline—'"

Wm Sultan gave a dry cough.

"'As my time,'" he resumed, "'is at present so largely engaged by my compilation of the Life & Letters of my uncle, the late Horace Seneca Sultan, that, *per se*—'"

It was then that the muted ring of the telephone had diffidently interrupted.

"What," inquired the secretary of the telephone, "will be the name on the tombstone?"

"It's the late Mr. Henry Harrison Perdue. I did all I could," Roberts insisted sadly. "I gave him 7cc of adrenalin, hot buttered rum, but the chill of the grave is upon him."

"I prefer the simple home remedies," said the secretary. "Have you tried putting a fresh young virgin on each side of him to warm him? Highly recommended in biblical times."

"I haven't got a one in my desk," Roberts objected.

The secretary turned to Wm Sultan.

"Where do we keep our virgins?" she asked. "Roberts is fighting an incipient case of rigor mortis in a Mr. Perdue who's tottered in to see you."

Wm Sultan said stiffly, "During business hours, Kelly, I prefer to hold to a little formality."

Kelly shook her dark head. "Not to my little formality," she said. She spoke into the telephone. "Carry in the corpse," she said. "We can bury him under the rug."

III

Mr. Henry Harrison Perdue beamed benignantly upon the blond employee when she re-entered the reception office.

"May I show you to Mr. Sultan's office?" she asked, and he was quite gratified by the dignified respect of her tone and her manner. It could not have been more nearly perfect had she been his own Miss Quilling, who was sixty. Nor could the tone and manner of the young man who rose from behind a desk and came forward to meet him have been more drily decorous, reservedly cordial, had he been sixty. Indeed, Henry Perdue had the comforting impression that in some ways Young Sultan's Boy *was* sixty.

"I feel about sixty," said Roberts, tottering into Kelly's office. "A little more of this and you can call up McBride's and get me a ticket to the old ladies' home."

Kelly's dark eyes remained grave under the frown that puckered her arched black brows.

"I'm not laughing any more," she said. "Not when I listen to this," she added, and flipped a switch marked *Listen* on the box of an inter-office communication system. She did not need to explain that she had surreptitiously switched on one marked *Speak* on its duplicate on Wm Sultan's desk as she had left his office.

A decorous voice was saying . . . "Confess I was somewhat surprised that dear Horace had kept them so long."

A decorous voice answered, "I've no doubt that he set particular value upon them."

Roberts laughed. "He only averaged about four letters a day for sixty years," she said, "and kept a copy of all 78,203 of them! And we know at least of 23,017 replies that he never threw away. Particular value, in sooth! Why—"

"Shhhh—" said Kelly, still unsmiling.

A desiccated voice was saying, "Not the least trouble to forward your inquiry, I assure you. I did it yesterday. Pity you had wasted time earlier trying to locate him. Should have come to us at once. Mr. Samuel Silliman was my grandfather's client, you remember, passed on in 1864. Then it was the elder son, Charles Silliman, who made his nephew, the Charles Silliman you've been trying to locate, his residuary legatee when he passed on in 1890, bachelor, you remember, and Young Charles was an orphan. For the first time in fifty-eight years, you know, Young Charles returned to this country just a month ago. Rather surprised to learn that Horace had had correspondence with him, mere lad of thirteen, you see, when he had left here in '89 with the Roylson Caldwells."

A desiccated voice explained, "There are only three letters in the series. There's an initial letter from Howard Caldwell to my uncle, the next in date from Charles Silliman to my uncle, and thirdly a holograph copy of a later letter from my uncle to Charles Silliman which apparently remained unanswered. As my inquiries might well have done had not other letters of my uncle reminded me that the Samuel Tilden branch of the Silliman family have been your clients for well over a hundred years!" There was a politely flattering laugh.

It was answered by a politely appreciative cough.

"That's what I mean," said Kelly tensely. "It's getting so you can't tell 'em apart. These animated mummies are turning him into one."

"By osmosis," suggested Roberts, scientifically.

"If you ask me," spoke up Morgan from her adjoining office, "they're replacing Bill's blood with a transfusion of starch."

"Quiet, Red. Grandpappy speaks."

A voice so reserved as to be inhuman was saying, "In compiling the Life & Letters of my late uncle, in accordance with the provisions of the trust fund bequeathed by him to that purpose, I usually find more gaps in the Life, I might say, than in the Letters." A dry laugh was answered by a dry laugh. "But this letter of Mr. Charles Silliman referred in rather glowing terms to some prior act of my uncle in connection with Howard Caldwell. Oddly, I think

I may say oddly in view of my uncle's usual correspondence habits, I can find no mention of it in later copies of
his own letters except one oblique reference to 'the affair
of Young Caldwell's toe.'"

A voice so reserved as to be inhuman replied, "Because
it was heroic, my dear boy! Modesty, becoming manly
modesty. Horace saved the boy's life, no less. I was there
myself, you see, when it happened. We were all in the
Berkshires, you remember. The Sultans, Caldwells, Silli-
mans, my own family. Yes, indeed, things do change for
the worse, but in those days those woods were filled with
people you could meet socially. Young Howard Caldwell
was in the woods with a hatchet, summer of '89 that would
be, and chopped off his toe. Unlucky lad always, well-behaved, but unlucky. He was just thirteen and would have
died then instead of at fourteen if Horace hadn't put his
finger in the dike. Stopped the bleeding, you remember,
with a tourniquet and carried the lad miles or yards, I forget just which, through the woods to a doctor. It will make
a heroic chapter in your Life of Horace, my dear boy!"

From her adjoining office, Morgan asked, "Didn't
Horace live in B.C.?"

"Yes, dear," Kelly said. "He was Bill's youngest uncle,"
she explained.

Roberts said, "I'm beginning to feel sixty-five."

Kelly said, "Listen to the senile old buzzards remi-
nisce."

Wm Sultan was saying, "And he died when he was fourteen, you say?"

Another octogenarian voice replied, "Off Capri. Always
an unlucky lad. Fell off the boat. The Roylson Caldwell's
were returning to Naples, you remember, to return to this
country because of Young Charles Silliman's inheritance
from Charles Silliman. Young Charles was with them, you
know, because he was an orphan and his mother, the last

to die, had appointed the Roylson Caldwells his guardians. Because her sister-in-law, Agnes Beltry—née Silliman, of course—had girls. Very sensible. He and unlucky young Caldwell were practically Damon and Pythias. So when the Caldwells received word that Young Charles's Uncle Charles had died they started to return to this country. Then their own son had to have his usual bad luck and fell off the boat. Young Charles felt responsible, I understand, because they were making the trip for him—you know how imaginative lads of that age are. Broke him up completely. Unable to make the trip home. Later went to school abroad. Married abroad. Had a child abroad. Son. Named Howard, in memory of his friend. He sent young Howard back here to school, in California, of all places. Never met the lad. He must have taken a fancy to that strange place— he married and died there. Married a western connection of the Leslie Lennoxes and lost her in childbirth twenty years ago, survived by a daughter, Leslie. Died about six months ago himself, only forty-five, cerebral hemorrhage. That's my theory about that California climate, dangerous, goes to the head." A dry laugh.

Answered by a dry laugh.

"This is most interesting, sir. Invaluable background for the Life."

Roberts said, "If he writes all this about one dull letter he's going to be an old man before he finishes the hundred thousand."

Kelly said, "He's going to be an old man in his thirties unless something blasts him out of this damned tomb."

In her adjoining office, Morgan said, yawning, "Turn that thing off, Kelly. It's too exciting. I can't stand it."

A disembodied voice was saying, "To see his granddaughter for the first time, no doubt. Has her with him at his uncle's former house of Greenwater on Bay Island.

For a fact, quite a family reunion. The young Caldwell children have been living there for some forty years, and even before his return Mr. Silliman cabled for his cousins to visit him, first cousins thrice removed, of course, the grandchildren of his aunt, Agnes Beltry, you remember. Charles, her brother, didn't leave her children anything, you know, because her husband, Bartram Beltry, was a very wealthy man. The fortune was dissipated by the girls' husbands, that stock-market speculation that some people dabbled in in 1929, and I understand the children had virtually no inheritance."

"I see. And Mr. Silliman intends to . . . Very thoughtful of him."

"Loyal to his blood."

"From his letter to my uncle after the death of his friend, Howard Caldwell, I'd say that loyalty had always been one of his qualities, *per se.*"

"Was this many years after Howard's death?"

"The entire series bear the date 1890."

"The very year! How interesting!"

"Let me have my file clerk bring them."

"I'd be very pleased," said Henry Perdue.

IV

Indeed, Mr. Henry Harrison Perdue could not recall when he had before been as pleased to see a file clerk. Neither could he recall when he had before seen a red-haired file clerk with green eyes and such a cuddlesome shape. Indeed, the more he thought about it, the more he came to feel that—

"Oh, yes, yes, yes! So these are the letters," he said. "How very interesting!"

"These are the ones from the boys," said Wm Sultan, selecting two identical in appearance in their schoolboy

Spencerian script, alike as peas in their earnest effort at formality proper to boys of fourteen writing to an aged senior of twenty-four in that lush but formal year of 1890.

Mr. Henry Harrison Perdue adjusted gold-rimmed glasses and approvingly mumbled through the stilted phrases of Howard Caldwell's letter. . . . He took his pen in hand. He was in Europe. It had been a rough crossing. He had been at breakfast every morning. French boys wore odd-looking clothes. They were going to Italy. He and Charles had seen many monuments but were also having a very good time. He had run a race with Charles yesterday and had beaten him. He remained ever gratefully your true and sincere friend. . . .

"His toe," said Henry Perdue.

"Yes, yes!" Wm Sultan affirmed. "I see now why he alluded to the race."

"Well-mannered lad, if unlucky," Henry Perdue agreed. "Not boasting."

"No, no! Simply offering evidence that despite the loss of his toe he was in no way crippled."

"Precisely."

Roberts mumbled, "Ah, yes, yes, yes, yes. Ah, no, no, no, no. Where the hell's my reticule?"

"Why, Roberts!" Morgan exclaimed from her adjoining office. "Haven't you been told about the bees and flowers?"

Roberts said, "All the old ladies I've ever read about have reticules. I'm seventy-five. *I want my reticule!*"

Kelly's cameo face remained grave as she listened to the disembodied voices from the office of the surviving, possibly, partner of Sultan, Sultan & Sultan.

One was saying . . . . "No copy of my uncle's reply has as yet been located. In such a mass of correspondence it will be some time before we can have it indexed and cross-indexed to the point of being able to locate every letter. I've no doubt but that he did make a copy. My grandfather, you remember, held slovenliness an abomination."

"A sound man on codicils," pronounced Henry Perdue.

Wm Sultan gave a dry cough of appreciation. "He drilled my uncle from his boyhood," he continued, "first to write a letter for substance, then to edit it, and finally to make a fair copy so that the recipient might read a letter without blemish or error. Uncle Horace continued this practice throughout his life and saved the original drafts. He was also, you remember, a man of orderly mind."

"Also very sound on codicils," remembered Henry Perdue.

Wm Sultan gave a dry cough of appreciation.

Roberts said, "After this even the radio won't bore me."

". . . But it is clear from this letter of Charles Silliman," Wm Sultan was continuing, "that my uncle had made a reply to young Caldwell's letter that was received almost immediately after the boy's death. And young Charles took on himself the sad duty of replying for his dead friend."

Roberts said, "What was in Charles' letter? Did Aunt Agnes have bats in her Beltry? Was Grandpappy Sultan a bigamist? Can a Sultan be a bigamist? Tune in any time, this station."

Mr. Henry Harrison Perdue was approvingly mumbling through the stilted phrases of Charles Silliman's letter. . . . Since he was too ill to travel it had been decided not to send his dear friend's body home but he had been buried in the English Cemetery. He knew that he should try to remember that it was God's will but he missed him terribly. He could not tell you how much it had meant to him to read your fine letter to Howard. You were the finest friend any boy had ever had. He would never forget how you had saved Howard's life. If you had been on the boat he knew that you would have been a hero again and have saved his friend's life. He would never forget you for all his life, for what a wonderful friend you had been to Howard. He remained, ever gratefully . . .

"A noble lad," said Henry Perdue. He looked from the letter in his right hand to the one from Howard Caldwell which he still held in his left. "Both noble lads," he said. He continued to nod in approval as he looked from one faded letter to the other. Then he stopped nodding and sat quite still. His hands holding the letters began to shake. He rose from his chair with startling suddenness. He opened his mouth as if to speak but did not. He put his right hand to his heart. He slowly sat down again. He leaned forward and put his forehead on the edge of the desk, and the senior partner of Debrosses, Perdue & Party was dead.

2

Strange Behavior of a Surviving Partner. A Ghost
and an Inquisition. A Violent Assault in the Room
of an Hotel. Vulgar Denomination of "Sultan's Harem."
A Bold Robbery. The Fatal Letters again.

When Wm Sultan entered the elevator of his office building on the morning following the death of the late Henry
Harrison Perdue he neglected, for the first time in his life,
to say, "Good morning, Captain."

It was not an omission to pass unregarded by a man
who for forty years, had received the "Good mornings,
Captain," of the Seniors of Old Firms, and particularly
not to pass unregarded when there were two young Juniors
in the elevator who did not appreciate his unique position. Captain made his feelings audible by shutting the
grilled door with a resounding clang.

Thus reminded that something was amiss, Wm Sultan
said, absently, "Good morning, Captain."

Captain acknowledged his due with his usual inclination of the head, a slow and ponderous nod it was, and
further added on this special morning a sympathetic sigh.

"Very sad," he sighed, "about the Senior of Debrosses,
Perdue & Party."

Behind him, Wm Sultan's voice said, "Yes."

Captain had expected something more sociable than just one curt word. What would the Juniors think? He tried again.

"Greatly respected."

"Yes."

By this time the elevator was at the second floor.

"Particularly sound on codicils."

"Yes."

Captain was becoming desperate. The roof of the elevator was at the third floor. It was unthinkable that in front of Juniors he should receive from the Survivor of an Old Firm nothing but a series of curt monosyllables, it was unthinkable but there it was and time was short.

He sighed again, a quick one. "And to think that only last week we carried out the Senior of MacTavish, MacLeod, MacKnoultie & Mack."

"Yes."

The third floor was waist high and sinking like his heart. It was then or never. He gambled all on the turn of a phrase.

"Not many of us left," he said.

"No."

That, certainly, was an acceptance of his comment and would show the Juniors that he had a right to name himself with the thinning ranks of the Seniors, and as such was victory. But a disaster so narrowly averted, like a near head-on collision with a truck, does not incline the heart towards the truck driver, and there was a malignant light in Captain's fat-shrouded eyes as he watched Young Sultan's Boy walk down the third-floor corridor.

When Roberts heard the door of the reception office open she turned with an expectant smile for the unfailing pause of Wm Sultan in the doorway of her adjoining cubicle and his invariably courteous "Good morning, Roberts."

She saw him pass her doorway without a glance or word and continue on into the mahogany partitioned corridor from which opened the private offices. The first in line was the one that had once been the seat of the Junior Partner. It was now the repository of sorting tables, index cards on filing cabinets, where Morgan sequestered the correspondence of the late Horace Seneca Sultan beyond recovery by any mortal except herself. Moved by that instinct which tells dogs and employees when their master is approaching, Morgan faced the corridor door with a welcoming smile in anticipation of its opening just far enough to admit his head and his precisely pleasant "Good morning, Morgan."

But the slight vibration of his footsteps went without pause on past the door. The next office in line, which had always been the seat of the Sultan next in line of succession, had been pre-empted by Wm Sultan's secretary one hot July day of the previous summer. It was cooler than the adjoining cubicle that was the designed place for a secretary, Kelly had condescended to explain her move. When he had, in half-jocular remonstrance, reminded her that it was traditionally reserved for the Heir Apparent, he had been informed that when it was apparent that he had an heir, legitimate, it had been added lasciviously, she would move over for him. And so, not wishing to take a high hand or to engage further in a low conversation, he had let her stay.

Petite and apparently cool on this hot July morning, she turned expectantly, if ironically, when she heard a dry cough in the corridor. She heard the door of the office of the head of the firm open and close before she could quite realize that there had been neither an impersonal morning smile nor a cautious, "Good morning, Kelly."

She went to the door. Morgan was standing in the doorway of the filing room. Roberts was standing in the doorway of the reception room. The three looked at each other and moved together to discuss, in whispers, what could be the meaning of the strange behavior of Wm Sultan.

II

Wm Sultan gave his hat to the mahogany clothespress that waited for it in the corner of his office. It was a large and solid clothespress that had in the course of sixty-odd years comfortably settled itself in the corner with a comforting air of stolid permanence. There was nothing swank or modish, like a foreign butler, about, the clothespress, but, as old-fashioned as its name, it had in its sixty years of performing the same daily service to the same family taken on the character of an old family retainer.

When it took a Sultan's hat, the creak of its aging hinges distinctly croaked a "Good morning, sirrrrr," and while it was not the custom of Wm Sultan to go so far as to reply, "Good morning, Pressy," it is an unquestioned fact that he did always close the door with a lingering of the hand that was like a pat on the back. Only, this morning, he was deaf to the greeting of the hinges and it was an unfeeling hand that closed the door.

He moved stiffly to his desk, his muscles tense with the tension of his nerves, and his long body sank wearily but stiffly, without repose, in his chair. In front of him on the desk was the morning mail, neatly arranged. Unseeing, he pushed it aside as he spread his arms on the desk and, leaning forward, he stared at the bare top of the desk between them. He was not of the temperament to see ghosts or apparitions of the conscience, and had one appeared his disciplined mind would have dismissed it as not being recognized in law, but, when his eyes slowly, unwillingly, moved to the soft glow of the old leather chair in front of his desk, his visual memory of Henry Perdue sitting on that chair was painfully clear.

Slowly, reluctantly, Wm Sultan opened the top drawer of his desk and took out two faded letters identical in their schoolboy handwriting. He sat gazing absently at them. When he first had read them in the routine of his faithful compilation of the Life & Letters, he had been left with the feeling that he had missed something. That feeling had persisted annoyingly after a second reading and exasperatingly through a third before, almost by chance, he had seen that those faded pages told an astounding, an almost incredible story.

It had amused him that his secretary had been bored by them, as bored as she was by any other two that she had read of the 101,220 letters and holograph copies of letters that reposed in the files. It had amused him to have the attention of the two other members of his staff particularly called to the letters and to find them as superiorly disinterested in such dull truck as was his secretary. As a man who, at least in his own opinion, put up with much, it had pleased his dry humor to have his staff look up old records in the surrogate's office, to transcribe from him letter after letter of inquiry, to be the active agents, in short, of the fascinating game that he was playing, completely unsuspected by them, under their little know-it-all noses. It had been amusing, that is, until he had found himself the active agent and the letters the instrument of Henry Perdue's death.

Wm Sultan looked up wearily at the opening of his office door. He saw that his secretary had opened the door. She was followed by his file clerk, who was followed by his receptionist, who closed the door. He watched Kelly lead the advance in single file to his desk and come to a stop with Morgan on her right hand and Roberts on her left. From left to right, he saw Morgan's green eyes look at the letters lying on the desk in front of him, he saw Kelly's brown eyes look at the letters, he saw Roberts's blue eyes look at the letters, and then he saw all three pairs fixed solemnly upon his own. Women are wonderful, he thought, gazing up into those inquisitorial eyes. They are too wonderful for this world. It is a pity that they are on it.

He said, "Good morning."

Morgan said, "Good morning."

Kelly said, "Good morning."

Roberts said, "Good morning."

The conversation came to a stop and as far as Wm Sultan was concerned it could stay there forever. But he saw Morgan look significantly at Roberts and Roberts look significantly at Kelly. He braced himself.

Kelly said, "You're upset over Mr. Perdue's death."

"Yes," he admitted.

"He was an old friend of your family," Roberts offered.

"Yes."

"But you, yourself, scarcely knew him at all," Morgan countered.

"No."

Morgan looked significantly at Roberts and Roberts looked significantly at Kelly. Sentimentality had been disposed of as a reason for the strange behavior of Wm Sultan.

Kelly said, "I made some fresh cracks about him."

"Yes," he agreed.

"So did I," admitted Roberts.

"Yes."

"But he didn't hear them," Morgan pointed out.

"No."

"And so you're not sore about it?" Morgan pinned it down.

"No."

Morgan looked at Roberts and Roberts looked at Kelly. Indignation with his staff had been disposed of as a possible reason for his strange behavior.

Kelly said, "He was eighty-one years old."

"Yes."

"And we all heard his personal physician say that he had repeatedly warned him to retire because of his bad heart," Roberts reminded him.

"Yes."

"So that there's really nothing surprising or unusual at all," Morgan came down to cases, "about a man eighty-one years old with a bad heart dying of heart failure, is there?"

"No."

Kelly took the final step, gave the final turn to the inquisitorial screw.

"But sometimes," she said, "an emotional shock may bring on a heart attack."

"Yes."

"And," Roberts blurted, "he was reading those letters when he had the attack."

"Yes."

"Is there—" Morgan swallowed. "Is there," she began again, "something in those letters that only a lawyer can understand? I mean," she went on, "we can't figure out where there's anything in them at all that isn't just the way Mr. Perdue said things were before he read them. But is there?" she pleaded. "Is there anything written in either of them that could have been a shock to him?"

"No."

Flat, monosyllabic and final, the word was like a closed door. Kelly was not fond of having a door slammed against the inquisitive tilt of her nose. She rapped on it in a temper.

"Then why," she snapped, "do we find you sitting here with them on your desk?"

"Because," Wm Sultan quietly turned the key, "you neglected to have them returned to the files yesterday, and so I dropped them in the drawer of my desk last night." He picked up the letters and handed them to his file clerk. His receptionist followed her from his office. To his secretary he spoke with a patience which she found galling. "Shall we attend to the mail?" he asked.

"In good time," Kelly promised, sitting herself down hard on her chair, "I'll attend to the male."

But her anger subsided, as anger will, and was replaced by a worried perplexity as the morning's dictation dragged on. And drag it did because Wm Sultan, for the first time in her experience, was absent-minded. And drag it did because, also for the first time in her experience, his gravity was unbroken by jabs of dry humor that were as enlivening as unexpected jabs with a pin. And drag as it did there was, unaccountably, a mounting tension. She was conscious of it in him, and the feeling in the office reminded her of the time she had waited at an airport for an overdue plane.

At eleven o'clock Mr. Charles Silliman called on the telephone, and with that call Kelly felt Wm Sultan relax, as if the tension of waiting were over, but when she heard his voice she knew that it had only been replaced by another, one that made her ears prickle as had the sound of the bell at the one and only prize fight she had ever attended.

The voice that Wm Sultan, and his switchboard operator, heard on the telephone was elderly but forcible. It said that it had been deeply shocked to learn of Henry Perdue's death.

"Most regrettable," affirmed Wm Sultan.

"Earlier in the day I had received your letter that he had forwarded."

"He told me that he had been kind enough to do so."

"He must have been as surprised as I to learn that your uncle had preserved a letter from Howard and one from me that I had written to him after Howard's death."

"He was most interested," agreed Wm Sultan. "In fact, he was reading the letters when he had the attack."

"I'd hoped to read Howard's letter today myself, and answer your inquiries about him."

"You're in town?" Wm Sultan asked.

"Came in first thing this morning. But, my health—evidently overestimated my strength—this shock, and the heat—I fear I shan't be able to make it to your office."

"Can't I call upon you?" asked Wm Sultan considerately. "In an hour, then," he concluded, and replacing the telephone he coughed a dry cough and said, "Where were we?"

His unusual gravity, even grimness, checked any questions, but to Kelly's dark eye he had a cat-who-has-swallowed-the-canary expression which, since she did not know the reason for it, she found infuriating. Thirty-five minutes later he looked at his wrist watch and said, as if licking his chops over the canary, "Will you please have Morgan bring me the Caldwell-Silliman files? She might," he added, "put them in one envelope. I wish to take them with me."

At precisely one hour from the time of the telephone call his name was sent up from the desk of the hotel that had been named by Charles Silliman. He was directed to room 1020 and rapped on that door.

A man's voice called, "Come in, come in."

Wm Sultan found no one in the room but from behind the partially open door of the bathroom an elderly but vigorous voice said, "Please sit down. My apologies, but I'm shaving; be with you in just a moment."

Wm Sultan looked for a place to sit. On one chair was a closed suitcase, on another the coat of a man's suit. The one unencumbered chair had its back to the bathroom door. He sat in it. Approximately thirty seconds later he was conscious, for the fraction of a second, of an explosion in the back of his head.

When he again became conscious he was lying on the floor and the taupe rug undulated before his eyes like an oily sea. Not far in front of his nose two rafts rode the waves. He watched them and they came no nearer and went no farther away. One of the craft that was anchored there was his billfold and the other was a brown manila envelope. He closed his eyes. He listened intently but could hear no sound in the room above the pounding inside his head.

He opened his eyes again and reached out a hand for his billfold and the brown envelope. He examined them, put them in a side pocket of his coat, and sat up. The room whirled. He closed his eyes and felt blindly for a chair and pulled himself to his feet. He opened his eyes on the open bathroom door. He lurched through it, banging his shoulder, and clung sagging, to the washbasin. He turned on the cold water and, supporting himself with his forearms on the basin, held his wrists in it.

His vertigo began to subside, his anger with himself to rise. He had walked into a trap that had been so obvious that he had refused to see it, a trap so crude as to be the acme of subtleness, a trap set by a trapper who had been contemptuous of him. He leaned forward on his hands in the swirling water in the washbasin, his lips pressed tight against an attack of nausea that was as much mental as physical as he considered the consequences of his negligence, his at least morally criminal negligence.

A few minutes later at the desk of the hotel Wm Sultan again faced the clerk who had announced him to Mr. Charles Silliman. He stood with his hands on top of the desk to steady himself and from the wet wrists of his coat and his shirt small but still surprising pools of water were spreading on top of the desk. He stood with his head tilted very far back. He had to keep his head tilted very far back in order to see anything, because he had to wear the sweatband of his hat on his nose to keep the back of it from touching the tender back of his head. It did not occur to him that he was not presenting his usually quite impeccable appearance.

He said, with what appeared to be a fine air of inebriated dignity, "I believe you were mistaken in directing me to room number 1010."

The clerk was looking at the two expanding puddles of water on the desk. He seemed bemused.

"I never," he said, at last raising his eyes, "ever saw you before in my life."

Wm Sultan looked at his wet wrist watch.

"Seventeen minutes ago," he said precisely, "after announcing me to Mr. Charles Silliman, you directed me to room number 1010."

The clerk checked himself on the point of giving a signal to a house detective and leaned over the desk just to confirm the seemingly obvious fact that there would be a reek of whiskey.

Wm Sultan said, "I am William Sultan."

Since he had heard it only seventeen minutes before the clerk remembered the name and with that assistance he recalled the face despite the disguise of the hat. Further, on the breath that pronounced the name there was no aroma or bouquet, much less a reek, of whiskey. Further, the voice that pronounced the name had an impressively unaccented self-assurance. The clerk began to lose some of his.

"Yes, sir," he admitted reluctantly, remembering a man who had worn his hat at a grave angle as befitted an impressively unaccented dignity. "But the room number," he remembered, "was 1020, not 1010."

"You seem to be confused," he was told. "Perhaps you'd better ring Mr. Silliman again, if you please."

The clerk looked at the puddles of water and he became unhappy.

"I'm sorry, sir," he said, "but Mr. Silliman checked out ten minutes ago."

"Nonsense!" said the voice under the hat. "Describe him!"

The clerk raised his eyes but could not face that hat.

"An elderly gentleman," he said to the puddles of water. "A large elderly gentleman," he plodded on. "A large elderly gentleman with a pointed nose. A large elderly gentleman with a pointed nose *and* a pointed jaw."

It occurred to him that there was something very fishy about all this. Or was it the pools of water that made him think of fish? While engaged in this trance-like perplexity he became aware that that was all that there was on the desk, the pools of water. Or were they puddles? At any rate there were no hands, no wrists, no wet shirt cuffs under wet coat cuffs. Just the pools, or puddles, of water.

He felt the finger of an assistant manager tap him on the arm and he saw another finger of the assistant manager pointed at the two puddles of water.

"What," he heard the shocked voice of the assistant manager demand, "have you been doing on the desk?"

III

In a letter dated the 14th inst. of April, 1901, Horace Seneca Sultan had written, "Revenge is sweet." At high noon on the 22d inst. of July, 1947, Captain was to find proof that that comment was true if not original. When Wm Sultan entered the elevator with his hat on his nose and the sleeves of his coat giving evidence that he had been on all fours in some particularly dank gutter, he gave Captain the courage to avenge his near humiliation of the morning.

The third floor was reached. Wm Sultan, leaning backward to see from under the brim of his hat, stepped not too certainly from the elevator. He stepped into the arms of a brunette, a redhead and a blonde who were waiting at the elevator to go to lunch. He was not released from the arms. He was practically carried down the corridor by the arms.

There was a low whistle in Captain's ear. "What," inquired the voice of a young fourth-floor attorney, "do you call that?"

"I," said Captain, and the vulgar disrespect of what he was going to say was already sweet in his mouth, "I calls it Sultan's Harem."

The young female employees of good character whom he so gratuitously slandered were, at that moment, propelling their employer into his office. Their hands that held and pulled him, their arms that supported and pushed him, were doing so with such energy that it was useless for him to resist, and their tongues were going at such a rate that it was useless for him to speak.

"He's stinking!" declared Kelly proudly.

"Drunk and disorderly!" Morgan agreed joyously.

"Always knew that he had it in him!" chortled Roberts. "Always knew that he'd come through some day!"

"My head—" Wm Sultan began.

"Look at that hat!"

"Never can say he's an old fossil! Never worry about that again, not that."

"I don't like his color," Roberts, athletically wise, suddenly decided. "I wonder if he's been in a fight?"

They drew back a step to peer at him and Wm Sultan had a chance to take off his hat. His head returned to a normal position. He also had a chance to speak.

"Are you quite through?" he asked.

Roberts said, "I don't like his voice."

"It sounds normal," Morgan agreed.

"Oh, my Lord," said Kelly in disgust, "sober again."

Wm Sultan sat down in his swivel chair and leaned back in it and closed his eyes.

"What's this about your head?" Roberts remembered him having mentioned it.

Wm Sultan's head, pride and conscience were hurt. The injury to his conscience was the most serious. In the back of his mind, so to speak, was the bitter, black knowledge that others were to suffer a great wrong because he had crawled out of his law books and played at being a man of action. He did not care to talk about that, he did not even care to think about it. But, also, there was in the back of

his head a throbbing pain and he was not unaware that
how he had received that pain was going to make him a
damned dramatic figure to his usually somewhat unappre-
ciative staff.

"When I was in Mr. Silliman's hotel room," he said
quietly, playing it down like a true ham, "I was hit on the
head." He waited for gasps from his audience.

"Hit on the head?" Morgan repeated, and from her tone
one might have thought that he had said that he had stood
on his head.

"Whatever hit you?" Kelly inquired skeptically.

Roberts yawned.

Wm Sultan tightened his lips in a grimace that was intended to make it clear that he was stifling a groan, and then
with ostentatious gentleness passed a hand over the back
of his head. There was very little swelling.

"Possibly a heel," he said.

"Only a heel," Roberts explained to the two other girls,
"would hit our Bill."

"A rubber heel," he said. "On a shoe."

Kelly looked at his rubber-heeled shoes and her eyes
narrowed suspiciously.

"With your shoes off," she mused. "Just *whom* did you
say you were in the bedroom with?"

"I have," Wm Sultan said with dignity, "no factual evidence of the identity of the person. A man purporting to
be Mr. Charles Silliman," he continued, "verbally admitted me to room 1020. I did not see him, as he was in the
bathroom allegedly shaving. I sat in a chair with my back
to the bathroom door. I was knocked unconscious. If," he
went on quickly, not caring for comment on that point,
"I accept the asseveration of the clerk, a man registered as
Charles Silliman checked out of the hotel very shortly after
my admittance to room number 1020. By a—ruse," he said,
finding some satisfaction in this part of his story—

"It's been months since I've had one," said Morgan wistfully. "Gave up desserts."

"He means a 'trick,'" Kelly explained, "'fast talk,' 'slick work.'"

"By a ruse," Wm Sultan resumed grimly, "I obtained from the clerk a description of the registered Charles Silliman. But since I did not see the occupant of room 1020 at the time of my entrance I have no factual evidence that they are one and the same man. I cannot prove," he admitted bitterly, the whole of his thoughts now upon the seriousness of the thing that had happened, "that the registered Charles Silliman did not, for some good and sufficient reason of his own, leave his room to check out of the hotel immediately before my arrival. I cannot prove that some second person, perhaps a hotel thief, did not then enter the room and accept the telephone call from the desk and invite me to enter for the purpose of robbery. Indeed," he concluded quietly, "since my billfold was emptied of one hundred and twenty dollars, and since Mr. Charles Silliman is a millionaire, that is the only possible conclusion that could be acceptable to the police."

Now, when he had forgotten them, he had the serious attention of his staff.

Roberts expelled her breath in a long sigh. "A bold old boy," she said.

"But a millionaire can't need a hundred and twenty dollars that bad," Morgan objected, frowning. "No matter how much they bellyache about taxes."

"Perhaps," Kelly explained, "he's just eccentric. So many old gentlemen are." She was giving Wm Sultan a long look. She held out her hand. "Now that you're back in the office," she said, "May I have the Caldwell-Silliman envelope for the files?"

Wm Sultan took it from his pocket. He did not wait for her to examine it. "The boys' letters," he admitted, "are gone."

3

Secrets of a Filing System. A Dead Man's Hand.
An Estate Attorney and an Invitation to
Greenwater. A White Coat. Interesting Views
of Nature. Arrival at a Scene of Tragedy.

Roberts, ever more interested in athletic action than in the, to her, practically unnecessary motives for action, for to play the game what motive was needed other than to play the game? Roberts, therefore, had been analyzing the game that had been played upon her employer and had come to the conclusion that, to use football parlance, he had been sucked into a "mousetrap." The mention of "letters" consequently caught her by surprise.

"What letters?" she asked.

"The letters," Kelly said, but still looking at Wm Sultan, "that Mr. Perdue was reading when he had his heart attack." She continued to look at Wm Sultan who did not look at her. "A singular coincidence," she commented. "Mr. Perdue reads the letters and drops dead. Mr. Sultan has the letters in his possession and is knocked unconscious and when he comes to his," she laughed slightly, "senses, the letters are gone. A very singular coincidence," she continued, and it was becoming distinctly cooler in the room, "because Mr. Sultan has assured us that there was not one word of any importance in either letter. In fact," she decided, "a practically impossible coincidence unless Mr. Sultan saw fit to lie to us about the letters. And," she concluded, rising, "I, for one, will not work where I am not trusted!" Then, remembering that she never lost her temper, she smiled courteously at Wm Sultan. "Will this be satisfactory," she inquired courteously, "or shall I put my resignation in writing? And you know," she added, stalking towards her adjoining office, "what you can do with it!"

"What?" inquired Wm Sultan with interest.

Kelly stopped short and her eyes opened very wide. Her mouth also opened and it seemed that she would speak but could not.

"You've hurt Kelly's feelings," Morgan accused him, "and I quit, too."

Roberts, who always played the game, said, "Me too."

"I'm afraid," said Wm Sultan, "that I've been somewhat at fault," and the atmosphere became a little warmer. He said it automatically, having learned in six previous mass resignations that a quick confession of his own guilt was a necessary preliminary. "When you put your inquiries to me about the letters," he continued, "I did not feel that I should volunteer a mere opinion of mine when that opinion had as its corollary a criminal accusation."

Kelly sat down again. "He suspected dirty work," she said aside to Roberts.

"Oh!" Roberts got it.

"However," Wm Sultan continued, "I answered your questions truthfully. The evidence supporting my opinion was not to be deduced from what the boys had written but how they had written it. In other words," he elucidated patiently, as to children, "the evidence was physical rather than declarative. Consequently," he said, "a typescript of the letters would have been meaningless. Photographic copies would still have been inconclusive without an examination of the physical condition of the letters to determine if they had in fact been written at the time of the dates they bore. Besides . . ."

He found it difficult to confess that his usual caution, and the temptation to put something over on his staff, had led him into playing a coy game in which, in seeming innocence and ignorance, he had depended upon the shock effect of his evidence. In one case the shock had been more than he had bargained for. . . .

"Besides what?" asked Morgan.

"For various reasons," Wm Sultan covered it, "I thought it better to use the originals. Their loss," he concluded, "is irremediable."

"I may be dumb," Roberts said, "but I still don't know what all this is about."

Kelly at the moment was not interested. She was concerned about Wm Sultan. "You seem to be taking this hard," she said.

Morgan was not sympathetic. "If people," she said, "didn't sneak in and take things out of my files without even telling me about it, maybe things like this wouldn't happen!"

Kelly took Morgan's hand and put the envelope in Morgan's hand and closed Morgan's fingers around the envelope. She said, gently, "You put the letters in here yourself."

"I did no such thing!"

Kelly spoke slowly that there might not be any error of understanding. "I," she said, "myself, personally, asked you to put the Caldwell-Silliman file in an envelope."

"All right," Morgan said, becoming indignant, "here it is!" She opened the envelope. "Every inquiry we made and every reply we got!"

Kelly took a deep breath. "And," she said, "if Howard Caldwell's and Charles Silliman's letters weren't filed in the Caldwell-Silliman file, may I ask, may I ask, may I ask just where they would be filed?"

"Where they belong, of course," replied Morgan, with dignity. "Under 'T.'"

Kelly swallowed. "'T'?"

"For 'TOE,'" Morgan explained patronizingly. "Subject: 'TOE.' Sub-classification: *'Caldwell's, Young!'*" She shrugged. "If you'd only told me that you wanted them," she said, "I'd have gotten them for you."

Wm Sultan was able to say two words. They were, "Get them."

She got them.

Kelly snatched one of them and began reading it while Morgan read it over Kelly's right shoulder and Roberts read it over Kelly's left shoulder. All in all, Wm Sultan thought, as awed thoughts began to creep back into his mind, it was not a bad little staff he had. He looked kindly upon their three heads bent together over the letter, red hair, black hair and blonde. They looked, he meant *worked* well together. Surprisingly, at times, efficient. It was for instance truly surprising how much it could mean to have a truly efficient file clerk.

Kelly finished the first page of the letter and began on the second. "This doesn't make sense," she broke off. "You've got them mixed up."

"And how," Morgan asked defensively, "am I supposed to tell them apart?"

And once that question was asked the secret of the two letters identical in their schoolboy's handwriting stared them in the face. The handwriting was, in fact, identical. The same hand had written the letter from Howard Caldwell and the letter from Charles Silliman.

"But this," Kelly said, "this means . . ."

Wm Sultan coughed a dry cough. "I must warn you," he said, "against making conclusions from what may be inconclusive evidence. In the meantime," he went on, "before you return from lunch you might have photographic copies made of the letters. The originals . . ." he paused thoughtfully.

Kelly nodded significantly towards the old-fashioned safe that snuggled in a corner under the shelves of the built-in bookcase.

Wm Sultan shook his head. "Perhaps the most secure thing," he decided, turning to Morgan, "would just be for you to file them." To Roberts he said, "When Mr. Party calls please tell him that I shall be back from lunch at two-twenty and can see him then."

"Thanks for telling me," said Roberts. "I didn't even know that you were expecting him to call."

"I wasn't," Wm Sultan said, rising. "But," he added, with a glance at the letters, "as you go on in life you may frequently find that, if you will pardon the cliché, circumstances frequently alter cases."

The cliché had carried him to the clothespress. He accepted his hat, closed the door with a pat of his hand, put the hat on his nose and went to lunch.

"A dead man's hand," Morgan whispered luridly, raising her wide eyes from one of the letters. "Written," she whispered, capitalizing it, "by a Dead Man's Hand!"

II

Roberts said deferentially, "Won't you please be seated until I can let Mr. Sultan know that you are here?" And, with a deferential bow, she disappeared into her adjoining office and plugged in the telephone in Wm Sultan's office.

Kelly's voice answered. "Yes, Roberts?"

Roberts' voice did not carry beyond the open door of the reception office. She said, "Mr. Party's face is white, his ears are red and his hair is powder-blue. His nose is short, his teeth are long and hang in public view."

"*My man!*" Kelly breathed. "Can he crawl in unaided," she asked, "or is it one of our cringe-and-carry cases?"

"Hell, Kelly, he's a mere kid in his sixties."

"O.K. then! Wipe his nose and give him a pogo stick." She put down the telephone and picked up her papers. "Mr. Party," she announced to her employer. She delayed her departure until Wm Sultan went around his desk to meet his visitor, at which time it was, as usual, no trick at all to switch open the inter-office speaking system.

Mr. Party was speaking when Morgan and Roberts joined Kelly in her office for the broadcast.

"They've said all the proper things about poor Mr. Perdue," Kelly reported. "We ought to be getting the real dirt soon."

Mr. Party was saying, "And as you can imagine it's thrown upon me a most, most unexpected, completely unexpected, it had never crossed my mind that poor Henry was about to do anything so unexpected as to throw all this unexpected burden of the Charles Silliman affairs upon me."

"No, of course not," said Wm Sultan.

"What?" Mr. Party's voice was disconcerted.

"Perhaps I should have said, 'Yes, of course'?"

"Well, I was rather expecting you to say 'Yes,'" Mr. Party agreed, his voice happier, "and when you said, 'No,' it was, well, unexpected!"

Kelly said, "Something stinks. Mr. Philemon Party doesn't pocket around a hundred and twenty-five thousand a year by being fuzzy-minded."

"Perhaps he's sound on codicils," Morgan suggested.

"He *is* sound on codicils."

"I still can't understand," Roberts could not understand, "how they rake so much money into these musty old offices."

"An estate attorney," Kelly told her succinctly, "is one who ends up with the estate."

"And so," Philemon Party was saying, "I was wondering, it's been broached with Mr. Silliman, of course, this very afternoon, very afternoon, if you would do me the honor to associate yourself with me as counsel to Mr. Silliman?"

Kelly rose from her chair. "What the devil is this?"

"And, of course, of course," Mr. Party was continuing, "you'd be named a co-executor of his estate, of the trust funds to be set up under . . . I should be most happy if you could see your way clear?"

"Happy as to lose his remaining kidney," Kelly said. "Why's Mr. Silliman forced him to do this?"

Wm Sultan said, "I shall be honored to be associated with you."

"No, no, it is I who am honored. Mr. Silliman is most anxious to, short notice of course, short, but would it be possible, he presses an invitation for a day or two at Greenwater, there's a train at six, give you time to drop by this afternoon, perhaps, familiarize yourself with a few things?"

"I accept with pleasure."

"Splendid! I shall call Mr. Silliman on the telephone. . . ."

Roberts hastened to return to the reception office as Mr. Party's fading voice indicated that he had risen from his chair.

A minute later Kelly stood with a set face in the doorway of her employer's office. Her employer was sitting with a smug expression while he flipped with the tip of a bony finger the lobe of a large ear, a crochety, elderly habit at which she usually winced and which at the present she did not even notice.

"Just what goes on here?" she asked in a voice of ice. "Blackmail?"

Wm Sultan stopped flipping the lobe of his ear and, instead, pinched it.

"It's possible," he said, "that Mr. Silliman may have made a conclusion on inconclusive evidence." He gave a dry cough.

"Blackmailers," said Kelly, "real or only suspected, sometimes have things happen to them. Conclusive things. Like tombstones."

III

At shortly past eight o'clock that evening Wm Sultan stepped from his train to the platform of the station of the old town of New Harbor. His head tilted far back, to see from under the brim of his hat, he watched men kiss women and women kiss women and men slap each other on the back and hatless men in sports coats or shirtsleeves pick up the bags of men who, as himself, wore business suits and hats, if few at the same angle as his own. These kissing, slapping people went into cars and the cars went away. He began to feel lonely and, since there was a land breeze, warm. He did not question but that another man might take off his hat and fan himself. A Sultan would as soon have thought of fanning himself with his toupee.

He became aware that a skinny brat, a slender youth of perhaps thirteen in bathing trunks was shuttling in and out of his immediate vicinity. The nosy runt, the inquisitive lad again approached him with a stupid grin, a fixed smile that slowly faded and then again drug his pants, slowly retreated to the side of an open convertible. A girl got out of the near side of the car and came directly towards him with unmistakable intention.

Wm Sultan put his head even farther back. The girl appeared to be wearing nothing on earth except a white, thigh-length coat and beach clogs. Watching her over his cheekbones as she came nearer he became convinced that she was wearing nothing except the coat.

She stopped in front of him and said, tensely, "Mr. Sultan?"

Wm Sultan removed his hat and bowed his head to get the kink out of his neck. When now he could look directly at her with open eyes he saw that the land breeze was molding the thin fabric of the coat to her female form and he felt positive that she was wearing nothing but the coat.

"Yes?" he said. Oddly, he heard no sound. He tried again, and heard it. "Yes?"

"I'm Leslie Silliman," she said. "I'm sorry to have kept you waiting but Bart—"

"Lemme carry your briefcase," said Bart pleasantly. Wm Sultan surrendered it and picked up his suitcase.

"But he was afraid to speak to you," Leslie Silliman said. "It was your hat," she explained with a shudder. "I hope you've had something to eat?" she asked as she got behind the steering wheel. "Toss your suitcase in back with Bart." He did. "Have you?"

"Yes, thank you, I've dined," Wm Sultan said, sitting beside her.

"We eat at Greenwater," said Leslie Silliman, and began unbuttoning her coat. "We eat," she continued, and continued unbuttoning her coat, "whenever our excuse for a cook finds that the victuals have become warm or discovers that they have burnt. We eat," she concluded, and took off the coat, "sometimes at five, sometimes at nine, but never well."

"Welllll!" said Wm Sultan. She *was* wearing something under the coat. She was wearing a bathing bra and shorts on her slender, tanned figure. But when he gave them a quick glance he understood why he had not detected them under the coat.

She threw the coat into the back seat and the car into gear. The windshield was down and the wind streamed her dark hair from her face. It was a slender, daring face with its sharp chin and its thin upper lip pressed down on its full, almost pouting lower lip.

"Ever been here before?" she asked.

"No, I haven't."

She jerked her head towards the harbor. "View," she said.

It was a very pretty view with the white hulls of pleasure craft glowing on the darkening water, and, beyond and ahead, some land offshore.

"Bay Island," she said. "Where we're headed for."

"It looks very attractive."

"From here," said Leslie Silliman.

The road, beyond New Harbor, ran beside mud flats, a far-extending bar, the figures of clam diggers small in the distance. A hand clutched Wm Sultan's shoulder and he turned his head.

"There," shouted Bart in his ear, pointing, "is where Mr. Caglett's body was found!"

"What?"

"He was washed up dead!"

"Didn't you know?" asked Leslie Silliman. "Or do you even know who he was?"

Wm Sultan gave a dry cough. "I was aware," he said, "that Beatrix Caldwell, the eldest of the Caldwell children surviving the death of their brother, Howard, in 1890, by drowning, off Capri, she was three years old at the time, married—later, of course—one Hector Caglett by whom she had a male issue, Roylson, at present residing with his mother at Greenwater. But," he admitted his carelessness, "I fear I neglected to pursue any inquiries as to the unhappy fate of her spouse. *However,*" and there was another dry cough, a complacently self-conscious dry cough,

"I *might* hazard a speculative opinion as to the time of
the old tragedy! By your grandfather's kindness," he said
graciously, "to his guardians, I understand that Greenwater, the former home of your great-granduncle, Charles
Silliman, became the family domicile of the Roylson Caldwells, in residence if not possession, and that, indeed, the
two younger children, George and Georgiana—twins, I believe?—have remained in residence until the present day.
But Mrs. Caglett, née Beatrix Caldwell, departed from the
family residence in 1912, wasn't it? and did not return until shortly before your grandfather's return to this country
a month ago, and at his invitation. Now," he gave a dry
chuckle, "let us see! Inasmuch as Roylson Caldwell was
born in 1912 and his mother has not been in residence at
Greenwater since that date, I think we may conclude, may
we not, that her husband met his death by drowning in
that very year? No doubt the tragedy with its sad associa-
tions was her reason for leaving Greenwater."

Wm Sultan became aware that the car had slowed almost to a stop. He saw Leslie Silliman give herself a slight
shake, following which the car leaped forward and main-
tained its racing speed. He saw her lips move.

"I beg your pardon?" he said. "Did you ask me something?"

"God help me," she said, "if I ever ask you another
question."

The car went even faster.

A hand clutched Wm Sultan's shoulder.

"I'll bet," Bart shouted in his ear, "you don't know who
I am?"

"Fool!" hissed Leslie Silliman.

"Why, I should hope I do, Bart!" Wm Sultan assured
him kindly. "You're Bartram Nollis, and you have a sister
Catherine who is here with you, who was named for her
grandmother, whose maiden name was Catherine Beltry,

just as you were named for your great-grandfather, Bartram Beltry!" Wm Sultan had to lean over the back of the
seat because Bart had slunk into a corner. "And," shouted
Wm Sultan, "since his wife, your great-grandmother, was
born Agnes Silliman, you remember, whose brother, Ben-
jamin, was Miss Silliman's great-grandfather, that makes
you," he awarded the prize, "a distant cousin of Miss Silliman!" He turned, beaming, to Miss Silliman.

Miss Silliman glanced into the back seat. "You asked
for it, kid," she said.

A village flashed past.

"Bayhead," said Leslie Silliman. "The issue of Hudson
Bay and Penelope Head, who was born Penelope Pin, you
remember." Her eyes flicked a sidelong glance at his face.
His eyes were modestly lowered to her torso. She took a
deep breath with effective results. The car entered upon
a bridge. "Another view," she said. "To the left the Bay,
opening beyond the east point of the island to the sound.
To the right and the west, Bayhead Channel, the issue of
Eliza Pin-Head and Chanel No. 5." She gave him another
sidelong glance, a more lingering one. "You're a damn faker," she said.

The car had made a right turn on Bay Island after the
bridge and, following a road near the shore of the channel, was going back in the direction from which they had
come. It was dusk. Behind haze and clouds in the west
there was an ugly half-light like the smoldering of a sulphurous fire. Wm Sultan Caught glimpses of the channel
between the trees and hedges and houses to his right, and
to his left there was—he did not look to his left, but ahead
of him was the dying light in the sky. He, clearly, was so
interested in the channel and the dying light that he had
not heard the conclusive comment of Leslie Silliman.

She repeated it, "You're a damn faker." The car was
running very slow.

Wm Sultan gave a dry cough.

"You weren't sore when I was kidding you," she said. "You were trying to keep from grinning. And you like views," she said, taking a deep, slow breath, "You're really very sharp on views."

Wm Sultan courteously turned his head and smiled politely into the smoldering laughter in her bold eyes. They were, indeed, so bold, that that is undoubtedly the reason that he lowered his gaze for a moment before again facing her eyes.

"It has been very kind of you," he said, "to show me the sights."

Leslie Silliman laughed. "Yes, sir, Bart," she said over her shoulder, "when you ask him for it you certainly get it!"

From the back seat Bart's voice came with that explosiveness of something which has long wanted to be said. "But he wasn't drowned in 1912!" he cried.

"Oh, indeed?" said Wm Sultan.

"No, no, indeed," said Leslie Silliman, and there was no laughter in her voice. "It was not in 1912, not by a little matter of thirty-five years. In fact, it was just the day after my grandfather arrived here that Mr. Caglett was drowned."

She turned the car into a dark driveway.

4

*A Haunted House. Terrible Twins. A Gaunt
Widow and a Plump Son. More Eavesdroppers.
Fateful Story of the Drowned Youth Who Wrote
a Letter. A Barrister Drinks Green Water.*

The size of the heavily shaded lawn between the road and
the house, comparatively shallow but stretching well to
either side, the size of the house that loomed darkly in
the dusk, were about what Wm Sultan's investigations that
afternoon in the offices of Debrosses, Perdue & Party had
led him to expect. He had learned that Charles Silliman's
present estate of a value exceeding two million dollars
had grown from an inheritance of an approximate value
of three hundred thousand from his uncle in 1890, and
Greenwater seemed about what one might expect as the
summer residence of a man of that wealth at that time.

Bay Island had become fashionable in the '80's and particularly fashionable along the strip of shore facing the
channel of the bay. The bay, formed by the eastern end of
the island lying at an acute angle from the shore, might
kick up a bit in stormy weather, but the back entrance
to the bay, the long, narrow channel lying between the
mainland and the parallel western end of the island, had
the more domestic qualities of a well-contained river.

In keeping with all other manifestations of nature that had come within the power of its settlers it had been further domesticated by smooth stonework retaining walls. More often than not, the back verandas of the fashionable cottages rose directly above their retaining walls on the channel. These verandas, this incomparable site for verandas, had been the irresistible lure accounting for the fashionableness of that shore in that age of fanatic veranda-sitting.

For the rest, these summer homes were built so flimsily that sixty years later it would have taken artillery fire to spring a leak in the roof. Built in a day of large families, of relatively inexpensive servants, of lengthy visits by other large families, their size was ample. They were built in a day when men had sideburns and houses had shingled turrets, and vied in presenting impressive fronts. But one thing Wm Sultan would have sworn to, when the car came to a stop before a dark, double-decked front porch that set back like the bar of a dumbbell from a huge protruding turret at either end, and that was that there was no house on that or any other shore that could exceed Greenwater in its oppressive gloom.

He got out of the car and set his suitcase on the steps. Bart got out of the car with his briefcase. There was no sign of life from the house. No sound. No light except a yellow lozenge that hung in the hallway beyond the dark porch and illuminated, at least from the drive, little except itself.

Leslie Silliman remained behind the wheel. She said, "I think I'll take the car around to the garage."

Wm Sultan politely took the hint. "Let me go with you," he said. "There must be doors or something to open."

"Sure!" said Bart, hopping back into the back seat as Wm Sultan resumed his. "I'll show you how," he offered.

Leslie Silliman sucked in her breath and said, "We appreciate that, Bart."

The driveway curved to join a service driveway that, screened by a hedge from the front lawn, ran back to the public road. At that end of the property, facing the road, was an old carriage house. The doors, both from the road and the spur from the service driveway, were open. The lights of the car showed three others parked in its littered, unkempt interior.

"We've only two slovenly 'hired girls' on the whole place at present," Leslie Silliman explained. The edge of temper in her tone could have been due either to that or to the continued presence of Bart.

"Cook's funny," Bart contributed.

"I'm told that a staff of servants was collected for my grandfather's arrival," she continued as they walked back down the driveway, "but the whole lot of them were fired, or quit, the day after he arrived. They quit," she gave her opinion conversationally, "if I know, those two Caldwell bitches."

Wm Sultan coughed to remind her that young ears were present.

"Bart," she said, "I left my keys in the car so you could run back and get them."

Bart laughed in the darkness. "Slick chick!" he said, and trotted back up the driveway.

"Still shocked," asked Leslie Silliman, "about my indelicate language in the hearing of young ears? Bachelors," she laughed, not explaining how she knew that he was one, "get very quaint ideas about the innocence of the young, and must have very short memories. Bart, my friend, has long known what a bitch is. Including the regrettable fact that one can have a son. He's had an example right in front of him right here." She paused, listening. Bart's whistle came from the carriage house. "I'm worried," she said in a lowered tone and one from which all note of mockery had gone.

"You are"—her face was very close to his—"worried?" asked Wm Sultan.

"I'm worried about my grandfather."

"Your"—her fingers were on his arms—"grandfather?"

Her fingers tightened on his arm. Bart's whistling was swiftly nearing, the young idiot was running.

"I must have a talk with you tonight."

"Talk"—some part of her body was pressing against his coat—"tonight?"

"I'll—I'll manage to see you in your room—" She turned with a quick intake of breath at a crunch of gravel a few feet away in the direction of the house.

A man's voice said, "That you, Leslie?" It was a young, cocky voice. A tall figure with a swagger to it became visible as he moved out from the deep shadow of the hedge. It was where the hedge ended at the curve of the front driveway and it was possible that he had only that instant come around it and had not been standing there.

"Why, yes, Alex," Leslie Silliman said. Her tone was cool. "I'm the little one. It's the tall stranger who's Mr. Sultan."

Wm Sultan said, "Mr. Redell," and was shaking hands with him when Bart came up and said, "Here's your keys, Leslie." He felt Mr. Alexander Redell's hand freeze for a fraction of a second.

"Hey, Alex," Bart urged, "ask him who you are."

"My God, no!" warned Leslie Silliman. "Not unless you want to stand here all night."

Alex said to her, "What about seeing if there's a new record in the juke box at Reilly's?"

"It's an idea."

"Like to go in the house?" Bart asked, and Wm Sultan thanked him and said that he would. Behind them, voices followed more slowly, more faintly.

"I'll have to get bathed and dressed."

"That never takes you long."

"It may, tonight. . . ."

Bart said, with enthusiasm, "This is some place, isn't it!"

"Like it here, do you?" Wm Sultan asked pleasantly.

"The swimming's keen."

"So I'd imagine."

"We swim a lot. Do you like to swim at night?"

"Very much."

"It's keen. But you have to watch out for the current," he warned.

"Oh! Really bad, is it?" Wm Sultan sounded as impressed with the peril as he was expected to be.

"Carried Mr. Caglett's body clear over to New Harbor from here, didn't it!" Bart clinched the matter, and turned to another that was even nearer at hand. "The house is keen, too," he said, in the tone of confiding a secret.

Wm Sultan sensed that having shown himself appreciative of the danger of the current he had been found worthy of a further, deeper confidence.

"How's that?" he asked with proper gravity.

They had reached the porch steps. Bart paused, a step or two higher, and turned with his head on a level with Wm Sultan's.

He said, quietly, factually, "It's haunted."

II

Wm Sultan had been carefully brought up to believe that for a haunted house a rattling of chains was the pre-eminent attribute, but the broad-mindedness of his education had recognized that that supreme distinction was, by the

chance of historical development, largely limited to the
admittedly superior quality of haunted houses in England,
and even there not to the common variety called Man-
or House with Priest's Hole, but solely to the definitely
top-drawer Old Castle with Donjon-Keep. As within the
continental limits of the United States the only private
castles were the rather recent seats of prosperous pants
manufacturers, a good creepy creak was accepted as par
for the course.

When, therefore, he was told that the house was haunted and immediately following the receipt of that information heard a creak in the darkness of the porch he listened
to the creak with some interest. He also heard it with a
definite sense of annoyance. Outdoors, where creaks are
difficult to produce except in the branches of trees in the
season of winter, an unexpected crunch of gravel is generally considered to be about the thing. Very well. He had
been given the crunch of gravel. Enough was enough. One
eavesdropper was annoying, but a second silent waiter in
the darkness gave an uncomfortable sense of being surrounded by stealthy distrust.

He drew the boy's head close to his own. "Don't tell any
secrets," he warned in a whisper good for a hundred feet,
"some sneak is listening in."

Bart laughed. "Oh, that's only Catherine!" he said.
"Hey, sis, this is Mr. Sultan!"

A female figure, clothed, appeared for an instant against
the dull light in the doorway, the screen door slammed,
and the figure disappeared inside the house.

Bart did not want his guest to be offended. "She's been
sore all the time," he dismissed it; "ever since we got here."
Inside the hall he set down Wm Sultan's briefcase and nodded towards an open doorway. "Guess you'll find them in
there," he said, and went back outdoors on his own boy's
business.

Wm Sultan coughed. When there was no response he formed a low opinion of the manners of the household and went to the open doorway that Bart had indicated. Under the light of a floor lamp, in a dim, circular room, there was a card table and at the card table two people were seated. One was a gray-haired man and the other was a gray-haired woman. They sat motionlessly and looked at Wm Sultan and Wm Sultan looked at the man. The man was the first on whom his eyes lighted and he did not look farther than the man.

An elderly man. A large elderly man. A large elderly man with a pointed nose. A large elderly man with a pointed nose *and* a pointed jaw. . . . The back of Wm Sultan's head gave a reminiscent throb.

He bowed slightly and said, "Mr. Silliman."

Then, for the first time, the two figures at the card table moved. The large elderly man with a pointed nose and a pointed jaw turned in his chair, and a large elderly woman with a pointed nose and a pointed jaw turned in her chair, and they looked at each other. Then, simultaneously, they burst into raucous laughter. They looked at each other and laughed, they threw back their heads and laughed, they faced Wm Sultan and laughed in his face.

"George Caldwell!" said the man with a wheeze of laughter.

"Georgiana!" said the woman with a wheeze of laughter.

And, with identical open-mouthed grins between their long, pointed noses and their long, pointed jaws, the identical twins sat staring at him like mocking children with some secret joke.

Behind and above him a man's voice said, "Mr. Sultan?" It was a fretful, flustered voice, and the plump, youngish man who came quickly down the stairs had a fretted, anxious manner. "Mr. Sultan, I've been waiting for you, I was waiting." His wide, brown eyes glanced aside at a chair in

the hall as if to say, "right there!" and then went apprehensively to a closed door in the hall. "But"—his voice
quickened and lowered—"when Miss Nollis ran upstairs
I—" he broke off as the closed door opened.

A gaunt gray-haired woman in black stood in the doorway. A gaunt gray-haired woman with a long, pointed nose
and a long, pointed jaw and a grim mouth between.

"Mother!" said the plump man. "Mother, Mr. Sultan.
Mr. Sultan, my mother. Oh, I've forgotten! I haven't intro-
duced myself. I—"

Wm Sultan bowed. "How do you do, Mrs. Caglett."

"Mr. Sultan," acknowledged the widow Caglett. It was
a voice without resonance, a voice as dull and flat as the
look in her eyes. She looked at her son. "Did you," she
asked, "introduce Mr. Sultan to your aunt and uncle?"

"No, Mother. No. I—"

"I thought I heard them talking," said the dull voice,
and it was an accusation as soft and as deadly as being
buried in sand.

Wm Sultan gave a look at the card table. Still motionless, still grinning, still avidly staring, it did not seem
that the two who sat there had so much as batted an eye.
With a polite inclination of his head, he again faced Mrs.
Caglett.

"Mr. Caldwell and Miss Caldwell," he informed their
sister, "were kind enough to introduce themselves."

The gaunt mother was staring fixedly at her plump son.

Roylson Caldwell said, "I went upstairs a moment, only
a moment."

She said, "Mr. Sultan is waiting to be shown to his
room." She watched her son obediently jump for the suitcase of the guest and the briefcase of the counselor-at-law,
and then to the representative on earth of Sultan, Sultan
& Sultan she said, "Mr. Silliman has had a trying day. He
will see you in the morning."

Wm Sultan gave a deferential bow. "That will be quite convenient," he agreed. "I shall be free in my office after," he considered, "shall we say eleven? Ah, no, no, no, no," he remembered. "My deepest apologies to Mr. Silliman, but I forgot, *as he did,* that I have an appointment. If it's quite convenient, I fear it will have to be tomorrow *a week,* after eleven." He considerately indicated that Roylson Caglett might set the luggage down again. "I shan't have to trouble you to show me upstairs, since," he explained to Mrs. Caglett, "when I find my *hostess* again, no doubt Miss Silliman can arrange for me to be conveyed to the train that leaves New Harbor at— I do believe it's nine-fifty, isn't it?"

Smiling courteously, he observed with interest that the skin had so tightened over Mrs. Caglett's long, pointed nose and long, pointed jaw that they had something of the appearance of two beaks of yellow, polished bone, and that her eyes, which in the dimness of the hall had appeared as dull as smudges of soot, had now, perhaps by some trick of the light, the reflective qualities of freshly broken pieces of anthracite coal.

Then, out of the corner of his eye, his attention was caught by a movement at the card table. He had been taught in his training for, and had learned by his experience in, the OSS in the late war, that the verge of the field of vision was the most sensitive to movement, and as it had been so in the case of that SS guard on the bridge at Lepois, whose back he had broken, and was now again correct in the hall of Greenwater, he was inclined to acknowledge that the evidence supporting the theory was strong, though, of course, by no means conclusive. At the card table the twins had again turned in their chairs to face each other and, again, they simultaneously burst into raucous laughter.

With that sound, Mrs. Caglett in a spasm of rage flung up her hand in a gesture that was as clear and violent as if she had literally flung Wm Sultan's luggage up the stairs. And with that speechless admission that Charles Silliman would, after all, keep his appointment for that evening, the door by which she had entered slammed behind her.

Wm Sultan turned with a polite smile to Roylson Caglett.

"Let me carry up the suitcase," he offered courteously, and, besides, his plump guide looked as though he might faint and drop it.

III

His room opened on a long veranda and the veranda on a wide view. There was still a faint saffron glow in the northwestern sky, to the northeast stars were out, below on the opposite shore of the channel were the fixed yellow lights of houses, the moving white headlights of cars. Wm Sultan did not go out on the veranda because it was obvious that should he do so he could not very well help but see into the lighted windows and doors of other bedrooms that opened on it. He doubted if, for that very reason, any one ever really used the veranda for veranda-sitting. It had an unused look. There was some porch furniture, wicker chairs and settees, but they were drawn back against the side of the house as if in storage out of the rain. On top of the shingled parapet some two feet high that guarded the front of the veranda there was a row of large ferns in large wooden pots, and while they must have to be watered now and then he had no doubt but that it was done only at discreet hours when the waterer would not transgress upon the privacy of those behind the windows and glass doors—Leslie Silliman was standing in his doorway.

Since it was the doorway of his bedroom and since she was wearing that short white coat that gave the impression that that was all she was wearing, Wm Sultan felt that the situation was one of questionable propriety. He wondered if, despite the informality of her entrance, she might not expect him to open the door to the hall? She came quickly into the room, and closed the veranda door behind her.

She came close up to him and said, "I could kiss you!"

"Well," said Wm Sultan. "Well! And to what," he asked quite heartily, "am I indebted for this flattering expression of an apparently favorable opinion?"

Leslie Silliman appeared for an instant to be somewhat baffled but her mood was too enthusiastic to be long dampened.

"Alex and I listened on the porch," she said, "and so help me if he hadn't put his hand over my mouth I would have cheered!"

Wm Sultan was less interested in her strangled huzzahs than in the admission, the fact, that she and Alex Redell had, in mutual agreement, deliberately stood in the darkness of the porch and eavesdropped upon his conversation with the relict Caglett.

"To see you," she specified, "kick that old bitch's teeth down her throat!"

Wm Sultan gave a dry, demurring cough.

"My grandfather's afraid of her," she said, in a changed, worried tone.

"Why?" asked Wm Sultan.

"I think it's her," Leslie Silliman admitted that she could not support her statement. "But he *is* afraid of something—" She put her hands on his arms. "You're my grandfather's lawyer, aren't you?"

"No, Miss Silliman." She was surprised. "I may," he explained, "become associated with Mr. Party as counsel, but that awaits the result of an interview with Mr. Silliman. I do not," he concluded, "expect the outcome to be favorable."

"Why?"

Wm Sultan looked at the floor. The floors of the house, in the tradition of summer cottages, were uncarpeted, and an inspection of the bare boards revealed to the discerning eye the location of a supporting joist. He followed it as if walking a tightrope to the door and there was not a single warning creak before he opened the door.

"Ah, Mr. Caglett!" he said.

"I—I was just going to knock," said Roylson Caglett. "My mother, I mean Mr. Silliman, would like you to join him on the veranda."

"It's very kind of you to—" began Wm Sultan and found himself brushed aside.

Leslie Silliman brushed him aside in order to have room for a motion of her extended arm. The motion began with her hand behind her and approximately on a level with the brief hem of her short white coat, and followed a swinging, rising arc that was concluded with a loud report when her open palm was arrested by the plump cheek of a face from which protruded an only slightly long nose and an only slightly pointed chin.

Wm Sultan averted his eyes and his own ear crinkled slightly around the edges. He thoughtfully went to the head of the stairs as other sharp footsteps clicked down the bare hall, their echo terminating in the slam of a door. He went down the stairs thoughtfully. If memory served him, Miss Silliman had boasted to him of having eavesdropped upon his earlier conversation with Mr. Caglett, and yet now when Mr. Caglett eavesdropped upon his conversation with her . . . His reflections upon feminine logic were broken by a cackle of laughter as he came within view of an open doorway at the foot of the stairs. He did not look in the doorway. He knew what he should see. The laughter followed him as he went, at a venture, to the back of the hall and the door which the widow Caglett had slammed behind her.

IV

Wm Sultan had seldom been more comfortable or more ill at ease. As he had expected, he had found the terrace on which Charles Silliman had been awaiting him to be directly beneath that of the bedroom floor, but it was a terrace that invited you to sit down and relax. Its chance grouping of chairs and tables, a scattering of magazines and ashtrays, were in themselves informal, relaxed and legs stretched out. Since his wicker chair had a leg rest he could sit that way himself without loss of dignity, and, perhaps as an after effect of the blow he had received on the head that forenoon, he felt that he could sit like that forever while his body soaked up comfort like a thirsty sponge. Further, after the roar of the city and the rumble of the train, after raucous laughter and slamming doors, it was quiet and peaceful on the terrace, all the more for the soothing lapping of water on the stone retaining wall beneath its stone parapet. He could not recall when he had been more ill at ease.

He had, in town, undertaken the journey with a throbbing head and a grim anticipation of a second meeting with a large elderly man with a pointed nose and a pointed jaw. If, after George Caldwell's introduction of himself, he had realized that a man did not necessarily have to be Charles Silliman to have registered at the hotel under that name, he had nevertheless not been able to get out of his still tender head the impression of a bold man of action.

To his left under the light of a lamp sat a timid little old man who was badly frightened and gravely ill. From his baffled blue eyes to his insignificant nose to his pursed mouth his face was the face of futility. If there was any strength at all in that ineffectual face it would be that of stubbornness, a certain tenacity in holding on, that last strength of the meek in spirit.

Wm Sultan wearily and reluctantly swung his feet to the floor, sitting sidewise on his chair, more nearly to face Charles Silliman. The letters had at last been mentioned.

"Yes, Mr. Silliman," he said, "Mr. Perdue told me the story. How your friend was drowned, Howard Caldwell, the son of your guardian, Roylson Caldwell. But there could be a different story, Mr. Silliman." He waited, but there was no word from the small old man who sat huddled in his chair.

"This other story," Wm Sultan began reluctantly, "is identical in every particular to the one we know with one exception. That exception is that it was not the son of this man who was traveling abroad with his family who was drowned, but the son's friend, the father's ward."

Wm Sultan rose and took a step towards the window open to the dark room behind Charles Silliman. There was a faint sound when some one moved away from the window. He did not believe that it was psychologically probable that the sixth, by count, eavesdropper of the evening would return to that listening post, but to be on the safe side, which his cautious nature always preferred when possible, he sat down on the parapet facing Charles Silliman and the window.

"We later have evidence," he continued, "that Roylson Caldwell was near the end of the fortune he had inherited. That evidence is in the very large sums you instructed your attorneys to have remitted to him the moment you came of age, the large annual sums you had remitted to him until his death."

The man huddled in the chair gave no answer.

"Two boys living in the same family," Wm Sultan went on, "two boys in a foreign port, two boys and one of them is dead and there is no one to question which one is dead, two boys and the one who is living only has to take the name of the one who is dead to inherit a fortune. I have only the deepest sympathy," he said gently, "for that son who obeyed his father and assumed the name of his dead friend. Nor do I think the father had any real idea of all that that act entailed. A man who extravagantly runs through a fortune usually is not a far-sighted man. At the time I think he saw no further than an opportunity for his son to come into a fortune with, of course, resultant benefits to himself. But I do not believe that he foresaw the necessity for a lifelong exile for his son, lest some old acquaintance of the boys such as my uncle, Horace, should recognize him and reveal the impersonation."

From the dark water came the sound of an outboard moving slowly up the channel. Wm Sultan listened to it, weary of saying what he had to say to the pitiful man in the chair. Out on the water the motor coughed and stopped. Wm Sultan again spoke.

"An obedient, affectionate boy of fourteen," he said. "A hero-worshiping boy, as who is not at that age, and his hero was my uncle. He had written a letter to my uncle from France, and in Italy he received a reply after the death of his dear friend. His friend whose name he now bore. His world turned upside down, heartbroken over the death of his friend, he could not resist replying to that letter, to saying farewell to his hero, even though he had to write of himself as if he were dead, and to sign his letter with the name of his friend who was dead, the name," Wm Sultan concluded, taking an envelope from his pocket and handing it to the man in the chair, "as you can see, of Charles Silliman."

He turned his back then on those shaking hands and leaning over the parapet gazed at the lights on the shore of the mainland, breathed the twang of the salt sea water, listened to its tamed waves lapping at the stone wall beneath him. He looked up just in time to see the tub of one of the potted ferns on the upper veranda as it came within the light on the roof. He was knocked over the parapet and unconscious sank into the swift current beneath the gently lapping waves.

5

*A Barrister Abed. Aboard the Cruiser. An Applicant
with a Strange Accent. A Signal is Seen. The
Rendezvous in Smugglers' Cove. A Doomed
Youth Plays a Strange Game.*

Wm Sultan quickly closed his eyes. He heard a "Thank
you," and the sound of a closing door. There was an assort-
ment of vague sounds and then there was silence and then
there was the sound of a faint, rhythmic drumming. He
cautiously opened the merest slit of an eye and saw a shoe.

It was a trim shoe on a small foot. It was suspended in
the air above the floor by a slender ankle and it was keeping time with the soft drumming. His slitted eye followed
nylon up the graceful curve of a calf to the hem of a skirt.
The hem of the skirt was just below a knee. On the knee
a hand was lying, and on the back of this hand the red-
nailed fingers of another hand were beating a tattoo.

It was then that Wm Sultan had his first suspicion that
he may have closed his eyes just a little bit too late. It
is difficult successfully to feign sleep if you have been
caught with your eyes open. To know the worst, he risked
a quick upward glance and knew it. Kelly was observing
him with a patient smile. It was a smile of a patience that
made his blood run cold. It was of a patience that has been

tried and tried again and doubts not but that it shall be tried yet again, the patience of a mother with a backward child, the patience that is beyond hope but cannot reach resignation.

"Really, Mr. Sultan," Kelly said, "twice in one day!"

Wm Sultan closed his eyes and damned the doctor who had failed to secrete him in some inaccessible hospital.

"I know," she said with threadbare indulgence, "that you don't *mean* to get yourself hurt, but it's getting so we can't let you go out of the office on the simplest errand without—!"

He might as well open his eyes. He saw Kelly distractedly shake her head. Then she sighed and took a grip on herself.

"It's getting so that every time the 'phone rings," she began in the monotonous tone of one who is uselessly repeating what has been uselessly said many times before, "I expect that, at last, it's the morgue. It's making a nervous wreck of me. Carrying you off elevators, wildly leaving my office work and rushing frantically to your bedsides!"

Wm Sultan closed his eyes again.

"Can't I make you realize how serious your thoughtlessness is?" she appealed. "You simply *mustn't* keep banging your head," she explained earnestly. "If you do it's only a matter of time until one of your playmates finds a soft spot."

Wm Sultan opened his eyes again and stared glassily at the ceiling.

"Oh, well—!" her sigh admitted that it was useless to point out to him the error of his ways. "And I suppose the rest of it's partly my fault," she admitted. "Since I knew you were coming to the shore I should have made you wear your waterwings."

Kelly shrugged it off. "Oh, well!" she said again, but brightly. "We won't talk about it any more now! We must keep you calm and relaxed, and that's what I'm here for! I'm not going to let a thing worry or fret or anger you! You must have a nice happy rest so all your concussions can heal up all ready for the next time! Now, let's see, what is there we can chat about to take your mind off things? Oh, yes—" she laughed, "the office is closed up!"

"*What?*" Wm Sultan lowered his head very slowly and gently back to the pillow; he must not do that again.

"Oh, yes! Since you're not there Morgan and Roberts might as well take their vacation now as any other time. And the telephone answering service will explain to any one who calls that we're only closed indefinitely. Of course, the Landlapper Executors *are* up for examination three days from now and there seems to be another point of view as to the legality of their authorization of that $87,643.27, *but* if they can't find their lawyer-man what's that to worry—" Kelly broke off, said normally, "I got a week's postponement," and laughed at him.

She stopped laughing when Leslie Silliman opened the door and came to the bed and sat down on the bed beside Wm Sultan and took his hand in one hand and with the other, and a dainty handkerchief, wiped the cold perspiration from his brow. She then had time to give Wm Sultan's secretary a reproving look.

"You mustn't worry Mr. Sultan with business," she said. "He mustn't be excited."

The secretary said, "If *I* were on the bed with him he'd be excited."

II

The small cruiser with a dinghy in tow pushed slowly up the channel. There was a break in the sound of its engine, it resumed again briefly, stuttered into silence. The small boat—it was of some twenty-four feet—lost headway and began to turn in the tide. A swimmer some distance from shore, evidently curious or willing to be helpful, half-drifted and half-swam alongside. The swimmer attracted the attention of the helmsman who had left the wheel and opened the engine hatch in the fore part of the cockpit. The swimmer was given a hand aboard.

"On the button," said Kelly, and sank, dripping, on a cushioned seat.

"How'd it look?" asked Roberts, and, remembering appearances, turned back to the engine.

Kelly, still breathing heavily, nodded. "Fine," she said. "Sounded fine, too. How'd you work it?"

Roberts, with a grin, untied double fishlines from a bar on a cut-off valve at the carburetor. "It ought to have sounded like a choked gas line," she said. "Choked it was."

"But it started up again. That's what made it so good."

Roberts rolled up the fishlines. "One to open, one to close," she said. "They're watching us over there."

"Be strange if they weren't when they saw me come aboard. Don't worry, they can't possibly suspect anything."

"My telephone call all right?"

"It was so cryptic," Kelly assured her, "that though I knew what to expect I could hardly decipher it. Stop fretting. This couldn't be arranged better. We've publicly struck up an acquaintance," she amplified, taking a look down the companionway: a galley to port, transom berths, an enclosed head forward. "Gives you the excuse to drop by and say hello now and then. Cozy," she commented, turning from the cabin. "Cozier with two."

"Who's the handsome blond thing who's waving?" Roberts asked. "At least he looks handsome from here."

"He is, and he's Alex Redell."

"Now I know all."

"He's one of the three descendants of the first Charles Silliman's sister, Agnes Beltry, née Silliman, who—"

Roberts rapped the engine with a monkey wrench. "Look, Kelly," she said. "There must be an easier way."

Kelly nodded. "The short of it is he's one of the three cousins who would get the dough if Charles Silliman isn't Charles Silliman."

"If? What do you mean, '*If?*'"

"If it can be proven."

"But with those letters there can't be any other answer!"

"Grandpappy says can be."

"Look, Kelly. All these cracks he's had on the head— I mean, he may not be feeling so good."

"Purrs," said Kelly. "Positively purrs!"

Roberts raised a grease-smeared face from the engine hatch. "I haven't heard this baby at a distance," she admitted, "but when you're aboard it sounds like *crunch-grunt, pog-pog.*"

"Purrs!" Kelly repeated, striking her fist on the coaming of the hatchway. "That lascivious kitten rubs herself up against him and he positively purrs!"

Roberts sat back on her haunches. "Do you really mean that some she-cat is trying to get our Bill to howl?"

"He's already purring. And it's Leslie Silliman."

The light of battle in Roberts' eyes became clouded by a thoughtful frown. "Do you think maybe we should have been kinder to him?" she asked. "When you look at it some ways, in some ways he's put up with a good deal from us."

"He's put up from us—?" Kelly took a deep breath. "When I think what I've— Oh, what's the use?" she dismissed it impatiently, and, in a changed tone, "They nearly got him, Roberts."

"Was the story you gave over the telephone straight?"

Kelly smiled. "The culprit," she said, "has even been found and punished."

"They found who—"

"Oh, my, yes. You see, one of the duties of one of the slatternly maids was to water the ferns. And so, *obviously,* she must have pushed it half over the edge and later vibration caused it to fall. She's been fired."

"That's a break," Roberts said.

"Yes."

"All right, now what really happened?"

"Some one overheard Bill tell the gist of the letter business to Mr. Silliman. Just before that tub of dirt fell on him he'd handed the envelope with those copies of the letters to Mr. Silliman. And since he hadn't mentioned that they were photos any one standing on the upper veranda would have thought that Charles Silliman had all the evidence in his hands. Everything else I told you was on the up and up except—"

"We'll have to start the engine," Roberts cut in. "Some kid's fooling with an outboard on that skiff."

"That's Bart. He's another one of the cousins."

"Once we're under way they may give it up," Roberts said. "Stay where you are, as if watching the engine for me, and when we get up there again you can give us more engine trouble and we can drift back here again if we need more time." The engine chugged to life and Roberts took the wheel. "But we'd better make it snappy because if they get that thing going they'll be alongside in two shakes."

Kelly said, "And except that I think some one pulled Grandpappy out of the water. He was found on the beach."

Roberts scanned the shore. The retaining walls had been built only in front of the houses, leaving between the native rock occasional short, narrow beaches of sand. There was one off the downstream end, so to speak, of the terrace of Greenwater.

"Why?" she asked, still studying the shore.

"Because," said Kelly, "the night after Mr. Silliman arrived here, the late Mr. Hector Caglett—"

"Never heard of him," Roberts interrupted.

"Beatrix Caldwell's husband," Kelly explained impatiently.

"Never have got these Caldwells straight."

"Howard Caldwell's little brothers and sisters, Howard of the Toe, you dope."

"That little devil's got that outboard—no, it's stopped again."

"Mr. Hector Caglett," Kelly resumed, "had a dizzy spell or something and fell off the terrace and *his* body was carried over to New Harbor."

Roberts' one comment on the coincidental demise of the late Hector Caglett was, "The next night? Didn't waste much time." Her blond hair blowing, her blue eyes intently studying the shore, she looked, thought Kelly, like a Viking on a raid. Not abstract reasoning, but a boat, water, the world of physical action was her element.

"We've got about thirty seconds," she said as the outboard changed the tune of its stuttering. "Yes," she decided, "a body falling from the terrace would be carried to New Harbor, all right. The sandbar of that beach wouldn't hold a body against the current. It would slow it down, though, give you a few minutes to wade out and fish it out. Who found Bill?"

"The fat character sitting on the rocks with the dumpy girl. She's Bart's sister, the other cousin, and fatty's Roylson Caglett, son of the late Hector."

"How soon?"

"Not too soon. Seems Mr. Silliman called out and Roylson, who was front-porch sitting with Miss Catherine Nollis heard him and went to him and found out what had happened and then ran down to the beach and—there was grandpappy. Unconscious, but, fortunately lying with his head out of the water."

"Nuts. Somebody saw him knocked in, pulled him out and left him on the beach, and but quick."

Kelly said superiorly, "Yes, Leif Ericsson, that's what I've been trying to tell you. The current from the bay—"

"The only currants you know anything about are in pies. Who slipped you this dope?"

"Bart."

"Here they come. When's the pay-off on the letters?"

"Mr. Silliman's sent grandpappy word he hopes to feel strong enough to see him this evening."

"Where's your room?"

"Two doors from Bill's."

"Wake up, Kelly! Which side the house?"

"This."

Roberts jerked her head towards the opposite shore. "See that cove?"

"Yes."

"I'll drop the hook there tonight, and pray," she commented, with a second glance at the shore. "If you need a task force flash your room light three times. Corny, but I'll be able to see it. I'll answer by showing a flashlight on deck. Give it three and I'll run *Bolivar* right up on the veranda."

"Who—oh, no!"

"Didn't you notice? Well, *Bolivar's* the name of this palatial yacht and if you don't think it's palatial wait until Bill sees the charter cost on the expense account he doesn't even know— You didn't tell him?"

"For heaven's sake."

They were speaking rapidly as the outboard propelled skiff was now rapidly nearing them.

"If you want an undercover conference flash it five times and I'll row over in the dinghy to—" she looked back down the island shore to a much larger beach at its western point, at which several people were bathing—"that must be a public affair, you can probably reach it from the road."

"But why can't you—"

"Row straight across against the current?" Roberts cut in. "If you want to wait an hour after calling me. Look, Kelly, just leave this sort of thing to me. Besides, there's too much chance of discovery if we meet at the house."

"All right."

"I think," Roberts said, "I'll go clam digging."

"Yes," Kelly affirmed, "it was clam diggers who first found Mr. Caglett's body. As they might have found grand-pappy's."

There was a blue light of battle in Roberts' eyes when she turned and said, "I'm mad as hell." But when she saw Kelly's quiet dark eyes and quiet smile she realized that she had not known what really deadly anger was.

The skiff swung into its turn to come alongside.

"Morgan?" Kelly asked quickly.

"I'll tell her. She'll do her part, all right," Roberts said confidently.

"Hey, taxi!" Kelly called, laughing, to Bart and Alex Redell in the skiff.

III

The slatternly girl slammed the flimsy door and its frosted glass panel rattled loosely but did not break. On the outside of the panel in chipped black letters was the name of the New Harbor Domestic Employment Service, G. W. Sander, Prop. Inside the dingy office G. W. Sander, and he suited the office perfectly, a little soiled, more than a little run down at the heels and resigned to it, wearily and a little sadly shook his head.

"I warned her," he said. "I didn't want to send her there at all even if the pay was good, very good. I warned her," he said wearily, "and she shouldn't hold it against me. But that's the way they are," he explained to the young woman sitting on the bench.

He had already made up his mind about the young woman sitting on the bench. Her clothes had baffled him only at first sight. Her dress looked like some sort of a maid's uniform and her hat something that cooks used to wear. A summer actress, that was the answer. She would want a cook-maid, only ten of us in the little cottage, and she was out of luck.

"That's the way they are," he repeated. "Because they can afford to be and they know it." He shook his head, not too regretfully because he was resigned to it, and said, "I'm sorry, but I can't help you out with—" he was momentarily tempted by the thought of Drunk Mary, but it was just no use, she *was* drunk—"any one at all," he concluded.

"Coooo—!" sang out the girl. "An' surre, Hi'm a-lookin' foah a job meself, suh."

G. W. Sander sat quite still for an instant, but realizing that the acoustic qualities of the office might be very poor he snapped himself out of it and turned his mind from the sound to the meaning of what she had said.

"You—you're an applicant for a place?" he asked. A real, live applicant?

"Coooo—!" replied the applicant.

"You—you haven't had experience? Not that it matters," he added hastily.

The applicant rose, opening her handbag. "May Hi hask yuh to refer to mine references?" she inquired haughtily, and, dropping a paper on the desk, sat down again.

G. W. Sander opened his mouth to speak, and then with a slight shake of his head closed it again and opened the recommendation. His eyes opened wider as he read.

"Why," he said, "this *is* a fine, a very, a very"—he began to reread the letter—"a most very fine recommendation."

The applicant said, complacently, "Hi thankee, suh."

G. W. Sander stopped cold, then shook himself and read on. "'Scullery maid—serving maid—ladies' maid—'" he murmured, with each more deeply impressed—"'downstairs maid—upstairs maid—parlor maid, bedroom and bath.'" He looked up. "Must have been a very large establishment."

"Hand wot else," inquired the applicant, "would youse be expecting, suh, from the noime of me employer?"

"Oh!" said G. W. Sander, looking at it again. "Yes," he said humbly. "Of course. 'Morgan.'"

"Coooo—!" said the applicant.

G. W. Sander rubbed his hand over his face. "Well," he said. "Well, certainly!" he said, when he really thought about it. "Certainly with such a reference as this you can have your pick! Now," he ran his finger down a card file, "there's the Chauncy Blug's. You won't have a thing to do—two old people with a house staff of nine, and two," he made it off-hand but got it over, "two young bachelors for chauffeurs! With *this* character—from a Morgan!—I know that you'll—"

"Wot," interrupted the applicant, "aboot ze yob that goil who-all wuz yust in heah gotta dismissed from?"

"For God's sake!" cried G. W. Sander, banging his hands down on the desk and jumping to his feet, *"What* nationality *are* you!"

"Hi?" asked the applicant haughtily. "Hi ham han hupper cluss Hanglish soivent! And vot else could yuh-all a-been a-thinkin'?"

"God," said G. W. Sander, weakly sitting down again, "knows." He put his face in his hands. "This other place is out of the question," he said. "As you heard yourself, the girl was dismissed on some ridiculous charge of having watered a pot of ivy or something. A short time ago an entire staff quit. No competent servant will go near the place. It's out of the question."

"Hi'll tike hit," said the applicant.

Speaking through his hand, G. W. Sander said, "Hit's yoot ob de question."

"Coooo—!" said the applicant.

IV

Since the investigation of remote causes is illimitable, one leading back to the other like the generations of man, and the successions of circumstances which had culminated in the presence of Bartram Nollis in the house called Greenwater would go in a direct line at least as far back as the date of two letters that had once been written to the late Horace Seneca Sultan, it is more practical to settle upon the climatic cause and to say that Bartram Nollis, at the age of thirteen, met his death because he wanted a drink of water.

Again to skip over the contributory factors, that he had been sun and salt dried all day, that he had helped himself in the kitchen to a noble slice of ham as a snack before going to bed, that he had been thirsty before going to sleep but had drowsed off while trying to make up his mind whether to get a drink, the climatic fact is that he did wake up in the middle of the night because, at least in his own opinion, he was so thirsty. He woke, got up, went into the connecting bathroom between his room and that of his sister, and drank a glass of water. He drew a second one and, while sipping it, leaned out of the open window facing on the upstairs terrace. He was yawning, and after finishing the glass of water should have shuffled sleepily back to bed and instant slumber, had he not seen a light from behind one of the windows on the terrace turn on and off five times. An adult might or might not suspect that such a thing was a signal, but no boy of thirteen would suspect it for a moment, he would know that it was.

Bart knew it with unquestioning certainty and he was instantly wide awake in a night that dreams are made of.

V

It was a dark night, and to two young female persons who were, by the environment of city streets, unaccustomed to the darkness of night, it lurked with waiting and pursuing dangers. Their state of mind may seem less censurable, particularly in female persons, if it is borne in mind that they had stealthily crept from a house in which an assault with deadly intent had been committed, that they had met each other surreptitiously and were, on their way to a secret rendezvous. But censurable or not, such was their state of mind that they had paused more than once to listen for the sound of pursuing footsteps before they reached the point of the island. Again their environment must be borne in mind when they stood completely in the open on a sandbar. They were, again, unaccustomed to open places that were unpeopled. They should have been acutely conscious of its loneliness had they stood on that bare spit in the daylight, the emptiness of water to either hand, and they should have felt strangely conspicuous. In the night they had the same sense of standing exposed themselves while imagination peopled the surrounding darkness. They shivered, and in unspoken accord went back up the shore to their left instinctively seeking their accustomed protection of walls, of something, anything, concrete to put between their backs and the night.

The shore swiftly narrowed and rocks began to stick up out of the sand and the water. They continued, in silence, not needing to confer as they followed their sure instinct, until an arm of rock barred their path and climbing over it they found themselves on a horseshoe patch of sand in the rocks open only to the water. They sat at once upon the sand, side by side, facing the dark water.

The flare of a cigarette lighter, like a candle flame, glowed in the tiny cove, flickering on the rocks of its walls, on its floor of sand, on the dark, lapping water, and

went out like a snuffed candle. It blazed again, was again
snuffed. Five times its light flickered on the rocks and
the sand and the water swirling over, a rock that raised
its head above the surface, striking crystal drops from the
dark water.

After a time, the flame again flared and died five times.

Later there was a creak of oarlocks in the darkness over
the water.

"It's like a smuggler's cove!" Morgan whispered.

"It's a good place," Kelly agreed. "I wonder if I should
keep the lighter on for her now?"

"I guess so, maybe. But it throws an *awful* lot of light."

Out of the darkness on the water loomed the white
prow of a dinghy, the face of an oarsman glancing over
the shoulder. There was a startled, choked exclamation, a
violent lunging upon one oar, the thud and scrape of wood
against rock, a splashing of water, a grating of sand, and
Roberts' long legs stepped overside.

"Give me that thing," she said, and Kelly gave her the
lighter. She examined the inside of the skiff and then
swung it broadside to the shore and said, "Take off your
damned landlubberly shoes and give me a hand with this."
They took off their shoes and helped her stand the skiff
on its beam ends so that she could examine its exterior. "I
don't know," she concluded. "We'll all sit in it while we're
here. Give me enough draft to find if it's shipping water.
Get aboard." She dropped a kedge anchor between two
rocks on shore so that the skiff floated but not much more
than that, and, taking her place, held it offshore with an
oar. "All right," she said, as they sat in the darkness in the
boat, "you thought I'd see the rock, along with the others you provided here. I would have if I hadn't assumed
that there was a clear channel to your light. For your
future advisement, it's an old nautical custom not to mark

a channel directly over a rock. Now," she dismissed the misadventure, and her voice was tense, "what is it?"

Morgan's voice said, "I don't know either. She's been waiting to tell us both at once."

"Mr. Silliman," Kelly's voice was low but crisp, "came to see Bill this afternoon about the letters. Now don't fall overboard, but he admits that he wrote both of them."

"Of course he did!"

"That's just what we've said."

"Only," Kelly said, "in reverse. The plain and simple story is that he wrote Howard Caldwell's letter from Paris for Howard Caldwell because Howard Caldwell had *hurt his hand* and could not write it himself."

The boat rocked in the darkness.

"But," Morgan asked, "why wasn't there anything in the letter about that? You know, 'I'm writing this for'—?"

"That?" said Kelly. "Oh! that's all been taken care of. Howard, you see, was already sensitive about his Toe, and Mr. Silliman remembers, with a chuckle, that Howard didn't want to admit that he'd hurt his hand because Horace Seneca Sultan would think that he was just always hurting himself!"

The water lapped against the boat.

"Is any one," Roberts asked, "supposed to believe this?"

The boat rocked and the water lapped against the boat.

"It isn't a matter of believing it or disbelieving it, but," Kelly said, "as grandpappy Sultan points out, of *disproving* it. As he further points out, Beatrix Caldwell, the present Mrs. Caglett, was three years old at the time and the twins were two, in short that they know from nothing, and all others involved are dead. You may say, 'Mr. Silliman, I don't believe you,' which, as our dear employer phrased it to me, 'will be a forthright expression of your personal skeptical predilection, but something short of admissible evidence.'"

"Did he really, Kelly?" Morgan asked. "Was he really talking like that?"

"Oh, yes."

"Then he's pleased about something."

"Pleased? He'd sprain his wrist patting himself on the back if it wasn't so sore."

"You mean he was expecting that was what Mr. Silliman would say?"

"He'd foreseen," the imitation of his voice in the darkness practically brought Wm Sultan into the gently rocking boat, "that such an answer could be made. And that," there was a modest cough that nearly choked her, "is why he has refrained from any precipitate and abortive action. Ah-hem."

"But, Kelly," Morgan said, her words tripping on each other in haste, "why'd some one try to kill him? Why was he hit on the head in the hotel? I mean, if all Mr. Silliman had to say was what he's said now! Why, well, if you ask me, this answer doesn't just answer anything at all!"

"No," Kelly said.

"What's Bill going to *do?*" Roberts asked.

"For one thing," Kelly said, "he's consented to act as counsel for Mr. Silliman in some financial transactions. For another, he's consented to obey the doctor's advice and stay in bed for two or three days. For another, he compelled his secretary to tell him to go to hell when he ordered her to return to town tonight."

"Tonight?"

"Oh, yes. After all, she'd be able to crawl in her little bed in the hot city about one a.m. and then she was to get up at six a.m., to catch a train back so she could be here before ten a.m., which was to give two busy little hours of business before she caught the twelve noon train back to the city where after two-something p.m. she would have ample time to do this and deliver that and get the next thing before she caught the six p.m. train back here which would give just nice time for some papers to be signed which she was to return with—*honest to God, now*—on the nine-fifty p.m. back to her hot little bed in the city at one a.m. again. Instead of that," Kelly concluded, "she is only going to have to go into the city in the morning, return in the evening, and *go back again to the city tomorrow night.*"

"Well," Roberts said, "I get the idea that he damned sure doesn't want you here at night. I wonder if he's expecting something to happen at night?"

"I don't know what he's expecting," Kelly said, and the words and her tone made them more sharply conscious of the darkness in which they sat swaying above the only deeper darkness of the water.

"But," she said, "he is making sure that his little secretary is not going to be here a minute that she isn't busy, not a minute to get acquainted with any one in the house, not a minute to be told, hear or see anything that might give her some idea of what's going on. No, sir! He's not going to have any feminine interference," she concluded bitterly. "He's going to keep his big secrets all to himself—and get his silly masculine neck finally and completely broken all by his little self."

"What excuse did he give you, Kelly?"

"Social error. Be an imposition on his hostess, whoever the hell she is."

"Mrs. Caglett's the only one I've seen," Morgan said.

"Bill doesn't know you're here?" Roberts asked.

"Not yet," Morgan said. "No more than he knows you're here."

"Yes, sir!" said Kelly. "All by his little self."

It began softly like the uncertain little chuckle of the water against the skiff, the chuckle that passed between them in the darkness.

Presently Roberts gasped, "If I could only see his face when he sees you—!"

"Coooo—!" exclaimed Morgan.

"My God. What was that?"

"Pardon mine haccent."

Kelly's tone was serious. "It's up to you two," she said.

VI

Morgan did not remember having left the kitchen door open. The only thing that would have been more unpleasant would have been to have definitely remembered having closed it. As one swallows bitter medicine in a gulp she wasted no time in tiptoeing across the dark kitchen with her shoes in her hand to the back hall and the service stairs. A light had been burning at the second-floor landing. It was out. The door to the front hall had been closed. It was open. But above the second floor was the third floor and the safety, as it then seemed, of her room in the servants' quarters. She went quickly but very carefully up the stairs.

From the darkness of the stairwell she could see into the dimly lit bedroom hall without danger of being seen. But what she saw was both so disarming and so strange that she would have stood in a lighted doorway, staring. Clad in his bathing trunks, Bartram Nollis was crawling on the floor on his hands and knees. He was crawling slowly, craning his head to one side and then the other as if the better to catch in the light some invisible trail that he was following on the floor. His course brought him to a bedroom door.

At that moment another door opened and the widow Caglett stepped into the hall. She stood quite still and the boy had slowly risen to his feet before she spoke, her voice low and dead.

"What are you doing?"

"Just playing."

"Go to your room and go to sleep."

The boy opened a door and it closed behind him. Mrs. Caglett moved to another door, put her ear against it, quietly opened it, peeked in, softly closed it. She passed to the next door in line, put her ear against it, quietly opened it, peeked in, and at the head of the front stairs Kelly gave a dry cough worthy of her employer at his best.

Mrs. Caglett turned and said, "I was wondering if you might want anything."

"Yes," said Kelly. "Privacy."

Morgan made her escape up the stairs to her room.

6

A Barrister on Holiday. A Troubled Pisciculturist. Jeepers.
A Bedside Manner and a Diagnosis of Death. A Tasty Dish
and a Hint of Foul Play. A Signal and a Swimmer.

Wm Sultan woke with the consciousness that it was late in the morning, and it was a pleasant consciousness, as when one is the possessor of eight, or even six, million dollars in tax-exempt bonds he may awake with the pleasant consciousness that a tidy sum of interest has collected while he has been asleep. He was pleasantly conscious that time, too, had been working for him while he slept. That even as he had dreamed a train had departed from New Harbor for New York City carrying with it the inquisitive, if classical, nose of his secretary.

He felt, and the still tender feeling of his head bore witness, that there might be at Greenwater some one with a tendency towards a certain impetuosity of action. And, which made it the more unpredictable, whose motives were obscure. Indeed, his own precipitation from the terrace into the current, so unnecessary in view of Charles Silliman's later explanation of the letters, suggested the presence at Greenwater of rather strong *cross-currents*—a pun at which he permitted himself a quite hearty dry laugh as he splashed in his tub, plumbing at Greenwater having anteceded the shower—the presence, then, of dangerously strong cross-currents of policy. Decidedly no place for the investigation of an inquisitive young person of the gentle gender.

It was a great relief not to have to be worried about her or to be worried by her. Yes, he would admit it; and never having been married he looked upon it as something of a discovery that persons of her sex had a certain, "Why did you get yourself hit on the head?" and, "What are you going to do about it?" persistence in interrogation which gave him a reminiscent feeling of a schoolboy under examination by his teacher. With teacher away, school was out. And that, with the further agreeable knowledge that the rest of his staff were on their vacations, pleasantly engaged upon their personal pleasures instead of sitting around the office criticizing him, gave Wm Sultan the feeling of being on holiday himself.

It was a sense of holiday so exhilarating that he whistled, under his breath of course, as he returned from the hall bath to his bedroom. It was there pleasant to find that during his matutinal ablutions the room had been made fresh as a daisy, his bed freshly made up for his convalescent reclining, while upon his bedside table reposed a beaker of chilled orange juice as an appetizing and vitamic promise of the repast soon to follow. He reposed his nether extremities under the light bedcovers, suitable to the temperature of the season, propped his back against the fluffed pillows, and sipped his orange juice.

There was a tap upon his door, and his unexpected but agreeable visitor proved to be Alex Redell. His health was the subject of an affable inquiry and a reassuring response. He invited his caller to be seated.

"Until your breakfast comes," Alex said, seating himself. "Then I'll leave you to the morning paper." He had brought it with him.

"Why, thank you! That's very thoughtful. I'm being spoiled."

Alex noted the room, the bed, the orange juice.

"Think I'll break a leg or something myself," he said. "That new maid—!"

"Very efficient!" Wm Sultan agreed heartily.

"What?"

"Efficient."

"Oh! Oh, yes. Just what I was thinking."

"Her performance—" Wm Sultan appreciatively sipped the refreshing juice—"is her best recommendation."

"The hell you say!" Alex Redell appeared, oddly, both startled and a little shocked. He quickly recovered himself. "Oh," he said, looking at the orange juice, "I see what you mean."

"'A well-spoken wench,'" Wm Sultan quoted, "'serves the board of the well-born master.'"

"Well-spoken," repeated Alex Redell in a tone of awe. He wagged his head. "Coooo—!"

Wm Sultan gave a violent start and splashed some orange juice on his hand. It was quite annoying.

"Sorry," Alex Redell said. "I should have thought. Does that to me too," he said, with another wag of his head.

Wm Sultan was, no longer, in a mood for a visitor addicted to vocal pranks of a particularly ugly sort. "Is there anything you particularly wished to see me about, Mr. Redell?" he asked.

"Why, yes," Alex Redell said, "there is."

He leaned back in his chair thinking things over, and when one realized that he was thinking and looked at him with that in mind it was something of a surprise to realize that he looked as though he might have quite a good mind of his own. It was a factor easily overlooked in the distraction of his unusually good looks, of his expression which was usually one of a cocky boldness, and because his

statuesque figure so strongly suggested the athlete rather
than the intellectual. His bronzed figure was something in
evidence this morning under a loosely-knotted bathrobe
over bathing trunks. After thinking things over for a moment he turned in decision to Wm Sultan and then paused,
blinked, asked:

"Aren't you warm in that thing?"

If, in mere decent modesty, Wm Sultan was wearing
his dressing gown over his pajama coat, he did not care to
have his propriety commented upon.

"I'm quite cool," he said, coolly.

Alex Redell nodded wisely, "Your vitality's low." He
further opened his loose bathrobe. "Hot morning."

Wm Sultan did not need to be told that it was a hot
morning. There was a band of perspiration where his dressing gown was rolled up against his back.

"Yes?" he inquired coldly.

"Well," Alex Redell again had his air of decision, "here
it is. Now I know you're Mr. Silliman's attorney, not mine.
I know it's your job to look after his interests, not mine.
But his letter inviting me here did cause me to give up a
job and with nothing happening I'm getting nervous as
hell."

"Is it your contention, Mr. Redell," Wm Sultan inquired, "that in his letter to you there were set forth certain promises conditional upon your acceptance of his
invitation which induced you to submit to a financial loss
in another quarter?"

"Skip it," said Alex Redell. "I'm not getting legal. I'm
not making any claims. The job was the only one I had but
I'm not claiming I was crazy about it. The only thing that
really interests me is pisciculture."

Wm Sultan gave a dry cough. "Sounds fishy," he said.

"My God, you have a sense of humor!"

Wm Sultan modestly cleared his throat.

Alex Redell relaxed. "Few people realize," he said, "that the artificial rearing of edible fish offers an inexhaustible supply of protein food. The entire science is in its infancy—" he broke off with a laugh. "And will remain there, I guess, for all of me. But when I got this letter from Mr. Silliman—it was practically an offer to stake me in whatever work I was interested in. Now don't get me wrong, I'm not claiming the old boy owes me anything. The whole thing was a bolt from the blue. Rich uncles are rare enough, but some distant cousin—! On the other hand I can't just sit here forever. The swimming's fine, the company's fine and," he glanced at the empty orange glass, "getting finer, but still and all I've a living to make. Now if the old boy's cooled off, changed his mind, that's his privilege, but he ought to let me know."

"Have you asked him his intentions?"

"I didn't try to until about a week ago," Alex replied. "Awkward position. I didn't feel like seeming impatient about it. 'All right, my dear long-lost distant cousin, hurry up and shell out the dough.'" He shook his head. "But awkward or not, in the past week I've tried a couple of times to find out what in hell he does have in mind. All I've been able to get are a couple of hems and haws before Mrs. Caglett's joined us. Now I know there's no reason you should bother yourself with my troubles, but, if he'd only . . ."

Wm Sultan said, "I'll bring it to Mr. Silliman's attention and strongly point out his obligation to give you a prompt and definite statement of his intentions."

"What?" Alex Redell slowly rose from his chair. "You'll—well, this is a damsite more than I expected! Thanks."

Wm Sultan accepted it with a deprecatory, "Not at all, a-hem, hum, hum, not at all," that was interrupted by a rattle of the doorknob.

II

It was later to occur to Wm Sultan that Alex Redell had
leaped to open the door. But that was much later. At the
time all else was, perhaps justifiably, blotted from his
mind by the red-haired maid with a breakfast tray who
sailed into the room.

"Coooo—!" she cried to Alex-Redell, and free and clear
it was, like a steamboat whistle. "Hi thankee kindly, suh!"
She docked at the bedside and straddled with the bed tray
the paralyzed form that she found there. "'Ere youse are,
suh! An' surre hit's de grand happetite you-all is a-guine
to 'ave dis bonny mornin'!"

"You," said Wm Sultan in a strangled whisper.

"Jenny Jeepers is me noime, suh!"

"Jeepers," breathed Wm Sultan stertorously.

Alex Redell's attention was, however unwillingly, drawn
from the maid. "I say," he said worriedly, "you don't look
so good."

"Hit's nothing!" Jenny Jeepers reassured him. "Hit's
merely a tetch of rigor mortis! Passes off like nothing wiz
ze Haigs!" She was peppering the eggs. Some of it flew
into Wm Sultan's eyes. He closed his eyes. "Hand shall Hi
a-salta dem for yuh, suh?" He replied not. "Hand two sug-
ar in de coffee, nu?" The spoon rattled in the cup.

Wm Sultan had rubbed the pepper from his eyes. He
looked at her through tears in his eyes. Such a pretty smiling face it was, with such a cold sea glint in her green eyes.

"Don't say a word, suh!" she exclaimed with touching
sympathy for his delicate condition. "Hin fact, soir, hi
would hadvise h-you not to say a word *out of turn*—hif Hi
might be so bold, suh." She dropped him an old-fashioned
curtsy and wafted herself to the door. Alex Redell was still
holding it open. "Coooo—!" Jenny Jeepers flung at him,
and went out the door.

"See you later," Alex Redell said to Wm Sultan and closed the door.

After a time, after a considerable time, Wm Sultan became aware of the rising aroma of food from the tray in front of him and raised the cup of coffee to his lips. He set it down again, having never developed a taste for salted coffee. His stomach, however, was painfully insistent upon the need for sustenance, and he took a bite of egg. He took only one bite, never having formed a liking for sugared eggs. Perhaps they were acquired tastes as that for olives, instead of natural as that for whisky. He was still sitting there, staring at the tray, when Doctor Benson came in.

Doctor Benson was a portly young doctor, not more pompous than young doctors are wont to be, who in sheer justice to himself was forced to take pride in his bedside manner; and of his bedside manners, for he had more than one, he took particular pride in his tongue-clicking. It was solemn yet stimulating, chiding yet cheerful.

Doctor Benson looked at the uneaten but not untasted tray and clicked his tongue. "No appetite! Not a bit of appetite this morning. Thought of food repulsive to us. Tch, tch, tch, tch! Well, a few more days' rest and we'll be eating like a longshoreman!"

"I'm getting out of bed today," said Wm Sultan.

"Tch, tch, tch, tch! With our concussion? Be dangerous for us!"

"Not," said Wm Sultan, "as dangerous as staying in bed. Most people die in bed."

Doctor Benson laughed as heartily as he always laughed at that particular witticism. "Serves me right for trying to argue with a lawyer! Which reminds me—as Mr. Silliman's lawyer perhaps you should know that his days are, I fear, limited."

"By disease," Wm Sultan inquired, "or because he is human?"

Doctor Benson remained in a good humor, tolerant of the bad one of a man who faced an uneaten breakfast, and explained that while Mr. Silliman suffered from a chronic organic disorder, although he did not call it that, since as all young doctors he spoke almost exclusively in Greek, an estimate of the patient's remaining days varied with the simple symptoms of how the patient looked and felt. There was, tch, tch, tch, tch! all too little else to go on since Mr. Silliman refused to enter a hospital for more controlled observation and scientific examination; who, indeed, carried his foolish antipathy for medical attention to the point of refusing to be attended by trained nurses, tch, tch, tch, tch!

Wm Sultan's right ear crinkled around the edges.

"A hypothetical question, Doctor," he said. "Could Mr. Silliman's present symptoms of distress be induced by worry, an acute apprehension, in a word, fear?"

"Fear?" Doctor Benson leaned forward and lowered his voice. "Of what?"

"Does it matter?" Wm Sultan asked, handing him the bedtray to set on the floor.

"Certainly"—Doctor Benson neatly covered his justifiable curiosity. "Fear may be a symptom of—"

"For the purposes of my question, Doctor," Wm Sultan interposed, "let's assume that the fear is justifiable."

Doctor Benson sat back in his chair and considered and shook his head. "Mr. Silliman," he pronounced, "is failing physically regardless of his state of mind. But it had been my impression," he continued, "since I was first called in about a month ago, that the deterioration of his observable condition has been hastened by some great nervous strain. Fear, of course, could account for his immediate condition and its removal might result in a marked improvement."

"In a word, then," Wm Sultan asked, "the answer is 'Yes'?"

"Yes."

"To go a step further, Doctor," Wm Sultan said, stripping his dressing gown from his perspiring torso, "once granting the existence of this justifiable fear, is it not possible, hypothetically speaking, that a patient's apparent weakness and declared feeling of illness may be," he neatly folded the dressing gown and threw it to a far corner of the room, "either consciously or subconsciously," he continued, settling back on the pillows, "a protective coloration, a means of isolating himself, in a word, faking?"

Doctor Benson was not startled. "Hypothetically speaking," he said, "in such a case as you outline and within the limits I have set upon the effect of the state of mind upon the basic condition of organic deterioration, the second hypothesis is merely a corollary of the first."

Wm Sultan beamed at him and favored him with a dry appreciative cough. It was a pleasure, a real pleasure, to meet a man who knew how to say, in a word, Yes.

"Interesting subject for reflection," he said.

Doctor Benson shook hands heartily. "I shall," he promised, "inform the family not to disturb you."

III

"Good Lord," appealed Mrs. Lumpey. "Good Lord above us, child, you don't think you're going to eat the family roast, do you?" She yanked the platter containing the luncheon roast from Jenny Jeepers' humble hands. It was a noble roast, if somewhat remarkable in color, being black on the left half and a pale liver on the right. "You don't think," she continued in outraged protest, "I'd put in my mouth the food I cooks for them?"

"Hi 'oped not," said Jenny Jeepers.

"I should hope not!" cried Mrs. Lumpey indignantly. "Can you imagine, Cora?"

"Them slops," wheezed Cora. Cora had a long, pale face and breathed heavily.

"Here," announced Mrs. Lumpey, opening the oven door, "is a little something for us!"

The little something proved to be breast of chicken in white wine, and not bad, not half bad.

"Hi must siy," concluded Jenny Jeepers on her conclusion, "that warsn't bad, not 'arf. Not 'arf, Hi siy."

"I do wish," sighed Mrs. Lumpey, loosening her apron, "that *I* was a high-class English servant instead of a low-class American one."

"As long as I eats good," wheezed Cora, "I say the hell with ambition."

"I learned this dish," said Mrs. Lumpey, chewing ruminantly, "from a high-class cook. Mary Fullswell, she is. And no better than me would she be if she hadn't been seduced when a kitchen maid by the Chauncy Blug's French chef. That was the makings of her."

"As long as I eats good," wheezed Cora, "I say the hell with seduction."

"You'll learn better when you're old as I am," pronounced Mrs. Lumpey authoritatively. "I takes Mary Fullswell's leavings, I do, and the only difference between us is the tricks that Frenchman taught her. One word to Mary Fullswell and she ups and quits on you, like she quits here."

"Coooo—!"

"I do wish you wouldn't do that unexpected, child; when my stomach's full it freezes it hard, it do. But true as I'm sitting here— Ah! My dyspepsia, it is."

"As long as I eats good," wheezed Cora, "I say the hell with gas."

"Ah— That's better. As true as I'm sitting here, it was Mary Fullswell as had this place before me. Oh, Lord love us, yes! nothing but the best staff was to be good enough for Mr. Silliman. *Only* and except, *only* and except, the

Cagletts' own man as they had brought with them! Lord above us! A *mean*-honest old pantry-watcher he was, Mary Fullswell says, which proved as clear as could be, says Mary Fullswell, that he'd never been a butler in his life before he came here. Odd jobs most likely, and paying for his keep by shopping so cheap. But *only* except him, good enough for the Chauncy Blug's was the whole staff and what, Mary Fullswell asks me and I asks you, happens?"

"Wot," asked Jenny Jeepers, "dooes 'appen?"

"What—ah! that dyspepsia again—happens? This is what happens. Mr. Silliman comes at night, and the next morning before he's as much as eaten a meal, before he's as much as set eyes on hide or hair of ever a soul, what happens? Complaints. That's what happens, complaints happens."

"As long as I eats good," wheezed Cora, "I say the hell with complaints."

"Lord love us, but you're not Mary Fullswell," pointed out Mrs. Lumpey. "One word to Mary Fullswell and she ups and quits on you, like she quit here. One word from Mrs. Caglett and she ups and quits and the staff quits with her. *Only* and except, *only* and except, the Cagletts' own man as they had brought with them to watch the pantry, and then, the next night, the very next night, Mary Fullswell asks me and I asks you, what happens?"

"Wot," asked Jenny Jeepers, "dooes 'appen?"

"He gets shipped off too, that's what happens! And why, Mary Fullswell asks me and I asks you, and why?"

"As long as I eats good," wheezed Cora, "I say the hell with why."

"Because," said Mrs. Lumpey, who could hold it back no longer, "because Mary Fullswell tells me and I tells you, *he knew something about Mr. Caglett's getting drowned that night!*"

"Coooo—!"

"Ah! Better than soda at bringing up gas, that is. . . . 'Mrs. Lumpey,' Mary Fullswell says to me, when I asks her about taking this place after she's quit, 'Mrs. Lumpey,' she says to me, 'I know how you cook and they deserve it, only before you go I'll teach you how to make one dish you can eat for your own sake'—"

"Hit warsn't bad," said Jenny Jeepers, "not 'arf."

"One month now," affirmed Mrs. Lumpey, "I've eat it noon and night—"

"Coooo—!"

"Good Lord above us, don't startle me so, child, it freezes it hard, it do. 'Yes, Mrs. Lumpey,' Mary Fullswell tells me, 'take the place and cure them forever of their complaining,' she says to me, 'but mark my words,' she says to me and I says to you, 'that Seever'—Lord love us! that was his name, Seever—'that Seever is living on the fat of the land some place,' she says, *because they probably had to give him part of the insurance money!'*"

"Coooo—!"

IV

The *Bolivar* rolled ever so gently at her anchor as if snuggling down for an afternoon *siesta,* and under an awning over the cockpit Roberts drowsed over a book. A *flick, flick, flick* of light on her eyes, on the shadowed page of the book, caused her to stretch out a little more, sink a little lower on the cushioned seat to escape the sun glare on the waves. *Flick, flick, flick, flick, flick.* She sat up abruptly and gazed across the channel at Greenwater. Then she saw it from one of the third-floor windows: the five-times-repeated flash of sunlight on a mirror. The third floor. The servants' quarters. Morgan.

Bolivar shuddered as her engine awoke her and she was cranky as she was turned down the channel. However, it *was* a nice day, and after turning up her peeling nose at a

fifty-foot flying bridge who went past her, as what honest
working girl hasn't the right to turn up her nose at a fast
hussy who's being kept by some old yachtsman? after turning up her nose and giving a contemptuous switch of her
stern she felt much better and enjoyed the run to the point
of the island more than her skipper. There was another
swing to bring her head into the current and she waddled
along within a stone's throw of the beach, of the rocks that
began to break the beach.

There was Morgan's smuggler's cove and there was—a
thirteen-year-old boy playing innocently in the sand.

"Hi!" called Roberts.

Without a response he ran straight into the water and
began swimming. Roberts did not think he could make it.
She throttled down *Bolivar* until she kept no more than
headway against the current, slipped a looped rope over
the wheel, and hauled in the dinghy. She did not need to
go after him. The young porpoise made it, just.

Roberts stood surveying him gravely once he was dripping in the cockpit. One thing they both knew. His blind,
racing crawl had forced her to wait for him.

"Tough fight, mom," he said, toughly, "but I won."

His eyes were glittering. "Can I have a drink of water?"

"Glutton for punishment! But sure, help yourself."

He was down the companionway as if to get there before she could change her mind. Roberts took the wheel
and gave *Bolivar* full throttle. She knew there was no need
to wait for Morgan. It presently occurred to her that her
boarding party must be trying to drink the tank dry. She
slipped the loop of rope over the wheel and took a look
into the cabin. The boy was standing with his back to her
facing, as if entranced, the closed door to the head.

"Go ahead, kid," she called. "You can use it."

He jumped at her voice, and then sneaking up on the
door jerked it open. He did not use it. He came back up
on deck.

7

Hot Young Blood. An Annotator Dictates the
Amazing Solution. He Sees an Amazing Illusion.
Suspicions Regarding a Servant. Tonight!

By looking out her third-floor window Morgan could see
the party on the terrace. The terrace, in the nomencla-
ture of Greenwater, referred to a strip of lawn immediately
adjacent to the seawall between the end of the veranda
and the end of the seawall at the "beach." A boat could
be docked, guarded from the wall by a boom suspended
by chains, and from the seawall one might dive into safely deep water although the only return was by the beach.
Shaded by a great tree and more open to the southern
breeze than the veranda it was that afternoon the resort
of the hot young blood. Or such, at least, was the sarcastic term which Morgan mentally applied to those who reclined and sported there and such was the temperature to
which the sight raised her own vital fluid.

After the first glance she had not given a second to
Catherine Nollis, whether diving or drying, or to the figure of Roylson Caglett which consistently accompanied
hers like a rotund shadow. After a second look out the
window, having in the meantime divested herself of her
clothes, a long and calculating look, she had even ignored

the bronze figure of Alex Redell. Her third and subsequent observations, between the use of a pair of scissors on a scarf, were devoted exclusively to Wm Sultan who reclined in state in a deck chair and to Leslie Silliman who paraded up and down the seawall in front of him.

It was Morgan's opinion that she dived only that saturation might make more revealing the scanty adornment of her bathing bra and trunks. Being a woman, she resented the immodest display but reserved her anger for the observant male.

Wait, she reminded herself, until she could tell Kelly! Look, she admonished herself, at the old goat's stupid grin! And if you think *that's* so wonderful, she promised herself, get ready to pick up your eyes!

Wm Sultan found the sight of Leslie Silliman and the tenor of his reflections refreshing. While he contemplated the one through half-closed eyes he pursued the other in almost half-uttered words.

"In compiling this Life & Letters," he mentally dictated, "this was not my first experience of the verity of the adage that 'from little acorns'—ah-hem, you may change the quotation, if you please, Kelly, to 'great oaks from little acorns grow.' But the particular incidents which have just been related have won their own unique niche in the memory of your humble annotator under the title of the Confusion of Coincidence. No doubt the gentle reader is beforehand and has been observing the lagging footsteps of my logic—ahem!—with many the indulgent smile."

He smiled broadly in illustration and Leslie Silliman answered it. He smiled again at Leslie Silliman. No doubt of it, he had the affair so clearly in mind it was a pity he could not dictate it instanter, but still as he looked at Leslie Silliman's female figure he could not but have a feeling that perhaps it was as well that he was on holiday from his secretary, just at the moment. The female figure dived and he resumed his dictation, with the pleasant privilege of being able to skip all the dull exposition.

"Obviously," he picked it up, "once we remembered that 'Truth is stranger than fiction,' and permitted our mind to accept the observed phenomena that coincidence is a stranger to fiction but not to life, chaos became order, the puzzle solved. The first coincidence to be accepted, and how unreasonably obstinate to refuse it! was that Howard Caldwell *had* hurt his hand in Paris and that his friend Charles Silliman *had* written the initial letter to Horace Seneca Sultan.—No, Kelly, we want this to be in the modern manner, off-hand, informal. Change 'Horace Seneca Sultan' to, simply, 'my esteemed uncle.' Now! Ahem, hum, hum— Obviously, before his arrival at Greenwater, Charles Silliman, for we must accept that it was Charles Silliman, since for the reason we have earlier pointed out it was obviously impossible that he could be Howard Caldwell—where were we, Kelly? Well, never mind. The point is that before he got here he intended to make some immediate settlement upon at least his distant cousin Alexander Redell—"

He broke off his dictation, said, "Thank you, Mr. Redell!" and accepted a Tom Collins with a sprig of mint in it.

"Made yours a light one," Alex Redell said; "your head—?"

"Very thoughtful of you!" He hastened to conclude his dictation before Leslie Silliman came out of the water and joined him for the drink that was awaiting her. "But over a period of a month," he said to himself quickly, "Charles Silliman failed to do so. Why? Because he was restrained from giving away his money by those who wanted it for themselves. What was this power of blackmail? What other than that, although Charles Silliman was Charles Silliman, the blackmailers had discovered a means of throwing serious doubt upon the fact? The letters would offer such an opportunity. This solves the two attacks upon my own person. The first, by George Caldwell, to gain possession of the letters for the blackmail of Charles Silliman, the second to remove me as a possibly competitive blackmailer! It is clear that Georgiana Caldwell is in the confidence of her twin brother, and, finally, the dominance of Mrs. Caglett over Charles Silliman makes it clear that she too—"

He waved at Leslie Silliman and indicated the glass on the arm of the chair beside his own. "Finally," he concluded his dictation, subject to later polishing, "what could be the one thing which taken in conjunction with the letters would seemingly provide the blackmailers with irrefutable proof that Charles Silliman was Howard Caldwell? What, indeed, except the final, the simple but staggering coincidence that Charles Silliman, as he had at some time in his long years of correspondence communicated to them, *had also lost a toe!*"

II

"I must say," said Leslie Silliman, taking up her drink and sitting on the arm of the chair, "that you look wonderfully pleased with yourself."

"How could I help but look pleased," protested Wm Sultan with dashing gallantry, "on such a pleasant afternoon?"

"Nice day," Alex Redell agreed, sitting on the grass.

"And then," Wm Sultan admitted because he could not help it, "I *have* had a little problem on my mind. Oh, nothing much, but I was a little slow in determining my future course of action."

"Slow?" Leslie Silliman repeated incredulously. "You? I say, Alex, did you ever hear any—" Her voice trailed off.

Alex Redell's eyes were wide and staring and his mouth was slightly open.

"Coooo—!" he breathed.

Wm Sultan followed his gaze and stopped breathing. It must be understood that he did not have time to think or analyze, he simply looked and saw. He saw a young female figure in that state of nature which was innocent in the Garden of Eden. He was startled, and in his defense it may be said that no doubt had he had time for reflection he should have been shocked. It must be regretfully admitted, however, that neither was his second sensation one of modest shame but one of unthinking astonishment that the form divine could be so divinely feminine. In a purely aesthetic sense, of course. His third observation was that this flamboyantly female and pulchritudinous figure was not in fact in a state of innocent nature, and here, as he later insisted strongly to himself, the only reason that he had felt regret instead of relief was that it had made very little difference. The fourth observation that penetrated his consciousness was that it was Morgan. Oddly, for the first time in his life he thought of her as Morgan instead of as his file clerk. But, as he was of an analytic turn of mind and naturally wished to determine the cause of the optical illusion which had given him the impression that she was in a state of nature, the fifth object of his observation *was* that cause.

He was aided in this observation by the circumstance that she was approaching him from the side and should within ten feet pass not more than a foot in front of his chair. Analytically considered, he saw that the primary reason for the illusion was that there was so little that was illusion. The little that there was divided into two sections which combined would have seemed inadequate for either of their divided purpose. The secondary reason for the illusion, and here he used the word in its technical sense of "a sensuous perception of an external object involving a false belief," was that the allegedly covering fabric was of the exact color, the precise glowing shade, of her skin. The third reason why it was *still* possible to receive an impression of a state of nature—she was now in front of his chair—was that the fabric, having no body of its own, amalgamated itself to hers. These first astonished impressions, succeeding each other in a space of time no longer than it had taken her to walk twenty feet, and culminating in the most astonishing impression of all, which was one of sheer beauty and essential innocence, were broken by as discordant a sound as ever awakened a man from a trance.

"Cooo—!" was the sound. The red-haired Aphrodite had stubbed her toe.

It was followed by another sound that, if possible, was even more grating. It was the sound of a whining, bitter, angry voice, and it cried, "What are you doing here!" and it came from the dumpy figure, would not you know it? of Catherine Nollis.

Jenny Jeepers did not look at Catherine Nollis. She looked with wide eyes at Alex Redell, but from her first words it is possible that her eyes also took in the glass in his hand with its sprig of mint, so remindful of a mint julep.

"Ah ain't doin' no wrong," she pleaded. "Mizzy Lumpey done tole me," she remembered her British, "that *H*i *h*am *h*entitled to t-*h*oo *h*-hours *h*-off *h*-in—" having huffed herself out of breath she fell back upon Brooklyn—"d' erfternern fert baitin."

"Then go to the servants' beach!" Catherine Nollis cried, and having taken another glance at Roylson's face her voice was still more angry.

Leslie Silliman's laughter was like "the tinkling of the ice in her glass." "When you can't compete, Catherine dear," she said, "why advertise it?" She looked at Jenny Jeepers with an odd half-smile. "Enjoy yourself on our little beach right here," she said. "Go on, it's perfectly all right." Her eyes went to Alex. "Perfectly," she repeated.

Alex took Jenny's arm. "I'll help you over the rocks," he said.

"Coooo—!"

They went to the end of the terrace and since she was not wearing shoes he had to carry her over the rocks down to the beach. To be exact, he had to carry her in a semicircle around the rocks before he found a place to take one step down to the sand on the far side of the beach.

Catherine laughed harshly. "Jealous?" she asked.

"Not jealous," Leslie said. "Alex and I were just bored to death around here, and for lack of better company," she looked matter of factly at Catherine and Roylson, "we've been flirting with each other." She looked at the two standing on the beach. "Thank God, that's all it was," she said.

Catherine Nollis rose as if the terrace had become contaminated. "Of all the shameless, vulgar . . ."

"Shameless?" repeated Wm Sultan in a voice of iron. "In the sense of neither feeling or in need of shame, yes! Vulgar, no!" *His* file clerk? How dare the bitch!

Leslie Silliman said, in at least the tone of one who wants to pour oil on troubled waters, "On some figures it would be vulgar." She watched Catherine flounce into the house and Roylson reluctantly follow. "You spoke," she said to Wm Sultan, "with a certain vehemence, my friend." There was an amused curl to her pouting lower lip, but her eyes were speculative. "One might have thought that you were defending a member of your family, or at least a dear old friend. You can stop watching her," she added. "If she gets that scarf wet I'll let you know."

Wm Sultan turned as if shot.

"She's not a servant," Leslie continued musingly. "At least she's never been one for the simple reason that no woman in her right mind would let her in the same house with any husband or son—who isn't a mamma's boy like Roylson. And then your exceptional sensitiveness. You know! I had the funniest idea for a minute! Yes, it just popped into my head that she might be an employee of yours."

"What!" said Wm Sultan.

Leslie Silliman shook her head. "But that accent! All ten of them!" She burst into laughter. "No, you'd have taken care of a detail like that. It's too fantastic that she expects any one to believe— No, for some unimaginable reason that babel must be natural to her. No one could be crazy enough to assume a half-dozen phony accents."

It occurred to Wm Sultan that he had, perhaps, not appreciated the genius of his file clerk. It was only that thought that caused him to take a look in her direction. She was in wading.

Leslie said, "I was going to tell you when she came out."

Wm Sultan coughed. "I was," he said, "watching that little cruiser"—he indicated one that had just come in sight.

III

Morgan waded briefly, careful not to be splashed, being of the opinion that the fabric of her illusion would become transparent if wet, and sat with her feet dangling in the water. She was not surprised that Alex had not returned to the terrace or that he sat down beside her.

"You look sad," he said.

Morgan looked at the solid and somber mass of the house and sadly shook her head. "I'm sorry Miss Nollis didn't want me to swim," she said.

"Forget her."

"Everybody here seems to swim an awful lot."

His tone was low and awed. "In all my life I never saw any one . . ."

Now was the time to be casual. "Does Mr. Silliman swim?"

"Good Lord, no! None of the older lot—oh, George Caldwell and his sister will take a dip now and then, but not, often. And Mrs. Caglett can't swim, always been scared of the water, they say. And Mr. Silliman's not feeling too strong, you know."

"Does he—wade?"

"Who?"

"Oh, Mr. Silliman."

"No, I've never seen him. But why?"

"Oh—it might be good for his feet."

"What's wrong with his feet?"

"Haven't you ever seen them?"

"No. What's wrong with them?"

"Wrong? Why, nothing, I guess." He was looking at her oddly. She decided to be more airy about it. "Ha, ha! Why should there be? What a silly question!" He was still looking at her oddly and Jenny Jeepers remembered her accent. "Wot," she repeated "a zilly question! Hi honly meant that salt water"—she felt that she had better finish it straight—"is good for the feet!"

She was pleased to see that Alex was smiling at her again, an open, candid smile it was.

"Feet!" he said. "Every one seems to be talking about feet. Or parts of feet. Just the other day I overheard somebody say something about a toe! Of all things! A toe. Let's see, I think it was—did you ever hear, I mean the cook or Cora say anything about 'Howard's toe'?"

He was so frank and straightforward she hated to deceive him, but she was saved from a reply by the imminent presence of a cruiser that seemed bent upon running aground.

"Coooo—!" she cried. "Hit's going to bitch!" It did not, however, beach. It sidled around the sandbar, headed straight for the seawall, let the current swing and straighten its stern, and slipped smoothly alongside the boom. "Coooo—!" she cried again. "Hit's birthing!"

Leslie Silliman said, "Something the matter?"

Wm Sultan had taken a long look at the skipper and put his hand over his eyes. "Nothing," he said hollowly. "Just the sun on the water."

"It's the girl who had engine trouble out here yesterday," she said. "She and your secretary scraped up an acquaintance."

"I see," said Wm Sultan. Now, he saw.

"Aren't you the lucky devil!" she commented to Bart as he jumped from the raised deck over the cabin to the seawall. "Come ashore and have a drink!" she called to the skipper.

"Plize, Miss," Jenny asked with an humble eagerness that was accented by the rapid rise and fall of her breasts from her run from the beach, "Plaze, Mees," she repeated, "wid hit be hall right fo' me to look down hat d' sheep? Hi've niver," she confessed touchingly, "seen one cluz up."

"It's quite a sight, cluz up, isn't it?" Leslie asked Wm Sultan. "Certainly, Jenny. Take your look—too," she added.

Roberts was having two words with Alex Redell.

"Picked him up down the shore," she said, "where's that mechanic I picked up yesterday?"

"Sorry, she's in town, but won't you come ashore and splice—"

"Cooo—!" he was interrupted. "Hit's got a little butt behind!" And excitedly leaning over to point at the dinghy Jenny Jeepers fell from the seawall into the water off the stern of the *Bolivar*.

Alex Redell dived like a plummet after her. Roberts turned off the motor. Alex Redell broke the surface with

Jenny Jeepers in his arms, tight in his arms. Roberts gave her a hand and pulled her aboard.

"Perhaps," she suggested with a pleasant smile to Alex, "you'd better not come aboard. The young lady seems to have lost her suit." But when she turned back to the young lady she saw that that was true only in a visual sense.

"Wait'll Kelly hears about this!" she said out of the corner of her mouth.

"Oh, Bartram!" called Leslie Silliman, rising indolently from her chair and picking up a beach coat, "I think you'd better come over and talk with Mr. Sultan."

"Roberts," Morgan whispered tensely, "I know how I can prove Mr. Silliman is Howard Caldwell!"

"How?"

"His toe!"

"What?"

"Howard Caldwell lost his toe, didn't he?" Morgan whispered vehemently. "Well, he hasn't grown a new one, has he?"

"Good Lord, you're right."

"I'll prove I'm right!"

"When?"

Leslie Silliman tossed a beachrobe. "Here, Jeepers," she said philosophically.

Roberts nodded. "Yes," she agreed, "that's the word for it, isn't it?"

She covered it with the beachrobe.

"When?" she asked under her breath.

"Tonight."

8

The Horns of a Dilemma. A Spry Invalid. A Check
is Written and a Check is Refused. A Smell of Gasoline.
Birds of Prey. A Scientific Failure and an Astounding
Success. A Question for a Coroner.

When Wm Sultan's secretary arrived shortly after six, having been picked up in New Harbor by Leslie Silliman, she
was directed to the terrace. It was, of the human kind,
deserted except for her employer. There were birds, and
there were gauzy-winged insects that slowly bounced up
and down through the nearly parallel bars of shadow and
sunlight. A soft southern breeze dappled the green wafers
of the channel and cooled the salubrious air. It was particularly gratifying to one who had evenly divided her day
between the close confinement of a railroad car and the
heat and roar of the city to find her employer reposing in
a scene of such peaceful quiet and equable temperature.

"I trust," she said, "that you haven't been working too
hard?" Her voice was surprisingly cool in view of her wilt-
ed appearance, to which the crispness of his haberdashery
made such an agreeable contrast.

The expression which, at her question, came upon the
large and rugged face of her employer bespoke of that
strong masculine temperament which will not whine under

hardship. It was with obvious reluctance that he permitted a sigh to escape him and he bravely tried to smile bravely.

It was a wan smile, of course, and the pathos in his voice was involuntary.

"I was with Mr. Silliman for fifty minutes."

His secretary continued to stand before him, one shoulder sagging under the weight of a laden briefcase which she held in her hand, and she seemed bemused by some mathematical problem as the mumbled numbers which escaped her thin lips indicated that she was counting.

"Oh," he said presently, "won't you sit down?" He had noted that her knees appeared to be shaking.

"You spoil me, Mr. Sultan," she said, and sat down.

His cough was deprecatory.

His smile was gracious, but brief; and to the experienced eyes of his secretary there was a look in his which suggested that he was playing the game absent-mindedly. She leaned back in her chair relaxing in its comfort and the coolness of the breeze. She listened to the chirping of the birds in their evening animation, she watched the gauzy insects bounce slowly up and down with doubtful purpose but hypnotic effect, and she gazed over the dappled water of the channel at a small white boat riding at anchor in a cove on the opposite shore. She breathed deeply of the air refreshing in its saline infusion, and waited for her employer to express an interest in the contents of the briefcase. When she waited in vain Kelly knew that Wm Sultan was in trouble.

"Mr. Silliman," he said at length, "desires to make a will."

"So," said Kelly, "the conference bore fruit."

"Conference?"

"While," said Kelly, "you have, as I understand from Miss Silliman, been either sleeping this morning or observing water sports this afternoon, Mr. quote Silliman's unquote bedroom has been the scene since early morning of a gathering of the Caldwell sept, to wit: George Caldwell, bachelor; Georgiana Caldwell, spinster; Mrs. Hector Caglett, née Beatrix Caldwell, widow; with occasional poppings in and out of Roylson Caglett, spinister, sole issue of the late Hector Caglett and his aforementioned relict."

Wm Sultan looked at her.

"If you will look closely," she said, "you will observe that I do not have on a hat but that my raven tresses are not windblown. In short, at Miss Silliman's humane suggestion, a lady's maid of the establishment conducted me to a bedroom where I might powder my nose. Chatty little thing. Red-haired. Perhaps you've seen her?"

"Practically," said Wm Sultan with dry precision. He took a note pad from his jacket pocket. "You can make a rough draft of the will from these."

Kelly read them. She put them in the briefcase. She said, "If memory and my curiosity this afternoon at the offices of Debrosses, Perdue & Party serve me, I believe that the will of Charles Silliman, the uncle, probated May 17, 1890, provided for his residuary estate to be held in trust until the 21st birthday of Charles Silliman, the nephew, or *failing his survival* to that age it was yackety-yack, yackety-yack to go to the nieces of the testator, Catherine and Gloriana Beltry."

"Yes."

"So that there can be no sort of question or doubt that, if Charles Silliman did not survive to his 21st birthday, the sole living descendants of the aforementioned nieces, respectively Catherine and Bartram Nollis and Alexander Redell, are the sole heirs at law of the real estate of dear old Uncle Charley?"

"No question."

"They might even bring suit at law to recover from one who had received it by fraud the value of the personal property?"

"It was under seventy-five thousand dollars."

"But throwing that trifle aside, the present value of the real estate is approximately a million and a half?"

"Approximately."

"A pretty penny."

"Very pretty."

"Much prettier than the hundred thousand which the present Mr. Charles Silliman's will splits up between them?"

"Much prettier."

"Which, just in case there *was* a little something smelly back in 1890 would make the Friend of the Court who draws up and must stand back of this document a party to a pretty raw deal?"

Wm Sultan shook his head. "I'm not much concerned with that speculation."

Kelly leaned towards him. "Are you serious?" she asked. "You really feel confident that Charles Silliman is not in fact Howard Caldwell?"

"The evidence to me seems—almost—conclusive."

"Then there is an almost? You will admit there is a tee-ny-weeny doubt?"

"Very weeny."

She smiled, thinking of Morgan. "You may," she said, "have to eat it with mustard." She touched the briefcase with her toe. "And the residuary estate is to be divided equally between the Caldwells and Leslie Silliman."

"Yes."

"His granddaughter. His sole surviving descendant on earth."

"'Surviving,'" said Wm Sultan, "includes 'on earth.'"

Kelly held her temper. "His own flesh and blood," she continued, "to her, one-half."

"Yes."

"And to the Caldwells one-half. Plus a little remembrance of a hundred thousand to Roylson."

"Yes."

"The Caldwells. No blood relation."

"No."

"Whom he has not seen for fifty-seven years."

"No."

"Not since Mrs. Caglett was three years old and the twins two."

"No."

"Unnatural action."

Wm Sultan twisted the lobe of his ear.

"Suggests," suggested Kelly, "undue influence."

"Coercion," Wm Sultan said flatly.

"And in your opinion do two letters reposing in the files of the late Horace Seneca Sultan have something to do with this blackmail?"

"Yes."

"So that if this will our client requires us to draw has been extracted by coercion it just sort of kind of makes us parties to the blackmail, doesn't it?"

"Yes."

"A nice position for Sultan, Sultan & Sultan."

"My God."

"Yes! I can just see all three of them spinning in their graves. Humm—the one in the middle is going in a counterclockwise direction. . . . But he might spin so fast he'd fly apart from centrifugal force if we surrendered the letters to our client, mightn't he? Because there is a little mustard-covered chance that we might then be aiding and abetting an even greater fraud upon the lawful heirs of Uncle Charley!"

Wm Sultan rubbed bony fingers through his sandy hair.

"An ethical dilemma," he admitted.

Kelly nodded. "Damned if you do and damned if you don't," she said.

Dinner was announced by a hail from the house, like a hog call. A red-haired maid turned back into the house.

"The cook," Kelly explained the hour, "wants to catch the early show at the picture house in New Harbor." She took pity on her employer's harassed expression. "It's a pity," she summed it up regretfully, "that you didn't go diving yourself this afternoon. I'm sure your head could have found a rock."

II

Kelly excused herself after the roast, wishing she had done so before, on the plea of the work she had to do. Her train time was approaching by the time Wm Sultan completed his examination of the final draft of the will.

"Well," said Kelly hopefully, "he may live a long time. In fact, just how sick is he supposed to be?"

"Seriously."

"He's spry."

"He's been confined to bed all day."

"Oh, yeah?"

Wm Sultan's right ear crinkled at that vulgar expression of mocking skepticism.

"It so happens," Kelly continued in the same tone, "that as I came upstairs—and every one was at the table—I heard something in the hall behind me and turned my head just in time to see his door closing, and the one to Mrs. Caglett's room was still swinging. He's spry."

"One of the servants."

"Which one? Cook was in the kitchen, Jenny Jeepers was serving and the other was wheezing in the butler's pantry. Also, it so happens that the one thing not tolerated in this house is what is called snooping. The girl before The Wheezer was fired for being somewhere around the house at an unauthorized time. And it was Mr. Silliman's door I saw closing. There's no escaping it, he's spry. And there's nothing wrong with his appetite."

"No?" Wm Sultan tried to disguise his interest.

"No. Much better than yours at breakfast, I hear." Wm Sultan let it go. "And good at lunch," Kelly continued. "And the little red-haired maid who brought me my coffee says as how she carried down an empty tray at dinner. There couldn't be a little faking, could there?"

Wm Sultan looked at the will. "Under certain circumstances—in a purely hypothetical case, of course—"

"Of course."

"Certain persons," he continued, "might be content to be named as substantial legatees of a dying testator where, if his health were better, they might insist upon"—he gave a dry cough—"a settlement less remote and speculative."

"So you do think the old boy may be foxing—! And that's why you're willing to play along?"

Wm Sultan gave a modest cough and looked at his wrist watch. "Mr. Silliman," he said, "is very anxious to sign this tonight."

The frail little man in the big solid bed was signing a check when Mrs. Caglett admitted them to his room. She admitted them and returned to the side of the bed to hold in front of him the portfolio size checkbook for his shaking hand. While he rested from the effort, his hand still shaking as it rested on the bedcovers, she tore a check from the book, put it on the bedside table, endorsed it, and turned to Wm Sultan.

"Mr. Silliman," she said, "wonders if you would be so kind as to have this deposited in my account in the same bank tomorrow?"

Wm Sultan took the check. It was for $50,000. "Certainly," he said.

"Thank you."

Mrs. Caglett put the checkbook in a desk and sat down with an air of permanence. Kelly wondered at the tension in the room. It had built up while Wm Sultan had waited for Mrs. Caglett to leave, his complete silence making it clear that he was waiting for her to leave and her deliberate actions declaring plainly that she had no intention of doing so, even before she had sat as she sat now, her rigid black figure and the stern white mask of her face almost a caricature of grim and secret resolution. But, oddly, she got much the same feeling from the relaxed figure and the familiar, the blandly expressionless face of her employer. But, more than either, she wondered about Charles Silliman.

An old ill man weakly collapsed against his pillows, and ill old man who had zipped across the hall before she could turn her head and who had eaten three squares, a nervously exhausted ill old man whose hand shook as it lay upon the bedcovers, whose hand for a reposing hand shook a little bit too much, a little bit too ostentatiously.

Without preamble, Wm Sultan said, "Mr. Silliman, accepting your legacies to your cousins as fulfilling your ultimate intentions, to at least Alexander Redell you have a present obligation which is unsatisfied."

Mrs. Caglett rose from her chair.

"He was induced," Wm Sultan continued, "to give up the position at which he made his living by the implied but clear promise from you of an immediate and substantial gift of money."

Mrs. Caglett stood looking down at Charles Silliman, and Charles Silliman looked up at her.

"No," he said, "no, the legacy is enough, enough."

"Unless," Wm Sultan resumed evenly, "it is your intention to inflict an immediate injury you should fulfill your promise by giving him a substantial check."

Charles Silliman looked at Mrs. Caglett and he beat his hand on the covers. "No," he gasped, "nothing more, nothing more."

"It need not be anything more," Wm Sultan said. "You may deduct it from the amount of his present legacy."

"No," Charles Silliman said in great agitation, "no! No changes in the will, no changes."

"There have been none," Wm Sultan said gently, "as you will find on reading it."

The bound papers fell from Charles Silliman's shaking hand. He rolled his head on the pillow.

"Later," he protested weakly, "later, I'm too upset, later . . ."

"It deserves your most calm attention," Wm Sultan agreed smoothly. "I had intended to return to New York with my secretary tonight, but it will not inconvenience me to do so in the morning."

"Thank you," said Charles Silliman weakly, "thank you."

They left the room. Kelly wanted to say, "That was much too pat. He got away with it too easily. Mrs. Caglett made no effort to have him sign it. There's something we don't understand here." But she had no opportunity for any word of warning because Mrs. Caglett accompanied them.

Mrs. Caglett was gracious. "My son will drive you to the station," she said. "He has been waiting to take Miss Nollis for a drive. They will take you to the station." She went downstairs with them. "Roylson?"

He was in the oval room watching Leslie and Alex glumly playing bridge against the twins, who were cackling with laughter. They entered. Catherine Nollis threw down a magazine.

"Well," she said, "at last!"

Leslie said casually, "You must have to practice a lot to be so bitchy."

It was that moment that Bartram Nollis chose to bang through the screen door and call, "Hey, Leslie, can I borrow the flashlight in your car?"

"Sure, kid," she said, and then looked at him with interest.

He had got back in his bathing trunks at some time since dinner and his skinny arms, legs and torso bore smears of oil. He gave off a rank smell of gasoline. "Douse your cigarettes!" she cried. "Or we'll have an explosion."

Bart grinned at her, and it was perhaps for that reason that there was an explosion from his sister.

"What have you been doing, you little pig!"

"Nothing."

"Get upstairs and bathe yourself and get in bed and stay there! Do you hear me?"

"Aw, it's early."

"You've been moping around half-asleep all day! Do as I tell you!"

"Well, I got to put something away first."

"Then put it away and do as I tell you!"

"Aw, all right," he shuffled out the door.

Alex Redell said, "Gasoline and that kid add up to only one thing and that's the outboard." The card playing stopped.

Mrs. Caglett said, "He will drown himself."

"He knows better than to fool around with that thing at night," Alex said. He looked at Catherine Nollis. "Instead of letting him run wild and shrieking at him once a week you better try to get in his confidence."

"That's all you know about it!" She laughed in furious mockery. "I don't have to try! He's never kept any secrets from me! And I don't have to be told how to rear my own brother!" She flung herself into the hall.

Mrs. Caglett said, "Roylson."

He jumped to follow.

Kelly said, "Good night, all." She did not have to say another word until she was dropped at the station. Then she said, "Thank you. It's quite unnecessary for you to wait for the train." She waited until the car drove away and then took a look in the waiting room. Roberts rose and joined her. "About to give me up?" she asked.

"You cut it pretty fine." The train was coming in.

"How do we get there?" Kelly asked.

"Walk. It's just a nice walk to the dock."

III

With Kelly's departure Leslie said to Wm Sultan, "I like her."

Wm Sultan coughed like a playful judge on the bench. "You are a great deal alike," he said. "She is impudent without malice and you are malicious without impudence." He became very fond of the twins. They stared at each other, at Leslie, then slapped down their cards and roared. He would have been even more gratified if it were not always such peculiar characters who appreciated his humor.

"All right," said Leslie, "now that I've been spanked—" her face became grave. "How is my grandfather?"

"He was quite fatigued," Wm Sultan said. "I hope to find him better in the morning. Which reminds me," he arrested Mrs. Caglett on the point of leaving the room, "since I'm to see Mr. Silliman again in the morning I'd suggest that he sign a new check." He took the one he had been given from his pocket. "His hand was trembling so that I know the bank would question his signature. Of course I could explain the circumstances, and since I'm his attorney—but," he smiled, "since it's merely a matter of writing another check?"

She snatched it from him but it was too late for her to escape from the room. George Caldwell's bridge chair lay upset behind him. He wrenched open her hand, took

the check, read it, gave it to Georgiana to read. Looking
at Georgiana Caldwell a neat descriptive phrase occurred
to Wm Sultan. The phrase was, "bedizened beldame." But
more than anything, as he looked at the three of them as
they stood for a moment motionless, facing each other,
he was reminded of a phrase that annoyed him because
of its triteness. But trite or not, with their long, pointed
noses and long, pointed jaws the three of them *did* look
like birds of prey. And there was terror in the eyes of one
because there were two against her. Georgiana held out the
check to her sister.

She said, with a little laugh, "Tear it up." And George
Caldwell laughed a little.

Slowly, not looking at it, Mrs. Caglett tore the check
into small pieces that fluttered to the floor, and all the
while the two others laughed a little.

"Try it once again, Bea," George said. "Just once again."

IV

Morgan rapped on the door and hearing some murmur
of acknowledgment entered. Charles Silliman gave a faint
smile on recognizing her. She was so dog-tired that for a
moment she forgot her accent.

"Shall I draw your bath, sir?"

"If you please."

"Thankee, suh."

She entered the bathroom, closed the door and turned
on the tub. It was an old-fashioned bathtub with legs and
it was not difficult for her to push the bathmat far out of
sight under it. She gave the tile floor a liberal dusting with
talcum powder.

As she returned through the bedroom she announced,
"Your 'ot milk in twenty minutes, soir."

Twenty minutes later she returned with a jug of hot
milk which she set on the bedside table and re-entered the

bathroom with fresh towels and to straighten it up after his bath. She again closed the door. She got down on her hands and knees. There were wet footprints in the talcum powder. But kind of sloppy. . . Then she found one that did not have a toe. That was the trouble. It did not have any toes at all. Perhaps he had curled his toes up as he stood on the cold tile? She was bitterly disappointed. It had been so brilliantly scientific and what was the result? Talcum on her knees. She cleaned up the bath and returned to the bedroom. He was pouring the steaming milk.

"Let me, suh!"

He let her. Some ran on the outside of the glass. She went to the bathroom to wipe it. She tested the temperature of the milk with her finger, humanely. She returned with a fixed smile and a clenched jaw. She stumbled when near the foot of the bed and the well-aimed contents of the glass hit the bedcovers over the indicated target.

Charles Silliman did not cry out or sit bolt upright or thresh around. With magnificent presence of mind he did one thing and one thing only and that was to get his feet the hell out of the bed. Then he sat on the edge of the bed and without wasting any time about it began pouring a glass of water over his steaming feet.

"I," said Morgan, "I—I'm so terribly sorry, sir."

She spoke with simple sincerity because her incredulous eyes counted a total of ten steaming toes. Not nine or any lesser number. But ten. Five to a foot.

V

The dark water lapped against the ghostly white of the dinghy beached between the dark rocks.

"But don't you see," Morgan's voice in the darkness raced to keep up with her imagination, "it's the only possible answer there can be! You just question the coroner or medical examiner or whoever it is at New Harbor and you'll find he had a toe missing, that's what you'll find!"

"Well," said Kelly's voice, "it won't do any harm, I guess."

"All right," Roberts consented. "I'll do it in the morning. We'd better break this up," she added. "That kid picked up our signals last night. He may be around."

At that very moment, in fact, his body was being carried past them in the dark current.

9

End of a Search. Foul Play or Misadventure?
Uncle Howard. Funeral Meats. Last Will & Testament.
Before Eleven! The One Without an Alibi.

As Morgan returned from the cove to the house she became, without acting, Jenny Jeepers. Where on the night before even in the company of another young female person every foot of the road had held an ambush, tonight although alone it only measured her dragging footsteps. The lively imagination of the file clerk which had so lightly created the literal maid-of-all-work sank beneath the torpid weariness of that selfsame drudge. When, therefore, she saw Roylson Caglett standing outside the kitchen door it was with the eyes of a sleepy hired girl whose only thought about him was that until he went elsewhere she could not sneak in. She waited grouchily in the darkness, the tub that was to wash away some of her grimy weariness seeming a mirage, her bed a dream.

Roylson stood in the light from the kitchen, his head bent, listening. He was wearing a dark crew shirt and dark trousers rolled to the knees. He was barefoot. He opened the screen door. He stood still, holding it open. He reached down and lifted into view the outboard motor. He stepped into the kitchen with it, opened the door of a

storage closet to the right of the screen door, briefly disappeared, came out without the motor, reclosed the closet
door and came back outside. He rolled down the legs of
his trousers. He sat on the steps on the edge of the path of
light from the doorway and pulled on shoes. He rose and
went around the corner of the house to the front, a darker
shadow in the darkness.

Morgan felt it was high time. She entered the kitchen.
Alex Redell came in from the butler's pantry. He appeared
very pleased to see her.

"You!" he said. "I thought you were in bed long ago. I
hung around out here for a while after you took Mr. Silliman his milk, but when you didn't show up I thought
you must have gone to bed. After the day you put in! You
shouldn't work so hard."

When you have been feeling sorry for yourself it is particularly nice to be understood. Morgan forgot that her
only interest in life was in her waiting tub and bed. She
sighed pathetically.

"Cooo—"

"You're not cut out for this kind of drudgery," he said
sympathetically. "I could see that this afternoon."

"Cooo—?"

"I mean you, a servant, simply no sense to it. As the
economists say, it's a waste of natural resources—well! I
mean, well you know what I mean?"

"Coooo—!"

"Well," he continued, "I wish I'd known you were up—
out walking—we could have had a talk. I've just been sitting around reading alone the last hour, came in for a
nightcap," he indicated the glass in his hand, had a happy
thought. "Won't you have one with—"

He broke off as Catherine Nollis entered the butler's
pantry. She was in a pink dressing gown. Her lips, cleaned
of lipstick for the night, looked white.

"Thank heavens some one's still up," she said in a low rapid whisper.

"What's the matter, Catherine?" he asked.

"It's Bart," she bit at her pale lips.

"Yes? What?"

"He's not in his room, hasn't been to bed."

Alex Redell set down his glass. "When'd you find out?"

"When I came back with Roylson. I looked in his room."

"But why didn't you—that was a couple of hours ago."

"You ought to know," she accused. "Saying I let him run wild. I didn't want to let everybody know he hadn't obeyed me."

"He went up to his room, all right, just a few minutes after you left."

"Then it was just to fool you! Deceive you just as he disobeyed me!"

It was an unpleasant surprise to Morgan to realize that Catherine Nollis' pallor and agitation were due not to anxiety but to anger.

"You mustn't," Alex's tone was sarcastic, "worry yourself too much, Catherine. He's just gone out in the skiff and the outboard's conked out on him." Catherine shook her head. "All he had to do so we wouldn't hear him leave," Alex explained patiently, "was to shove off from the beach and let the current carry him away before starting it up." Catherine's smile was mocking. "I heard one at some distance a little while ago," he informed her. "Where he is depends on where the motor failed."

Catherine Nollis gave a scornful laugh. "I'm not in the least worried about him being any place on the water," she said. "Because *I* thought of that two hours ago and went to see for myself and both the outboard and the skiff were here."

Alex looked in the storage closet. "It's still here," he said, and appeared perplexed. "If he were out in the skiff, couldn't get home," he argued, "that would make sense. But where else the kid could be at this time of night . . ." He turned to Morgan. "Would you put on a pot of coffee? And you'd better get dressed, Catherine, while I wake the others for a searching party."

The search ended at New Harbor at low tide on the following morning, on the clam flats a half mile from shore, in a crying of sea gulls.

II

Mr. Ashley had tactfully absented himself from the three men who remained in the parlor of the Ashley Funeral Home. When the others had departed, after visiting the mortuary, he had tactfully stepped outside with them and even more tactfully closed the door upon those remaining. The closed door brought a cloying stuffiness to the room that made the state police lieutenant and the medical examiner even more impatient to go about their business. But they, too, were tactful, and if the lawyer representing the family of the deceased wanted to talk around and about the matter to further pointless purpose they could humor him a little longer.

The counselor-at-law in question was aware of their attitude. He thought that it was both natural and sensible. The body of a boy in bathing trunks had been found at low tide. The body had been identified as that of a boy for whom a search had been under way since the middle of the night and who had last been seen in bathing trunks. The boy had last been seen on the channel shore of Bay Island and the point where the body had been found was where one would be carried by the current of the channel. The boy had been fond of swimming at night. On the night of his disappearance he had been ordered to bed by his sister and had gone up the front stairs—and presumably right down the back ones again since he had known that his disciplinarian was to be absent from the house for some time. At night it was easy to misjudge distance and get too far from shore, with the swift current an ever-present danger. To the least panic, an exhausting attempt to swim against it, it would be deadly. Aside from all of which, every now and then, day or night, fair weather or foul, rough or calm, some one who goes in swimming gets drowned. And Doctor Benson's superficial examination indicated that drowned he had been. Oh, of course, he would perform an autopsy, but—!

But Wm Sultan did not want the autopsy to be as superficial as it was likely to be with human nature being what it is and the opinions of the responsible police and medical authorities being what they were. He had a strong feeling himself, and he resented such hunches, as they were not conclusions from evidence, that the evidence of the autopsy would establish that the boy had, in fact, been drowned. But though he had no doubt that water would be found in the lungs he was, perhaps inspired by the still tender back of his own head, intensely interested as to whether a fractured skull might not also be found, or a concussion, or other contusions or injuries suffered before death which might indicate the possibility that Bartram Nollis' death by drowning had not been altogether the result of misadventure. That answer he must have beyond the suspicion of a doubt, but he must insure getting it without showing that he had the least suspicion of such a possibility. . . .

Lieutenant Orprey was idly speculating upon the effect of the latest tragedy upon real-estate values on the channel: people would be saying the water was a lot more dangerous than it really was, though he didn't fancy it for bathing himself.

"One thing I know," he concluded, suppressing a yawn while Doctor Benson glanced surreptitiously at his watch,

"I'd hate to try to sell that house after this. Two drown-
ings in five weeks from it, get a bad name that'll stick for
years. Of course," he admitted quickly, with a smile to the
family attorney, "while you might blame a low parapet on
the veranda for an old gentleman falling in, you can't very
well blame anything on the property for a kid who goes
out swimming in the channel! But that's the way people
are, makes it a better story to say the house has a curse on
it, or something."

"Ah, yes, yes, yes, yes," said Wm Sultan, catching a
glimpse of light and stumbling towards it. "Yes," he said,
finding his footing, "I'm very worried about the gossip the
coincidence of these two deaths may cause."

"Oh, well now, I don't think you need to be worried
about that," Lieutenant Orprey said reassuringly. He spent
a great deal of his time reassuring people, frightened citi-
zens and overly ambitious prosecutors, and was very good
at it. Without even half trying there was much that was
reassuring in simply the calm intelligence that was reflected in his round, pleasant face.

"There's been nothing," he explained, "to start up that
kind of talk. I know what you mean, and you're right if
there's anything to give it a chance to start. If I'd believe
all I'm told a wealthy man has never yet died by accident
in this state—they've all been murdered!" He laughed reassuringly. "But Mr. Caglett didn't even leave any insurance. So you see," he concluded, rising, "there's nothing to
start up that kind of talk."

"Perhaps there hasn't been," Wm Sultan fought on, if
hopelessly, "but now there's this second death. There's
something about a coincidence," he said, lecturing from
personal experience, "which the human mind refuses to
hold in fee simple. It insists upon a partnership with an
occult or other illogical explanation." Lieutenant Orprey
sat down again in sheer surprise. "Since the undisciplined

mind," Wm Sultan continued, "refuses to believe in the coincidence it has no recourse other than to destroy the coincidence by altering one of its constituent parts. Therefore in this particular coincidence, the mind of gossip will begin to have second thoughts about even the first death."

He felt his summation had been rather neat, and was somewhat chagrined to see that Lieutenant Orprey only shook himself, as a man who has been momentarily stunned, and rose again.

Doctor Benson looked up from his watch.

"You know," he said, "I'm afraid—tch, tch, tch, tch— Mr. Sultan's right."

"I don't question it," Orprey said quickly. "In principle," he added reassuringly.

"I'm not speaking in generalities," Doctor Benson said. "I'm thinking of a young woman who came into my office just before I answered this call. I didn't think of it then, but there'd been time for her to have learned of the boy's body having been found. That explains it."

Lieutenant Orprey sat down again. "What?"

"She began by asking me if I were the medical examiner and if I'd performed the autopsy on the body of a man washed up here on June the 18th. When I told her I had she wanted a description of the man. Well, tch, tch, tch, tch! in these cases I've learned I save exactly half my time if I don't ask questions myself, so I told her that he was about seventy, five foot eight, rather emaciated, blue eyes, a face without any distinctive features. Then the girl—a tall blonde, an athletic-looking girl, fine tibia!—she said that was the spitting image of her Uncle Howard."

Wm Sultan choked on something. "Her uncle who?" he asked.

"Howard. So I told her that the corpse in question couldn't be that of her uncle since it had been identified within a few hours of death by the wife and son of the deceased. But *that* didn't satisfy her and she asked if the corpse hadn't been missing one toe."

Lieutenant Orprey said, "A what?"

"A toe. She said her Uncle Howard had lost a toe when a boy. So I assured her that the corpse had had all ten tootsies and she left."

Orprey said, "There's been no missing person reported answering that description."

"No," Doctor Benson agreed, "I'm afraid Mr. Sultan's right. I'm afraid this second death's going to start a lot of curiosity about the first. And, tch, tch, tch, tch, I'm afraid it isn't just idle or innocent curiosity because—I saved this for the last—this girl said she feared that her uncle had suffered from foul play."

"Oh, Lord," said Lieutenant Orprey.

Doctor Benson nodded. "And so she wanted to know if the autopsy had revealed any injuries before death that—! Fortunately," he admitted with wry humor, "she didn't ask about poison."

Wm Sultan said, striking while the iron was hot, "That will probably be thought of in the case of the boy. With horrible young women like the one of whom you've told me running around you see what we're up against. Doctor, for the good name of my client and his household this autopsy report must go beyond what common sense would require. It must cover the remotest possibility of foul play."

Doctor Benson nodded. "I see your point. It will be most thorough," he promised.

III

"Funeral meats!" exclaimed Mrs. Lumpey. "Lord love a duck, if it's one thing I have a tooth for it's Funeral Meats. It's knowing our own good fortune, Mary Fullswell says, as makes them taste so good. Down on our luck we may be, she says, but at least we know that we're not down in the ground with the worms."

"As long as I eats good," wheezed Cora, "I say the hell with worms."

Morgan sniffled.

"There, there, child," chided Mrs. Lumpey, "it's the way of life, it is, and Mary Fullswell says who was seduced by the Chauncy Blug's French chef—though it was the makings of her as a cook—once as you gives way to it you can weep all your life over men and deaths. You just have to learn to enjoy what you can of it, she says, from Wedding Cakes to Funeral Meats."

"As long as I eats good," wheezed Cora, "I say the hell with men."

"You might as well!" Mrs. Lumpey cheerfully agreed, surveying her. "But some is built different, like Jenny," she pointed out. "And now, child, do wipe your eyes and look for the silver lining. This ain't the first death this house has known and it won't be the last, not with the signings of Last Wills and Testaments."

Morgan's eyes opened wider.

"Well may your eyes open," affirmed Mrs. Lumpey. "It's a real pity you had to go to sleep after being up all night for you missed it good as a movie. Of course Cora didn't fold her hands in front of her but *only* and except that, *only* and except that it was good as a movie. There we stood the two of us at the foot of the bed of the ill Master and the Will being held for him and him Signing it on his Death Bed, it was beautiful, it was. And I don't mind saying that when Mrs. Caglett carried it to a table and I Signed Witness my hand shook more than his had done!"

"Mrs. Caglett," said Morgan under her breath, her face setting at the name.

"Mrs. Caglett," affirmed Mrs. Lumpey, still in her Great Scene mood, "and this very minute she is with the Lawyer."

"He's come back?" asked Morgan, rising.

"With the Doctor," affirmed Mrs. Lumpey, "not two minutes ago." She wagged her head. "A sight enough to make you pity the devil," she sighed, "doctor and lawyer arriving together. It do seem rubbing it in, it did." A second sigh was broken by surprise. "Lord love us, Jenny," she exclaimed, "aren't you going to finish your coffee?"

"'E may want 'is tea."

Morgan went through the downstairs finding no one and then up the front stairs and down the hall to the open doorway of Wm Sultan's bedroom. Mrs. Caglett was standing rigidly shortly within the doorway. Wm Sultan was facing her.

"—is provided for," he was saying, automatically turning to the covering provision. "The form here used," he said, "goes back beyond the wireless telegraph to the days of stage coaches and sailing ships when it was entirely possible, and I dare say not unusual, for legatees to have been dead for months when the will naming them was signed. That is why that even in this last half century," he gave a modest cough, "Sultan, Sultan & Sultan have never deviated from it."

Morgan could see that Mrs. Caglett was trembling.

"A little verbose perhaps," Wm Sultan conceded, scanning it, "but it does have the virtue of covering all things which human experience has taught could have happened before signing or may happen before probate. And so, in regard to your particular question, the death of Bartram Nollis before the will was signed does not effect the testator's intention that either the sister or the brother should receive the other's legacy in the event that only one should be surviving at the time of the death of the testator."

She half-turned to leave, but his drily formal voice held her, dry as the rustle of legal papers, formal as the sentence of the judge, dry as the throat of the prisoner in the dock.

"Indeed, Mrs. Caglett," he said, "you will find that the real intentions of the testator," the end of his bony finger unerringly found the signature, *Charles Silliman,* "will be carried out despite fire or water, riot or murder."

The gaunt widow turned with a face of death.

"'E may want 'is tea," Jenny Jeepers explained her presence.

Mrs. Caglett did not seem to see her as she walked stiffly to another bedroom and closed its door. Morgan quickly stepped within that of Wm Sultan and closed its door.

"You think she did it, too!" she said. Her voice was a little uncertain. "Now please don't try to lie to me, Mr. Sultan. I know you too well!"

He looked into her brimming eyes and said gently, "There's no evidence yet that it wasn't an accident."

She brushed that aside. "But when there is? Why do you think it was she?"

Wm Sultan shook his head. "I've no evidence to support such a—"

"Oh, how can you!"

Wm Sultan threw the will on top of a table as though, in this exceptional circumstance, putting aside legalities.

"His sister," he said, "found that he was missing when she returned at eleven. The boy had disobeyed her in leaving the house. I think that if he could have returned he would have returned well before there was any chance of her returning."

"You mean he was," she swallowed, "he was already— before that—"

There was a tap on the door.

Wm Sultan hastily picked up the will and said, "Come in." When the door opened he was reading it.

Doctor Benson put his head in, saw Jenny Jeepers, and drew his head back somewhat so that it might be thought that the door blinded him, like a horse, from seeing Jenny Jeepers.

"Just thought I'd report on Mr. Silliman," he said, and with a shake of his head gave his report in a word, "Shaky."

Wm Sultan looked at the firm signature in his hand. "No doubt he feels stronger in the mornings," he said, relishing the dryness of his humor clear down to his toes because it was quite impossible for the doctor to get the least taste of it.

"Just thought I'd let you know," Benson said, enjoying his own little joke: some of these dry sticks were pretty hot stuff!

Wm Sultan thanked him, the door closed, he dropped the will back on the table and said, "There's no evidence as to the time, but I think he would have been home had he not been drowned before eleven."

Morgan said desperately, "Please!"

"Miss Nollis and Mr. Caglett," he said, "were with each other until their return at the time. All the rest of us, with one exception, were downstairs together."

Morgan said, *"Mrs. Caglett."*

Wm Sultan said, "I must warn you against jumping at conclusions. But—she did go upstairs a few minutes before Bart came in and I saw nothing of her for the rest of the evening."

"Then she's the only one who could have—could have—*hurt* him. Oh!" She buried her face against him.

Wm Sultan coughed. It blew a curl of her red hair. He cleared his throat. That did not seem to soothe his file-clerk. He put his arm around her and patted her shoulder. The door opened and he looked into the eyes of his secretary.

10

*The True Name of an Invalid. A File-clerk Loses a Toe, and
a Barrister Loses His Temper. A Secretary's Suspicions.
Sultan's Harem Discovered. An Autopsy Report.*

"Well, well!" Kelly said, shutting the door. "Quite a period piece. The gentleman and the pretty parlor maid. My, my!" She had stalked up to where they were standing. "But I thought," she said, "that a gentleman of the old school always chucked 'em under the chin? Like this!"

The illustration bounced Morgan's head back like an uppercut. Kelly contritely put her arm around her.

Wm Sultan coughed. "You made a quick trip from the city," he said.

His secretary looked at him coldly. "I called the office a little while ago," she said, "and got your message to return from the telephone answering service. I didn't have far to come. I'd spent the night on the *Bolivar* with Roberts."

Morgan said, "Kelly, do you know?"

"Yes," Kelly said, "I know." She looked levelly at her employer. "You're doing something?" she demanded.

"A little," Wm Sultan said. "Perhaps, however, nothing quite so creative as giving birth to deceased uncles."

"Oh," said Kelly, "that."

He inclined his head. "Just in morbid curiosity," he said, "I should like to know why any one conceived the notion that the corpse identified as that of Hector Caglett might have been that of Howard Caldwell?"

Morgan's tear-stained eyes were lowering. "I don't like your tone, Mr. Sultan," she said.

Wm Sultan passed his bony hand over his head. "An ill-timed pleasantry," he said humbly, pulling at his hair.

"I don't," said Morgan, "see how you can be pleasant at a time like this."

"I've stopped," he pointed out, twisting his ear out of shape.

"All right," Morgan conceded reluctantly. "It's very simple," she explained. "I thought they must have killed Mr. Howard Caldwell who's been impersonating Mr. Silliman all these years and had Mr. Caglett take his place *because* the way Mrs. Caglett bullies him no man except a husband could be bullied like that by a woman, could he?"

Wm Sultan let it pass, let it pass. He went to the table, held out the will.

"Do you recognize that?" he asked his secretary.

"Mr. Silliman's signature."

"You've seen it before?"

"I should give that a silly answer," Kelly said. "But yes, in the weary hours I spent at Debrosses, Perdue & Party I've seen it on a filing cabinet full of papers going back fifty years."

"Including the past month since his return?"

"Of course."

"As, for example, the date this was witnessed it—"

"July 24, 1947—" she broke off with a gasp. "But that means— Oh for heaven's sake, why didn't I think!"

"Whoever else he may or may not be," Wm Sultan affirmed, "he is—per se—the same man who has been known as Charles Silliman for the past fifty-seven years."

Kelly sat down on the bed.

"Bill," she said, "What's the answer to this?"

Wm Sultan cleared a dry throat. "You no doubt have heard," he said, "the results of a delicate investigation Morgan conducted as to the number of Mr. Silliman's toes?"

"Yes, I know."

"And," he said, tapping the will, "we know that the man we know as Charles Silliman is the same one who has been known by that name since 1890?"

"Yes."

"And that therefore he must be either Charles Silliman or Howard Caldwell?"

"Yes." Kelly sat up straighter on the bed.

"And we know that Howard Caldwell lost a toe in 1899?"

"Yes!" Kelly rose. "And the third thing we know is that *this* man—"

"Who is either Howard Caldwell or Charles Silliman—"

"—Has *all* ten toes—"

"—And therefore must be—"

"—The *true*—"

"—Veritable—"

"Charles Silliman!"

Through thick and thin, through employment offices and scrubbing bathrooms and smugglers' coves in the night, Morgan had held, as steadily as a compass needle to the north magnetic pole, to Young Caldwell's Toe. Now they took her toe away from her, at a stroke, as it had been taken from Young Caldwell in those woods in '89. She sank weakly upon the bed.

"Then why's anything?" she asked distractedly. "If *somebody* hasn't got a missing toe then I just don't know what this is all about and I don't think you do either. No, I don't. You can say Mr. Silliman's Mr. Silliman all you want but if somebody didn't find somebody's missing toe I don't see how anybody can be blackmailing anybody!"

"That," Wm Sultan affirmed, "is precisely what this means. One entire 'criminal' case has been, you might say," he gave a dry cough, "kicked over by a toe."

Kelly went thoughtfully to the door of the upstairs veranda and stood looking over the green water. Morgan sat on the bed shaking her head.

"But, Mr. Sultan," she cried, "there's the letters—!"

"Mr. Silliman," Wm Sultan said firmly, "has explained the letters. Since it's now proven that he is Mr. Silliman that is the only possible explanation. The letters are quite 'innocent.'"

"But some one tried to rob you of them!"

"That was my own impression at the time," Wm Sultan admitted, "because I was then under the impression that the letters were incriminating. But since they are quite innocent no one could have wanted to rob me of them— and, *in fact,* the only thing that the hotel thief took was my money."

"But, Mr. Sultan, somebody tried to kill you!"

"Why?" he asked. "Ah, yes, yes, yes, yes, yes. That stops us now, doesn't it? I'm afraid we can no longer avoid accepting the simple fact that flower pots do now and then fall off of narrow ledges. If it had not struck me not a second thought would have been given to it. That it did does not make it the less an accident."

"Then . . ." said Morgan, not willing to face it . . . "then . . ."

"The great conspiracy," Wm Sultan concluded for her, "and the series of heinous crimes against myself have existed only in our imaginations."

"I don't believe it," Morgan flared. "I just can't," she admitted distractedly.

Wm Sultan felt like giving a great sigh of relief, but that might give things away. He knew that without a toe to stand on his file-clerk would soon come down to earth. She just needed a little more time.

Kelly said, still looking out the doorway, "If we forget about toes getting lost we may remember a couple of other things happened." She gave a little jerk of her head that seemed to indicate the white boat that rode at anchor across the channel. "Oh, yes," she said, "Roberts and I had all night to think of them. First the servants quit or were encouraged to quit and then . . ."

"Mr. Caglett was drowned," Morgan whispered.

"Well!" Kelly said, "Let's not be coy about it." She turned facing her employer. "Who could have had a motive to drown Mr. Caglett?"

Wm Sultan glared at her, his temper rising in resentment.

"There was no insurance," he said as if that ended it.

"Fine," Kelly said. "That eliminates Mrs. Caglett. But it doesn't eliminate Mr. Silliman— And you may stop wiggling your ears, Bill! Something's very wrong here. Terribly wrong. We all feel it. We don't need evidence to know it. And don't try to tell me you haven't thought of this yourself."

"In the presumable privacy of one's mind—" Wm Sultan demurred bitterly.

"Mr. Sultan, we're not in front of a grand jury. Now just let down your hair and listen to me. Morgan's picked up from backstairs gossip that it was from Mr. Silliman that the complaints came that caused the staff to quit. All except some old codger who had come with the Cagletts. Now just let's assume—hypothetically! hypothetically!— that Mr. Silliman *did* have some reason for wanting Hector out of the way. He might first need to clear the decks by getting the servants out of the way, might he not?"

Wm Sultan looked at his file-clerk, saw the wheels of her imagination whirling, and could have cursed.

"And so," Kelly continued, "he disposed of Hector and the Caldwells caught him. From what you've seen of them would you say they'd run to the law for blood or just take blood money? Yes.

"So now, in turn," she said, "the Caldwell clan need to clear the decks and bundle off the remaining servant, who just might know a little something even if he, himself, didn't even know he knew it. But safer not to have him around, wouldn't it be? Particularly if that little something might indicate that *our dear client had been framed?*"

Her employer wondered only if she would never shut up.

"And, indeed," she amplified, "the hundred thousand for Roylson in the will, additional to his mother's share, could be a little additional compensation for the death of his father, just couldn't it? Yes."

Wm Sultan looked from the inquiring, or challenging, eyes of his secretary to the widening and tear-stained eyes of his file-clerk. He had a strong impulse towards, and had not his auditors been members of the gentler sex he should have indulged in, profanity. Such an indulgence would have been unusual; he was not one of those men who by frequent practice can curse for five minutes without repeating themselves, his maximum was two. But the present impulse was so strong that even though his auditors were members of the female sex he might have permitted himself a short burst of fifteen sulphurous seconds had there not been the further restraint that they were his employees. It is true that the restraint of the relationship at times appeared to him to be a little one-sided, but there it was and he respected it.

"To the best of my knowledge and belief," he began quietly, "I've spent my civilian maturity in the study and practice of contractual law, in which I have never, to the best of my recollection, ever set foot in a criminal court or a police station. And unless memory further fails me for the past year my principal vocation has been compiling a certain Life & Letters. In that quiet and lucrative occupation I have been assisted by you, as my secretary, I believe? And by you, as my file-clerk, I believe?"

Neither answered.

"Then may I suggest," he said in a quiet fury, "that we remember who and what we are? The fatuous puerility, the trifling asininity, the moronic ineptitude, the plain God-damned foolishness of our playing detectives! unfit, un-qualified and incompetent as we are! should now be obvi-ous enough, I'd think! to bring us all to our senses. *Per se.*"

Morgan was facing him in rage and tears.

"I come down here and work like a dog," she said, "work as a *servant,* to stop people bouncing things off your head, Mr. Sultan, and now this is the thanks I get!"

"I'm very grateful, but—"

"And you call it *playing!*"

"You misunderstood, I—"

"And you called me plain God-damned fool! Mr. Sultan, I don't know how you could use such language to any girl!"

Alex Redell had opened the door. He came on into the room.

"Just what is this?" he demanded.

Kelly's cameo face had become truly cut from stone. She shrugged. "I just came in myself," she said. She shrugged again. "You know how some men are with servants." Alex turned towards Wm Sultan. "Mr. Redell! There has been a death in this house. No scenes, please. Just take Jenny out quietly."

Alex took Jenny by the arm. "Come on with me."

She sniffled. "Cooo."

II

Wm Sultan stood facing the door which had closed behind Morgan and once or twice seemed on the point of beginning a speech to it. He turned with an air, a gesture and a sense of exasperated futility unique in his experience if not in that of husbands. He sank wearily in a chair.

"Oh, what the hell's the use?" he muttered.

"None whatever, Bill," said Kelly.

He had momentarily forgotten the presence of his secretary. He looked at her apprehensively but was relieved to see that she did not appear to be in a temper.

"I don't know how she could so misunderstand me," he grumbled. "I appreciate that she's meant well— I didn't mean— I was referring to the future."

Kelly shook her head and smiled somewhat. "If it will make you feel better—which I doubt—but if it will make you feel better, I assure you that Morgan didn't misunderstand you in the least."

"But, you heard what she said?"

"She said 'No.'"

"No?"

Kelly again shook her head. "As I said a moment ago," she said, "it's not a bit of use. You're not going to be able to bully her into leaving." She nodded at his expression. "Yes, I know. You're worried about her, aren't you, Bill?"

He shook his head. "I've no reason to be."

She nodded hers. "And that's why you're so worried, isn't it?" she said very quietly. "Not knowing whom to fear," she continued musingly, her voice hushed, "or where the danger lies. Not knowing when she may pour hot milk on the wrong toes, when she may see the wrong thing. Not even knowing that she hasn't already. Bart must have seen the wrong thing. Perhaps she saw the wrong thing when she saw Bart crawling in the upper hall, does Mrs. Caglett know she saw him? Or the some one else whom we don't suspect at all? Or did she see the wrong thing when she saw Roylson Caglett with the outboard motor last night?" Kelly stirred herself from her abstraction. "Yes, indeed," she said, "did she see the wrong thing then?"

Wm Sultan rose. "I can take care of that," he said.

"How?"

"No one knows where I was. I could have seen him."

"I see. If some one else knows about it—"

Wm Sultan shook himself. "Our entire attitude's preposterous!" he objected. "We haven't the slightest evidence of foul play or even of motive for there having been foul play!"

His secretary said quietly, "It's no use."

"There's every presumption that it was an accident!"

"You're not even fooling yourself."

Wm Sultan faced his secretary. "At least I trust you'll agree we might wait for the autopsy report before assuming murder?"

"Why?" she asked. "We haven't any doubts as to what it will be, have we?"

Wm Sultan turned away from his secretary and went to the door.

"Mr. Sultan."

He paused with his hand on the doorknob.

"Because you're a man," Kelly said, "oh, don't look startled, I'm not going to make any improper advances, but because you're a man one of the strangest things that's going on here just might escape your notice. But let me, as a woman—perhaps you've noticed?—let me assure you that it's most unusual for a woman like Mrs. Caglett to push, shove and throw her son at a girl."

Wm Sultan coughed nervously at this reference by his secretary to what was, in his own opinion, a dash of abnormal psychology.

"But for a fortune," continued his secretary, "a nice, whopping fortune a temporary sacrifice could be in order. I say temporary because wives sometimes die."

Wm Sultan looked bored and so she knew that he was thinking very intently indeed.

"If—hypothetically speaking of course—" his secretary went on, "there were some large inheritance that could come to her, why, not having a brother any more that inheritance would be just twice as whopping, wouldn't it?"

Wm Sultan put his hand on the doorknob. "And if some misfortune should happen to her cousin, Mr. Redell," he said wearily, "it would again be just twice as 'whopping.' And all this presupposes that Mrs. Caglett has it in her power to—shall we say, 'double-cross'?"

"Let's."

"To double-cross the twins and switch Mr. Silliman's fortune into a new line of inheritance." He did not sigh but his tone indicated that he felt like sighing. "But this is reverting to the exploded notion that Mr. Silliman is Howard Caldwell, isn't it?"

"I know," Kelly apologized. "I stumbled on a toe," she explained.

III

The upper hall had a withdrawn look with its closed doors. Wm Sultan went downstairs and through empty rooms. There was no one on the porch or the veranda nor from the veranda could he see any one on the terrace. He sat down on the veranda overlooking the gray-green, the blue-green, the brown-green water and waited, as the house was waiting.

It was an hour later that he heard footsteps in the dining room behind him. He went in, saw no one, heard a clink of glass in the butler's pantry and pushed open the swinging door. Roylson Caglett was pouring himself a drink. He gave a start at the opening of the door. "The house is so quiet," he excused himself.

"Yes. I suppose every one's trying to get some rest. Think I'll join you."

"Yes, yes, of course. Here's some ice."

"Thank you. How's Miss Nollis?"

"Catherine?" His hand was shaking. He put down his glass. "I haven't seen her, not since we got back, but Mother's with her. Mother's being wonderful."

"I'm sure she is. Can't escape a feeling of responsibility myself about this. I suppose any adult must, a feeling one should have foreseen, prevented."

Roylson Caglett's face had turned the color of lead.

"If you don't mind," he said, "I was lying down, I thought a drink may help me rest."

"Certainly, don't let me keep you! I know," he added as Roylson pushed open the swinging door, "that you didn't have any sleep at all last night, getting in just before Miss Nollis gave the alarm."

Roylson Caglett stopped a step within the dining room and stood there without turning, the door held open by his plump figure.

"It must," Wm Sultan suggested pleasantly, "have been nice on the water."

For a moment more Roylson Caglett continued to stand with his back to the butler's pantry, quite motionless, and from the glimpse Wm Sultan had of the side of his face he appeared not stunned but absorbed in thought. That impression was fortified when he slowly turned a composed if still leaden face and spoke with a firm decision that was far from his usual fretful, flustered manner.

"You must have seen me bring the outboard to the house," he said. "I hadn't been able to get to sleep, and

I'd got to wondering if Bart had left it on the skiff. I went down to see and he had, so I put it away. I had to wade in to get it, but I wasn't on the water."

The door swung to. Wm Sultan opened it.

"Mr. Caglett."

Roylson turned. "Yes?"

Wm Sultan stubbornly smiled and held the door open until he returned. "I was very thoughtless," he said then. "My only excuse is that I didn't know you at the time of the other tragedy—I'd forgotten how doubly painful this must be to you."

Roylson stared at him very hard and then relaxed somewhat.

"That's all right," he said. "There's no reason you should have thought of it."

"That's very kind of you, but inexcusable of . . ." He shook his head, took a drink.

"It does bring up memories," Roylson admitted.

"Wouldn't wonder that you'd hate the very sight of salt water. I've noticed, why your mother hasn't been in swimming, I suppose?"

"Well, no," Roylson said, "she doesn't know how to swim, but I don't imagine she'd care to now if she did."

"Doesn't swim?" Wm Sultan said in surprise. "Unusual, I mean spending her summers here as a child."

"It's a phobia," Roylson explained. "Mother's *so* sensitive, really all nerves. Even when the poor brave dear was a child she had this terrible phobia of the water—and living here! Uncle George and Aunt Georgiana joke about how they used to tease her because she was afraid to go in the water, tease her about how much fun it was to swim. You can imagine how miserable they must have made her!"

"Ah, yes, yes, yes, yes, yes."

"Well—I *will* go up now."

The door swung to, and he was gone.

Wm Sultan went back to the veranda and waited, as the house waited.

IV

Morgan sat with her head resting against the back of the car seat and the breeze that blew sparks from her red hair was cool on her face.

"Feel better?" asked Alex Redell.

"Mmmmmm."

"It's about the best thing, next to a dip."

"Please, Alex."

"Sorry."

"No," presently, "I was wrong. We can't be afraid to mention taking a dip, or swimming, or sailing, or channels or bays or the sea."

Alex listened with a half smile, but when he looked aside at her, and he was driving slowly enough that he might do so often enough and long enough, he saw the tears in her sea-green eyes.

"You're tired out," he said. "And your nerves are on edge."

"That's it mainly, I guess."

"Sure it is. You scarcely . . ."

"I know. I only saw him a few times. But . . . I feel responsible."

"You?"

"In a way."

"What way?"

"I should have watched out for him."

"Why?"

"I should have known something might happen to him."

"How could you have known that?"

Morgan shook her head, sat up a little straighter.

"Oh, I just meant being around at night—swimming."

"You know what you're saying doesn't make sense?"

"I know."

"Can't you tell me what you really have on your mind?"

"Would you like to help?"

"Spill it."

She turned on the seat to face him. "Alex—"

"Yes?"

"Mr. Caldwell—Mr. George Caldwell—have you ever seen his feet?"

The car swerved.

"His feet?"

"Yes!"

"His feet? What is this feet routine? First Silliman, now George—"

"Please, Alex!"

"His feet! When would I see his feet?"

"You said he went in swimming now and then."

"Well, yes. I've seen him in once or twice."

"Then you have seen them! Alex—how many toes has he got?"

"How many toes? Seventeen."

"Alex!" She was angry.

"Well, I'll admit I've never counted, them," he said. "I guess his feet are tender. He's worn tennis shoes when I've seen him."

"Oh."

"Now just what do you know about this toe business?"

"I can't tell you."

"Why not?"

"It's a secret."

"Coooo—!"

Morgan looked at him with suddenly startled eyes, remembering that she had forgotten that she was Jenny Jeepers.

"We'd better go back," she said.

"No hurry."

V

"Hello."

Kelly looked up from her book at Leslie Silliman in the veranda doorway of the bedroom.

"Oh, hello!" she said, "Won't you come in?"

"Thanks."

She came in and sat down. They looked at each other. Kelly thought, "She's a hell raiser with that pushed-out lower lip. Morals of a cat." She took another look at the veranda doorway of Wm Sultan's bedroom.

"Know my way, don't I?" Leslie Silliman said. "But don't worry, I don't prowl at night."

Kelly had been holding the book as if wondering how long it might be before she could resume reading. She laughed and put the book on a table beside her chair.

"It's just secretarial jealousy," she said. "I hope."

Leslie smiled.

"Where is he?" she asked.

"I don't know. He walked out on me a couple of hours ago."

"I didn't see him downstairs. But he may be on the veranda. I don't want to go out there."

Kelly nodded understandingly. "He seemed a likable boy, the little I saw of him."

"I liked him."

"I saw that you did."

"What's wrong here?"

"Wrong?"

"Cooo."

"You mean Jenny? What about her?"

"Jenny my eye. Look, my room's next to this one. I was standing in my doorway a couple of hours ago. I couldn't hear much, not in words. But I do know that you and Mr. Sultan wouldn't be having a conference with a servant. She's planted here. And I think that little boat you went on board, that's been anchored across the way ever since, is also keeping an eye on this house. Now I know I'm only the client's granddaughter—but can't you give a girl a break?"

Kelly was glad that she had shown the way out. She might have been too disconcerted herself to think of it. She shook her head.

"I'm sorry, but it's simply impossible for me to discuss either Mr. Sultan's or his client's affairs."

"I was afraid of that. But why look so worried? I won't talk."

"I was wondering if any one else may suspect what you've mentioned."

"I couldn't say."

"I was afraid of that."

Leslie smiled. "Mind if I wait?"

"For Mr. Sultan? I can—"

Leslie shook her head. "No, just wait. No one's around. This whole damned house seems to be just waiting." She shrugged. "For something."

VI

It was late afternoon before Doctor Benson called with the report that the autopsy had revealed that Bartram Nollis had met his death by drowning; and it had not disclosed any fractures, concussions, bruises, abrasions or injuries of any kind, type or variety received before death which could have in the opinion of the examiner in any wise incapacitated him; and that therefore the official finding was that Bartram Nollis had been drowned by misadventure; and that was that; and closed doors opened in Greenwater and those who had been waiting behind them came forth again.

11

Conclusive Evidence. Sink or Swim. Dangerous Pressure. A Clock Starts. Terror. Wild Remorse. "Beast— Liar—Sneak!" Seever again. A Mine Field. A Secret Overheard. In Stocking Feet. The Corpse in the Current.

Wm Sultan had said, with goose pimples on his spine, "Thank you, Doctor, that's splendid, splendid. Ah, yes, yes, yes, yes, yes."

He was thankful, as he paced his room awaiting Kelly's return, that he had anticipated the report and had fore-gathered the last item of evidence for an air-tight case. The death of Bartram Nollis was an air-tight accident.

The very circumstances which in the event of foul play would have made suspect Mrs. Caglett had as clearly excluded any one else. Catherine's outraged indignation at the discovery of her brother's disobedience on the night of his death was the best evidence that he never openly defied her authority. It was morally certain that he would have returned to his room before her return had he been capable of doing so. The only person without an alibi for that period had been Mrs. Caglett. There had never been any question of her having a struggle with the boy; it would have been heard. The one possibility had been that she had knocked him on the head and that later Roylson had taken the body out in the skiff and dumped it overboard. But the findings of the autopsy had ruled that out; Bart had not been conked on the head or otherwise incapacitated.

But, having had some experience with the mental state of his staff earlier that afternoon, which now was responsible for the anxiety in which he paced his room, he was thankful that he had not stopped with that negative finding but had explored the only remaining possibility: one swimmer could drown another.

Ah, yes, yes, yes, yes, yes. That could have been not too difficult of accomplishment. The undersized and spindly boy of thirteen could have fallen easy prey to an unexpected and murderous attack by an adult swimmer. But there were two things that proved that such an attack could not have taken place.

Wm Sultan nodded emphatically. The alibis still held and even more strongly. Roylson had been with Catherine Nollis. He himself had been chatting with Leslie and Alex while the Twins had played their interminable game of double solitaire. The Twins had once adjourned to the butler's pantry to mix a drink, which they had done quickly to get back to their game. Alex had twice left the room to pour a round of drinks, but had taken no more than enough time to do so. Leslie had once gone upstairs for perhaps five minutes. None of the four had had enough margin of time to have stripped off his clothes, jumped into the water on a fortuitously waiting Bart, drowned him, climbed out again and dressed again. Only one person had had time.

And Mrs. Caglett could not swim.

There it was; and it was air-tight. On the one side, conclusive evidence. On the other, only the uncomfortable sense of secret dealing and mutual spying natural to a household where several people were working against each other to get what they could out of a dying millionaire; that and the feeling that if there did happen to be a murder around Mrs. Caglett looked capable of having done it.

Wm Sultan felt that his secretary had seen that it was sheer insanity not to admit it. He felt that she could not help but be successful in making his file clerk see that further snooping was simply silly, and to give up her onerous and menial labor in the house. God knew he hoped so. Because his own secret belief was that there were one or two too many coincidences, and that if there were some one had developed a method of murder too secure for any one's safety.

Wm Sultan stopped short in his pacing when Kelly opened the door. He put on a bland expression.

"Find a chance to tell Morgan?" he asked casually.

Kelly nodded. "She says she'll find out," she said.

"Find out?" he repeated. "What?"

Kelly considered him a moment before making her reply. Then she shrugged and said, "God knows."

II

When, a few minutes later, the file clerk of Sultan, Sultan & Sultan plunged Mrs. Caglett from the veranda into the channel on a sink-or-swim basis it became reasonably clear to Young Sultan's Boy what it was that she had determined to find out. If his secretary had been something less than honest in implying that she had not known what it was that Morgan had wanted to find out, it would be unfair to say that she had been an accessory before the fact.

When Morgan had asked her, "But how do we *know* she can't swim?" and then had answered her own question with the assertion that she would find out for herself, Kelly had not taken it as a promise of immediate scientific and criminal experiment. It had seemed to her, a woman, no more

than an expression of a suspicion that Wm Sultan might
be putting something over; a suspicion in which, logic be
damned, Kelly concurred.

That which was to cause the death of a member of her
sex she took into consideration scarcely at all. She should
have been forewarned by Morgan's having given the milk
test to Mr. Silliman's feet the night before. That had been
something that one might have taken as a matter of course
from Roberts. Even as if it had been Roberts who had announced that she would find out for herself if Mrs. Caglett
or any other human could swim, Kelly would simply have
begun listening for the splash. But that Morgan, who lived
in her imagination, should have turned to physical action;
that Morgan, with her ardent and too tender sympathies,
should have forced herself to an act that must have seemed
to her not less dastardly than acid-throwing; that—should
have forewarned her of the dangerous emotional pressure
that had been built up in every person in the house. It was
to burst forth from George and Georgiana Caldwell, from
Roylson Caglett, from Catherine Nollis; it was to impel
Morgan to plunge Mrs. Caglett from the veranda into the
channel and result in murder. It was the more strange that
Kelly did not take it into account because she felt it herself.

Had she done so she would not have walked downstairs
with Wm Sultan but would have run. As it was they arrived
just too late to do anything about it.

The clock had started ticking with the arrival of Doctor Benson. He had given the autopsy report to Wm Sultan. Wm Sultan had gone up to his room and the doctor
to see his patient. The doctor had told Charles Silliman of
the official finding and then had dropped in to see if he
could be of any aid to the bereaved sister. He had found
her lying on the bed with Mrs. Caglett in attendance. As
different people take the shock of a loss differently their

requirements are different, and the attending physician must make the best guess that he can.

It was Doctor Benson's feeling that the girl was, to a certain extent, doing what she thought was expected of her, and was, however subconsciously, bitterly resenting her isolation with her considerate but grim companion. He had "ordered" her to get up, to "try" to go downstairs, and the alacrity with which she had responded had confirmed his diagnosis. Before departing he had, with practiced delicacy and indirection, let them know that the boy had not suffered any "painful injury" before death.

As he had gone down the hall the doors of George and Georgiana Caldwell had, by chance, simultaneously opened. When he had whispered the result of the autopsy they had insisted on seeing him to the front door and had bid him a hearty farewell. They had then adjourned to the butler's pantry for a drink and had had two. They had poured another and had come out into the dining room when Catherine Nollis and Mrs. Caglett reached the veranda.

In the meantime, Wm Sultan had found Leslie Silliman with his secretary and told them both the result of the autopsy. Leslie Silliman had gone downstairs and aimlessly out the front door to the lawn, where she had found Alex Redell walking in thoughtful circles. They had ambled around the side of the house to the terrace and sat in chairs somewhat back from the sea wall so that little of the veranda was visible to them beyond the steps at its end.

In less than three-quarters of an hour from the time Wm Sultan had gone to his room Kelly had returned from her mission to Morgan and they started downstairs together. Roylson Caglett was shortly ahead of them. They were halfway down when he reached the foot of the stairs and they heard Mrs. Caglett's cry.

III

From Morgan's later confession it is clear that she acted with that incredible directness of the person who does not dare let himself think what he is doing. From the door of the butler's pantry she saw Catherine and Mrs. Caglett on the veranda. To reflect her state of mind it would be more accurate to say that she saw the sister of a murdered boy and his murderess. She ran past George and Georgiana in the dining room and out the dining-room door to the veranda. She ran straight for Mrs. Caglett.

She called, "May Hi git youse some—"

She faked a stumble, and it is significant that she did not change the pattern of the creaming of Charles Silliman's toes; flung her arms around Mrs. Caglett and carried her over the parapet. They landed at full length on the water, checking their fall, and as they went on down only their legs bumped against the shelving rock. Morgan released her hold on Mrs. Caglett and watched her with interest through the clear water. Mrs. Caglett was moving her arms and legs but she was moving only with the current. She was not going up and it was necessary to go up at once. Morgan gave her a shove upwards and shot up herself. They broke the surface together and then Mrs. Caglett with a very strange and ugly expression on her face began to go down again. Morgan suddenly realized that that strange and ugly expression was that of terror and that the story of Mrs. Caglett's hydrophobia was true and that she could not swim.

Mrs. Caglett's harsh cry as she felt herself carried over the parapet did not sound loudly in the front hall and it might have come from almost any direction. It was not a scream. It sounded as though she had called out an arresting command. Roylson at the foot of the stairs and Wm Sultan and his secretary above all recognized her voice. Roylson went out on the front porch and after a quick look around came back in and went hastily, but not running, to the back of the hall and through the intermediate room to the veranda. He was followed reluctantly, and at the width of the room, by Wm Sultan and Kelly. In any normal household both would have gone in the opposite direction as they anticipated with distaste some unpleasant quarrelsome scene. They began to run when half across the room because Roylson began to run on the veranda.

He ran a few steps towards Catherine, who stood watching two struggling figures in the water. There was the flail of an arm, a head would go under, bob out. They were beyond the end of the veranda. Georgiana was standing beside the girl, a glass in her hand. Quite unconsciously, she raised it to her lips. A broken glass was lying where it had been dropped on the floor by George Caldwell who was lumbering towards the steps leading from the veranda to the terrace.

Roylson suddenly screamed, "Mother!" He struck Catherine on the shoulder with his fist, as if knocking on a door, stepped on top of the parapet and leaped into the water.

On the sea wall at the terrace Alex Redell pulled off his shoes, stepped out of his trousers, literally ripped off his sports shirt, the while sizing up drift and distance, and sliced the surface of the water in a racing dive. Leslie Silliman, who had got stuck in pulling her dress over her head, followed in his wake.

Wm Sultan's secretary was leaning over the parapet, holding to a pillar of the veranda. He touched her on the arm.

"Shall we," he suggested, "go down to the beach?"

To her astonishment she realized that he was perfectly right. Alex's dive had carried him within one stroke of the struggling figures and Leslie had just joined them. There were already one too many people in the water. Roylson's hysterical jump seventy-five feet away from those to be rescued, when he might have got within fifteen by running to the terrace, effectively illustrated how helpful it was to lose one's head.

Kelly's hand held tightly to her employer's right arm as they went quickly down the veranda towards the terrace and the beach. She was unaware of those who were preceding them to that scene that was to give birth to murder. She was not even aware that Wm Sultan's coat was over his left arm and that he was carrying his shoes in his left hand. Neither took their eyes from those in the water.

IV

Between the time that Morgan had carried Mrs. Caglett over the parapet and they sat draining on the beach many seconds less than a minute and a half had elapsed. In that period Morgan had had time to suffer some of life's most unpleasant emotions and almost complete exhaustion. She had in wild remorse sacrificed her strength completely for Mrs. Caglett. It had been not over forty-five seconds before Alex had relieved her of that burden and Leslie had supported her. Without that rescue the full minute and a half might have seen the end of her. She knew that and her ringing head was filled with a fearful astonishment. A passably good swimmer, she had mentally brushed aside the possibility of taking care of Mrs. Caglett as being no problem at all. It simply had not occurred to her that she had never before been in swimming in a maid's uniform and oxfords or that she might find her first actual attempt at rescue another unpleasant surprise. Nor as she sat draining and recovering her breath and strength did it occur to her that the very boldness of her attack had made it seem the most unquestionable accident. She thought: *They'll send me to jail.*

Mrs. Caglett sat on another rock a few feet away. She sat with her hands on her knees, her head bent, her streaming hair hanging over her gaunt cheeks. Her sopping black dress, her dead white hands and face, made a bleak picture. She breathed deeply and harshly.

With the exception of Roylson those from the water reached the beach at the same time as those from the land. Kelly started to go to Morgan but Alex and Leslie were standing beside her, there was nothing to be done, and the thing that really stopped her was that now that she saw Morgan safe she felt more inclined to slap than sympathize.

Georgiana, seeming as out of place in that scene of rock and sand and broad salt water as some aged and battered orchid, washed down avid gazes at her sister with sips of whisky and soda. George Caldwell stood looking at Catherine Nollis joyously. Catherine was holding her shoulder as she had held her shoulder since Roylson had beat his fist upon it. She stood waiting, her staring eyes never leaving his approaching head in the water.

Wm Sultan sat down and turned his back to put on his shoes. The entire scene was to be over before he had the laces tied, like a childish quarrel. That seemed its quality. A moment of voices raised in petty temper and spiteful dislike. Wm Sultan found it embarrassing because it was cheap, sadly lacking in the elemental dignity of wrath and passion.

Roylson Caglett waded from the water, his plump, fully clothed figure the more foolish-looking because of his belated arrival, and staggered up to Catherine Nollis.

"Why hadn't you tried to save her?" he cried shrilly. "You were standing there, just standing there, watching Mother drown!"

"You little beast!" she cried. "How dare you strike me?"

"But you were just standing there," his tone had become plaintive, "and Mother—"

George Caldwell had been panting with laughter as he watched them. "Could have kept her from falling!" he said. "Only had to reach out her arm."

Catherine spun on him. "You liar!" she cried. "You dirty liar!"

George Caldwell laughed and leaned towards Roylson. "Don't believe it!" he said. "I saw it all. She didn't know I was there but I saw it from the dining room! Ha, ha, I was watching!"

"You lying sneak!" Catherine Nollis cried. "Always sneaking and spying on me, like you were last night! Oh! So you didn't think I saw you sneak into the back hall from the kitchen when I came in from looking at the skiff? Well, I did!" She laughed tauntingly. "And then you thought you hid yourself standing on the back stairs but like the old fool you are you didn't go up high enough and I could see your feet!" Her laughter rose shrilly and then broke off as, on a thought, she suddenly remembered Roylson and turned upon him. "And as for you, you little beast, you little half-man, I'll teach you to strike me!"

She slapped him in the face with the back of her hand and ran sobbing to the house.

Mrs. Caglett rose. Her black eyes appeared dead in her white face. She looked at her son.

"You are a little beast," she said in her dead voice. "Hadn't the girl been through enough today?" Her dead eyes shifted to the face of her brother. "And you did lie," she said. "Catherine had no chance to . . ." She turned from him as she saw him begin to laugh at her and looked at Jenny Jeepers. "Get out of this house in an hour," she said.

Georgiana Caldwell stepped between them. "She'll do nothing of the kind!" she cried. "She does all the work in the house now!" She began her panting laughter. "I wouldn't let her go for anything. Funniest thing I've seen since George and I used to get whipped for doing the same thing to you! She's the last servant in the world I'd ever let go!"

Mrs. Caglett started for the house, passing between them.

George flung out, "Bea never could keep servants!"

"No!" Georgiana picked it up. "Not even Seever!" They roared.

"Yes! Why'd you ever let Seever go, Bea?"

"Yes!" Georgiana turned to her brother. "I can't imagine, can you?"

He shook his head. "I can't imagine."

Then they stopped laughing as though discouraged by her retreating back and that was the end of it.

V

Midsummer it might be, but a chilly night it was on the half-damp sand in the pocket in the rocks by the lapping water. The three girls sat huddled together for physical warmth and spiritual comfort. Roberts had been told and Roberts had listened. After a silence Roberts spoke.

"Do you really think the Boss thinks everything's O.K, here?" she asked.

"I think," Kelly said, "he thinks it's none of his business any longer and I think he's right. As long as Bill felt that the letters were causing trouble he felt responsible."

"I get that," Roberts said. "No toe, no Caldwell; no Caldwell, no blackmail."

Kelly snorted. "And no rightful heirs!" she said. "You know, Grandpappy's really been on a spot. I don't wonder he's been 'Ah, no, no, no, yes, yes, yessing' to himself. With that hyperthyroid integrity of his, to wonder if he were helping some one blackmail his client or helping his client to steal a couple million from the rightful heirs—!"

Morgan said, "I ought to be getting back, Kelly." She
had said it twice before and so she was ignored.

"But that's cleared up," Kelly continued. "And now
the—the other thing's cleared up."

"Seems as how," Roberts agreed. She added inconse-
quentially, "One sweet swimmer, that Alex."

Morgan rose with her indignation. "Roberts, I don't
know how you could make such a nasty insinuation against
such a nice young man! I'll have you know he's been very
helpful to me and I trust him implicitly!"

"All I said—" Roberts began. "This cruise is going to
do you good," she said. "Your nerves are shot, though I
should worry if I had your figure. Do you a lot of good
too," she added to Kelly. "We'll have a time! Give the Boss
a great big hug and kiss from me. Darned if I don't think
it's one of the most generous and thoughtful things I ever
heard of."

"I have an idea," said Kelly, "that we really have no idea
just how thoughtful it is."

"Kelly," Morgan broke in again, "I really *must* be going."

"Why the devil didn't you quit this evening?" Roberts
asked. "You could have spent the night with me on the
boat."

"I couldn't! I mean, well, I— Kelly, I must get back!"

"May we walk?" Kelly asked. "Or don't you trust him to
wait as implicitly as you say you do?"

Roberts laughed. "See you both in New Harbor in the
morning."

VI

It had not been late but it had been something of a day and
Morgan had found that there was no one still up downstairs on her return. While she waited with the door on
the crack at the bedroom landing of the servants' stairs the

thought that Mr. Caldwell may have already gone to the bathroom was maddening. Of all feelings that of being too late most distresses with its sense of unnecessary futility.

There were tears of vexation in her eyes when his door opened and, in dressing gown and slippers, George Caldwell went yawning to the bathroom that he shared with Alex Redell and Wm Sultan. Morgan waited until the bathroom door closed behind him and then darted to his bedroom door. Her hand, which for the past quarter hour had been so tightly gripping the little purchase she had made in Bayhead village that afternoon, withdrew it from her apron pocket. With speed and yet with care she sowed a minefield of carpet tacks, No. 2's, in front of Mr. Caldwell's door and then hastily returned to her vantage point, by chance dropping one or two along the hall on the way.

Presently, still yawning, George Caldwell came out of the bathroom and came down the hall to the door of his room and stopped yawning.

"Grawm—" he said and jerked up his foot and hopped on the other for balance and then sat down when he tried to jerk it up too.

Jenny Jeepers started to open the door but another door opened first and Alex Redell stepped into the hall in dressing gown and slippers.

"Hello! What's the matter?" he asked, and hastening to George Caldwell took two steps too many and found out twice.

Jenny Jeepers opened the door and tripped into the hall.

"Cooo—!" she said. "Hand may Hi be of some 'elp to you-all, suh?" She gave not so much as a glance to Alex Redell, who had bought the tacks for her. She stared steadily upon the feet of George Caldwell.

Since his first atavistic ejaculation George Caldwell had eschewed conversation in favor of concentrating upon removing his slippers from his feet with that which attached them to them. He had removed one. Five toes. He withdrew the attachment out of the pierced sole of the other slipper and waved it at Alex Redell who did not notice because he was similarly occupied.

"The damned thing's a railroad spike," he said, more in surprise than anything else. Then he removed the second slipper to look at the sole of his foot.

"Oh, *no!*" said Jenny Jeepers. Five more toes. She sank to her knees and listlessly swept up the tacks in front of the door.

George Caldwell began to give some thought to causes as the shock of the effects wore off. "But how the devil?" he wondered.

"I did it," Morgan said. "I'm terribly sorry."

"You mean," Alex Redell said, "you'd dropped the box but hadn't realized some of them had spilled?"

Morgan did not reply. She put the last of the tacks in her pocket. She felt too low to care what explanation was given. She rose, avoiding their eyes, and hastened with bent head back to the stairs.

"I got them for her myself this afternoon," she heard Alex continuing. "Said she wanted to stick up some pictures in her room. It's just one of those things . . ."

Morgan dragged her feet on up the stairs and down the third-floor hall.

"—*Only* and except, *only* and except," Mrs. Lumpey's voice came from behind the door of Cora's room, "you again didn't fold your hands in front of you, even better than the first one, it was! Dying in front of your eyes, as good as, his hand shaking so's you wonder he could hold the pen! Oh maybe we haven't been seduced by French chefs or been born with high-class accents, but you can see who's the servants Mrs. Caglett trusts in this house! And twenty dollars and an evening—" her voice broke off.

Morgan's feet plodded on down the bare hall. The door opened and Mrs. Lumpey looked out.

"Lord love a servant, you do look played out, child." Morgan nodded wearily. "Well," Mrs. Lumpey yawned elaborately—"time I get to bed myself. Just been sitting around with Cora all evening telling her about some of the dinners I've known Mary Fullswell to cook."

"As long as I eats good," wheezed Cora, "I say—"

Morgan plodded on into her room and the door closed slowly behind her. She sat down and took off her shoes. After some ten minutes she rose and listened at her door, cautiously opened it, slipped out, quietly shut it. She sped down the hall on tiptoe, down the back stairs to the second floor and down the hall to Wm Sultan's door. She dared not knock. She closed her eyes and slipped inside. Wm Sultan was reading in bed. He lowered his book. Morgan opened her eyes and looked apprehensively towards the veranda but the door was closed. She went quickly to his bedside.

"Mr. Sultan," she gasped, "Mr. Silliman's signed a will!"

Wm Sultan gave a ghost of a sigh and put his finger in his book to mark his place.

"I mean a new will, another will, tonight," she specified. "I overheard Mrs. Lumpey talking to Cora and they have, they've witnessed another will tonight! And then she heard me in the hall and when she opened the door she didn't have a thing to say about it and that means it's a *secret* will! But he can't do that, can he?" she asked indignantly. "How can anybody sign a will unless you draw it? It can't be any good!"

Wm Sultan coughed. "Conceding that," he said, "it's still possible to copy my inimitable product changing only the beneficiaries or the amounts to the beneficiaries."

"Then this is really important?" she said eagerly. "I have found something really important?"

"Yes, Morgan," Wm Sultan said, "it's really important. But just for me," he added, "just in a legal sense. You may embark upon your nautical vacation tomorrow without a worry."

When she slipped out of his door again he took his finger from the book and closed it. He got out of bed and limped to a chair. He could worry as well lying down but he could think better sitting up.

Morgan recovered her room without being seen by any one except Kelly. Instead of going to her room on her return to the house Kelly had sat on the front porch to think things over. When from the front stairs she saw Morgan slip from a certain door in her stocking feet to the back stairs, she was given even something more to think over while she lay in the dark in bed.

For long hours from Wm Sultan's room a light shone out over the dark current which bore the body of Catherine Nollis.

12

*An Accident Aboard the Cruiser. Who else? Jonathan
Edwards Seever. Terrible Discovery. "Cursed—Haunted!"
A Blue Dinghy. Another Body is Found. A Missing Toe.*

Wm Sultan took a modest pride in his ability to wake up
when he wanted to. Instead of being a slave to an alarm
clock he could on retiring fix his mind upon the hour at
which he wished to awake, and without fail he would never
sleep past that time. It was two in the morning when he
turned out his light and set his mental alarm for seven.
As usual he awoke before that time, at four. This was the
reason he took only a modest pride in his ability.

However, he decided that it might be all for the better.
He could catch the six-thirty instead of the eight-thirty
train for the city and by leaving at this hour, alone, could
pursue a line of inquiry that might be exceedingly helpful.
He left a note for his secretary, wishing her bon voyage on
her vacation, which he pushed under her door, and one for
his host, explaining that he felt it imperative to be early in
the city. At four-thirty he started down the road at a brisk
walk, swinging his bag, quite like a vagabond.

Within five minutes he was, to his considerable surprise, given a lift by an inebriated couple who deposited

him, at his request, on the roadside above the cove opposite Greenwater. Due to this unexpected saving of time
it was in the first faint dawn that he stood on the shore
contemplating the water between him and the *Bolivar*. He
was on private property. He was on a small dock belong-
ing to a house that was so close it seemed that he could
hear the breathing of its sleeping occupants through the
open windows. There was a dory tied up to the dock and
there were oars in the dory. Not caring longer to trespass
he put his suitcase in the dory and rowed out to the *Bolivar*. He rowed quietly, not wishing to disturb perhaps very
hard-working people who needed their sleep, and mindful
of how sounds carry over water he was very quiet about
boarding the *Bolivar*.

But, as a little lie leads to a bigger one, his unexpect-
edly early awakening seemed to be leading him into more
and more unexpected complications. He had not planned
on boarding a boat containing a young female person
asleep in bed. Of all situations on earth capable of being
misconstrued by the general public *and* the young female
person . . . And there was the dory and there were the open
windows of the house and there was that stillness of dawn
in which breathing seems noisy.

He put his head in the open companionway and whispered, "Roberts." He tried it again, more loudly. A third
time, still more loudly, and looked apprehensively over
his shoulder at the house. The impropriety of entering the
cabin was such that it never even occurred to him, but he
felt that one step down to remove his voice from the amp-
lifying waters would make up in discretion what it would
infringe in propriety. He took one step down and his foot
was snatched out from under him and he took a belly dive
into the darkness of the cabin that ended with a dazing
crash of head, arms, ribs and legs upon the cabin floor.

Lights flashed in his head, went out, became a blinding white glare.

A shocked voice came to him faintly, "Well, of all people."

Wm Sultan became aware that the blinding glare was from a flashlight. Since he would have to know sooner or later he tried to move. It worked.

"Just keep your head down a minute," Roberts' voice said sternly. "I sleep raw." Wm Sultan closed his eyes while there were various soft sounds in the cabin. "All right," she said, "you can sit up now!"

He felt that the statement might be unduly optimistic but upon putting it to the test found that he could.

He said, "Good morning, Roberts."

"It just goes to show you," she said musingly, and as if shaking her head, "you never really know."

"I came to ask you a question," Wm Sultan said with dignity.

"The answer—" Roberts began.

"On the way to the train," he cut it off. "The six-thirty from New Harbor," he made it specific.

"Why," she said in surprise, "it is getting light!" Her voice became the one to which he was accustomed. "Holy cats, Boss, here, let me help you up!"

He sat on her berth. She had switched on the cabin lights. She stood in front of him anxiously, looking boyish in her shorts, not boyish in her crew shirt.

"That's a honey of a bump on your forehead," she said. "Can't understand how you didn't split it open." She added, in frank admiration, "You certainly do have a hard head, boss! *Nothing* can break it. No sir," she insisted, "nothing!" She went to the companionway and unhooked a dark thin line like a wire that was visible against the pearly background of the sky. "Summer two years ago," she said, "an eager beaver from a schooner hit my pure life line and *he* needed six stitches and a new nose."

Wm Sultan found it unpalatable that a comparison could be drawn between him and an eager beaver from a schooner.

"If I'm to make my train," he said stiffly, "I haven't much time."

"I'll run you over to New Harbor," Roberts offered.

"Thank you," Wm Sultan said, molding his kneecaps back into a semblance of their former shape. "The question I have to ask you," he continued, wincing, "is in reference to the time—ummmmm—when, so I'm told, Bart signaled—ooooph—you from the house?—ahhhhh."

"I've some rubbing alcohol," Roberts suggested, "if you want to take off your pants?"

"And, you picked him up at the beach!" Wm Sultan said loudly, his ears turning red. "I'd like to know if he said anything—well, anything at all that might have given a hint that his having signaled you was anything other than just a prank?"

"He didn't say anything, but he expected to find some one else aboard."

"Some one else? That was definitely your impression?"

Roberts nodded. "It's the reason he signaled and it's the reason he swam out to the boat," she said confidently. "The second he was aboard he wanted to get below decks. Then I saw him standing here staring at the door of the head, so I told him he could use it"—Wm Sultan's ears crinkled at this subject, which was never mentioned as being mentionable in *Godey's Ladies' Book*—"and," Roberts was continuing, "he jerked the door open like he expected to find Captain Kidd and then turned around and came back on deck."

"Thank you," Wm Sultan said, "that's very helpful."

"Look, Boss, what are you up to?"

"I'm merely picking up those little odds and ends of information which my staff has not seen fit to confide in me."

"Can I be of any help?" Roberts asked.

"Yes," Wm Sultan said emphatically. "You may take Kelly and Morgan on their vacation cruise today. I want you to forget this entire affair. Perhaps it would be best if you don't even mention to Kelly that I have asked you about this."

"Yeahhhh," Roberts agreed, starting on deck. "Maybe it would. She knows I sleep raw."

But Wm Sultan was in far too good a humor to let any comment long disconcert him. There are few things more intellectually satisfying than, as with Columbus on his first sight of birds heralding the nearness of a New World, the discovery of signs presaging the verification of a theory. He sailed on more confidently.

He had breakfast on the train, a change of clothes in the city, and gave some signed authorizations to the assistant cashier of the Pine St. Bank & Trust Co. He commented that it practically completed the liquidation of Mr. Silliman's portfolio. Some $540,000 in securities had been sold since the first of the month and the proceeds deposited. Which reminded him that Mr. Silliman wanted an immediate check of his account. A statement to date and the canceled checks were brought to him. There was a balance of $17,000. The cashier understood that that small balance was to be brought more in line? that Mr. Silliman was going to liquidate some real estate? Oh, yes, yes, yes, yes, yes. There were canceled checks totaling an even $500,000 that had been endorsed with the name of Jonathan Edwards Seever.

II

Morgan wanted to wait to tell Mrs. Caglett that she was leaving and did not see her before breakfast. In the meantime she carried on. Breakfast was at eight and was promptly attended because it was at eight only. When Mrs. Caglett entered the dining room Catherine Nollis was the only other not present.

She said, in her dead voice, "Has any one seen Catherine?"

Some one said, "She's not down yet."

"She's not in her room," Mrs. Caglett said. "I may be mistaken," she continued, "and you, Leslie, are familiar with her clothes and might also look to see if anything you recall is missing."

They had all stopped eating now. Morgan moved behind Kelly's chair.

"Last night," the full flat voice continued, "I persuaded her to have a hot bath and then thought she went to sleep. I noticed that her bathing suit was hanging in the bathroom. It is not there now."

Leslie Silliman sprang up and went out on the veranda a step ahead of Alex Redell. George and Georgiana Caldwell went after them. Kelly and Morgan followed, paused behind the others, who stood looking with sick eyes at the empty green water, knowing that if they saw any swimmer it would not be the one they sought.

Leslie Silliman said, "I could kill myself for not having been any help to her."

Roylson Caglett put his face in his hands.

Morgan, clinging to Kelly's arm, put her lips to her ear. "I'd better not now, had I?" she whispered.

Kelly shook her head. "I don't think the police would want any one to leave before the autopsy."

"Where's—"

"In town. Left early."

They stopped whispering then, knowing that they had not been noticed by any of those who stood staring at that bright water and then uneasily turned from it as if fearing to look in its face too long; but their whispered conference, in pantomime as clearly a conference of equals as had the words been heard, did not pass unnoticed by the gaunt widow who, forgotten, watched it from the dining room.

III

Having suffered from Mrs. Lumpey's cooking, Wm Sultan made amends to himself by lunching at the Codicil Club. The Codicil Club was one of the three remaining in New York that at lunch poured more wine than cocktails and that at lunch or even dinner disposed of more snuff than cigarettes. It is, however, a canard that at the last national election ten per cent of the membership wrote in the name of McKinley. Wm Sultan sat, in the least favorable chair of course, at the Sultan's table in the most suitable of company, the ghost of Young Sultan's Brother to his right, of Young Sultan to his left and *Mr.* Sultan in the chair that had a view of the room. Since it was a hot day and he wanted something light he had iced coffee, and some Little Necks, broiled salmon with Bechamel sauce, a mutton chop, new potatoes, escalloped sweetbreads with green peas, a tossed green salad and some orange sherbet. It was three o'clock when he reached his office and, not feeling very peppy somehow, it was three-thirty before he picked up the telephone and called the answering service. Yes, his secretary had left a message that morning. It was, and clearly the girl thought it was a honey, "Miss Nollis is not here in her bathing suit."

He caught a cab to his garage and drove through New Harbor after six. He stopped at a state police car parked beside the road at the clam flats. Lieutenant Orprey was waiting glumly.

"There doesn't seem a doubt of it," he said. "It doesn't mean anything she hasn't washed up as soon as her brother. It doesn't deliver on railroad schedule, you know. If we don't get it this tide it'll be after midnight."

"What were the circumstances?" Wm Sultan asked.

"Oh, it seems she had her brother's death on her conscience pretty much, I got that much talking to her yesterday— My God, *yesterday* her brother and today—

There must be a curse on that house, or haunted or something."

Wm Sultan said, "Yes, Lieutenant."

"Doc Benson feels like hell about it," Orprey continued. "Blaming himself for not keeping her doped up for a couple of days, but how could he tell if she had it in her head to go out the same way the kid did?"

"I thought there was a theory that a swimmer can't drown himself?"

"You mean can't keep himself from trying to swim, don't you, Mr. Sultan? All she'd have to do would be to undertake more than she could finish and she'd drown like any other swimmer who does not wanting to. Get exhausted and the chop where the Sound runs into the current of the channel off the point of the island out there will finish you."

"You'll call me at once, of course?"

"I certainly will. And one thing, Mr. Sultan," he called him back, "you don't need to have to ask for a thorough autopsy this time."

"I'd imagine not."

"And while I'm trying to be suspicious, how much dough has Mr. Silliman got? Here's what I'm getting at. Had he left her any important amount of it in his will?"

"By the terms of a will that he signed yesterday, fifty thousand out of upwards of a million and a half."

Orprey laughed. "Go ahead, tell me I'm as bad as the old gossips you were worrying about yesterday. I admit it. This thing's beginning to get me."

"I think I know how you feel."

Wm Sultan was pleased to drive away. He wanted to get as straight a story as he could, perhaps from Leslie Silliman, before he committed himself. He drove fast, which he disliked to do, and nearly got in trouble braking when he saw the *Bolivar* still lying at anchor in the cove. Roberts came on deck at his hail and rowed to the dock.

"Don't blow up," she said. "No one's playing detective. But there's a man with black puttees at the driveway of the death house. He's there to shoo sightseers away. But if Morgan wanted to leave before the autopsy makes everything officially innocent he might want to ask her a couple of questions. And if she tells who she is it's going to leave some funny explaining for you."

"I know, I shouldn't have instructed her to take the position. But now that you're still here . . ."

"Name it."

"A blue dinghy."

"Green do?"

"Yes."

"Red?"

"But dark."

"Oh, yes. All dark."

"When you come to anchor again I'll know you've found it."

"Right, Boss."

"You can pick me up here."

"Right."

IV

Kelly had repeated Mrs. Caglett's exact words to him. "And that," she had concluded, "is every last damned thing we know."

"No doubt it's all there is to know," he had said soothingly, and had suggested that they sit on the veranda. Leslie and Alex Redell had joined, them. The rest of the household were behind closed doors. A half hour later he had said he wanted a drink of water and as he had hoped had found Morgan in the kitchen: even better than he hoped he had found her washing up some dishes alone.

"Mr. Sultan," she said, "there's something wrong here. I don't care what you say about evidence, you can't tell me this has been a normal week."

"I came out," Wm Sultan said, reassuringly, "to tell you that you'd find everything all cleared up very shortly. Now will you do something for me this evening?"

"You know I'd love to!" Her voice was thrilled, and this was the part that Kelly and Alex Redell, who had also discovered that they were thirsty, heard just outside the butler's pantry door.

"Wait for me in your room," he said coaxingly.

Morgan would have replied, but Alex and Kelly came in the butler's pantry just then and she nonchalantly resumed her dishwashing, dropping a glass, and flushed with excitement. It did not last her through the mountain of dishes and pots and broilers. It was just after dark and she was just cleaning up in slow motion when she heard the telephone ring. She slipped through the back hall and into the front hall and managed to be the first to reach it.

"Doctor Benson speaking. Mr. Sultan, please."

She gave the telephone to Mr. Sultan, who was waiting, as Kelly was waiting and Alex and Leslie were waiting. She walked very slowly back to the back hall. She heard:

"Yes, Doctor? . . . A half hour ago? . . . I understand . . . You're going ahead with it at once? . . . Oh, yes. Thank you, Doctor."

Morgan did not completely close the back-hall door and so she heard more. Through the crack of the door she saw Mr. Sultan put down the telephone and saw him turn solemnly to the others.

He said, "Her body was found a half hour ago. It appears to be a plain case of drowning." He was bending over the telephone table, writing. "Kelly, I'd appreciate it very much if you'd take this note to Doctor Benson." He folded a paper, put it in an envelope, sealed it and gave it to her. "And you, Mr. Redell, as the next of kin, had better go along for official identification. I'd appreciate it if you both would wait until the autopsy is completed."

It seemed to Morgan that Kelly and Alex were looking at each other rather oddly. Leslie was sagged against the newel post.

"I'd go myself," Mr. Sultan explained, "but I have to go out on some other business."

"Go right ahead," Kelly said.

"I must run now," he agreed, and with a nod went out the front door.

Leslie lurched up the stairs. "I'll tell the others," she said.

Morgan went back to the kitchen. She put away dishes and glasses. She washed the sink and went outside to empty the garbage can. She emptied it. She noticed the lights of Roberts' cruiser riding at anchor in its usual place. She wished she were on it. She was dog-tired. She sank down on the steps of the veranda and lit a cigarette.

Then she held the match until it burned her fingers as she stared like Robinson Crusoe at a footprint. It was a wet footprint on the step beside her. It was the print of a bare foot. It was clear and distinct and complete except that it was missing a toe. The big toe.

Some one moved on the veranda behind her.

13

*A Sea Serpent? The Bolivar Sails. "Ram Him!" Boarders
Away! Young Caldwell's Toe. Upstairs. The Exile's Story.
A Servant Alone. A Few Seconds! Cold Murder.*

Roberts was waiting for him beside the road.

"You can leave your car in the driveway," she said. "I got permission."

They went quickly to the dock.

"Doctor Benson called," Wm Sultan said, "just as I saw your lights swing to."

"Yes, I know. They found the body."

"How the—"

"The whole shore knows it. What did the doctor have to say? Same thing?"

"The preliminary, yes."

"Not a mark? Pull up into the current more."

"Apparently not."

"Our obliging friend here," Roberts indicated the house on the shore, "has a theory. A sea monster—*Ship that oar!*" She swung aboard the cruiser. "A big serpent," she continued, making the dinghy fast, "coils up around them and drags them down."

The *Bolivar* quivered with the life of her engine. Wm Sultan went forward to raise the anchor. When he returned to the cockpit Roberts told him that they were heading for the bay.

"I looked at New Harbor first," she said. "I'd noticed a green job there the other day. But there were a couple of women on board, so—"

"Right."

"Took me some time to beat it back up the channel here to the bay. Nearly dark when I spotted this job. Looks about right to me. Say, just a few minutes before you got here I heard an outboard. You don't suppose it could mean anything?"

Wm Sultan shook his head. "Much too early."

The *Bolivar* pushed on over the dark water, the lights of the mainland falling away to the left and those of the island to the right as the channel opened into the bay. The stars were as bright. The sound of an outboard motor gave them a brief stern chase, passed ahead unseen in the darkness.

"It isn't far now," Roberts said. Presently, "It's the one to the right."

They bore down on the lights of a single cabin cruiser of more modern vintage than the *Bolivar*. She was beam on. Through the ports of her cabin they saw some one at her controls.

"He's getting under way," Roberts said. "He can walk away from us."

"Douse your lights."

The *Bolivar* ran in darkness.

"Ram him."

"Right."

"Allow for his increase of speed as he overcomes inertia."

"Right. By the way, Boss, what is this, piracy?"

"I'm under the impression that it's barratry in an anchorage"—his tone was testy as he did not like admitting his ignorance of admiralty law. Or did it even come under

admiralty law in territorial waters? Women could think of
the—

The cruiser had seen them and was swinging hard to
starboard. The *Bolivar* was alongside with a grinding
bump and William Sultan leaped through a wild splash of
water. He landed full length in the other cockpit.—Of the
damnedest questions at the damnedest times, he concluded the thought irritably. When he picked himself up the
Bolivar was astern. Through the companionway he looked
at the man who stood at the controls. An elderly man. A
large elderly man. A large elderly man with a long, pointed nose. A large elderly man with a long, pointed nose and
a long, pointed jaw. White hair showed at the temples beneath a dark-blue beret. His pullover and his trousers were
dark blue. His feet were bare. His left foot was missing a
toe. The big toe.

"Suppose you heave to, Mr. Caldwell," Wm Sultan suggested.

II

Morgan wondered who it had been that she had heard behind her on the veranda. She had not waited to find out.
She had run to the kitchen. The lighted kitchen was comforting. She wanted desperately to tell some one about the
footprint. But there was no one to tell. Kelly had driven
off with Alex. Mr. Sultan had left before them. She remembered that Mr. Sultan had told her to wait in her room.
She went into the back hall. The back stairs looked dim
and lonely. She wondered if stairs and corridors looked
lonely because there wasn't anything on them that you
lived with like the homey but companionable equipment
of the kitchen.

She started up the stairs reluctantly and stopped short
when the door at the second-floor landing opened. A gaunt
black figure stood in the doorway looking down at her.

Mrs. Caglett's dead voice said, "Will you please prepare some milk toast for Mr. Silliman? You may take it to him when it's ready. Be careful not to boil the milk."

Morgan turned and went back down the stairs. She heard the door close behind her. She was, at first, more pleased than not to have an excuse to return to the kitchen, but she was so tired and her attention so wandering that the milk-toast making became a task. First she burned the toast and then while watching more toast the milk boiled over.

But eventually it was on the tray and she carried it up the stairs and down the hall without meeting any one. The house might have been deserted, it was so quiet, but it did not feel deserted. She was conscious of the people behind the closed doors.

Mr. Silliman was alone and looked very ill and lonely. She helped him sit up a little more against the pillows, and put the tray on the bed and poured the hot milk on the buttered toast. He dabbed at it with the spoon. He's old and ill and lonely, she thought, and looks frightened maybe because he's old and ill, and she did not have the heart to leave him to eat alone.

She sat down beside him smiling and said that she had better hold the bed tray steady. He brightened up considerably and, though very slowly, spooned it up to the last drop. She helped him settle down comfortably in bed again before carrying the tray back to the hall. Then back down to the kitchen again and wash up the dishes on the tray and put them away and start back up the back stairs again.

In her weariness the excitement of her discovery had been replaced by doubt. When she recalled a mental picture of the footprint it was fuzzy around the edges. She was still certain that she had not seen a toe but less confident that it meant that the foot that had made the print had not had a toe. She had been mistaken so many times about toes.

She passed the second floor and went on up towards the third. Mr. Sultan had told her to wait there and so she would, but she did wish that Mrs. Lumpey and Cora hadn't been given the evening off after dinner leaving all the work for her to do and leaving her all by herself up here.

But she was too tired and hot and dirty to be much concerned over anything else.

III

Wm Sultan had called to Roberts to drop her hook and come aboard. When she entered the cabin her expression caused Howard Caldwell to give a grim smile and a nod to Wm Sultan.

"You can imagine my homecoming," he said. "I knew something was wrong by the servant's expression as he looked at me when he answered the door. But then when I entered the room and the four of us looked at each other —my God!"

Wm Sultan could see them. He could see Mrs. Caglett and the twins, their faces with their prepared expressions for the welcome of Charles Silliman. They would want him to see that they were humbly grateful for a half century of generosity. They would want him to see that sight unseen they loved this unremembered friend of an unremembered brother. And so they had faced each other—the three and the one, the four peas from the same pod—faced each other for a moment incredulous of the thing they recognized.

"I assume the twins laughed," Wm Sultan said.

Howard Caldwell nodded, and it might have been George Caldwell, save that the man who swept the beret from his white hair was a dozen years older in fact and five in appearance, save that his expression was intelligent, lacking the hint or more of arrested development common to both the twins.

"That's all there was to it at first," he said. "The funniest thing that had ever happened. Here brother Howard had been putting something over all these years and he was caught. But something had to be done at once. My granddaughter was on her way from the coast, young Redell and Catherine Nollis and her brother were due in a couple of days. One look at us and any one would know we were brothers and sisters. Even the servants—only Seever had seen me, we got rid of the others the next day while I stayed in hiding."

He rose with a fierce gesture as if to strike something down, his expression bitter as if, striking, he knew that the thing at which he struck was impalpable, as beyond the reach of a blow as the air.

"An embezzler!" he said. "An embezzler at fourteen at the persuasion of a father? Then later helpless to do anything without sending *him* to prison. Of course I should never have married. But I was an exile, and lonely, and I was *young,* Mr. Sultan." Momentarily his expression softened. "But I already know you understand. I heard you the night . . ."

"Ah, yes, yes, yes, yes, yes," said Wm Sultan. "I've been wondering if it weren't you who'd saved my life."

"After first striking you down in the hotel because I thought you were a blackmailer and then being responsible for your near murder, you don't owe me thanks. Besides," his smile was sardonic, "I'd thought of an answer to the letters and you were no longer dangerous."

Wm Sultan let it pass. "I'm surprised you didn't count the consequences the second time, Mr. Caldwell," he said. "The first substitution to gain a fortune, and wreck your life, the second to save it, and—?"

"You're forgetting the pressure of time. There was one day. One day. To turn myself in as a criminal after a half century, leave my granddaughter penniless—or to try to save something."

"Only," said Wm Sultan quietly, "Seever wouldn't agree. From what I hear of him," he continued, "I understand that he was a narrowly honest man? Was it necessary to murder him, Mr. Caldwell?"

"It was an accident. I don't expect you to believe—"

"I've rather imagined it was. Otherwise it would rather upset the pattern, wouldn't it? A boy accidentally falls off a boat at Capri, and at Greenwater—?" Roberts saw him look at his wrist watch.

Howard Caldwell said, "He was a blackmailing drunkard. We were having an argument about terms when he backed against the parapet and fell off the veranda. I went down again and again. It was ten minutes before I found him and dragged him out on the beach. I worked on the corpse for an hour, though it was foolish, I've seen too many drowned people."

Wm Sultan nodded. "Up until then you had intended only to go away and leave some excuse for your granddaughter and cousins, I imagine?"

Howard Caldwell smiled somewhat. "That's a mild way of expressing what it meant to go back into exile, Mr. Sultan." He shrugged as a man who has suffered what he cannot expect others to understand. "But, yes," he said, "that was it. It was, however, going to be damned difficult because of Henry Perdue. He'd met the twins, and so I wouldn't dare see him. But with Seever's death all that was changed." His voice had hardened. "I was offered the alternative of the substitution or of having them make a deal with the legitimate heirs, cutting my granddaughter off without a cent and sending me to prison. So I agreed. *Foolishly,* you say!"

"Two lives, Mr. Caldwell."

"My God, you can't hold me responsible for accidental deaths."

"Ah, no, no, no, no, no. But murder, yes."

"Murder!"

"Any one is entitled to two points of view, Mr. Caldwell. That you've simply given it up as a bad job now that you've signed the will and are going off with the half million you deposited under your new name of Seever. No, no, I don't think you took the name callously, but as a warning to the others that they're in this too when they should find what's happened on receiving Charles Silliman's bank statement on the first of the month. But the other point of view is that the moment any one learns of your existence they learn that you've had both motive and opportunity."

"Good God, Mr. Sultan, when I came back to do what I could for the rightful heirs and intended to make full restitution in my will, can you think I'd drown a boy and a girl to save myself from whatever might happen?"

Wm Sultan said, "A girl? What makes you so certain that Catherine Nollis has been drowned?"

"I've just come from Greenwater."

"You weren't seen?"

"I may have been. But only by one of the maids. We were talking on the veranda when she sat down on the steps and lit a cigarette. She looked at my footprint, the wet grass—"

Roberts grasped her employer's arm.

"Look here, Boss, maybe I put things together wrong but it seems to me that somebody named Alex has been getting somebody out of the way ahead of time, if you know what I mean. He's at the house," she added in a breath.

Wm Sultan shook his head. "There's nothing to worry about. I sent him with Kelly to New Harbor and asked them to wait until the completion of the autopsy."

"People don't always do what they're asked to."

He shook his head again. "Morgan's all right. I told her to stay upstairs with the cook and the other maid."

"Oh!"

Howard Caldwell said, "I don't know what's concerning you, and so I don't know if it means anything to you, but I was told that the other servants had been given the evening off."

Wm Sultan turned and ran on deck. "Your outboard, please!" he called over his shoulder.

Roberts helped lift it into the blue dinghy drawn alongside.

"I'm going along."

"Ah, no, no, no, no, no. It can carry one faster than two. A few seconds faster at any rate."

IV

In the back of Carmichael's Pharmacy, pharmacist Carmichael said, "Well, there you are!"

Lieutenant Orprey softly beat his fist against his leg. "Murder," he said. "Cold murder."

Doctor Benson was saying, "And it never even entered my head. How did he know? How the devil did he know?" He stared again at the note from Wm Sultan which he already knew only too well by heart.

"My dear Doctor," he read, *"I have no doubt that your preliminary report of death by drowning will prove correct, but would you mind determining whether the water you find in the lungs is salt or fresh?"*

14

Morgan knew that she could not feel really alive again until she had a bath. If she hurried up and took it right away she would probably be all through long before Mr. Sultan got back.

She undressed hastily if wearily, sagged into a dressing gown, and shuffled down the hall. She stopped cold with her hand on the knob of the bathroom door. She was certain that she had heard the click of a latch on one of the doors of the rooms behind her. Her pause in time was only the fraction of a second. She must be like Roberts: she must not imagine things: imagine Roberts imagining doors opening on a floor where no one was except herself!

She went into the bathroom and turned on the water in the tub; she would have given her eye teeth for a shower but a deep soaking tub had its advantages too. She wanted a nice warm bath, just blood temperature, to soak out the grime and weariness. She felt half dead. It was a close night. Not much air came in from the window overlooking the channel. She left the bathroom door open for ventilation with the steam of the hot water rising. She thought of Mr. Sultan as she took off her dressing gown? But no, a thousand times no! If he came to the head of the stairs and heard splashing in a tub he would be the last person living . . . Morgan shook her head to start it again like a stopped clock. She was so tired that thoughts stopped midway. Mr. Sultan would be the last person living to take one step down such a hall. She was as safe as safe could be.

And the noise of the running water was companionable. It sang in the pipes quite cheerily. It sang in the pipes that ran through another bathroom directly below. The person who had been waiting heard it singing and the door of the bathroom was opened and closed and cautious footsteps went down the hall and the door to the back stairs was opened and closed and the cautious footsteps mounted the stairs to the floor above.

Perhaps the stairs creaked as the stairs in old houses will, but creak ever so loudly it is certain that Morgan could not have heard them above the friendly gushing of the bright fresh water into the tub. It had a rushing sound now, as the tub was nearly as full as it could be if she were to get in, and she could have told by the sound of it alone that she could not let it run much longer, that there was not much time left.

She turned it off and stepped into the tub, slowly lowered herself. Awwwwwww. She had her hair done up in a bun on the very top of her head and could slide down in the tub with her legs and arms limp and the water lapping at her chin. The bun on top of her head made a good grip for the strong fingers that seized, the strong arm that thrust down.

II

With the outboard given full throttle the blue dinghy stood on its tail like a rearing horse but moved much faster.

There was a breeze from the west quartering the current and the channel was like a diagonally plowed field. The dinghy exploded against each furrow and tried to roll over like a bronco, to free herself of the man who drove her. He drove her, now, towards a square of light on the third floor of a house. The single square of light of a bathroom window. It was driven full throttle at the beach, struck and leaped like a skipping stone, lay still. Its driver went over its head like a rider thrown over the head of a bucking horse, rolled head over heels like a hoop through water and sand, was on his feet and running to the house.

Wm Sultan flung open the screen door, went through the kitchen, into the back hall and up the back steps. The door of the second-floor landing opened ahead of him. Alex Redell stood on the landing.

"Where," he asked, "do you think you're going?"

Wm Sultan did not have much breath left.

He said, "Upstairs."

"That's what you think," he said. "A nice kid like that!"

Wm Sultan hit him on the kneecap knocking his leg from under him and as he leaned forward charged on up under him. He was coming out from under the weight on his back into the clear when a wildly clawing hand caught the toe of his shoe and spilled him face down on the stairs. It was his own fault. He knew better. He should have paused for a half beat when the weight of the other man's body had fallen on his back and straightened himself with a jerk. He had, however, not wanted to throw a fine-looking young athlete like Redell clear through the air to the bottom of the stairs.

He was picking himself up when a hand again clutched his foot jerking his leg straight out on the stairs. Since protecting the other man any longer was out of the question he did not waste time thinking about it but rolled over on his back and had his other leg drawn up to kick him in the head when there was a scream from the hall above them.

III

Kelly screamed in the doorway of the bathroom and Mrs. Caglett straightened from the tub. For an instant the gaunt woman with the dead black eyes did not move, and then a light came into her eyes and she rushed forward brushing Kelly aside. She flung open the door of an adjoining room, disappeared inside.

Kelly did not watch her. Kelly swayed back into the bathroom, whimpering. Morgan's wet red topnot came out of the water. It was followed by Morgan's wet red face. It was followed by Morgan, wet and red from the hot bath. Kelly was at the side of the tub laughing absurdly in relief when Morgan, wet and red, wet and red in body and hair and red in temper, stepped from the tub.

"So it's so funny, is it?" she said. "You push my head down in the water and hold it there until I nearly bust and it's just a big laugh, is it?"

"But, Morgan—" Kelly backed away from her.

Morgan, wet and red, wiggled a finger at her. "You just come here and you'll find how funny it is!"

"But, Morgan, you don't understand, I saved you!" Kelly cried, still retreating.

Morgan's wet, red finger wiggled. "Just come here and I'll save you just the same way!"

"But Morgan—" Kelly retreated into the hall and into the arms of, jointly, Wm Sultan and Alex Redell.

Wm Sultan said, "Thank God she's . . ."

Alex Redell said something, perhaps, to himself.

"Morgan," Kelly said with terrible patience, "don't you think, dear, that all things considered you might step back and shut that door?"

Morgan, snapped out of it, stopped standing there wiggling her wet, red finger.

IV

Wm Sultan's file clerk, a dressing gown over her and her feet under her, sat on a chair on the arm of which sat Alex Redell. When she looked at Wm Sultan's secretary, who sat on a sofa to his left while his receptionist sat on the same sofa to his right, a definite coolness, like the North Atlantic in February, came into her sea-green eyes. Oh, yes, she had been told. Well, she hadn't said anything, but when she started believing a story like that! Just when. Just, for instance, what had Kelly been doing on the third floor? Just what, Kelly?

The secretary understood the look. She understood it only too clearly. Just what, Kelly? It was, fortunately, the sort of question which would occur seriously only to another young female person. To any man it was enough to say that she had just happened to go up there and he nodded wisely. It would have been so awkward to say that she had been, because of a mistaken interpretation which she had put upon an assignation which she had overheard, altruistically concerned about the preservation of the good conduct of an insouciant young fellow employee of the same sex.

She found it much more comfortable to meet the understanding eyes of Alex Redell. They, because it would have been utterly impossible, did not need to disguise from each other the motive which had caused them to drive like fiends to New Harbor and without waiting for any report to drive like fiends, green-eyed ones, back again and take their respective measures concerning a projected meeting between an employer and one of his employees.

Wm Sultan, however, looked favorably upon his file clerk. Within the past few days he had come to look more and more favorably upon his file clerk. He felt that in these past few days she had shown herself to better and better advantage. He also looked favorably upon his receptionist, who had her hand on his shoulder in a comradely gesture. Sitting on her hip, with her long blond legs bent to the right, for they had the same quality in coloration as her hair, she was naturally forced to lean against him in the comradely fashion of a fellow pirate, or was it barrator? Again miffed by the admiralty, he put her out of his mind for the moment if not the consciousness of her comradely nearness and the pressure of her hand on his shoulder, and looked with favor and the only smile he had in his system upon Leslie and her grandfather sitting together and holding each other's hands. As a matter of course, he conveyed the warmth of his feeling for the grandfather to him by smiling at the granddaughter.

Alex Redell had inquired, with some vehemence, if some one might be so good as to give him some slight inkling as to what anything was about; and Wm Sultan, graciously overlooking the several expletives which accompanied the request, had courteously complied. If for some time Alex had felt that he was lost in some genealogical forest somewhere in the Berkshires, his guide had gently led him by the hand to a clearing where he had seen Young Caldwell with his hatchet, a well-behaved lad but unlucky, dissociate himself from his Toe. He had seen Horace Seneca Sultan, later so sound on codicils, then so handy with tourniquets, to the rescue.

He had been whisked from the woods to France and had seen Young Caldwell, still well-behaved without his Toe, take pen in hand and write a dutiful letter to his arterial benefactor. He had been conducted to the melancholy scene where the also young Charles Silliman, probably also well-behaved and certainly even more unlucky, had departed this life in the Bay of Naples. He had been made aware of the temptation of Roylson Caldwell, the father, and the compliance of Young Caldwell, the son. He had seen Young Caldwell, still well-behaved and still unlucky, again take pen in hand and again write to his hero, signing himself Charles Silliman. He had followed him on his fifty-seven years of fearful exile, his hopeful return when it had seemed that at last all chance of recognition must be past.

Alex Redell had had only to look from him to the twins, who sat together like naughty children expecting to be spanked, to see how that hope had been killed by the fatal family resemblance of that generation of Caldwells.

He had then been conducted to the properly musty offices of Sultan, Sultan & Sultan, where he had been informed of the projected Life & Letters of the late Horace Seneca Sultan and of the two letters reposing in the files of his correspondence which had, upon their perusal by the speaker, unmasked to him the impersonation. *Per se.*

Alex Redell had whistled. "That was using the eye," he had said.

Wm Sultan coughed a modest cough and smiled at the exile's granddaughter.

"But the second impersonation," he said to the grandfather, "of Mr. Caglett for you, most successfully duped me. The very lack of any family resemblance, when your two sisters and your brother bore such very marked ones, made me most doubtful of my earlier interpretation of the letters. Then the unquestionable personality of your signature was for a time a most impenetrable mask. With one of my exceptional naïvety, it was only necessary for Mr. Caglett to make an excuse to hold papers overnight, when you would sign them."

Roberts' comradely hand gave a pal-like squeeze to the back of his neck and her unhostile voice whispered with friendly warmth in his ear, "Stop running yourself down, Bossy."

Wm Sultan shook his head and pulled unhappily at his opposite ear.

"Had I had the wit to appreciate it," he said, "I was told the entire situation within ten minutes of the time I arrived here. Before I ever set foot in the house, Bart told me that it was 'haunted.' And what is a haunted house other than one with more than the known living in it? Ah, yes, yes, yes, yes, yes, it must have indeed seemed a ghost to him the first time he caught a glimpse of you, Mr. Caldwell," he looked at Howard, "when he knew that Mr. Caldwell," he indicated George, "was elsewhere. Because I assume that you had had to call at night to give instructions to Mr. Caglett and to sign papers for Mr. Perdue?"

Howard Caldwell was looking at his granddaughter.

"Yes," he said, not turning his head. "I usually called in the small hours and left before dawn, but sometimes I stayed over until the following night. Either because there was business to be transacted the next day about which it could not be waited until night to consult me, or—" he spoke solely to Leslie—"after waiting all these years, I spent a few days watching you when you were outside from behind a window curtain." Then he did turn his head. "Mr. Sultan, if I could tell you what this means to me . . ."

"Very likely it was on one of those days that Bart saw you!" Wm Sultan said hastily.

Kelly, sitting as straight and solitary as a lamppost, had a negative corner of her eye on Roberts' fingers stroking the back of Wm Sultan's neck. Outdoor girl. The athletic type. Always so physically active.

"Then it must have been you," she said, "instead of Mr. Caglett, that zipped across the hall behind me as I came upstairs from dinner?"

"Yes! You very nearly caught me."

"And so it was also you instead of him who ate those big meals of his that day!"

"And when you'd arrived the night before," Wm Sultan interposed with a glance at his wrist watch, "you'd been seen by Bart, and he'd followed you upstairs and trailed your still damp footprints, damp enough at least to disturb the film of dust on a bare wood floor, to Mr. Caglett's door. There was something else he'd seen that night, and that was certain, ah, signals between the members of my staff here in the house and on the *Bolivar*. So when you came in your dinghy he naturally assumed that you came from the *Bolivar*. Indeed, the thing that convinced me that he had seen you arrive by water was his later evident expectation that there was a man on board the *Bolivar*."

"Hummm," Kelly said, her eyes narrowing as she looked at the skipper's head on the employer's shoulder. "I wonder."

"And on those occasions when you were going to stay over," Wm Sultan continued quickly, "I assume that Mr. Roylson Caglett would tow your dinghy back to your cruiser so that it would not be found here the next day?"

Howard Caldwell nodded.

"And then he'd take you back in the skiff that's here when you wanted to return the following night?"

"Yes," Howard Caldwell said, "and that's all that he had to do with it."

"His mother needed no accomplices," Wm Sultan agreed. "She saw Bart in the very act of trailing you to her husband's bedroom. Perhaps she was doubtful that he had actually seen you, but the very next evening when she learned of his intention to take the skiff out on the channel at night she could have no doubt but that he had seen you arrive the night before and was hot on your trail with all of a boy's curiosity. She knew that sooner or later the boy would be bursting to tell some one, and that if one word reached me her game was up. His sister ordered him upstairs to take a bath and he was never seen alive again. I," he said bitterly, "assumed that he had disobeyed his sister and sneaked back down the back stairs. But, no. The poor lad, well-behaved but unlucky, took his bath and was drowned while taking it. Then she put his bathing trunks back on him and pulled him through his bedroom to the upstairs veranda and dumped him over. Exactly as she later did to his sister."

"But why her too?" Howard Caldwell asked, aghast.

Wm Sultan said, reluctantly, "Because she had seen you on the stairs and mistook you for Mr. George Caldwell. She died because she mentioned that she had seen 'George Caldwell's'—" he cleared his throat nervously at the anatomical reference, not because of any psychosis but simply because it seemed to him an invasion of personal privacy—"feet."

Morgan sat forward like a shot, her dressing gown recoiling from her shoulders.

"His toe!" she cried.

Wm Sultan again looked with favor upon his file clerk. "Ah, yes, yes, yes, yes, yes," he agreed. "She could not have failed to notice the result of the digital amputation which had taken place in the Berkshires in '89. We may assume, I think?

"We may," said Kelly, glaring at where Morgan's dressing gown was not.

"That sooner or later she might comment upon it. By then that 'might'—any mere possibility of the fortune that she felt that she had in her hand being taken away from her—was enough for Mrs. Caglett. Because, after her first experience, she believed that she had hit upon an absolutely safe method of murder."

"And you might," Kelly reminded Morgan, "you just might remember that I saved you. God knows why."

"What," Morgan asked, "were you hiding in one of the servants' rooms for, Kelly?"

Wm Sultan coughed violently, having some dry sand in his throat.

"Poison!" he said, coughing. "Poison. In fact, she loaded her victims with a 'poison' that had only to be suspected to be discovered. Fresh water in the lungs of a person presumably drowned in salt water providing as conclusive evidence of the method of murder as had she used arsenic. I don't particularly dislike to speak evil of the evil dead," he concluded firmly, "and to me the evidence also seems conclusive that Mrs. Caglett was a very stupid woman. To me the most weighty evidence is the 'secret' will that she—'bullied' was the term you used, Morgan?"

Morgan was leaning against Alex's arm.

"Bullied," she said complacently.

"In the secret will," Wm Sultan continued, "which she bullied her husband into signing last night."

Howard Caldwell would have leaped to his feet had not Leslie's hands held him down by holding tight to his.

"What?" he demanded.

"Ah, yes, yes, yes, yes, yes," Wm Sultan affirmed. "Your bargain was not to be kept, Mr.—may I call you Mr. Silliman since Howard Caldwell has been so long legally dead? The sacrifice of the legitimate heirs and half the fortune to the Caldwells was not to be enough. I doubt if there would have been murder if it had not early occurred to Mrs. Caglett that once her husband was accepted as Charles Silliman he could make any will that he chose. An ill man, the signature a scrawl, with two witnesses that Charles Silliman had penned it. But when he signed it at Mrs. Caglett's dictation she had in fact herself given the game away. She had started on her way, shall we say? out the third-floor window."

"I see what you mean," Howard Caldwell said. "You knew that I'd given all that I would."

Wm Sultan glanced at his wrist watch and spoke more crisply.

"Certainly," he said. "Since the will had been kept secret from all except Mrs. Caglett it was obvious that it had been drawn almost exclusively in her favor. With, perhaps, enough of a sop to her brother and sister and to your granddaughter to make all three of you hesitate to strike in mere anger at a *fait accompli* when to do so you would lose everything. But as there seemed no existent circumstance in which an authentic Charles Silliman would have to agree in advance to further sacrifice, I was forced back upon the assumption that the man posing as Charles Silliman was not Charles Silliman."

"Toe or no toe!" said Morgan, crossing her legs and receiving a favorable smile from her employer.

"But since," he continued, "the man posing as Charles Silliman had one toe too many to be Howard Caldwell, and inasmuch as an authentic Charles Silliman could have no reason for being in hiding, but since one or the other had been signing that name all these years, it was—as you see—perfectly obvious that Howard Caldwell was hiding some place in the immediate neighborhood. The moment even such a possibility occurred to one, one saw instantly— of course—the significance of Bart's words and actions, and consequently that Howard Caldwell would be found upon the water in some craft with a dinghy of a color that would blend with his necessitously nocturnal visits."

Roberts patted the back of his neck in congratulation. He coughed involuntarily.

"One also saw," he continued, "a motive for Bart's murder; and when Mrs. Caglett with his sister repeated that method, the coincidence of baths being the last known acts of both victims reminded one that there is water in such a tub as well as the sea."

Oddly, it also seemed to remind him of Morgan. He looked at her a moment, caught himself, and spoke crisply to Alex Redell.

"Mr. Caldwell," he said, "has never alienated any of the real property of the estate. Since you are the one who profits by it, it might not be uncharitable to conclude that through all these years he has felt that he was holding it in trust for eventual return to the true heirs."

Alex Redell leaned forward on the arm of Morgan's chair.

"What would you do?" he asked. "I think that will be good enough for me."

Wm Sultan gave an embarrassed cough, but with that preliminary out of the way he said directly, "I'd let Mr. Silliman transfer to you the real property, its value's something over a million and a half. I'd forget everything else. And if you shouldn't, Mr. Redell, I wouldn't, even if I were you, trust my file clerk to find the two letters that are the only evidence on earth that you have any claim to anything."

"A million and a half," Alex said in quiet awe, "ought to do a lot for pisciculture."

Leslie at last let go of her grandfather's hand. She came over to Wm Sultan with her lower lip puckered out. "I think you're sweet," she said, and kissed him.

The brakes of a car screeched on the road.

"For what?" Morgan asked, looking up at Alex.

"And," said Wm Sultan hoarsely, his throat tightening as he looked at Kelly out of the corner of his eye, "and," he tried again, "if we give her unfortunate son and husband a chance they may now have many peaceful years ahead of them. And I venture to predict," he predicted, trying to wipe lipstick from his lips surreptitiously, which is very difficult to do, "that the present entering authorities"— there were footsteps on the porch—"will delve no deeper if we forget all else in the charitable assumption that any member of the gentle sex who behaved so inhumanely as Mrs. Caglett, was—insane. *Per se.*"

"What?" Alex repeated to Morgan. "Oh!" he explained. "I'm a pisciculturist."

"Cooo—!" said Morgan, rising primly. She came to the sofa. "Move over, Roberts, I want to sit down," she said.

Kelly said nothing.

THE MILKMAID'S MILLIONS

1

$3,000,000. Sultan, Sultan & Sultan and Kelly,
Morgan & Roberts. Life & Letters. A Wild Old Love.
A Cad and a Chorus Girl. A Dairyman's Daughter. Miss
Zenobia's Secret Son. A Threat and Its Dire Consequences.

We always think of the wrong people. When Zenobia Beal, tightly clasping her well-worn handbag, caught the New York train that morning at Cobb's Mill her thoughts and speculations were fixed upon Sultan, Sultan & Sultan. In her well-worn and tightly clasped handbag was a letter that began, oddly and dully enough, "In compiling the *Life & Letters* of my uncle, the late Horace Seneca Sultan, I find the copies of a series of letters from him, beginning the 10th of October, 1902 . . ." and it was signed, "Wm Sultan." Her thoughts, therefore, as she went over and over in her mind the story that she was to tell at the interview from which she calculated she might get three million dollars, were concerned with Wm Sultan and the firm of Sultan, Sultan, & Sultan, Counsellors at Law. She did not give a single thought to Kelly, Morgan & Roberts. She did not so much as know of their existence; but had she been informed of their existence their status would have seemed too minor and subordinate to have distracted her thoughts from the wrong people.

II

When Wm Sultan, the surviving partner, entered the reception office of Sultan, Sultan, & Sultan on the morning of the 10th of that warm October of 1947, his nose gave an appreciative twitch and his ear a gratified wiggle. To be more exact, since this is a legal affair, it was only the tip of his nose that gave the twitch, which was just as well because it was a nose of a size at least adequate to his bony face and had the entire structure twitched it would have been a rather startling thing to see. Again, to be precise, it was only his right ear that gave the wiggle, not that his left ear was of a less demonstrative temperament but that it had been rendered a mite deaf by enemy action in the most recent German war.

A man of steady habits, his nose gave an appreciative twitch *every* morning on his first breath of that aroma so proper and peculiar to the offices of old firms of estate attorneys. It was not an atmosphere that can be successfully imitated by some johnny-come-lately outfit in a chromium suite in a skyscraper. It was a distinctive smell compounded of furniture polish on old mahogany, of saddle soap on old leather, and of dry mold. While the sound which so gratified his ear was the rhythmic clicking of a typewriter from beyond the open door of the adjoining cubicle that was the office of his receptionist-switchboard operator-typist. The clicking of the keys, so rapid as to be a blur of sound, was a gratifying promise that he should not have long to wait for the completion of the Forty-Second Chapter of the Second Volume of that monumental work that was to be the *Life & Letters* of the late Horace Seneca Sultan.

As was his invariable custom, Wm Sultan went to the door of the cubicle and said, with formal politeness, "Good morning, Roberts."

Roberts said, "Good morning, Bossy." She continued to type.

As usual, Wm Sultan's ear winced at the informal appellation of "Bossy," but it was not usually said in such an acrid tone. Further, Roberts usually turned her blond head to show him a pleasant smile. But, this morning, she did not so much as raise her eyes from the working manuscript. Because he was perplexed by her unusual concentration Wm Sultan hesitated, and because his was the pride of authorship he was betrayed into an incautious hope. He gave a self-conscious cough.

"Interesting?" he suggested.

Roberts stopped typing. She turned in her chair and faced him, her blue eyes bleak.

"Thrilling," she said flatly. "Particularly the twenty-seven thank-you notes he sent for presents received on his fourteenth birthday. Each and every one of the twenty-seven. Simply thrilling."

Wm Sultan decided not to interrupt her longer and entered the book-lined corridor from which opened the private offices. As usual, he stopped at the door of the first in line, formerly the office of the junior Sultan, opened the door, and said, "Good morning, Morgan."

His file clerk was seated at a large table covered with stacks of letters, softly yellowed by age. She was cross-indexing the contents of one of the drawers, it stood open, of one of the filing cabinets that now lined the walls of the office. In this room, the repository, in round numbers, of 78,000 copies of letters sent by, and 24,000 originals of letters received by, the late Horace Seneca Sultan in his long life of fairly active correspondence, the aroma of dry mold was particularly noticeable. His file clerk raised her red head from the faded pages of a letter to the editor of *The New York Times,* dated October 10, 1897, containing a vigorous and exhaustive defense of the horse cars, and her green eyes peered at Wm Sultan over the top of a stack of equally topical letters to the same editor.

"Good," she said, "morning, Mr. Sultan," and no doubt the better to see she pushed the stack of letters off the table.

Wm Sultan decided to continue on his way to the next office in line, which had traditionally been the seat of the next Sultan in line of succession. When his secretary had decided to occupy it instead of the cubicle more proper to her station, he had, very tolerantly, decided not to argue with a high-tempered woman. He now opened the door and said, "Good morning, Kelly." He was somewhat piqued to find, after speaking, that there was no one in the room, and he went on to the office that for three-quarters of a century had been the throne room of the reigning Sultan.

He there found his secretary looking out the window, and to the straight back of her petite figure and to the back of her sleek dark head, he said, with his usual formal little bow, "Good morning, Kelly."

III

Wm Sultan's secretary sucked in her breath at the impersonal courtesy of his tone and she closed her eyes when in the reflection of the window glass she saw his old-fashioned little bow. Through thin lips she said, "Good morning," and she opened her eyes again, large and dark in her cameo face, in time to see him give his hat to the old-fashioned clothespress that had waited in its corner of the office for generations of Sultans' hats in the morning.

She thought, *If he pats that door again today with his hand when he closes it, I'll scream. If he does one more crotchety, elderly trick . . .*

As unaware of her thoughts as he was that at the ripe age of thirty-five he had the mannerisms of an over-ripe seventy-four, and even less aware that the grandfatherly attitude which he so scrupulously observed towards the young female persons in their twenties who composed his staff was insult enough to turn any member of that fair sex, matron or spinster, into a manic depressive, Wm Sultan closed good old Pressy's door with a friendly little pat and faced his desk and his secretary with a hearty, "Ah-hum, a-hum, a-hum! And what have we this morning?"

"Galloping senility," suggested his secretary.

Wm Sultan let it pass, let it pass, and sat down at his desk to read the obituary column of the morning paper opened there for his perusal. His secretary did not need to turn from the window to know what he was doing. She knew that in the adjoining offices of *Jessup, James, Jordan & Dounce* old Jessup and old James and old Jordan and old Dounce were reading the obituary columns in their papers; and that next to them in the offices of *Wickerworker, Bradley & Broom* old Wickerworker and old Broom were reading the obituary columns in *their* papers, as old Bradley would have been reading it had Bradley not already appeared in it. Indeed, on the floor above and the floor below, throughout that old building of law offices in that quiet backwater of the financial district, Kelly could see all those silver and pewter heads nodding above the death notices that would inform them what clients had been lost and what juicy Trust Funds and Foundations gained. She turned and fixed bitter eyes on the sandy hair of her employer. *It might as well be white,* she thought bitterly.

Wm Sultan gave a dry cough and dropped the newspaper, with its obituary column, in the wastebasket.

Kelly, who had already read it, gave a curt nod. "No hits, no runs, no errors," she summarized, and came to the desk. "And we didn't have much luck with the morning mail either," she continued, "except this reply from Mr.

Zacharia Attley." She handed it to him. Wm Sultan took
it, eagerly, and read:

> "Fairview Farms
> "Cobb's Mill
> "Oct. 9, 1947

"My dear boy," ran the shaky handwriting.
"Life & Letters, hey? Wait until I can tell you
about the night Horace and I were at the Hay-
market. That was real life, my boy! Saved copies of all the letters he ever wrote, did he? By
Jupiter, that's a lawyer for you. Yes, at one
time I did think there was something between
Horace and Zenobia. Might be some letters in
the attic. Having them looked up. So Horace
left you a Trust Fund for the work, hey? Well,
that's better than having to leave it to great-
grand nephews or whatever the devil mine
are. Better dust off that will of mine. Half
a mind to draw one to a Cat Hospital or a
Society for the Advancement of Something.
Don't mind me. Just lonely since Zenobia was
killed. Never thought I'd outlive her when
here I've been a sick man for twenty years
ever since that fool operation I had when I
was sixty-four. Imagine it was a surprise to
Zenobia, too.

> Yours very sincerely,
> Zacharia Attley."

"This," pronounced Wm Sultan on his conclusion, "is
most interesting. An invaluable contribution to the *Life.*"

"Do you mean," Kelly inquired, innocently, "the Hay-
market incident?" And her attentive smile was innocent.

Wm. Sultan's right ear flushed with embarrassment. The question, he realized, betrayed the innocence of ignorance; but the allusion by a young female person to what in its long-ago heyday had been infamous as a "sporting place" was, he reflected, the more embarrassing by the very innocence of his fair interlocutor. Fortunately, his throat was quite dusty and he passed over the question with a series of dry coughs.

"I was referring," he said, "to the fact that it is, *per se,* confirmation that Uncle Horace held Miss Zenobia in the greatest esteem."

"He might," Kelly suggested, "have tried holding her in his arms instead."

Wm Sultan coughed. "Firstly," he continued, "we have his letters— Ah, perhaps you wouldn't mind having them brought from the files?"

He became aware that she was holding them out to him.

He extended his hand for the file folder, closing his fingers on the nearer edge, and then, while her hand still held to it he paused, looking at her.

Every woman knows when admiration, warm admiration, enters the eyes of a man; and because of that instinctive knowledge Kelly recognized the light that came into the gray eyes that looked first at her blue-black hair, then at her cameo features, then at the warm red of her lips, and finally into the dark depths of her own. She saw those eyes, usually so reserved in their expression, become warm; and she saw the slow warm smile that melted the ice-like mask of formality that usually frosted his rugged face. Even before he spoke she knew that she would hear that same warmth in his voice. She did.

"*Very* efficient!" Wm Sultan complimented her, and opened the folder. "Firstly," he continued, removing the holograph copy of a letter, "we have this." He opened a folded letter and read it aloud:

"My dear Miss Attley:

"As you can see, I have respected your confidence. You are aware of my feelings on this, but you may rest assured that neither now nor in the future shall your trust prove unfounded.

"By your father's instructions in preparation for his departure for Central America on the 14th inst. I have deposited $5,000 to your account in the Fifth Avenue Bank.

"Permit me to remain,

"Your most sincere and respectful friend,

"Horace Seneca Sultan."

Wm Sultan put down the letter and sighed.

"A love letter," he sighed, "if ever there was one." He withdrew a second letter from the file. "And if that were not enough," he said with a little chuckle that showed how absurd the very idea was, "we have," he concluded triumphantly, "this second exhibit!" After a preparatory cough, he read the letter aloud:

"August 23, 1903

"My dear Miss Attley:

"Your father has informed me that he will return from Central America by the 15th of next month. I must confess that I will doubly welcome him because it will also mean your own return from your long sojourn with your Aunt Unice. Please give my most respectful regards to her and to Mr. Trumbo Pease. May I hope that after this absence of nearly a year I may again pay my respects to you as a most sincere friend?

"Permit me to remain,

"Your most sincere and respectful friend,

"Horace Seneca Sultan."

Wm Sultan placed the letter neatly on top of its predecessor. "An open avowal," he said, "almost embarrassing in the passion of his esteem. And now," he triumphantly picked up the letter of Zacharia Attley, "we have the further confirmation that his hopeless devotion had even been noted by her father! I think," he nodded thoughtfully over the letters, "that we may truly call it the *grande passion* of his life."

Wm Sultan rubbed his hands together and removed from the folder its final content, a faded newspaper clipping. Its date was written on it in pencil, *October 17, 1902.* It read:

MURDER AND SUICIDE
IN TENDERLOIN FLAT
Young Man About Town
Slays Woman Tenant
And Shoots Self
Has Been Seen in Society

In a double tragedy early this morning the careers of John Host Devers, a young man about town, and that of a young woman known as Miss Fifi La Belle, of the theatrical profession, came to their ends. The tragedy occurred in the flat of Miss La Belle at—

On the margin was written in the bold and inimitable hand of the late Horace Seneca Sultan, "MY GOD!" Then, as upon second thought, he had written quietly, "Good riddance."

Wm Sultan sat back in his chair and tugged at the lobe of his ample ear. "I feel," he began—

"I doubt that," said his secretary levelly; and when he looked at her for the first time since so graciously complimenting her upon her efficiency with the folder, he found

that Kelly's eyes were as level and as black and as disconcerting as the mouths of guns. She pushed back her chair
and rose as if to take better aim. But, before she could
fire, the telephone rang. She closed her eyes, took a deep
breath, picked up the telephone and said, "Yes, Roberts?"

"Was," Roberts asked from her cubicle adjoining the
reception office, "grandpappy ever a traveling salesman?"

"Were you," Kelly inquired with cold courtesy of her
employer, "ever a traveling salesman?" Wm Sultan shook
his head. "He says not, Roberts."

"That's strange," said Roberts. "There's a farmer's
daughter here to see him."

"Ah!" said Kelly. "No doubt from the *Hay*market?"

"No," Roberts said. "Fairview Farms. A Miss Zenobia
Beal."

Kelly repeated the information to Wm Sultan and then
again spoke into the telephone. "Send her in," she directed. "He's practically drooling. Or shall I," she added,
knowing the usual age of the clients of the house, "roll out
the wheel chair?"

"Look Kelly," Roberts said gravely, "this number hears
more whistles than a grade crossing."

"Oh," said Kelly.

"Yeah," said Roberts.

Kelly put down the telephone, picked up some papers
from the desk, in the process of which she managed to
snap on the little lever labeled *Speak* on the interoffice
communication box on the desk, and stalked to her office.

IV

When Wm Sultan rose from behind his desk on the entrance
of Miss Zenobia Beal to his office he mentally noted, and
not without pleasure, that she was a young female person
with loam-brown hair, with a peaches-and-cream complex-
ion and with cornflower blue eyes. He further noted, and

still with pleasure, that she appeared to have that vigorous but not unshapely constitution nurtured by clean country living. He observed that she crossed his office with that slow and steady stride that tells of the hillside pasture, the sweet sod underfoot occasionally broken by the rugged rock that is the backbone of the elevated acreage, and is so readily distinguishable from the rapid and nimble step of the urban dweller. And, within the vicinity of his desk, she extended her hand with the open yet bashful gesture of frank innocence.

"You're very kind to see me, Mr. Sultan," she said gratefully, "when you don't know who I am or why I'm here but I'll tell you if you'll let me!"

"Assuredly," Wm Sultan agreed, and invited her to sit down. She sat on the edge of the chair and he resumed his own.

"I'm Zenobia Beal," she said quickly, as if in fear that he might change his mind, "and I've lived all my life at Fairview Farms because my father managed the farms for Mr. Attley. He also," she went on, and her robust rural lungs did not have to pause for a new breath, "lived at Fairview Farms all his life or almost because his parents came to work there for Mr. Attley when my father was only three years old."

"I see," said Wm Sultan.

"Before that," Zenobia Beal continued, "his parents had been employed for years and years by Mr. Attley's sister, Unice, who was married to Mr. Trumbo Pease."

"That's very interesting," said Wm Sultan, and meant it.

"And when my father grew up he went to agricultural college and met my mother and they came back to live at Fairview Farms and he managed Fairview Farms for Mr. Attley."

Wm Sultan had known clients who took hours to tell less; there it was, the story of three generations as compact and complete as an—egg. He felt that the simile would be appreciated by a pastoral person, and he opened his mouth to tell her that her story was as complete as—

"They're all dead now," she said.

For some obscure reason it was a surprising announcement, and Wm Sultan closed his mouth.

"Mr. Attley's sister has been dead for years," Zenobia Beal came down to cases, "and her husband Mr. Trumbo Pease has been dead for years too, and my mother died when I was twelve and—" her voice faltered—"and then two years ago both Grandmother and Grandfather Beal—and then last year . . ."

Then Wm Sultan remembered something that he had been told by Zacharia Attley concerning the death of his daughter, Miss Zenobia Attley. The name of the farm manager had not seemed important at the time and had quite gone out of his mind.

"Then it was your father who—" he said gently.

Zenobia Beal took a grip on herself, faced him with steady eyes and a firm chin. "Yes, Mr. Sultan," she said. "Father was driving Miss Zenobia to the Holstein auction when there was the accident and they were both killed. Since then," she continued, "I've been doing a little clerical and secretarial work for Mr. Attley." She smiled. "Since he's been completely retired for several years there's really hardly anything for me to do, but he knows that Fairview Farms is the only home I've ever known and that I wouldn't feel right about staying on unless I was doing something to earn my keep."

Wm Sultan was touched by her modest frankness and sympathetically watched her fumble with girlish nervousness at her well-worn handbag. He accepted a letter which she took from the bag and read, below his own letterhead:

"My dear Mr. Attley:

"In compiling the *Life & Letters* of my uncle, the late Horace Seneca Sultan, I find the copies of a series of letters from him, beginning the 10th of October, 1902, addressed to your late daughter, Miss Zenobia Attley. Two of the series express his respectful esteem in terms which can only lead me to believe that his intentions were as ardent as they were honorable. Knowing your lifetime association with my uncle, I am emboldened to hope that you might be willing to assist me in the work that was so dear to his heart by . . ."

Wm Sultan put down the. letter. "Ah, yes, yes, yes, yes," he said.

"When Mr. Attley received this," she explained, "he asked me to go through some old trunks in the attic that had belonged to Miss Zenobia."

"Ah, yes, yes, yes, yes! I received his letter," Wm Sultan indicated it, "only this morning. And may I hope that you found something?"

"Yes, sir," acknowledged Zenobia Beal. "I did. Here." With artless impulsiveness she handed him several papers.

The first was an envelope addressed to Miss Zenobia Attley in Horace Seneca Sultan's holograph, and on opening it Wm Sultan found the original of the 1903 letter. The second was freshly written in a girlish hand and he raised his eyes in surprise to the wide and troubled eyes of Zenobia Beal.

She shook her head in pretty distress. "I only made copies," she said. "Oh, perhaps I should have brought the originals," she confessed in a gush, "but I didn't feel they belonged to me, and I shouldn't, but I did so want to talk with you, ask your advice, before I showed them to Mr. Attley, if I should?"

V

In front of the inter-office communication box in the office of Wm Sultan's secretary, Kelly, Morgan and Roberts were listening to the broadcast from the office of their employer. It was not to satisfy idle curiosity but solely to promote efficiency that his office force felt obliged to keep informed of what was going, on, particularly when it was a farmer's daughter.

"Ah, yes, yes, yes, yes," they heard Wm Sultan say, and then, after a pause, "This is a copy of a marriage certificate?"

"Yes, sir."

"Performed October 7, 1902," the dry voice went on, but with a note of self-congratulation not unfamiliar to his staff, "between John Host Devers, bachelor, and Zenobia Attley, spinster."

Kelly half rose from her chair.

"Good heavens," she gasped, "she was secretly married to the man!"

"What man?" asked Roberts, completely in the dark about the whole thing.

"Devers," Kelly said impatiently. "He shot himself in the Tenderloin."

"If you mean the thigh," Roberts said testily, "why don't you say so?"

"Old Broadway, you idiot! And besides tenderloin steaks don't come from the leg but— He murdered a woman and killed himself!" she concluded, exasperated at the continued interruption of the broadcast.

"It's very odd," Roberts persisted skeptically and stubbornly, "that I haven't read anything about it."

"It happened," said Kelly faintly, "in 1902."

Morgan, whose lively imagination had run far beyond that old date, spoke excitedly.

"But, Kelly," she said, "then that means that Miss Attley was never really Miss Attley ever after that but was really and truly Mrs. Devers!"

"That," Kelly agreed, "is the whole point."

"Mr. Sultan," Morgan said perplexedly, "didn't sound surprised."

"No," Kelly admitted. "And what I'd like to know is how he guessed— Hush!"

"Ah, yes, yes, yes, yes," a dry voice was saying. "And here is a letter—"

"It's from her Aunt Unice," the girl's voice interrupted.

"Ah, yes, yes, yes, yes. Mrs. Trumbo Pease." There was a preparatory cough and then the slightly altered tones of the reading voice of the head of the house of Sultan:

> "August 4th, 1904
> "Zenobia darling—it's simply madly danger-
> ous to write you like this but you force me to.
> I'm enclosing a picture of your Darling and
> you can see for yourself how utterly impos-
> sible it would be for the Beals to bring him
> to your father's home. When he gets a year or
> two older perhaps he won't be the image of
> you that he is now. At any event, you must
> give yourself time to get yourself in hand."

There was a series of tactical coughs while Wm Sultan absorbed what he had read. Morgan clutched Kelly's arm.

"She must have had a child after his death," she whis-pered. Her eyes widened. "A Secret Child!"

Wm Sultan was again reading:

> "Your Aunt Unice must now talk to you like
> a Dutch Uncle. You must remember, my poor
> dear, that the Beals could have adopted some
> other child, and have adopted him legally so
> that no one could ever take him away from
> them. Instead of that, out of the goodness of

their hearts they consented to take little John
Host as their own son and that is something
you must never take away from them. You had
your choice of revealing your marriage to a
man who had been a murderer, of bringing
black shame on yourself and your father and
your son. I think you made the nobler choice,
but, for better or for worse, having made it
you must never go back on it. In good time
I and Trumbo will write to your father and I
know that at our request he will find a place
at Fairview for the Beals. My heart bleeds for
you, my poor darling, but I know that this
picture of your darling baby will help yours
until you can see him.

"Your loving Aunt Unice."

Kelly said, "Morgan, close your mouth."

Morgan closed it and then opened it again. "But, Kelly,
doesn't that mean—"

"Shush!"

From the other office a girlish voice said, "My father's
name was John Host Beal."

In the silence that followed Morgan whispered, "But,
Kelly, doesn't that mean—"

"Mr. Zacharia Attley," Kelly nodded, "has just been
given a new great-granddaughter. All nice and grown-up,
too."

VI

Zenobia Beal was twisting her fingers in her lap.

"Mr. Sultan," she said, "I was always told that I was
I named Zenobia for Miss Zenobia Attley because she'd
been so kind to my mother, and that Grandmother and
Grandfather Beal persuaded my parents that it would make

her very happy." She caught her breath, and then went on steadily. "But did my grandparents know that Miss Attley had a very great reason for wanting me to be named after her? Mr. Sultan, tell me! Does that marriage certificate and that letter that I found in her trunk mean that Miss Attley was my *real* grandmother?"

"Well," said Wm Sultan, "ah-hum, ah-hum, ah-hum."

"Does it mean," Zenobia Beal persisted, "that Mr. Attley is my great-grandfather? I didn't want to show them to him until I could talk with someone, someone who knows all about law and legal things, because, well, this has been such a shock to me I hardly know what to think. Please tell me, Mr. Sultan!"

Wm Sultan scrubbed his hand over his face. "Well, of course," he said, "as you can understand—*per se!*—*per se, per se*— Ah, yes, yes, yes yes, as Mr. Attley's counsel—examine the originals—investigate—perhaps find other records— or the absence of them! Ah, yes, yes, yes, yes, and—"

"Mr. Sultan," Zenobia Beal broke in, not in rudeness but in simple inexperience of the legal mind, "Mr. Sultan," she broke in, beating her clenched hands on her lap, "do you know of anything that proves otherwise? Of any reason why I shouldn't show these to Mr. Attley? If he is my great-grandfather," she cried, "he's the only close relative I have on earth!"

"Well," Wm Sultan began, and then remembered to cough a few times. "Well," he began again, "to my own and definite knowledge at this moment—but then in these matters one never wants to jump to conclusions! Or on the other hand, to be precipitate, you know, and so—" He broke off as his secretary entered the office.

Kelly came diffidently to the desk. She placed a scratch pad in front of him. There was writing on the scratch pad.

"A message from Garcia," she explained and tripped back to her office.

Wm Sultan read the writing on the scratch pad. He
read:

Dear Boss:
Thaw out and give the kid a break or have a
new staff in here after lunch because we won't
be.

Kelly

Morgan

Roberts

Wm Sultan sighed.

"Miss Beal," he said, "I know of no reason why you
shouldn't show Mr. Attley what you have found at once."

In the office of Wm Sultan's secretary, Kelly winked
at Morgan, and Morgan nudged Roberts, and Roberts
grinned at Kelly.

"I thought," Kelly summarized it complacently, "that
that would bring him around!"

And nothing was further from their thoughts than that,
in forcing those words so unwillingly from their employer's legalistic caution, they had slipped the noose over his
neck for the murder of Zacharia Attley.

2

A Codicil. About Beavers. Hazards of Marriage.
Fatal Fruit. Two Evil Names. Violence! The Man
on the Steps and the Girl in the Doorways. A Barrister
Views Bananas and Hears the Sound of Death.

It was late that afternoon, and Kelly was idly doodling on the top of the switchboard with the eraser of a pencil, when the long-distance call came in. She had just delivered to Morgan, among other items, a list which read:

For Chronological Index, Life & Letters:
Sub-class: His *Grand Passion*

1902: Horace Seneca Sultan pays "respectful addresses" to Miss Zenobia Attley.

Oct. 7, " : Zenobia secretly marries one John Host Devers, a cad.

Oct. 10, " : H.S.S. informed of marriage and foresworn to secrecy by Zenobia. (Be ready to change this one, a wild guess, say I)

Oct. 14, " : Her father, Zacharia Attley, departs for (approx) 11 month trip in Central America, leaving daughter in care of Aunt Unice (Mrs. Trumbo Pease)

Oct. 17, " : John Host Devers murders girl
friend, Fifi La Belle (oh you kid! some
monicker!) and commits suicide. (Probably heard her try to speak French)

July — 1903: (July is just a shrewd guess)
A son, surnamed John Trumbo, born to—
she's still known as Miss Zenobia Attley.

Aug. 23, " : H.S.S. renews "addresses" to Zenobia.

Sept. 15, " : Mr. Attley returns from Central
America.

Aug. 4, 1904: Copy of letter from Aunt Unice
to Zenobia establishes (1) to protect her son
from disgrace of his father's name Zenobia has (2) let him be secretly adopted as
own child by couple named Beal.

Oct. 10, 1947: Original of Horace Seneca
Sultan's letter of Aug. 23, 1903 found in
effects of late Zenobia Attley means (so
says Our Boss) that she cherished it and
consequently reciprocated "esteem" etc.
and brushed him off only because (quoth
Wm) she could not in honor marry him
without telling of son, and could not in
honor tell. (unquoth)

There had been tears in Morgan's eyes when she had
raised them from that conclusion.

"Kelly," she had sighed, "have you thought what a wonderful youth she had? In love with a wild young murderer
and hopelessly loved by a mature man old enough to be
her father!"

"What?" Kelly had asked, and she had been somewhat
taken aback because she had *not* thought of it.

"Yes, Kelly! I was just figuring it out a little while ago. When she was eighteen and Mr. Horace Seneca Sultan was hopelessly and madly in love with her he was *thirty-eight!*"

Kelly had gone to the door.

"Oh, well," she had said, "sultans aren't what they used to be." She had slammed the door. She had then dropped in on Roberts to deliver a note which read:

> Note on typing *Life & Letters:*
> If names "Zenobia" or "Attley" inadvertently appear in ms. they are to be deleted. Mr. Attley is to be referred to as "a respected client," and Miss Attley as "a young lady of proper station" (but whether Pennsylvania or Grand Central grandpappy saith not) or as "the fair object of his honorable ardor."

Roberts was a mumble-reader and she had come out particularly strong on "honorable ardor." She had rested her blond head on her hand and had read, and mumbled, it again. Brows puckered, she had looked up at Kelly, doodling on top of the switchboard.

"Say, Kelly, back in those days didn't they have," she had dropped her voice to a whisper, "s—e—x?"

Kelly had shaken her head and the switchboard had buzzed.

"Those times were known," Kelly explained, "as the Stork Ages."

"Well," Roberts persisted, "what about the storks?" She listened in until the connection was completed and then, on the point of disconnecting herself, continued to listen in. She covered the mouthpiece with her hand.

"Great-grandpappy Attley," she reported, "for Bossy."

"Gentlemen of their age," said Kelly sweetly, doodling a dagger, "should have much in common."

"She's told him!" Roberts reported in an excited whisper. "The old boy's almost incoherent with joy. Say, am I glad we made Bossy— He's drawn a new will!"

"*What?*" Kelly dropped her pencil. "Without consulting—"

Roberts shook her head impatiently. "It's only to cover things for a while until he can have Bossy—it's only one of those 'codicil' things—"

"Only," said Kelly weakly.

"He's already mailed it!" Roberts impatiently dismissed the matter and went back to listening.

Kelly's face would have reminded the perspicacious beholder, had only one or two been present, of those marble and moronic features which so nobly delineate the character of Law in courthouse statuary. Her face, such was the effect of the atmosphere which she had so long inhaled, was as would have been the faces of Jessup, James, Jordan & Dounce had *they* just been informed that a will which they had drawn, a will subtly providing for every contingency, sternly guarding against any contest, was now modified and superseded by a little postscript dashed off in haste by an idiot—but which they would have to attempt to defend if . . . and then Kelly thought of how the surviving Sultan must be feeling on learning that there was a little codicil in the mail for him; he would have preferred a time-bomb.

"Bro-ther!" Roberts enthused. "Did we get action!"

Kelly was laughing. "When," she gasped, "is Bill leaving?"

"How on earth did you guess?" Roberts asked in surprise, pulling out the plug. "He's catching the first train this evening."

Then Kelly had another thought and she was not laughing any more. "He certainly jumped at the chance to visit them, didn't he?" she mused.

Roberts gave a matter-of-fact nod. "He certainly did," she agreed. "Say, Kelly, what's about a codicil to make Bossy such an eager beaver?"

"Ask," said Kelly, turning to the door, "the other beaver." Roberts gave Morgan a ring. "Say, Red," she said perplexedly, "what's about beavers that I haven't been told yet?"

"Well . . ." Morgan considered a moment, and then said, "They cut down trees."

"That I've heard."

"And they make dams."

"Ah, ah!" said Roberts. "I get it." She hung up and gave Kelly's office a ring. "I get it!" she reported, and then continued with that surprised pride of a non-humorist who has, *mirabile dictu,* conceived a pun, "You mean—our beaver is going to make a dame!"

Kelly, like Queen Victoria, was not amused.

II

Wm Sultan was not amused when in the course of his three-hour train ride to Cobb's Mill he had ample, but no more than sufficient, time to reflect upon the hazards of marriage. Unless it should seem preposterous that any mind could cover in three hours what has engaged the lifetime and morbid meditations of several members of both sexes, it must be made clear that his melancholy thoughts were not concerned with the hazards of the parties to the dispute but only to those suffered by innocent bystanders; and of innocent bystanders in general only to those who were estate attorneys in particular.

Since April in '46, no, it had been in 1845, the Upjohn Johns had been well-behaved clients of Sultans. If for the last two or three generations their estates had comprised little more than a few heirlooms of little intrinsic value, they had always disposed of them by Sultan Incontestable

Last Wills & Testaments, and had never sent poison-pen letters or codicils through the mails. Then, on a fateful day in '83 a daughter had married one Zacharia Attley, and Sultans, in courtesy to his connection, had consented to act as his counselors at law. His forefathers, Wm Sultan reflected bitterly, might have foreseen that this train ride of his would be the inevitable consequence of their rash acceptance of a new client.

The life of that client, which was to culminate in the sending of a codicil through the mails, had begun in the bedroom of a farmhouse. When, eighteen years later, Zacharia Attley had left the ancestral acres for the city it had been with an unwillingness only less than the willfulness of his father in the opinion that a son who would never make a farmer had better seek his fortunes elsewhere. He had departed in reluctance, and in homesickness had found work in the nostalgic atmosphere of a produce market. With a sniff of a barrel of Red Pippins he was back in the family orchard. But his very homesickness had given rise to a resentment against that parental agriculturist who had banished him as unworthy of the rearing of a McIntosh. With his first sniff of a banana he had found his fate. It had been almost too good to be true. It had satisfied his nostalgia by being a fruit and his resentment by being one that his father could not raise.

He had plucked five million from that tropical tree when he had sold out to competition at the age of forty-five. He had by that time for many years been maintaining the ancestral acres as a summer home, and when by the age of fifty he had dropped three of his five million in assorted speculations, having proven as easy to skin as his favorite fruit, he had let himself be persuaded to retire on the old homestead. Had his wife been living, which that daughter of the Upjohn Johns had not for fifteen years, she might have preferred Society to solitude, or had not his daughter, Zenobia, by that time demonstrated every intention of remaining an old maid, he might have felt it his duty to her to remain in the city; but with no such restraints he had permitted her to persuade him, particularly as it had been his lifelong hope to return in triumph to those acres from which he had been exiled in failure.

Not the least part of that triumph, even as had not the least part of a Roman Triumph been the captives chained to the chariot of their conqueror, was that in the progress of the succeeding thirty-five years he had by the chains of expectation made dependent upon him the grandson and the great-grandson of his late brother, Zolicopher, who had not been exiled from the family fields but had in the opinion of their mutual but discriminating sire been a veritable Johnny Appleseed and Burbank of a farmer. Bright expectations which had, sadly, been nipped before harvest by an untimely fall from a silo.

A series of equally untimely takings-off had left of Zolicopher's descendants only a grandson, Zolicopher Hay, and a great-grandson, Trumbo Gates. The importance of those surnames had been made clear to Wm Sultan on the occasion of drawing a new will for Zacharia Attley after the death of his daughter, Zenobia, in her untimely automobile accident the year before. With the uninhibited frankness of age and in the freedom of a man speaking to his lawyer, he had made it clear that if there were two names on earth that he loathed the first was Zolicopher and the second was Trumbo. It was hard lines, indeed, that his late brother Zolicopher should win the final triumph by having his descendants inherit his, Zacharia's, fortune. It was rubbing it in that one should be the namesake of his dearly detested brother and that the other should be the namesake of his not less detested brother-in-law.

Zacharia Attley had, at that time, been in his first grief for the death of his daughter and had with great bitterness

HUGH AUSTIN

told the reason for his detestation of the very memory
of his sister, Unice, and her husband, Trumbo Pease. His
story had been that in the years 1902-03 he had made
an extensive inspection of banana properties in Central
America, leaving his eighteen-year-old daughter in the
care of her aunt and uncle, and on his return some eleven
months later had found that they had practically usurped
his proper place in her affections. It had been his opinion
that having no children of their own they had tried to
steal her from him, and had been so far successful that as
long as they had lived he had always felt that they were in
some *secret way* closer to Zenobia than himself. And now,
if you please! he was to leave his fortune to a Zolicopher
and a Trumbo. But his pride of family in general, greater
even than his prejudice against them as individuals, gave
him no other choice. There was a blight on the stock, it
was dying out, they were the only two left and to them he
must, with whatever bitter reluctance, leave the inheritance of the Attleys.

And now, like a reprieve from the horns of his dilemma, a great-granddaughter of his own loins presented herself to him, the veritable child of his own child's child,
the lovely namesake of his beloved daughter, Zenobia . . .
Wm Sultan was twisting the lobe of his ear as the train
slowed for Cobb's Mill. Under the circumstances and considering his age, which was hard on eighty-six, one might
not, perhaps, wonder at post-haste codicils in her favor;
but one might wonder if Zacharia Attley had weighed all
the evidence with judicious calm and had treated his heirs
of standing with impartial justice.

III

"Mr. Sultan?"

Wm Sultan acknowledged the query with a courteous
bow. "Yes?"

"I'm Trumbo Gates."

It was stated aggressively, and, in the light of those lamps of patented dreariness peculiar to railroad platforms, the speaker, a rugged young man with a grim expression, appeared to be taking an equally dim view of Wm Sultan.

Wm Sultan smiled politely and extended his hand. "Kind of you to meet me."

Trumbo Gates ignored the hand, perhaps because he was stooping so quickly to pick up Wm Sultan's suitcase. Indeed, such was his haste in courtesy that his shoulder struck Wm Sultan in the stomach with a certain violence.

"Thank you!" said Wm Sultan, appreciating his good intentions.

"This way," said Trumbo Gates, and as he turned to lead the way the suitcase swung against the back of Wm Sultan's knees with a force that nearly knocked him from his feet.

Wm Sultan realized that it was an awkward thing to handle and that perhaps he should not have been in the way.

"I beg your pardon," he said courteously.

If Trumbo Gates made a reply it was no more than a thin smile. He led the way to a car at the end of the parking field.

"In here," he said, and as he flung open the door he quickly stepped backward with calculated violence. His feet were knocked out from under him and a force greater than gravity yanked at the back of his collar. His back and the back of his head struck the packed cinders of the parking lot with momentarily stunning violence.

"May I suggest, Mr. Gates," Wm Sultan said testily, "that it's scarcely sporting to jostle a man under the guise of accident. It is, *per se,* an imposition on one's courtesy."

Trumbo Gates got slowly to his feet.

"And if I smack you one," he said, "I suppose you'll see to it that the old fool cuts me off without a cent?"

"No," said Wm Sultan. "But I have attained an age where I regard fisticuffs as being both highly unseemly and possibly unhealthy for me."

Trumbo Gates laughed a little, his lips parted over clenched teeth. "You know," he said, "I think you are going to be so right." He flexed his shoulders.

"Consequently," Wm Sultan said, "I'd not recommend any 'smacking' unless you had paratrooper or commando training in the late imbroglio, which I doubt from your very slow reactions."

"You scare me to death!" protested Trumbo Gates. "I suppose," he continued in mock fearfulness, "you were one of those cloak-and-dagger boys who can break *necks* and *backs* and *arms* and *legs* with just a snap of your wrist?"

With the word he snapped a hard, straight left. There was no stopping it. It kept on going, his arm in back of it, his shoulder following his arm and the rest of him following, in an effortless somersault, his shoulder. He again lay on his back on the cinders. He felt completely paralyzed, unable to breathe.

"Yes," said Wm Sultan.

It was Wm Sultan's distinct impression during a silent ride to Fairview Farms that he had definitely antagonized Trumbo Gates. The injustice of it, both to himself and to Fate, was annoying. To himself, because he had been most considerate: to Fate, because despite his own considerate intentions only a telegraphed blow had made possible such a harmless counter. But if he were superficially annoyed with Trumbo Gates' attitude, he was deeply disturbed by the incident's violence. It had brought to him for a moment a certain feeling which he had hoped never to experience again. It was a feeling that was composed of a whole set of feelings, physical, mental and emotional. Physically, four of the five senses seemed preternaturally acute, sight and hearing, the sense of smell and the sense of touch, so that the body was suddenly aware of its clothing and a groping hand could feel the warmth of another body when still too far away to strike. Mentally, there was that incomparable alertness and quickness so that the mind seemed both clairvoyant and electric, and so terribly concentrated upon the sole and single problem of keeping alive for the next five seconds. Emotionally, there was that co-existent combination of fear and exultation in all their primitive force of animal fear and animal blood-lust.

Wm Sultan had profoundly hoped never to have that feeling, which was composed of that set of feelings, again. He had learned to loathe it from his heels up. He had for too long had to experience it. With the end of that necessity he had in his civilian life sought with single-minded determination and singular success to crawl into his peaceful hole and pull it in after him. He wished to heaven that he *were* living in the 1880's. Peace. All that he asked was a little peace and now this character—!

Wm Sultan caught himself just in time. He had half-turned in his seat towards Trumbo Gates. He sat facing straight ahead again, his eyes closed, his bony fingers tugging at his ear. He shut his ears to it, that wild skirling of bagpipes that was his temper. It went down presently but left him shaken by what could have been its consequences. He really must keep a better watch on himself. What, and it was a thought to chill the blood, if *his staff* had seen him in such a rowdy exhibit as that on the parking field? What would they think to see grandpappy, for Wm Sultan was aware of his staff's aged and honorable appellation for him, cutting such a caper? They would, he feared, be disillusioned. He must not let that happen. He must live up to their high expectations. He gave a dry cough, just to keep in practice.

IV

Zacharia Attley had retired in the frank and un-aesthetic
year of 1912. It had not occurred to him, it had not occurred to his architect, it had not occurred to *anybody* that
he should "preserve" by endless alterations—the unspoiled
charm of the old farmhouse that was his birthplace. Did
he not have money enough to tear down the old wreck and
build a brand new house for himself? He did. So, he did.

He built a big, square, three-story house of yellow
brick with white trim. Across the front there was a wide
white porch with a heavy-looking roof supported by spindly white columns, which had, however, held it up for
thirty-five years without a sag. The front door was in the
middle of the front porch and in front of it and above
it from the ten-foot ceiling of the porch there hung by
chains a large white globe. By the light from this globe
Wm Sultan saw a man standing on the porch when the car
turned into the long driveway.

The man walked to the steps at the end of the porch
as the car came to a stop. Wm Sultan got out of the front
seat, took his suitcase from the back and closed the door.
The car instantly shot forward on the driveway which ran
straight to a large garage a full hundred yards to the rear.
No word had been spoken. Wm Sultan was left facing the
man on the steps.

His first introduction to Zolicopher Hay had been some
twelve years before. It had been made by Horace Seneca
Sultan on an occasion when Zacharia Attley had called
at the offices in company with his grand-nephew. Since
then he had met him perhaps two or three times, briefly,
the last occasion having been the year before when he had
drawn the new will following the death of Zenobia Attley.
On that occasion Zolicopher Hay had not looked younger than his years, which were the mid-forties, as scarcely
could be expected of a man who was portly and chanced

to have thin, graying hair, but on the present occasion, when he turned on the steps from following the car with his eyes, he could have been in his mid-fifties.

He extended his hand, and, apparently, with no thought of violence.

"I'm afraid you've had a cold welcome," he said, with an indicative glance at the receding car.

Wm Sultan gave a deprecative cough. "Oh, no, no, no," he said. "Rather warm, if anything."

Zolicopher Hay drew back the corners of his mouth, spreading his lips against his teeth in an expression of petulant but futile disapproval. It had the mark of a mannerism, so that seeing it once one seemed to see it repeated back through long years of practically constant annoyance about which there had been practically nothing that he could do. "Trumbo's been taking this very badly," he said, mounting the steps. "He has a very violent disposition and has never learned to restrain himself."

"'Experience,'" Wm Sultan suggested, "'is a great teacher.'"

Zolicopher Hay came to a stop on the porch and turned with a wry smile.

"We do learn that we have to make the best of things," he admitted. "I'll not pretend that this has not been a great shock to me. No, I don't mean that," he corrected himself. "It would be a shock to anyone. No doubt it's been a shock to the servants. It's been such a shock to Mr. Attley that he's in a state of collapse."

Wm Sultan expressed concern.

"Oh, it's nothing serious," Zolicopher Hay reassured him. "Or so I'm *told,*" he amended, again spreading his lips. "He shut himself in his room this afternoon and has refused to see anyone. Except Zenobia—" he seemed to have more to say on that subject but then dismissed it with a shake of his head. "What I meant to say," he resumed, "was that this has been more than simply an astounding surprise to me. Both Trumbo and I are familiar with the terms of Mr. Attley's present will, and I'm not such a hypocrite as to pretend that it isn't a devil—"

He broke off as Zenobia Beal opened the door. She stopped in the doorway with a bashfulness which Wm Sultan found as becoming as the simple gingham dress which artlessly clad her shapely figure.

"Ah!" he said, with a courteous bow. "Miss Beal!"

"I—I thought I heard Trumbo drive up," she explained, excusing her intrusion. She spoke diffidently to Zolicopher Hay. "Should I call—" she paused, and it was clear that she was wondering what to call him, and then with a pretty toss of her head she said, sturdily, *"my grandfather now?"*

"If you please," Zolicopher Hay said with a pleasant smile.

But Wm Sultan observed that she evidently found something forced in it, for her eyes went on to his own with a lingering glance that was touching in the trusting warmth of its welcome, as if to her only friend in a world of enemies. He followed her into the house.

"I'll show you to your room," Zolicopher Hay said behind him, closing the door, "after you've seen Mr. Attley. I didn't want old Sedgwick hanging around downstairs this evening," he continued. "Perhaps country 'help' don't gossip more than servants in town, but the difference here is that everybody more or less knows everybody else."

Wm Sultan turned from watching Zenobia Beal, a lonely if robust figure in the big hall, trip to a door at its back.

"A friendly interest," he said understandingly.

Zolicopher Hay nodded understandingly. "I told Trumbo that he was a fool to resent your part in this," he said. "As Mr. Attley's attorney it was your duty to examine the evidence of her claim and report your honest conclusions. For my part, I feel better about it that someone competent has passed upon the authenticity of the documents—or whatever they are."

Wm Sultan coughed, and on second thought gave another one. "You, ah, have not examined them yourself, Mr. Hay?" he asked.

Zolicopher Hay gave his expression of annoyed frustration. "Mr. Attley's always been very quick-tempered and—well, I'd call it high-handed," he said, neither of which items was news to Wm Sultan. "Unfortunately," he continued, "Trumbo had been informed of this business first. I understand that he *began* by calling it a damned fake that only an old damned fool would believe . . ." and to Wm Sultan's surprise Zolicopher Hay had it in him to laugh, if somewhat resignedly. "So naturally by the time I saw Mr. Attley *he* began by accusing me of thinking him an old damned fool, too. He waved some papers at me," he continued wearily, "and swore they'd show who was the damned fool. After managing all his business affairs for him for fifteen years, I think I've at least learned when to let him have his way without question or protest. He always cools down and becomes reasonable later. In fact, he'd cooled down enough before I left him to assure me that I wasn't going to suffer. 'Surely there's enough for three,' was the way he put it."

"Surely," Wm Sultan agreed perfunctorily.

Zolicopher Hay was looking at the door behind which Zenobia Beal had disappeared, and again his lips drew back against his teeth in a grimace of long-suffering frustration.

"I'll wait in here," he said heavily, and went into a front room to his left.

It was only a moment before Zenobia Beal entered the hall. She again paused immediately on her entrance, as she had on entering the porch, and took a moment fumbling with the knob to close the door to the back hall behind

her. Wm Sultan was again favorably impressed by her lack
of composure, so natural in so momentous a time in her
life, as eloquent of her lack of worldly experience, of her
innocence of that sophisticated self-possession which can
falsely assume an air of nonchalance.

She was breathing quickly in her excitement when she
came to him. "Mr. Attley will see you at once," she said,
and he was pleased to note that, since she sensed that he
was not antagonistic to her, she did not again defiantly
use the term, "my grandfather." It was, he felt, a tactful
admission that she was leaving that to *his* judgment after
his examination of her *bona fides* to that claim. "He will
be dressed in just a few minutes," she added.

Wm Sultan frowned. "But if Mr. Attley's not feeling
well," he protested, "can't I—"

"No—" in girlish impulsiveness she put her hand re-
strainingly on his arm. She bit at her lip, and then, with
a little laugh, told him the reason. "He's very sensitive,"
she said, "and very proud of being so vigorous and able to
take care of himself completely at his age. And I think it's
wonderful of him, too," she concluded proudly, making it
clear that she felt that if his vanity were a thing to smile
at it must be an admiring and sympathetic smile.

Wm Sultan smiled sympathetically.

"If you'll wait in his study?" she said, going to a door
towards the back of the hall. Unspoiled by the social graces,
she opened it for him. She indicated another door at the
back of the room. "He'll be in in just a few minutes." She
lowered her voice in explanation. "He's had his bedroom
on the ground floor for many years—the stairs—" Wm
Sultan nodded understandingly. "And now if you'll excuse
me?" she begged, backing out the door. "I couldn't bear
to be present while you—until everything's settled!" she
explained in a rush.

Wm Sultan again smiled sympathetically as she closed the door upon herself. He sat down and looked at the room. The room was dark brown and was cluttered with dark brown furniture: a rolltop desk, sectional bookcases, a large table and two or three small tables as obscure of purpose as they were to sight in the brown gloom, and large brown leather chairs loomed all over the place as if a herd of them had overrun it. It should be possible, he decided, for Zacharia Attley to make a complete tour of the room, of every object in it including the windows, without ever over half-rising from a squat. Once or twice he heard obscure but promising sounds from the adjoining bedroom and sat up hopefully, but after a time he wearied of staring in a brown study at brown furniture in a brown room and got up to look at the pictures on the walls. That was always quite proper and even flattering to one's host.

The walls were covered with pictures variously framed and of all sizes, but as his inspection of them proceeded he found that they all were faded brownish photographs, all tropical, and all featuring bananas. There were bananas on trees, on dinkey railroad cars, on ships. There were short and swarthy men under sombreros, there were tall men under panamas, and there were pale women under parasols, but one and all holding, with reverence, bananas. There were . . .

Wm Sultan was peering intently in the brown gloom at a particularly dim picturization of something to do with bananas, and he blinked his eyes twice before he realized that the lights in the room had gone out. Yes, despite the gloom, he remembered that it had been lights in the plural: one on the large table and one on a small table but both under chocolate shades. Since there had been two of them burning the law of averages was slipping badly if both bulbs had chanced to burn out precisely the same instant, and a simple exercise of the process of elimination left it as a reasonable conclusion that a fuse must have blown out. He recalled that Zenobia Beal had reached inside the room to switch on the lights, which precluded the possibility that someone passing in the hall had switched them off because the door had not been opened.

At that moment a door was opened, not the door to the hall but, and he was quite certain of the direction, the door to Zacharia Attley's bedroom. He had to judge it by direction because there was no glimmer of light in the blackness. He started to say something but before he spoke he heard a sound in the darkness that once heard, and he had heard it before, is not readily forgotten: it was the click of a gun being cocked.

3

Bull's Meat. A Secret Code. The Thirteenth Time.
A Frightened Secretary. Chalkmarks on the Rug.
A Swinging Door. The Wrong Window.
A Terrible Story. A Fatal Accident.

When Wm Sultan's staff, after meeting for breakfast at their usual drugstore, and after walking together the distance from its soda fountain to the address of their employment, and after turning from the sidewalk and entering between the pink marble pillars of that dignified structure's formal doorway, and after walking across its marble lobby, spotlessly scrubbed, the smell of good yellow soap rising to the mezzanine floors above, when in this post-participial condition they came to the grillwork elevator in its grillwork shaft they were met by the robust bellow:

"Bull's meat!"

Then, from the tail of his rheumy but roving eye, Mr. Waldo Wickerworker caught sight of the staff of Sultan, Sultan & Sultan, and the senior partner of Wickerworker, Bradley & Broom swallowed further words that were rising in his throat in such a gulp that his strangled coughing turned his face a slightly richer shade of purple. His embarrassment in having mentioned before young female persons of unmarried status, for he had made it a point that summer to note their ring fingers, as lifelong habits will outlast their day of usefulness, his embarrassment in having mentioned in the hearing of such delicate ears a word appertaining to *sex,* and his delicacy in uttering no further offensive syllable, were not, perhaps, fully appreciated by those fair auditors.

To understand if not condone their attitude it may be sufficient to say that they had the morning mopes, that morbidly melancholy outlook on life and all that it holds that is particularly virulent at five minutes to nine. There has been a night to recover from whatever slight interest work may have held the day before, and with the cheerfulness of a drunkard returning to sobriety the too sane mind sees all too clearly The Job for the Alcatraz that it is. There is the memory of the pigeon outside on the cornice, *still* outside on the cornice! in the morning sun! without a thing to do but selectively watch the hats of the superior animals entering their prison. In atavistic revolt some old instinct of lost freedom glares upon the place of its confinement with loathing, and likes not to be reminded of its long imprisonment; it is the time of day when most *Ten Year Man* buttons are surreptitiously swallowed.

By those two little words, "Bull's meat," Waldo Wickerworker had, had he but known it, called up to the staff of Sultan, Sultan & Sultan the entire period of their servitude. In that building of aged gentlemen of a certain eccentricity, for having been formed before the machine age they were not all stamped from a mold, being stiff shirts instead of stuffed shirts, there was not one who rode his mental hobbyhorse with a stronger view halloo than the Senior of Wickerworker, Bradley & Broom.

While waiting for the elevator upon the mezzanine third floor Kelly had listened to his bull-like voice discoursing upon it on the first; while waiting upon the first floor Morgan had often been showered with its booming

notes from the third, and while riding up and down between Roberts had too often heard it awaiting her at either
destination. They exchanged a bitter glance, they stalked
grimly from the elevator when it reached the third floor,
they slammed the door of the law offices of Sultan, Sultan
& Sultan.

"Bull's meat!" cried Kelly, snatching up the morning
mail from the floor.

"The only meat fit for a man to eat!" shouted Morgan,
storming ahead to her office.

"What makes a man?" demanded Roberts, kicking open
the door of hers.

"The food he eats!" Kelly responded, stomping down
the booklined corridor.

"*Bull's* meat!" bellowed Morgan in the file room.

"*Masculine* meat!" cried Roberts from her cubicle.

"For *men!*" Kelly shouted in the distance.

"What's the matter with this country?" demanded Morgan.

"*Steer* meat!" came back the voice from Kelly's office.

"*Emasculated* meat!" roared Roberts indignantly.

"*Ha!*" cried Morgan significantly.

"Oh—!" Kelly cried, and her voice brought Morgan
from the file room and Roberts from her cubicle. They
ran down the corridor together. Kelly was standing in
her office holding a telegram. She gave it to them. It was
addressed to her. It had been sent at seven-thirty that
morning from Cobb's Mill. It read:

> Please bring letter in morning mail from the
> late Zacharia Attley as I am peremptorily de-
> tained here by circumstance of his death.
>   Wm Sultan.

"The 'late' . . ." Morgan began.

"'His death' . . ." Roberts concluded.

"Oh," said Morgan, "the poor thing! Just when he was so happy because of . . ."

Roberts shook her head. "He was pretty old, wasn't he?"

"Eighty-six," Kelly said absently, leafing through the mail.

Roberts nodded. "I suppose the shock was too much for him."

Morgan sniffled. "I kind of wish we hadn't had anything to do with it."

"There's no letter here from Mr. Attley," Kelly announced. "Maybe I dropped it?"

The three went back down the corridor together like hounds on a scent. They turned into the reception office. They shook their heads.

"Do you think he'd want you to wire or phone him or something," Roberts asked, "and let him know it won't be until a later mail?"

Kelly was reading the telegram again. "It's hard to tell from this just what—Oh, great heavens!" she broke off, and ducked into Roberts' office. "It's in code, of course!"

"Code?" Morgan repeated, her eyes widening. She glanced over her shoulder and her voice fell to a whisper. "I never knew we had a code here!"

Roberts watched Kelly opening desk drawers and since it was her desk she frowned. "Look, Kelly," she said, "I can tell you now there's no code book in—"

"Ah," Kelly exclaimed, snatching a book from a drawer, "here it is!" She slapped the book down on the desk.

"But that's a dictionary!" Morgan protested.

"Bill writes in English," Kelly explained impatiently. "Sometimes he even speaks it. Safest code in the world . . . Per-perem—here we are! 'Peremptory: by absolute command.'" She looked up and her eyes were grave. "Write that down," she said. Roberts wrote.

"'Detained' is next," Morgan whispered.

Kelly leafed quickly. "D . . . d . . . d . . . 'detain: keep in confinement'—" her voice fell—"'imprison.'"

"But, Kelly!" Morgan objected.

"'From Latin, *tenere* hold,'" Kelly concluded. "That cinches it. What's next?"

Morgan looked at the telegram. "'Circumstance,'" she said, "but everybody knows—"

"Quiet, Red," said Roberts.

"Here we are," Kelly announced. "*Circumstance:* the time, place, and manner . . .'—" She straightened. "Read it, Roberts."

Roberts read, "'As I am by absolute command kept in confinement here by the time—'"

"Substitute 'owing to' for 'by,'" Kelly directed, closing the dictionary.

Roberts read again, "'As I am by absolute command kept in confinement here owing to the time, place and manner of his death.'"

"Now who, and only who," Kelly inquired crisply, "can by absolute command confine or hold a person—"

"The police!" Morgan gasped.

"Now," Kelly snapped again, "What's police and 'the time, place and manner of his death' sound like?"

"*Murder!*"—Morgan whispered, her eyes brightening. "Murder!"

"All right," Kelly said thinly, "how does this sound: 'As I am being held by the police on circumstantial evidence for the murder of Zacharia Attley!'"

Morgan swallowed. "Frankly, Kelly," she said, "it doesn't sound so good to me."

II

"And then," and State's Attorney Hastle's voice was ever so friendly, "you heard the cock of a gun?"

The first time Wm Sultan had heard the question, the night before, from an officer of the state police, he had said, "Yes." He had said it as flatly as if he had heard someone whistling and had been asked on requestioning if he had heard someone whistling. On the fifth or sixth time that he had been asked the question the night before he had said, flatly, "Yes." Now, on the fifth or sixth time that he had been asked the question this morning, he said, flatly:

"Yes."

"Well . . . Thank you very much, Mr. Sultan!" said State's Attorney Hastle. He rose. "Now, if you don't mind, I think it would be very helpful to me if you would go over the scene with me."

"Certainly," said Wm Sultan.

"Thank you," said Hastle, leading the way across the hall.

"Not at all," said Wm Sultan, two state policemen following him.

"Remarkably warm weather we're having, isn't it?" Hastle inquired, courteously opening the door of the late Zacharia Attley's study.

"*Per se,*" Wm Sultan agreed, stepping through the door.

By daylight the brown study was still brown; about the only noticeable change was that the bananas in the photographs on the walls stood out more clearly.

"And Miss Beal," inquired Hastle, "left you at the door?"

"Yes," said Wm Sultan.

Hastle closed the door. The two state police officers stood inside the study with their backs to the door.

"We will assume," said the state's attorney, "that Miss Beal is now outside."

"*Per se,*" said Wm Sultan drily. The assumption was self-evident, Miss Beal *was* outside.

State's Attorney Hastle flushed. Although like all his breed he was primarily a politician he was also a lawyer, of sorts.

"I am referring," he said, "to the *story* you told about last night." And his voice was a whiplash of sarcasm.

Wm Sultan smiled happily. He had thought that a little needling would probe the depth and sincerity of that friendly manner.

"Ah, yes, yes, yes," he said.

Hastle was quite annoyed with himself. He did not want to force things. He had thought that his friendly manner had gone over in a big way. It was still a necessary tactic. He let himself become lost in thought long enough to get over the idea that he had been lost in thought and while thinking of other things may have said something in a tone that could be misinterpreted.

Then still somewhat absent-mindedly, but in a companionable sort of way natural to two friends who are trying to work something out together, he said, "Let's see . . . Yes! You know, I think it might be helpful here if you'd just go ahead and do what you did when you came in last night. I've been trying to get the picture from words— don't need to tell you that, the number of times I've gone over it!—Hate to ask you to do this play-acting, but—"

"Ah, yes!" said Wm Sultan, and, to Hastle's surprise, snapped his bony fingers. "Play-acting" had given him the cue; he had been wondering what Hastle's monologue reminded him of: it was, as usual, in Shakespeare, something to the effect that, "methinks the man doth protest too much."

He sat down in the chair in which he had sat the night before. There was enough of the ham in him that he really threw himself into the spirit of the play-acting. He looked around at the room and his expression made it clear that he found it a *bore* to look at. He crossed his legs and looked *expectantly* at the closed door of the bedroom. He uncrossed his legs and looked *hopefully* at the closed door of the bedroom. He shifted his weight in the chair and looked *curiously* around the room again. He rose with *decision* and weaving his way between chairs and tables, went to a wall and looked with *interest* at a photograph of bananas. He looked at another photograph of bananas. He went along the wall, in and out around the furniture, *inspecting* a score of photographs of bananas.

Hastle's eyes narrowed. "You're quite sure that you looked at so many of those?" he asked skeptically.

"I was interested," Wm Sultan explained with dignity, "to see if I could find one without bananas."

Hastle stiffened. Then he forced a smile.

"Please continue," he said.

Wm Sultan continued until he came to the faded photograph at which he had peered in such perplexity the night before, and in the better light of day he was now pleased to decipher the source of his confusion: it was a close-up of a tarantula sitting with arms akimbo and a contentious expression on the upturned end of a banana. Because of the angle of the photograph the fore-shortening of the banana was quite interesting.

"May I ask how long you looked at that?" Hastle inquired thinly.

Wm Sultan coughed. "I didn't," he confessed. "The lights went out."

"Well, you've been staring at it for thirty seconds now!" Hastle controlled his temper, mentally deducted thirty seconds, and said, "So you were in here not over five minutes, possibly not over four, before the lights went out?"

"That was the estimate I gave you, I believe," Wm Sultan agreed.

Hastle became very friendly again. "And then?" he asked.

"Then in fifteen or twenty seconds the door opened."

Hastle smiled encouragingly. "I suppose you looked at the luminous dial of your wristwatch?" he suggested helpfully.

"No," said Wm Sultan.

"But you're quite certain that it was as long as fifteen or twenty seconds before the door opened?"

"No," Wm Sultan said. "It might have been a little less or a little more, but that's my estimate."

"And what did you do during this estimated time?" inquired Hastle.

"Nothing," said Wm Sultan.

"You just stood there?"

"Yes."

"Just stood there. Didn't move around at all?"

"No."

Hastle gave a laugh of good-fellowship. "Waiting for a streetcar?"

"I did not," said Wm Sultan, "desire a streetcar."

"Then," still friendly, with a little chuckle, "just what were you waiting for?"

"Someone to open a door."

"Ah! Then you were *expecting* the door to open!"

"Certainly."

"Certainly?"

Wm Sultan inclined his head. "I understand that it is common practice to have the circuit from a fuse serve more than one room. Consequently, I assumed that the lights must be out in other rooms and that some member of the household would presently bestir himself to see how I was faring."

"It didn't occur to you to 'bestir' yourself?"

Wm Sultan glanced at the cluttered furniture with only winding lanes between. He said, "I preferred not to try to navigate through here in the dark. Particularly," he continued precisely, "since in looking at these photographs on the wall I'd taken no notice of the location of objects of furniture behind me."

Hastle nodded understandingly, and then, quite clearly, he suddenly remembered something. "Oh, yes!" he said. "When you lit your cigarette in the other room I meant to ask you—just slipped my mind—*why didn't you light a match*, Mr. Sultan?"

"I'd used my last one on the train."

"Oh, yes," said Hastle, "that's right! I believe you borrowed a slip of matches from one of the officers last night, didn't you?"

"Yes."

"And so, since you carry matches it's hardly necessary to ask you if you carry a cigarette lighter—or is it?"

"No."

"Hate the things myself," Hastle said affably. "And so—once the fuse was blown you had *no means whatever of making a light*, did you?"

"No."

Hastle nodded affably and, indeed, with that point nailed down he was beginning to feel affable. He disliked only those who made things difficult for him.

"And then," he said, "the door opened?"

"Yes."

"Ah, yes. And what did you think of that, Mr. Sultan?"

"I assumed that it was Mr. Attley."

"Ah, yes. But you didn't speak to him?"

"No."

"You just *waited* again?"

"It was," Wm Sultan repeated for the thirteenth time, "only a matter of a few seconds. I was somewhat surprised that he did not speak after he opened it as he knew that I was waiting in here. After a moment's hesitation I did start to speak his name."

"Ah, yes. But then you heard—?"

Wm Sultan nodded. "The sound," he said flatly, and for the thirteenth time, "of a firearm being cocked."

State's Attorney Hastle nodded, the two state police officers nodded. They were becoming quite fond of that reply.

"Perhaps there is one little thing that escapes me," the state's attorney conceded, hanging his head bashfully. "Mr. Attley was a client of yours?"

"Yes."

"And a very old client of your firm's, I understand?"

Wm Sultan shook his head. "Quite new," he said.

"But I understood— How many years *has* he been your client?"

"Sixty-four," said Wm Sultan.

Hastle started to say something and caught himself just in time. He was, he realized, being psychologically jabbed off balance; every time he got the tension wound up for a good blow this dry stick would give him a distracting jab, take the sting out of the punch. He decided to stop boxing and start swinging for a knockout.

"All your life then!" he said. "And in that time have you ever known him to exhibit homicidal tendencies?"

No self-respecting attorney could reply to that except by the demurrer that he was not competent to give medical testimony, but Wm Sultan also wanted to bring things to a head and so, though it saddened him, he said simply, "No."

"And yet you come to his house at his invitation," Hastle drove ahead, "and you know that he knows that you are waiting for him in this room. But when he opens his door, and you have given it as your own opinion that at the time you thought it was he, but when he opens his door in the darkness and you hear a metallic click you instantly assume that it is the sound—" his voice became scary—"of a firearm being cocked!"

He turned away as if it were more than he could bear, swung back again. "Now, under the circumstances as *you* have stated them, was that a likely assumption for any sane man to have made? Or for any sane man to believe!"

"To your latter question," Wm Sultan said, "perhaps not."

Hastle approached him with short steps. "Then why," he demanded, "do you ask me to believe that you ever made such an assumption!"

"Because I heard the sound of a firearm being cocked," said Wm Sultan.

Hastle nodded, the two state police officers nodded.

"Very convenient, wasn't it, Mr. Sultan?" he asked.

"Why?" asked Wm Sultan.

Hastle smiled, the two state police officers smiled.

"Very well, Mr. Sultan," he said. "I'll show you why!"

He turned towards the door to the bedroom, paused at an interruption at the door to the hall. One of the state police whispered to another outside and then beckoning the state's attorney whispered to him. Hastle considered a moment, gave a decisive nod.

"We may as well clear that up first," he said. "Send her in." He turned with an affable smile to Wm Sultan. "Your secretary to see you, Mr. Sultan," he announced.

III

Wm Sultan gave his little old-fashioned bow and said, "Good morning, Kelly."

Kelly swallowed and said, "Good morning, Mr. Sultan."

Wm Sultan gave another old-fashioned little bow and said, "State's Attorney Hastle."

Hastle said, "Good morning. I assume you've brought the letter in answer to Mr. Sultan's wire?" He held out his hand.

Kelly looked at him, as at some not particularly interesting bug, and crossed the room to Wm Sultan. She opened her handbag.

"Look here!" Hastle snapped, following. "I want that!" He held out his hand commandingly.

Kelly shrugged resignedly, dropped her lipstick into his open palm, and turned back to Wm Sultan.

"Perhaps he only uses it for kissing babies," she said, as if trying to view the thing in the least unfavorable light.

Wm Sultan coughed.

Hastle threw the lipstick on the carpet. "Now my dear young woman—" he began.

"I beg your pardon," said Wm Sultan coldly, and looked at the lipstick on the carpet.

Hastle took a deep breath, picked up the lipstick, returned it to Kelly, and said quietly to Wm Sultan, "I did not mean that the letter should not be delivered to you. But from what you have told me I consider it as evidence in this case, at least until I read it."

"Certainly," Wm Sultan agreed. "If I may have it, Kelly?"

Kelly shook her head. "It hadn't arrived when I left," she explained.

Hastle shook *his* head. "So this *alleged* letter hadn't arrived when you left? Well, well, well . . ." He came to a decision. "We'll take that up later. Just at the moment," he faced Wm Sultan, "we may as well conclude our business in here."

Kelly also faced Wm Sultan, and stubbornly. "You'll want me to stay," she told him firmly. "You have, you know, such a poor memory."

Wm Sultan said, "My secretary is completely in my confidence."

Hastle's eyes were narrowed as they went from one to the other.

"No objection at all!" he said, and then went on quickly, as if in fear that either one of them should have a change of mind. "And now, Mr. Sultan," he said, "we have the fuse blown out, and you standing where you are and you hear the door open and then in the darkness you hear a metallic click which you instantly assume is—" his eyes shifted to Kelly—"the click of a revolver being cocked!" He noted Kelly's frown and repressed a smile. "What *then?*" he asked.

"Nothing, for a time," said Wm Sultan for the thirteenth time. "And then in about a half minute I heard someone breathing in the doorway."

"Weren't you *afraid* whoever it was could hear you?"

Wm Sultan wished that he had not been quite so precipitate in permitting his secretary to stay. "No," he said. "I had my mouth open," he explained.

"And how much longer," Hastle inquired, "did you stand here in the dark with your mouth open before anything else happened?"

Wm Sultan did not look at his secretary. He felt that the picture that Hastle had drawn was not flattering.

"In about five minutes," he said stiffly, "I heard something that I thought might be a window being opened."

"And what," Hastle asked in a tone of awe, "did you do then?"

"I got down on my knees," said Wm Sultan.

"You heard a window open," Hastle repeated, "and so you got down on your knees."

Out of the corner of his eyes Wm Sultan saw his frowning secretary bite her lip, and he began to realize that perhaps he had not been sympathetic enough with Hastle's incredulity.

"I thought it might be a ruse to lure me into giving my position away," he explained patiently, but feeling a certain bitterness.

"Ah-hah!" said Hastle. "And *then?*"

"I crawled towards the doorway."

"That was very brave of you," said Hastle admiringly. "And how long did it take you?"

"I should say about ten minutes."

Hastle looked at the door. It was about fifteen feet away.

"And during that time," he asked, "did you hear any other *sinister* sounds?"

"No," said Wm Sultan.

"No more clicks?" Hastle persisted. "Or breathings? Or windows being raised?"

"None."

"And so?"

"And so," Wm Sultan said, "I concluded that whoever had been in the room had left. Particularly," he amplified, "when I reached the doorway and could definitely feel the breeze from an open window."

"And then?"

"I went inside the room and came upon the body."

Hastle smiled. "So we're in the wrong room now, aren't we!" His voice hardened. "Let's go in the other one."

He went quickly to the bedroom door and opened it. Kelly found that there was a white chalk outline on a dark green carpet. It began shortly within the room from the doorway and extended straight back for several feet.

"Does that," she heard Hastle ask Wm Sultan, "coincide with your recollection of the position of the body?"

"Yes."

"It does," Hastle confirmed, "with this photograph."

Kelly stood behind Wm Sultan, peeking at it from behind his arm. It was a photograph of an old man in a dressing gown stretched straight out on his stomach on the floor. His shoulders appeared hunched up and the dressing gown pulled up around his shoulders as if . . . as if, Kelly suddenly realized, someone had drug him over the floor with their hands under his shoulders! And his feet were stretched out that way, too, the toes dragging . . . She did not want to look at his head, it seemed turned at a peculiar angle . . . Her eyes turned quickly to State's Attorney

Hastle because he had closed the door and he was looking
at Wm Sultan with a peculiar expression.

"Let's reverse things, Mr. Sultan," he said. "You are in
the other room and you say that someone in here opens the
door. Very well, let's open the door!"

He did so, slowly, swinging it back and forth once,
twice, three times, and Kelly was biting her tongue to keep
from crying out because the door was swinging over part
of the chalk marks on the floor, what would be the shoes
and part of the legs.

"And perhaps you can explain," Hastle said, swinging
the door over them again, "how Mr. Attley's murderer
could have opened this door without knocking his legs
out of the way? Because if you can't," he cried, "I can!
He didn't, that is how!" He flung the door wide and went
to an open window. "And this was the window you found
opened, wasn't it?"

"Yes," said Wm Sultan.

"It's too bad," Hastle said, "that you have never visited
here before, Mr. Sultan. It's too bad it was a dark night,
or you might not have picked the wrong side of the room
for your murderer's 'escape'!" He jerked a pointing finger
out the window.

Kelly moved with leaden feet behind Wm Sultan to the
window. Below the window in the bright morning light
was a wide flower bed, evidently of bulbs that had been
taken up for the winter some days before, because its surface was smoothly raked, and that surface was unbroken
by any imprint except the evenly spaced and weathered
furrows of the rake.

IV

Kelly turned slowly from the window at Hastle's voice.

"You have told me a story, Mr. Sultan," he was saying
quietly. "It's only fair that I should now tell you one." Kelly

found his eyes upon her. "But we need not stay in here," he said considerately, opening the door to the study. "I see that your secretary is badly upset. Murder's such a shocking thing, and the crime seems so vivid in here, so clear."

But when they stood in the brown room again he left the door open to the bedroom with the white chalkmarks on the green carpet, and the open window below which . . .

"My story," Hastle was saying, "is about a man—oh, let's call him a lawyer! A lawyer," he continued, "who finds it necessary to kill his client. The lawyer is waiting for the client in a room like this one—in fact, let's say in this room."

Kelly leaned against the back of a big leather chair, her hands holding to it behind her.

"And," Hastle resumed, "let's say the client was Zacharia Attley." He jerked his hand towards the open doorway. "And Zacharia Attley enters this room to meet his lawyer, and in *this* room he is killed by . . . but that's a mere detail, although a very interesting one, very, which I shall go into in another part of the story. Now it's enough to say that this old, this very old man was slain without bloodshed. And now, with him dead, his lawyer is faced with the problem of trying to avoid the consequences of his crime."

Hastle pointed his finger as at a corpse at their feet.

"To begin with," he said, "he certainly must not be found in here where the lawyer was known to be waiting for him, and so he is—" he gestured towards the bedroom, "drug in there." He shook his head, clicked his tongue.

"But that, obviously, is not enough. Can the lawyer claim that he heard no word of outcry, no sound of a body falling, or that hearing those things he just quietly sat in here instead of running to the door and opening it?" He again shook his head. "No, that would be a little too thin. And how did the murderer enter and escape? The lawyer does not know the house, he does not know where everyone is, it would be far too risky to leave no possibility except that the 'murderer' had entered and left by the bedroom door to the back hall—it may be under observation, and the other members of the household may be together or variously in sight of one another. No, no, that won't do at all. A way must be left open for it to have been some outsider, a sneakthief perhaps. And so a window is opened—but it is a dark night and the lawyer cannot see what lies below the window."

Kelly did not know that her fingernails were leaving permanent marks on the leather back of the chair. She dared not look at her employer, and had she dared she could not have taken her eyes from the hard, smiling face of the state's attorney. She saw him frown, and bite his lip, and shake his head.

"But the lawyer knows that this sneakthief business is very thin. There has been talk of a change in the murdered man's will, it should be very easy to throw suspicion on almost any member of the family, if only he can give them a better opportunity and make his own position more helpless—if only the lights were out!"

Hastle clapped his hands together and the sudden sound went through Kelly like a jolt of electricity.

"Perfect!" Hastle exclaimed. "He can claim that he heard something that did make him wonder if Mr. Attley were all right—after all, he has been waiting several minutes for Mr. Attley, and he had been told that Mr. Attley would see him at once, and when a man of eighty-six!—Yes! It will make his own story very simple and plausible. And it would have been very nice for him to have had a simple and plausible story, wouldn't it, Mr. Sultan?"

But Kelly saw that the state's attorney was looking at her, looking at her so pointedly and fixedly that she felt Wm Sultan's eyes also turn to her; and then she understood Hastle's purpose in letting her stay, that he was trying to break down Wm Sultan by letting him see the crushing effect of the evidence upon his own secretary. By the time she realized that, it was at that moment too late to do anything about it; to dig her fingers out of the leather of the chair or to put a different expression on her face.

Hastle smiled. "Yes, indeed!" He answered his own question. "Such a simple, plausible story. He can say that he went to the door and spoke Mr. Attley's name but received no response. Then he heard a window thrown up and opened the door—but couldn't see who climbed out of it *in the dark*. Yes, indeed, it could have been anyone!"

Hastle again clapped his hands. "And what—" he broke off; Kelly was clapping hers. Enthusiastically.

Wm Sultan coughed.

Hastle jerked his thumb towards the hall door.

"That will be all for you!"

Kelly was indignant. "But I don't think it's fair," she protested, "that you should put me out just because I applaud you, *too.*" She appealed to the two state police officers. "And I don't think anyone else *I tell about it* will think it was fair either!"

Hastle looked at the two state police officers who had turned their backs and were carefully examining the paneling of the door.

"It's nothing to me what you tell!" he said boldly. "Or whether you go—or stay," he added. He swung back to Wm Sultan. "And what can be easier?" he demanded. "Why, it can even be done with a coin. Unscrew an electric bulb from a lamp and insert a coin in the socket. So simple. And so well known. And that is exactly what this lawyer does. And the fuse *does* blow out, and he needs only to remove the coin and screw back the bulb and go to the hall door *there*—and wait, oh, say five minutes—and then stumble into the hall and give the alarm—or someone else may have been aroused by the blowing of the fuse and will come blundering into either room—which will add to the confusion and make everything that much better! Such a simple, plausible plan—wrecked by such a simple little accident."

Hastle shook his head in mock commiseration. "Wrecked," he repeated, "by a little accident that delayed this lawyer. That delayed him minute after frantic minute, delayed him until it was a full twenty minutes since he had entered the room and dared not delay longer in giving the 'alarm.' Already there were twenty minutes that had to be explained away—in which he must account for his silence—and for doing nothing—a delay that could be explained only by some danger that kept him silent and from doing nothing—a delay that at all costs must be explained away, however implausibly, by—by—by something like having heard the cock of a gun in the darkness!"

Kelly told herself that she must try to look nonchalant, or smile, or something . . .

"Now I wonder," Hastle said, "I wonder what that accident could have been?"

A coin fell from his hand, rolled across the rug, came to a stop under a table. Hastle walked around a chair, got down on his knees under the table, picked up the coin, rose, and put it in his pocket.

"But it was night," he said. "And the fuse had been blown. And this lawyer had used his last match on the train. He had no way whatever of making a light. But the coin must not be found in this room. It would prove that the fuse had been blown from this room—where the lawyer had been waiting. So he must get down on his hands and knees in the dark and feel blindly over the rug for the coin, and minutes pass, minute after frantic minute passes, and still he blindly, desperately searches until at last he knows that he can delay in giving the alarm no longer. *That* is the accident that could have happened!"

Kelly, unconsciously, was again leaning against the back of the chair.

"In fact," Hastle cried, "that was the accident that *did* happen!"

He flung aside the chair against which Kelly was leaning so suddenly that she almost lost her balance and fell, and then she swayed as she saw on a part of the rug that had been covered by the low-legged chair a white chalk circle, and in the middle of that chalk circle a quarter, a quarter with a bluish smudge in its center.

4

The Guilty Three. To the Rescue! In France.
Strange Spectacle. The Edge of a Hand. In a Country
Parlor. A New Client. Startling Disappearance.

Roberts turned from her typewriter to the switchboard and slipped on the headset.

"Good morning," she said, "The offices of—"

"Roberts—"

"Kelly!"

"—get Morgan in on this."

There was for a moment a certain confusion of questions.

"Pipe down both of you!" snapped Kelly's voice.

"All right," said Roberts.

"And listen to me!"

"Yes, Kelly," said Morgan. "Only—"

"Quiet, Red!" barked Roberts.

"Shut up, you!" said Kelly.

"But all I started to ask—" began Morgan.

Roberts pulled out the connection to her telephone, and let a count of three go by before putting it in again.

"Yes, Kelly," murmured Morgan, humbly.

"Oh, no," said Kelly. "Keep it up. We have all the time in the world. Only any second a cop is likely to step in and ask me am I through. I'm calling from Zacharia Attley's residence—the *late* Z. A.'s residence—I'm calling from a room they call the office—which has a separate telephone—and I'm calling at the special *request* of the state's attorney. In case you Manhattan cut-ups don't happen to know, that means he's the same as a district attorney."

"Whee-whewh!" whistled Roberts.

"Oh," breathed Morgan.

"Yeah," said Kelly broadly. "And for your further information," and there was something in her voice that made them both begin to feel a slight draft up and down the spine, "if he has any hayseed in his hair it's because it's worth a lot of dough. And it so happens," she continued, "that this smart potato has a case of circumstantial evidence against Bill that's the kind that ends up with a judge saying, 'And may God rest your soul . . .'"

Morgan and Roberts waited in silence. Kelly's voice had broken on the last word. It was crisp and clear enough when it began again.

"To clear up the excuse for this call first—has that letter arrived from Zacharia Attley?"

"No, Kelly."

"No, Kelly."

"All right then. Now get this. The three short-brained meddlesome morons who had to stick their long noses in Bill's affairs are the three bright bitches who are responsible for him being on this spot. And in case you'd like to forget their names, as I would, they are Kelly, Morgan and Roberts!"

"Yes, Kelly," said Morgan.

"Yeah," said Roberts.

"Now listen fast," Kelly commanded. "We know how much chance there is that grandpappy could hurt a fly! But other people don't understand him as we do, and with the story he's telling it's enough to convince anyone that— What's happened to him," she interrupted herself, "is too much to have been an unlucky accident. He's been framed—*beautifully* framed—in the kind of a frame you hang! And I for one am going to do anything on earth to get him out of it."

"Count me in," said Roberts.

"To the last drop of my blood!" cried Morgan.

"Heh, heh," said Kelly drily, "it's more likely to be to the last inch of your attractive skin. I don't know who's framed him, but I do know we could use some information, and one of the characters here, name of Trumbo, looks to me like he would not find a redhead repulsive."

"What train do I get?" asked Morgan.

"The first."

"Where was *he?*" asked Roberts.

"In the garage. Fiddling with the car. Had just driven Bill, up from the station. Things happened fast. Our farmer's daughter was upstairs. Zolicopher Hay—you know him, he was in the office list year—was in a room adjoining the study where Bill was waiting. So they say. But though none of them can prove it that doesn't help Bill any. Not any."

"How was he killed?" asked Roberts, ever factual.

Kelly's voice was strained. "I think he had his neck broken. I'm not sure. The state's attorney was starting on that and then switched to Bill's war record and Bill suggested I call about the letter." There was a pause and then her voice was angry in its defensiveness. "Well, was it Bill's fault that he was a lawyer? I suppose he did spend the war sitting at a desk in the adjutant general's office, so what? Men did what they were told to, didn't they? Nothing to be ashamed of! Even if the silly does feel embarrassed about it and would rather that we didn't— Oh! So it hasn't come yet? Well, as soon as it does, please bring it, Roberts. That's all, thank you."

There was a click and the phone went dead.

II

"Oh, so you were?" said State's Attorney Hastle. "Adjutant general's office, I suppose?"

"Well," Wm Sultan temporized, "not exactly."

"No? And just what did you do—exactly?"

"Well, a-hum, hem, hem, you see, I happened to be in France at the time."

"The time," Hastle inquired, "of what?"

"Oh—the German invasion."

Wm Sultan was becoming seriously embarrassed. As he had felt from the start and throughout the whole business, he still felt that there had been something a little melodramatic about the whole business for a then junior partner of Sultan, Sultan & Sultan.

"Affairs of a client," he hastened to explain. "Franco-American family, American branch clients, one died, you see, necessary—France."

Hastle was grimly amused by his embarrassment, seeing a different reason for it.

"And what," he inquired, "did you do after the invasion?"

"Oh, well, French branch, almost clients, too, after manner of speaking, stayed on, any little services."

"Such as?" inquired Hastle, smiling.

Wm Sultan coughed. "Well—oh—there was the Resistance, you know." It was what Hastle had expected and yet he stopped smiling. He shrugged irritably. Whether he was beginning, despite himself, to like this dry stick was entirely beside the point that a stick could kill. Particularly this stick.

"So you engaged in the Resistance?" he said. "And after we entered the war?"

"Oh, just very much the same sort of thing."

"Must have been rather rough work now and then?"

"Oh, well, a few little incidents, perhaps."

Hastle turned his head to one of the officers at the door. "Mr. Trumbo Gates and Willy Nebbit, please."

In the light of day Trumbo Gates was, if anything, an even more lowering and powerful looking young man than he had been by the dim lights of the station platform. He stood shortly within the room and his expression, when he looked at Wm Sultan, was that of a man holding his temper.

Hastle, with a wag of his finger, called Willy Nebbit forward and forward Willy Nebbit bounced. He was a slender mite of a man who seemed on the point of bouncing out of blue jeans and a leather jacket that were too big for him. But Wm Sultan was soon to learn that if he bounced when he moved he bounced more when he talked. He bounced from heel to toe, and his shoulders bounced, and his single whispy curl of hair bounced with him.

Hastle said, "You were at the station last night, Willy?"

"Get off my dairy feed order!" The words bounced out of him. "Feed dealers are robbers around here!" His eyebrows bounced. "Put it right slam in the mailcar!" His eyeglasses bounced to one side of his nose.

"Did you see," Hastle indicated first Trumbo Gates and then Wm Sultan, "these gentlemen there?"

"Dam-nest thing I ever seen!" His cheeks bounced, and his eyeglasses went to the other side of his nose.

"Suppose you tell us."

"Well, Trumbo—you know Trumbo!" He smacked his fist against his palm with such violence that his chin bounced up and down beneath his protruding teeth. "Smack! And a man's out. You can count ten! Twenty! Thirty!"

"Yes," said Hastle, "I know Trumbo."

"Well, Trumbo starts roughing up this ge'man here— bumping him around platform with suitcase—funniest thing I ever seen!" He laughed, and when he laughed his eyelashes bounced, his chin bounced, his cheeks bounced, his hair bounced and his eyeglasses did a tap dance on the bridge of his nose. "So I hung around to see the fun! Then Trumbo *bangs* back from opening the car door, this ge'man standing behind him, *bangs* back fit to knock over a truck, and—*Bang!*" Again he struck fist against palm. "Trumbo's digging up the cinders with the back of his head!"

"And then?" said Hastle.

"Well, you know Trumbo—*up* he bounces!" and Willy Nebbit bounced a foot. "And *back* comes his elbows! And says I to myself, you can count *ten!* You can count *twenty!* You can count *thirty!* You can count *forty!* You can count—"

"Yes," said Hastle, "I can count, Willy."

"And so—" Willy wound up his arm—"he lets her go!" And in the violence of the illustration he bounced out of the off shoulder of his leather jacket. Then he stood stock still. His voice came in a tone of subdued awe. "Dam-nest thing I ever seen. Dam-nest thing I ever seen. You'd think he'd been tied to his fist, like a tail to a cow, the way he follows it. And he turns a somersault right there in the middle of the air. And when he comes down on his back on those cinders this time it—*bounces the station platform!*" And Willy Nebbit bounced with it.

Trumbo Gates was weaving slightly backward and forward. "Is that the story," he muttered, "that you're telling around town?"

Willy Nebbit bounced around to him. "It sure is!" he affirmed. "And you can do anything about it you want to as long as you won't mind a pitchfork in your belly!"

Hastle said, "There'll be no trouble out of either of you. Now, Willy, when you talked to officer Jim Calfedge last night you told him that you could hear these men talking. Something about the war."

"I sure did! This ge'man here, polite as a boy to his girl's folks before they're in-laws, he says to Trumbo,

polite! that he wouldn't recommend Trumbo doing any—"
fist hit palm—"unless he'd been a parytrooper or a commando in the war. Dam-nest best advice I ever heard, way
it turned out!"

Hastle nodded. "And what did Trumbo say?"

"Oh, Trumbo says something about this ge'man being
a cloak-and-dagger boy and after Trumbo had *bounced the
platform!* then, still polite, this ge'man answers him and
says, 'Yes.'"

Hastle said, "All right, Willy, thank you, and give my
regards to the Missus."

"That I will!"

"And you may go back with the others, if you please,
Mr. Gates."

A scowling Trumbo followed a bouncing Willy from the
room.

State's Attorney Hastle deliberately turned his eyes
from Wm Sultan and looked at the chalkmark on the green
carpet in the bedroom. He did so not for effect on anyone
but himself, and when his eyes returned to Wm Sultan
they were the properly grim eyes of a prosecutor.

"OSS?" he asked quietly.

"Well, only by accident, you see," Wm Sultan protested
depreciatingly. "Being there at the time—had made con-
nections—merest fluke of chance."

"But I take it you did pick up a few knacks of taking
care of yourself?"

Wm Sultan pulled at the lobe of his ear. "By what means
was Mr. Attley's neck broken?" he asked.

"I'll give that an honest answer," Hastle agreed. "Because of the collar of his dressing gown we can't tell. It
could have cushioned the blow of a stick—there *are* some
walking sticks in the coat closet in the back hall, or of a
fire poker—there *are* some in the house though neither in
here nor his bedroom—so that the characteristic bruise of

a hard weapon may have been modified. But would you
have needed such a weapon, Mr. Sultan?"

"Well—hypothetically speaking, of course!—I'd say,
simply from my cursory observation of the attenuated
physique of the corpse, you understand, and the advanced
age of the deceased, that perhaps I should not have experienced too great difficulty in achieving the result by a blow
with the edge of my hand."

"Precisely," said Hastle, "my conclusion, Mr. Sultan."

An officer put his head in the hall door. "She's back
again."

"And has the letter been received?" Hastle inquired
with a smile.

The officer shook his head.

"No," Hastle said, "I hardly thought so." He rose. "Now
we'll get together and clear up this thing."

III

In leading the procession across the hall to the room where
they were waiting, Kelly felt that she was walking the last
mile. An officer on guard opened the door of the room and
then it closed again after Wm Sultan and the state's attorney entered behind her.

Bananas or no bananas, millions or no millions, it was
evident in his home that Zacharia Attley had remained a
Yankee farmboy at heart. Kelly saw that the room was not
a drawing room or a reception room, it was a country parlor. Outsize, certainly, as was the house for a farmhouse,
but the spirit was there, the unused stiffness of a special
place where one sat only on Sundays and at funerals . . .

She found that though, truly, her chair was not up-
holstered in horsehair, its green plush was not less stiffly
resentful of being sat upon. She saw that Trumbo Gates
was sitting in another green chair in a corner, and for once
looked more thoughtful than angry; she saw Zolicopher

Hay in an identical chair in the opposite corner, the reflection of the light on his eyeglasses hiding his eyes, but the corners of his mouth were drawn back, his lips flattened against his teeth in an expression of long-suffering petulance. Green chairs, green drapes, a green carpet not unlike the one bearing the chalkmarks in the bedroom.

Her eyes turned unwillingly, afraid to look, to Wm Sultan as he sat down on a green sofa at the other end of which sat Zenobia Beal in a gingham gown. Kelly did not know what sign of despair she had expected to see, but it was almost more disconcerting to see him as perfectly at ease and undisturbed as if he were totally unaware of being involved in anything more dangerous than a taxi ride. If at least he were only aware of his danger! But how could he be, she reflected bitterly, when in all his law-book sheltered life he had never known any danger greater than that of misinterpreting a *whereas*.

As he sat down she saw him give his little bow and his patented grandfatherly smile to Zenobia, but Kelly was less certain that the smile that Zenobia returned was altogether grand-daughterly. It was wan enough, and of course it should be trusting, but not necessarily so trusting that it amounted to her jumping into his lip and cuddling up there. Her attention jerked around to the door at Hastle's voice.

"Miss Beal," he said, and his tone indicated that he had asked the question before and was repeating it only for the information of others, "did Mr. Attley give you a letter in a sealed envelope yesterday afternoon addressed to Mr. Sultan?"

"Yes, sir."

It could not have been because Kelly was prejudiced that she was beginning to dislike Zenobia Beal's little-girl voice.

"What did you do with it?"

"I put it on the table in the hall with the other letters—so that—"

"What time was that?"

"About five o'clock."

Hastle spoke to Trumbo Gates. "Did you see it there?"

"I didn't notice one way or the other."

"Did you?" he asked Zolicopher Hay.

"I put a number of letters there myself about four-
thirty," Zolicopher Hay replied. "I don't know what may
have been added later."

Hastle opened the door. "All right, Mr. Sedgwick," he
said.

Mr. Sedgwick followed his chin into the room. First
there was his chin, and then there was a dead heat between
the point of his nose and the lenses of his steel-rimmed
spectacles, and then his squinting, faded blue eyes, and
then his white-haired head, and then his scrawny neck,
and then his knees, and then, in an arch between, the rest
of him.

"What time did you take the mail down to the village
yesterday?"

Mr. Sedgwick's outthrust chin chewed on his words quite
lengthily before he rolled them out over his lower lip.

"Some after five. Always leave to get them there before
five-thirty." He chewed some more words. "No other mail
goes out after till next day ten o'clock."

Hastle handed him an envelope. "Was this among those
you picked up yesterday afternoon?"

Mr. Sedgwick began chewing violently. He started
holding the letter out further and further from in front of
his chin and then suddenly slapped it back into the hand
of the state's attorney.

"I can drive a car as good as any man here and better'n
any woman!" he cried defiantly. "My eyes as good as ever
at a distance—even better!"

"O.K., Eagle-Eye!" Trumbo Gates spoke in a tone of weary anger. "But you buy your own fenders from now on."

Hastle opened the door and turned Mr. Sedgwick around and closed it after him.

"And what do you know about this letter, Mr. Gates?" he asked.

Trumbo Gates spoke on a take-it-or-leave-it basis. "I got the old boy's dander up when he gave me some song and dance about Zenobia being his great-granddaughter, just all at once, and he said by God just to prove it he'd write to his lawyer right there and then and tell him to put her in his will. Maybe he did, maybe he didn't, I don't know."

Hastle nodded, turned. "And you, Mr. Hay?"

Zolicopher Hay said, "I saw him immediately after Trumbo had." He gave his expression of unending misfortune. "He was still very angry and told me much the same thing."

"But you did not see him writing such a letter, he did not show such a letter to you?"

Zolicopher Hay shook his head. "We only had a few words. I left him to cool off."

Hastle said, "Did, later, anyone else tell you anything about the letter?"

"Yes. I asked Zenobia about it when she told me that Mr. Sultan was coming here last night and she said Mr. Attley had given her a letter to him to mail."

"And you, Mr. Gates?"

Trumbo nodded. "I asked her too. She told me Zack had called his lawyer on the phone, written him a letter."

Zenobia Beal spoke up for herself, if timidly. "He, Mr. Attley, wrote the letter right after talking to Mr. Hay."

"Thank you," said Hastle. "It's so hard to remember that anyone actually saw this letter. It's too bad, Miss Beal, that an angry threat to write something is no proof that it has been written."

Wm Sultan coughed. "The subsequent asseveration of the writer that he had, in fact, written such a 'letter,'" he said, "had given to be posted, I should say, a codicil to his extant last will and testament—is a corroboration of his previously twice reiterated intention which, I think—ah, yes, yes, yes, yes—which, in my considered judgment, is not to be brushed aside, skipped over or, shall we say? crawled under. And certainly one which, *per se,* may not be simply ignored."

Hastle smiled. "Am I to understand that you are acting for Miss Beal?"

"Oh—if you only would!" pleaded Zenobia Beal, and Kelly observed that she slid along the sofa towards him.

Wm Sultan smiled in embarrassed appreciation of her confidence, and inclined his head in affirmation of its acceptance.

"Speaking for my client," he said, and Kelly could have cursed, *"and,* in that capacity," he continued in a quiet tone but one which halted an interruption from the state's attorney, "I refer only to the present criminal investigation, as in any matter relating to the disposition of the estate of the late Zacharia Attley I am exclusively engaged by the intentions of the testator. *But* in my present capacity, and I shall—heh! heh! heh!—certainly be the first to advise Miss Beal to seek competent counsel in the particular field of your official activities if such an unlikely necessity should arise! *But,* just at the moment, I must decline longer to be used as a stalking horse for a possible criminal charge involving Miss Beal."

No-no-no-no-no-no-no-no-No! Kelly kept saying to herself. You're practically admitting your guilt when you fall back on that constitutional rights business. Can't you see Hastle's pleased as punch, just letting you talk, giving you enough rope . . .

"Your assumption," Wm Sultan was continuing, "quite clearly from the start, your only tenable assumption unless you wish to prove that I am a homicidal maniac, is that I and Miss Beal have acted in collusion to perpetrate a fraud upon my client, Zacharia Attley. But I must remind you that Miss Beal's purported claim rests not upon hearsay but upon certain documents that were in the possession of Mr. Attley. Since these documents effect the disposition of his estate, as the executor of that estate I request that they be produced for examination."

And when she saw Hastle's expression Kelly knew, intuitively, what was coming. Hastle turned to Trumbo Gates.

"Perhaps you examined them, Mr. Gates?

"As I told you," Trumbo stated, "I got his dander up. I got his dander up by demanding to be shown these 'proofs.' So he said he'd be damned if I could demand that he do anything. He slapped the pocket of his dressing gown and said there they were and there they would remain."

Hastle smiled. "And you, Mr. Hay?"

Zolicopher Hay said, in a tone of weary suffering, "The temper he was in, I knew better than to try to question him. I left him to cool off."

Hastle nodded. "And so," he said, "no one else saw these wonderful documents . . . Where did you last see them, Miss Beal?"

Wm Sultan nodded. "You may answer that."

"In the pocket of his dressing gown!" Zenobia exclaimed.

Hastle nodded. "But now," he said, "but now, oddly enough, they are not there! And a very thorough search has shown that they are not in his bedroom. In fact, they have just vanished like they had never been! Or," his voice dropped significantly, "as if they were fakes that could not bear examination."

Kelly saw Zenobia slide a little further along the sofa until she was huddling against Wm Sultan's shoulder with the hurt and pouting expression of a milkmaid accused of drinking the cream.

5

A Cough & Its Consequences. Motives Revealed.
Three Mice. A Circuitous Secretary & an
Unscrupulous File Clerk. Several Things of
Hidden Significance. Mata Hari at Work.

Wm Sultan coughed. It was a cough that, first of all, arrested the attention. It was a cough that, secondly, said that he had been most patient and most forbearing. It was a cough that, thirdly, concluded that the time had come for forbearance, like the worm, to turn.

"I have tried to forbear," Wm Sultan said with an air of forbearance, "from jumping to conclusions on inconclusive evidence, but I have for some time anticipated that the disappearance of the original documents was an inevitable corollary of the violent death of Zacharia Attley."

Hastle gave a cough in his turn, and Kelly looked at him pityingly, and Hastle looked both surprised and embarrassed. No doubt he had an adequate courtroom cough, it might even pass company with the judicial cough, that catarrhal pride of the race of bench-warmers, but to give utterance to it while the ear still retained the inimitable overtones, the exquisite nuances of a cough by a member of the Codicil Club, venerable and drafty, from which men have been blackballed for a cough that would make the reputation of a superior court justice, *that* was a rashness for which he paid by learning to his own surprised embarrassment what a pitiful thing was that noise he called a cough in comparison.

"To be precise," Wm Sultan continued precisely, "there were two documents. Since there were only two, am I correct," he asked, "in assuming from your use of the plural that both have disappeared?"

"Yes," said Hastle, and it was then that Kelly began to sense some subtle change in his attitude towards Wm Sultan.

"A marriage certificate?" Wm Sultan pinned one down exactly.

"Yes," said Hastle again, and Kelly's impression of a change in his attitude was reinforced.

"An item of relative unimportance," stated Wm Sultan.

"Of relative unimportance," Hastle agreed.

"And a letter to the late Zenobia Attley," Wm Sultan continued and still precisely, "signed, 'Aunt Unice,' whose identity we may, I think, reasonably accept as being the late Zenobia Attley's only paternal aunt, Unice Pease,' née Attley, the wife at that time of one Trumbo Pease, particularly," he pointed out, "since Zenobia Attley had *no* maternal aunts and the signator, 'Aunt Unice,' refers in her letters to one Trumbo, to wit, 'Trumbo and I will write to your father?'"

"All things considered," Hastle again agreed, "I think we may safely assume that 'Aunt Unice' *was* her aunt, Unice."

Wm Sultan gave a cough that expressed his appreciation of this bold concession, and that made Hastle bite his lips with envy. But, although Kelly had been long enough associated with members of the legal profession fully to appreciate the moral superiority which is conceded to a superior cough, she shrewdly surmised that while it may

have given Hastle pause in his attack upon her esteemed
employer, that attack had come to a dead stop only because the state's attorney had foreseen that it was heading
for some legal rocks.

"And that letter," her employer began pointing out the
shoals for all to see, "the only discovered evidence of the
hitherto unsuspected parentage of Miss Beal's father, is of
primary importance to Miss Beal?"

"*Per se,*" said Hastle, and seemed quite pleased with
himself.

Kelly began to feel like a stranger playing cards with
two sharps on a ship. She took a quick glance at Trumbo
Gates and Zolicopher Hay and saw that they too were uncomfortably aware that the two erstwhile opponents were
working hand in glove.

"It is of primary importance to Miss Beal," Wm Sultan
said, as one who spells it out for children, "because it is
the only discovered evidence that the late Zenobia Attley,
or Mrs. John Host Devers, ever had a child?"

"Precisely," said Hastle.

"And, further, identifies that offspring as a male child
known under the name of John Trumbo Beal?"

"I understand," Hastle agreed as blandly as a gambler
looking at a marked card, "that such is the purport of the
alleged letter."

"And consequently," Wm Sultan dealt an ace from the
bottom of the deck, "its disappearance leaves Miss Beal
without evidence to support a contest of the extant last
will and testament of the late Zacharia Attley?"

Hastle inclined his head in agreement and Kelly saw
him shift his feet a little as if turning from Wm Sultan to
the other side of the room.

"A situation," Wm Sultan deftly dealt another ace,
"which would be completely altered were there in existence a codicil to that will naming her as a beneficiary, as

her claim would not then rest upon proof of relationship but upon the expressed intention of the testator in exercising his right to dispose of his property?"

Hastle again accepted the card with a bland inclination of his head, and shifted his feet a little further.

"But," and Wm Sultan dealt a third ace, "the absence of such a codicil leaves her without any claim whatever upon the estate?"

Kelly saw him pat, in grandfatherly sympathy, Zenobia's hand; and she saw Zenobia clasp that bony hand in both of hers with a responsiveness that no doubt was as artless as it was ardent.

"Consequently," and in an off-hand casualness Wm Sultan dealt the fourth ace, "unless *heh! heh!* one enter the realm of purely speculative hypotheses, quite incapable of proof, Miss Beal is left without any expectation of gain by the death of Zacharia Attley and, therefore, *without any motive for his murder.*"

Kelly felt like a sucker for card tricks. They had been plainly enough marked from the start, goodness knew, for all to see, and she knew that Hastle had foreseen what the hand would look like when it was turned face up; but her own surprise left her mentally agape.

She saw that State's Attorney Hastle was facing Trumbo Gates and Zolicopher Hay. He faced them with that quiet assurance of the gambler who knows not only his own cards but also those held by those with whom he is, and how, playing.

"I understand," he began, "that you both were familiar with the terms of the will that Mr. Attley made about a year ago, shortly after the death of his daughter?"

Kelly saw that Zolicopher Hay nodded at once, and that Trumbo Gates, after a glance at Zenobia, did the same.

Hastle also evidently saw the glance, for he said, "Yes, I understand that it was Miss Beal who informed you that you were the residuary legatees." He turned to Zenobia Beal. "Even before your father's death," he said, "you'd been doing a certain amount of—oh—clerical or secretarial work for Miss Zenobia and Mr. Attley?"

Zenobia nodded her loam-brown head. "I used to keep the Herford records for Miss Zenobia," she sniffled, "and help Mr. Attley with his correspondence about the Banana Pioneers Association. He was President Emeritus."

Wm Sultan and the state's attorney both inclined their heads in respect, and Hastle turned back to the two residuary legatees.

"And since she learned the terms of the will before you," he purred like a cat with a mouse, or in this particularly happy instance, mice, "it would kind of look, wouldn't it, that she was more in his confidence even a year ago than either of you, now wouldn't it?"

Trumbo Gates gave a snort. "You mean in a better position to read his wastebasket!" he said.

Zolicopher Hay gave his long-suffering expression and inclined his gray head in agreement.

As when a plowshare turns the loam-brown soil did Zenobia Beal's head curve and bow upon her maidenly bosom.

"It's true," she murmured in confession. "He, Mr. Attley, kept writing it out different ways before he went to have Mr. Sultan—" her eyes fluttered up clingingly to that rugged face—"draw it up legal for him. But Zolly and Trumbo were so worried I just kind of peeked at his papers when he'd tell me to take them out and burn them, so I could tell them and they could stop worrying."

Kelly saw her employer give a sympathetic smile to Zenobia Beal, and when he looked down the extensive length of his nose at Zolly and Trumbo that large but sensitive organ seemed to smell something, bad, like ingratitude.

Hastle, on the contrary, smiled at them.

HUGH AUSTIN

"And you believed her?" he asked.

They nodded.

Hastle nodded.

"And since you believed her the first time," he said, "I think we'll agree that you must have believed her the second time? When," he specified, "she told you yesterday afternoon that a codicil had been written which changed the will." He paused, accepted their silence as agreement. "And you've both stated," he continued, "that Mr. Attley gave you no opportunity to examine the evidence of Miss Beal's parentage, and so, of course, you couldn't know whether it was true or false."

"Per se," murmured Wm Sultan, and Kelly saw Trumbo Gates half rise from his chair.

"We have, by the way," Hastle said in an off-hand manner but with the claws showing, "only your unsupported words that in your separate interviews with Mr. Attley he did not, in fact, show one or both of you the evidence, and that you were convinced that it was authentic—"

"And conclusive," concluded Wm Sultan.

Hastle accepted the conclusion with that polite nod with which one thanks those dear people who speak the "missing" word for you before it is a physical possibility for you to speak it yourself, and Kelly's sense of relief began to evaporate.

"But in either case," he continued to Trumbo Gates and Zolicopher Hay, "each of you stood to *assure* himself of a great sum of money by killing Mr. Attley and removing the evidence in support of Miss Beal's claim—"

"Including the codicil, which would of itself establish a claim," interposed Wm Sultan, as a mother to a child who has forgotten a line of recitation.

Hastle momentarily choked, but smiled and nodded; and Kelly became very worried.

"Including the codicil, which would of itself establish a claim," Hastle repeated dutifully, "before either could reach the hands of Mr. Attley's attorney and executor. In short," he concluded for himself, for once, *"you* both had motive!"

"Per se," said Wm Sultan, and Trumbo Gates rose from his chair.

"Per se," the state's attorney echoed, and by that more than mortal patience Kelly learned, and the knowledge tip-toed with little icy footsteps up and down her spine, that Hastle was playing not with two mice but with three. And as a cold, high wind howled around the nape of her neck, and no place else in that still, green room, she was informed by a dry, a complacent little cough from Wm Sultan that that was exactly what he had set out to learn, and had learned, for himself.

II

Under the late afternoon sun, at Cobb's Mill, on the station platform, Kelly was walking around in circles when a train came in and a redhead stepped out of it, carrying a coat, wearing a skirt, and sprayed with a sweater.

"Where's this Trumbo?" Morgan asked.

Kelly gently took her by the elbow and led her around the corner of the station so that the expressman might return to his truck and the conductor signal to the engineer. Morgan took a look around and her expectant smile faded.

"I don't see him," she said.

"It won't be vice versa," Kelly assured her absently, taking the coat from Morgan's arm and draping it over her shoulders.

"Look, Kelly, I'm warm!" Morgan protested, shrugging it off.

"That," Kelly said, still absently, "is the understatement of the year."

"I don't know," Morgan said doubtfully, "but half the things you're saying don't seem to make sense to me."

"Only half?" Kelly appeared encouraged. "Guess I'm improving. Do you know what I've been doing while waiting for this train? Walking in circles!" She pointed her finger at the station platform. "Around," she said, circling her pointing finger, "and around and around. In circles."

Morgan peered at the indicated terrestrial area with interest.

"Why? Drop a quarter," she asked, "or something?"

She was surprised when she turned to look at Kelly to find that Kelly, with her eyes closed, was sinking down on a bench with its back against the station. Kelly slapped the slatted seat so that a little cloud of the dry October's dust erupted like smoke from an explosion.

"Sit down here!" she invited in such a tone that Morgan sat before the dust could settle. "And," she said, "I'll tell you something about dropping quarters! When I got here this morning . . ." she began. "Close your mouth, Morgan," she concluded.

Morgan opened it again. "Which one did he arrest?"

"Which one," Kelly asked in return and bitterly, "would you arrest?"

Morgan shrugged impatiently, and in the late afternoon sun, so demonstrative of the lights and shadows of texture, the undulation of the knitted contours of her sweater, knit three pearl four, as perceived from behind a grimy window, so stirred the aesthetic sensitivity of the station master that he dropped his stub pen.

"I don't care who we pin it on," she said indifferently, "just so long as it isn't Mr. Sultan."

"Of all the unscrupulous . . ." said Kelly, but as if trying to figure out a way. She shook her head. "Here's the set-up," she stated. "Between Trumbo the Bull and Zolly the Prissy you pays your money and you takes your choice.

Trumbo *could* have hot-footed it back from the garage and waited until Miss Beal—a title which I think that dear, dear! is intending to change as soon as may be, by the way!—Well, he could have waited until she went back into the front hall and then stepped in and been through with the job before Bill entered the study. Or Zolly *could* have managed it the same way by entering the study from the room where he was waiting and on into the bedroom while our dear hand-patting employer and Zenobia—that sweet, sweet!—were still in the hall. Either could have. I think one did. But there's no proof."

"What," Morgan asked shrewdly, "about the butler?"

"I'm sorry," Kelly apologized, "but we ain't got no butler. There's four 'help' in the house. An old codger named Sedgwick and his wife and two fiftyish sisters named Sipley. Soon's supper was over, by cracky, the four of 'em gathered as usual in the 'help's' sittin' room on the third floor a-listenin' to the radio and eatin' cookies and drinkin' hard cider. All they know about last night is that the radio wasn't any good but the cider was."

"Then nobody's in jail at all?" Morgan asked, and as if she thought it was a very odd way to handle a murder. "Everybody's just still running around loose?"

Kelly nodded. "Free as flies. Until the state's attorney picks the one to swat." Her dark eyes were worried. "He's being very cautious, and when he makes an arrest I think it'll stick. I don't think he's overlooking much, and I'm very sure he isn't forgetting those chalk marks on the rug or that quarter under the chair."

Morgan shook her head. "It's too bad Mr. Sultan dropped it," she said.

Kelly jumped to her feet.

"Do you mean to tell me," she demanded, "that you think that *he*—?"

"Oh, Kelly, for goodness' sake, stop worrying!" Morgan protested. "We'll pin it on somebody else."

Kelly closed her eyes.

"That car horn that's been blowing for five minutes," she said numbly, turning towards the sound, "is Mr. Sedgwick, who," she added absently, "is so blind he won't even whistle when he sees you."

"Mr. Sedgwick?" Morgan said, picking up her overnight bag. "I must say, Kelly, I don't think you're managing things very well. Why isn't it this Trumbo? Why waste so much time?"

"This Trumbo," Kelly said dully, leading the way to the car, "does, for one thing, not live at Fairview but in bachelor's quarters of his own about a half mile away. And, for a second thing, This Trumbo is, like everybody else, busy as a little bee getting the estate tied up in a neat little package for the income-tax people and for the surrogate's court. Bill's been down to the Cobb's Mill National Bank this afternoon, which was controlled by Mr. Attley, with Mr. Zolicopher Hay, who was its nominal president, and I've been working my little stenographic fingers to their tender bones, and This Trumbo, who except on days after murders works as an assistant cashier at the bank, has been away somewhere working on this and that, and even dear, dear Zenobia has been working on the inventory of the farm, and, believe it or not, Mata Hari, you're also going to go to work!"

"I thought," Morgan said aggrieved, "that I was going to go to work on Trumbo?"

"That was my idea," said Kelly, and her temper began to dispel her despondency. "But when our dear, sympathetic, hand-patting, simpering employer heard that you were on your way here—I told him that you were bringing up a few little things I'd need to stay the night, and since grandpappy does need me here even he can scarcely expect me to commute on three-hour train rides, when they run—he said, with a cough, how very, very fortunate that you would be here to help Miss Beal, that sweet, sweet!—to make a search through the effects of her late grandparents for some new evidence that they may not have been her true grandparents, he hopes. You see," Kelly continued, and in free-wheeling temper sprung the car door as she opened it, "this calf-eyed little package—and I mean a package, but not little—has had no experience in business or legal matters and wouldn't know what was important and what was not, in fact," Kelly said, and, with a strength that one might not have expected in her petite figure, she tossed in Morgan's overnight bag; so that it bounced from the opposite side of the car into the front seat beside Mr. Sedgwick, "she's just too dang dumb to know one thing from the udder!"

III

Since the death of Zacharia Attley his ancestral acres, had they been located in those equatorial climes favorable to the growth of that lush but sensitive plant whose fruit had founded his fortune, would have traveled some twenty-four thousand miles on the spinning surface of the inevitably dizzy world; but inasmuch as those acres were fixed in the intemperate climate of the north temperate zone where the latitudinal circumference may readily be determined by reference to a globe but is certainly a great deal less than at the equator, those acres and the people upon them had traveled *less* than twenty-four thousand miles in those twenty-four hours but still several thousand miles further than suspected by the state's attorney, who had ordered them not to travel at all.

They were, indeed, even during that very hour, to travel a great deal further towards the end of the world for one of them than suspected by the most of them. The obtuseness of some of them should, perhaps, be excused on the

grounds of fatigue. It has for some time been the general
custom of mankind to go to sleep approximately every six-
teen hours, awakening ever the sadder, never the wiser.

When, Wm Sultan reflected, this period of alleged consciousness is more than twice prolonged it is difficult for
the average man, and he pretended to be no more when it
suited his purpose, to retain an avid interest in figures.
Figures arranged in columns, Morgan was in another room.

He regretted that circumstance, as an employer, since
he found a vicarious pleasure in observing that the sti-
pends with which he rewarded the labors of his staff were
adequate to clothe them in warm woolens of good quality.
As a man who favored tweeds and homespuns he had a
good eye for good wool, and, offhand, he could not recall
ever having seen a better molded fabric than that which
was knit upon his file clerk.

He feared that in this textiliar appreciation Miss Zenobia Beal, bereaved child, was as sensitive as himself, but,
poor penniless waif not yet in possession of three million
dollars, more envious. After all, her simple, low-cut gingham gown which in her innocence she did not realize had
been laundered a few too many times for a shrinking fabric
which could shrink no further, naturally appeared a crude
affair in comparison with those long-wool contours. She
had taken one look and had pleaded fatigue; and, without
waiting even for an early country supper, but only after
a solitary and simple repast in the kitchen, probably of
curds and whey, had retired to slumber in her chamber,
slamming the door.

Even his secretary had appeared to view his viewing
of such superior needlework with a jaundiced eye. Perhaps, Wm Sultan reflected, for most women such a sweater would be an extravagance in its precise meaning of
something more than necessary, or practicable, or capable
of fulfillment, and raising a wearily confused eye to the

comforting precision of his secretary's cameo features—O
Rock of Ages, cleft for me! and he blearily wondered why
that hymn should occur to him—he made a mental note to
raise her salary.

"$8,529," said Kelly wearily.

"$8,529, preferred stock and accrued dividends antici-
pated March 15, '48, Banana Refrigeration Suppression
Co., Ltd.," repeated Wm Sultan and wrote it down.

"That does it," announced his secretary, sprawling a
sheaf of reports on the desk.

Wm Sultan added and said, yawning, "$4,009,687 gross
assets."

Zolicopher Hay pursed his lips. "$4,009,606," he cor-
rected primly.

"81—9—transposition," said Kelly,

There was a long silence and then Zolicopher Hay
rubbed his eyes and said, "I'm very sorry. It was in that
Cobb's Mill Grain & Lumber item of $346,009."

Wm Sultan quietly broke a pencil into three pieces,
tossed two of them on the desk and ate the third. "Liabil-
ities?" he asked through clenched, and blackened, teeth.

"$684,818," Zolicopher Hay offered timidly.

"Check!" checked Kelly.

"Net, $3,214,869, before tax," said Wm Sultan.

"Check!" said his secretary.

Wm Sultan looked grimly at Zolicopher Hay.

"Check," said Zolicopher, without checking.

"Then," said Wm Sultan, "or perhaps I should say 'now'
that we are in agreement on this tentative total, I fail to
see where there is much more that we can do until we hear
from—" He paused thoughtfully as the door of the room
gave the impression of having been kicked open.

It was, Wm Sultan felt, and by every instinct he was
inclined to be more than chivalrous to the feminine gender, a sad commentary upon Emily Post that so few of the

sort who receive their breeding by post, so to speak, like chicks from a hatchery, had been imbued with the instinct of taking their murders with a proper sang-froid or even with calm and becoming decorum. Zolicopher Hay, for instance, had remained in a patently peevish mood ever since he, Wm Sultan, had directed upon him the suspicions of the state's attorney. While Trumbo Gates had even gone so far as to threaten violence, from which he had been dissuaded only by the state's attorney and two state policemen. Wm Sultan had hoped that the intervening hours might have brought to the latter's disturbed disposition a greater degree of composure. He feared, however, that such was not the case when Trumbo Gates followed the door into the room.

Kelly was just plain scared stiff. Had he come storming into the room after having practically torn the door from its hinges, there might not have been time to become frightened or it might have seemed like bluster, but he paused in the doorway while she held her breath and then came slowly and steadily into the room in a direct line to the desk where they were sitting. Wm Sultan was sitting with his back to the door and after a glance over his shoulder at its opening returned his attention to the financial statement he had been preparing.

When Kelly looked at the black-browed face of the man who slowly approached the desk, and Wm Sultan's back, she was transfixed by the capacity and desire for violence she saw on that young and not unhandsome face. Indeed, had it been the face of an older man it would have been less frightening; but with his youth, such rage appeared uncontrollable.

Zolicopher Hay said peevishly, "We've been waiting a quarter of an hour. Eighteen minutes, to be exact. I don't know why you can't be more punctual. Did you finally get arrangements completed with Mr. Swanson?"

Trumbo Gates was looking down at the back of Wm Sultan's head. He flung some papers on the desk and they slid into the lap of his second cousin, once removed.

"There's the dope," he said. "I don't want to spend any time here talking about it," his teeth bared, "or anything else! I have other business to—"

"Trumbo!" said Zolicopher Hay sharply but softly. "Trumbo!" he repeated.

Kelly saw Trumbo Gates slowly, reluctantly turn his head, and for the first time since he had entered the room his eyes left Wm Sultan.

Zolicopher Hay's lips flattened in prim martyrdom against his teeth, but his spectacled eyes, raised to the face of the younger man, were steady and commanding.

"I think my wishes deserve some consideration from you," he said. "Good night, Trumbo."

Trumbo Gates turned from the desk so that he did not face Wm Sultan as he turned and strode from the room. When he stopped in the doorway as if shot Kelly did not need to know what had happened. But, being of that feminine gender known for its cat-like qualities—such as curiosity—she did look; and she saw Morgan's sweater go out the front door to the porch and she saw Trumbo follow, not instantly, but not slowly once he got under way.

Zolicopher Hay nervously examined the papers in his lap. "Sometimes I fear I've been too lenient," he said pettishly. "But," he sighed, "he's young, and when I think what I went through with Mr. Attley when I was young . . ." He shook his head. "Young men are so bull-headed."

Kelly said kindly, "I'll buy him if I ever get a pampa." She attracted her employer's attention with an arching brow. "What's the address of this Banana Pioneers Association?"

Zolicopher Hay said, "321—or is it 312?—" and Wm Sultan opened an address book that was on the desk. He turned to "B." He read:

Banana Pioneers Ass—
Bureau of Documentary Certification . . .

After a moment, a long moment, he coughed and returned his eyes to the initial line and read aloud the address for Kelly.

Zolicopher Hay was nervously pleating a sheet of paper
in his fingers at which he would glance doubtfully, and
then look away and think, and then glance again.

"Well," he said doubtfully, "everything seems to be tak-
en care of." He passed the sheet of paper across the desk
to Wm Sultan. "The funeral arrangements," he explained.

Wm Sultan ironed out the pleats and read:

Swanson promises to meet all trains up to the
10:30 the day after tomorrow. I've insisted
that the services at the family cemetery be not
later than 11:30—so I suspect they may actually take place not later than 12:30. Casket
as ordered by Zack. Mausoleum as ordered by
Zack. Mourners, as ordered by Zack:

Car 1—You and I.
Car 2—Dear Zenobia.
Car 3—Sedgwick and Sipleys.
Car 4—What's left of farm help.
Car 5—Banana Pioneers Association, if any
    have answered your telegrams.
Car 6—Mr. Sultan (and any of the dames who
    work for him, I suppose).
Car 7—Cobb's Mill National Bank stooges.
Car 8— " " " " "
Car 9— " " Grain & Lumber Co. yes-men.

From here on, to stop making enemies, we can let them straighten it out privately and without making any acknowledgment of any-body's claim for precedence.

All for tonight, see you tomorrow—if not in jail—

Trumbo.

"Now, Mr. Sultan," said Zolicopher Hay, rubbing his eyes, "in regard to those International Fruit Company Debentures . . ."

A half hour later, Kelly yawned ostentatiously when, at last, she heard a car depart, and said, "I'm sleep-happy." With that explanation she rose and she departed, not neglecting to close the door behind her. It was nice timing and she met Morgan as Morgan entered the door from the porch. Kelly took her firmly by the arm and shook some of the stars from her eyes.

"Learn anything?" she whispered.

Morgan nodded. "Practically everything."

Kelly's fingers tightened. "What did he tell you?"

"What?"

"What," and Kelly's fingers scraped the bone, "did you talk about? What did he tell you?"

"I," said Morgan, moving towards the stairs, the light of the Aurora Borealis in her green eyes, "told him the story of my life."

6

The ages-long and once universal custom of stabbing, strangling, stoning or otherwise doing to death the bearer of ill tidings may have been a little rigorous, although this conclusion has been questioned in reference to gossips and the eager friends of a friend's misfortune, but, for good or ill, it has in the last few centuries fallen into such general disuse that it seldom enters the expectations of a Western Union boy bringing advance notice of a visit by relatives. On the other hand, the one not holding a dagger, the bearer of good tidings may still expect a larger tip.

Roberts had, therefore, the custom of centuries behind her in her anticipation of a joyous welcome at Fairview Farms, and she was pleasantly entertained during her train ride by little imaginary scenes of grateful joy flitting past her car window. At least she was certain that a mere peccadillo such as her having closed up the office, leaving it unattended except for the Telephone Answering Service, would be overlooked and even commended. Since when an excuse to take a holiday presents itself it is ever wiser just to take it instead of giving someone else a chance to think of some way to do you out of it, Roberts had not committed the folly of telephoning before she had caught the ten o'clock train. This business of being left on the bench, so to speak, while the rest of the team were playing on the field, was one which Roberts' conscience had, without a qualm, assured her that she could do no wrong in righting.

The assurance of custom and of conscience were given a favorable omen when she alighted, virtually alone, and within two minutes stood alone, on the station platform of Cobb's Mill looking in vain for that passenger pigeon of the city streets, a yellow taxi. She was approached by a sepulchral man in black who smiled sadly.

"A guest of the late Mr. Attley?" he asked.

Roberts nodded, and smiled to herself. Despite the trick costume and manner this country cabbie was as much on the beam as his cousin cabbies in the city who could with unerring eye pick just the right place to suggest to the out-of-towner poised indecisively in front of Penn Station.

The Cobb's Mill Charon conducted her to a black seven-passenger cab that, oddly enough, reminded Roberts of her Uncle Robert's funeral. By the time he had taken his seat behind the wheel Roberts had observed that there was no meter in the cab.

"How much?" she asked succinctly.

"That," sighed the sepulchral man with a Lugosi smile, "has all been taken care of. There will be no charge."

Roberts returned his smile. She had also been offered free cab rides in Li'l Old.

"O.K. bub," she said cheerfully, removing a long cut-glass vase from a holder, and the knobbed blackjack balanced nicely in her hand, "but the first wrong stop you make will be your last."

II

Let a man who hates mountains and hates traveling be informed that he may not take a trip to Tibet, reflected Wm
Sultan, and he will begin to feel so hemmed in that the
rest of the world will seem a confinement. For a quarter
of a century, Wm Sultan estimated, Zolicopher Hay had
resented his every and infrequent departure from the vicinity of Cobb's Mill, and for the same twenty-five years he
had looked upon the yellow brick manor that stood upon
the acres of Fairview Farms as a reasonable approximation
of heaven upon earth. And yet such was the effect of a hint
by the state's attorney that any departure by him from the
jurisdiction of the State would be officially circumvented,
that those marble (yellow brick) halls (walls) were beginning to afflict him, observed Wm Sultan, with claustrophobia. He also, no doubt from some weakness in his nervous
constitution, found his digestion impaired by the fact that
he was, with his cousin, one of the two principal suspects in
a murder. Wm Sultan shrewdly surmised this from a *burp*.

It was this later complex which caused Zolicopher Hay,
an hour after the completion of a noonday country dinner, to toss aside some financial statements and to rise
from the desk where he had been reading them. It was
the former sense of claustrophobia, in the opinion of Wm
Sultan, which caused him, more than any desire to view
the ambient countryside, to step out of the house and to
pace up and down the front porch like a tiger in its cage,
but unlike a tiger or other of the essentially sane animals,
reflected Wm Sultan, he was a man and did not need bars
for his confinement.

He, Wm Sultan, quit work and went outside for entirely different reasons, which were simply that he wanted
some fresh air and felt a little restless. The circumstance
that his secretary had joined his file clerk and Miss Zenobia Beal after lunch in the tenant residence of the latter's

late alleged grandparents had nothing to do with it. He, of
all men, was not a man to miss feminine companionship.

The tenant house, at present occupied by a man who
was the successor of Miss Beal's late father, and his wife,
occupied the usual position of a farmhouse in relation to
the farm buildings, and it was merely by chance that Wm
Sultan decided that a stroll to the farmyard would be of
a proper length to settle his luncheon. He coughed, to
demonstrate to himself that his throat was raw from cigarette smoke and that he needed a breather of the refreshing salubriousness of the rural atmosphere, so fragrant of
the autumn countryside, the fair agricultural fields bearing four tons per acre of fresh manure.

Those fields so fertile of stones some few of which had
been laid into picturesque walls, locally called fences,
gave, he reflected, to the New England landscape a rugged coziness that has ever been its peculiar and strongly
comforting charm. Houses, he reflected, were peculiarly
appropriate to such a landscape, and he cocked an eye at
the attic window of the tenant house.

Zenobia Beal turned from that window, by whose light
she had been examining a shawl exhumed from her grandmother's trunk, and observing that Morgan and Kelly were
busily engaged in discussing something of more importance, she slipped downstairs without interrupting them
by any explanation of her departure. She had a sudden desire to take a look at the barn when she emerged from the
house, and with no more than one glance in the mirror of
her compact to make sure that she was being followed she
returned that useful reflector to the pocket of her gingham
gown and continued on her innocent and lonely way.

Wm Sultan was touched when he saw the dairyman's
daughter who, unaware of his presence, walked ahead of
him with her head slightly bowed under the loss of three

million dollars. She turned into the doorway of a low structure that projected from one end of the barn and behind which rose two huge concrete silos. Following, but at a dignified pace, Wm Sultan found himself in an enclosed passage with a closed door to the barn. Two protuberant arcs in the wall indicated the position of the silos. At each the iron rung of a ladder went up into a dark hole in the roof which must be the beginning of the concrete tube which his attentive eye had observed from without ran to the top of either silo. Beneath one of these holes there now rested a cart and from out of the hole and into the cart there was falling a steady non-liquid rain of what his logical mind instantly deduced was hay, fodder or other nutritious sustenance from the silo. Standing with her back towards him, silently observing this fall of cow-manna from heaven, was the daughter of that dairyman who had departed this life in company with his unknown mother while on their mutual and ill-fated way to a Holstein auction. It was a touching scene.

Wm Sultan was, again, touched. But, manfully eschewing bathos, he felt that the best small service which he could render to the lately bereaved daughter and granddaughter, the so recently bereaved great-granddaughter, was to assume a cheerful mien and speak the cheerful word. He was, but only momentarily, given pause by what might be the most proper and fortuitous word of salutation to a young bucolic female in her natural environment.

"Hay, hay?" said Wm Sultan with a witty little chuckle.

"Why, no," replied Zenobia Beal, "for roughage we prefer corn silage. You see, on the storage basis alone a cubic foot of long hay in the mow contains only about 4.2 pounds of dry matter, while the same unit measure of silage amounts to 10.7 to 11.3 dry matter."

Wm Sultan coughed modestly in advance. "Rather a dry matter, isn't it?" he said, again wittily.

"Oh, no," replied Zenobia Beal, "even with its high moisture content, on total weight three pounds corn silage equal one pound good hay, net dry weight basis."

Wm Sultan realized perfectly well that he could not be becoming confused by such a typically simple rustic occupation as feeding cows, but he was beginning to feel that way.

"Or another way of looking at it," said Zenobia Beal, putting her head on one side and thoughtfully watching the silage fall, "is that one ton of corn silage has the equivalent value—for dairy cows—of 4.6 bushels of corn and 270 pounds of mixed hay."

"Ah, yes, yes, yes, yes," said Wm Sultan.

"Of course it must be remembered," she continued warningly, "that while cows have eaten as much as 60 pounds c.s. per 1,000 live weight—" and Wm Sultan winced at such tautology because obviously a dead weight cow was not interested in eating—"you *must* remember that their mineral and vitamin needs must be adequately met by supplementing the silage with suitable compounds!"

"I assuredly will," said Wm Sultan. He was beginning to eye the cart nervously. It was almost full.

"Where corn silage," Zenobia Beal said lovingly, "forms most or all of the roughage it's desirable to use a comparatively high protein feed for the concentrate mixture. While of course there are many, a very simple and satisfactory formula to remember is that a 24 per cent grain mixture can be made by using ground corn 360 pounds, ground oats 280 pounds, wheat bran 250 pounds, corn distillers grains 640 pounds, either linseed or soybean oil meal—according," her voice hardened, "to price—400 pounds, iodized rock salt 20 pounds, ground limestone 20 pounds, and dicalcium phosphate 20 pounds!"

Wm Sultan nodded absently. "Hadn't you better call up to whoever's heaving this down?" he asked, indicating the full cart. "There must be enough in the air now—"

But at that moment there was a click from a gadget on the wall, a distant hum of machinery ceased and the shower of silage ceased.

"An automatic unloader," Zenobia Beal explained. "You set the hydraulic winch for the amount of silage you want and a time clock starts and stops it automatically. On a man-hour basis, and amortization at ten years, the investment will show a return of—" her voice broke. "The Holstein herd," she gulped, "was sold off by Mr. Attley after Miss Zenobia and my father were killed going to the Holstein auction. There are only," she sobbed, "just a few left for me to remember him by!" She shook her head. "Oh, Mr. Sultan," she said, "as you can see I'm just a simple country girl and I don't know what I would do if I didn't have you to depend upon!" And with a little choked sniffle she crouched against him.

"Well, now, a-hem, a-hem, a-hem!" said Wm Sultan modestly, and he comfortingly patted her trembling shoulder. To be exact, he patted it twice before his hand froze out in the middle of the air as his eyes met those, and they were blue, and one of them winked, of an employee standing in the doorway.

"Well, Bossy!" Roberts greeted him gaily. "And how'd you like a codicil?" She held an envelope out to him.

III

Zenobia Beal's departure from the attic had not passed unobserved.

"Now I wonder," Kelly said, "where that little heifer is sneaking off to?"

"Oh, Kelly, for goodness' sakes!" protested Morgan. "Don't stop, this is *important!*"

"Yeah," Kelly agreed absently, and resumed work.

"I simply can't believe it yet!" Morgan declared.

Kelly shook her head. "Neither can I," she agreed, fastening the last of the hooks and eyes. "*Those* women had to be laced to get in one of these things. And padded up above to fill 'em out," she added as Morgan pirouetted.

"I simply," Morgan announced again, flouncing her bustle, "can't believe it! To think that her *grandmother* had the New Look!"

But Kelly was not looking. Kelly was looking towards the window with narrowed eyes. "I wonder," she wondered, "if that little homogenized milkshaker saw something? Or someone," she added, and went decisively to the window. She jumped back a foot.

"Roberts!" she cried, and tore down the stairs.

Morgan tore after her, but she did not, precisely, tear down the stairs. To be precise, she tried to walk inside the hem of her skirt and bumped down the stairs on her bustle. On, or at, the landing, she took a deep breath and exhaled it from puffed and florid cheeks to blow disarrayed curls of red hair out of her, momentarily, red eyes. To make up for lost time she did tear down the hall to the head of the flight of stairs to the ground floor, and at the foot of the flight of stairs she again rose from her bustle, again blew hair out of her eyes, and in a temper as red as that anatomical attribute exaggerated by the bustle, she tore for the barn.

She did not fail to observe that Mr. Sultan and Miss Zenobia Beal were walking towards the residence of the late Zacharia Attley, but Kelly was approaching Roberts, who was awaiting her at a doorway of the barn, and it was to them that Morgan tore. Since she was now holding the New Look some inches above her knees she did not fall, even once. Whether she breathed deeply, or expanded centrally, with exertion, there was a constriction about her waist which constrained her to listen a moment before finding breath to speak.

". . . came in this morning's mail!" Roberts was saying happily. "Bossy's gone in to call the state's attorney or whatever he is so he can be here when it's opened. Well! I guess this will show that hayseed Hawkshaw that there was nothing phony about this codicil biz!"

Morgan knew that she was red, but she observed that Kelly was quite white from her run downstairs and across the farmyard.

"Hi, Morgan!" Roberts continued gaily, and whistled. "Holey Hudson Tubes," she exclaimed, looking Morgan down, "who's the Cobb's Mill *couturière?*" Then she looked Morgan up, and whistled again. "Ba-bee!" she said. "You're foaming out of that like a strawberry ice-cream soda!"

Kelly was looking after the retreating figure of Wm Sultan. "No," she said faintly, "you can't have brought it. You can't mean it."

Long and blond, Roberts took a complacent stance, like something in *Vogue.* "I not only mean it," she said, and winked a blue eye, "but I know what's in it!"

Kelly grasped her arm. *"What?"*

Roberts' blue eyes were looking towards the tenant house, from which had just emerged the spouse of that dairyman who had succeeded if not replaced the father of Zenobia Beal.

"Unless we scram," she said sotto-voce, "we're going to have company."

"In here!" Kelly said, and pulled her through the doorway, Morgan following. "How," Kelly demanded, "do you know?"

The door from the barn opened and a pleasant-looking middle-aged man entered. Seeing them, he smiled pleasantly. He started to move the hand truck of silage and then looking Morgan up he swallowed, and still smiling pleasantly, did not move the hand truck.

"Hello," said Morgan politely.

"Hello," said Kelly coldly.

"I think your wife's looking for you," said Roberts.

And, with a sigh, the man stopped smiling and pushed the hand truck into the barn.

"Grand Central Station," muttered Roberts, and looking around for some more private place spotted the ladder. "Up!" she said, and, virtually with the word, her long blond legs took her out of sight.

Knowing Roberts when Roberts was on the move, Kelly did not waste time in protest but followed as fast as she could. Morgan also saved what breath she had for climbing, which turned out to be just as well, and foamed up the iron rungs after them. If Roberts were surprised, once she was under way and her eyes adjusted to the gloom above, to find that the ladder did not simply lead to a room above the one which they had been in but was like a ladder up the inside of a high chimney, she was, of all of her sex, the last to turn back on any course of action once undertaken. Like a moth to the flame, she flew upwards towards the light at the top.

Her athletic extremities tingled pleasantly under the stimulus of exercise, and in contrast to the emotions of those below, she thoroughly enjoyed herself, spurred on by a sense of accomplishment, like a mountaineer on his first peak. This was her first silo. She felt an instinctive affinity with, and understanding of, the structure. She recalled its aspect from without; a round tower with a tube running up the side; and now, deep in its secrets, she comprehended that that tube must be the one enclosing the ladder on which she so nimbly mounted that her companions' curses were now only a murmur, as of a distant mob, far below. The rungs of the ladder were set in a vertical nitch in the concrete wall, reminding her of a crevasse in a glacier, and she perceived that behind the iron rungs were wooden doors one above the other. With this, observation she understood the aperture at the top of the silo from which a spout projected as if looking down at her.

Attaining that aperture she found as she had anticipated that the doors from that point up had been removed, giving access to the silo proper. The interior of the silo, as illuminated by the skylight of its conical roof, was some eighteen feet in diameter and was completely straddled by an evil-looking mechanical spider whose arching tail, like that of a scorpion, terminated in the spout that projected into the tube enclosing the ladder.

Roberts hopped down some three feet to the level of the silage and found that while it was fairly firm from the tons of pressure which once had pressed upon it from above it was a damp and slippery footing. She sat down on one of the radial booms that formed the legs of the mechanical spider and was quite refreshed by the time that Kelly and Morgan stood in panting expectation before her. Roberts rose to the occasion.

"When the letter came this morning," she began, sludging back and forth before them from the body of the spider to the wall of the silo, her hands clasped behind her and her head thrown back, "it occurred to me," and she coughed modestly, "that I had better ascertain if the envelope in fact contained what might be hoped for from the return address and name upon the exterior of cover. I forbore," she continued, taking a long stride and skidding slightly, "from jumping to—"

But her succeeding words were drowned out when all hell broke loose. The spider gave a *whirring* growl and filling its lungs with a great *whoosh* of air began to spin around in the silo.

"Jump!" yelled Roberts, but too late; and one of the boomlike legs swept against Morgan's bustle and laid her like a rug. Kelly's petite figure, with unexpected alacrity, went straight up in the air and she came down again on her feet just in time to go up again to escape another boom on its scythe-like sweep. Roberts cleared both easily, in her stride, so to speak, and plucked Morgan from her prostrate position as a silage-scraping boom with curved teeth swept upon her. She tossed Morgan over a following boom and Morgan, displaying a fine instinct of self-preservation landed like a cat on her feet with the New Look safely tucked around her waist. Roberts was surprised and relieved to observe that despite her quite unusually shapely legs Morgan could jump like a kitten.

"Hey!" Roberts yelled at Kelly, who was tearing around the silo like a circus horse in a ring, overtaking and leaping everything in her path. "No—sense—chasing—'em!" she shouted, and grabbed Kelly's arm as Kelly whizzed past. Kelly was swung to a stop just in time to leap for her life.

Spinning on its booms, the spider breathed like a furnace, its wicked teeth skimming the silage towards its voracious mouth, its breath discharging the shredded result through the arching tail that emptied into the tube enclosing the ladder. Three abreast, like a trio of hurdlers in a dead heat, Kelly, Morgan and Roberts cleared each passing boom.

Above the *whooshing* roar of the mechanical Araneida, above the sibilance of its slicing teeth, Roberts reported:

"Went down to the drugstore" (*jump*) "had a pot of tea" (*jump*) "teapots steam, you know" (*jump and leer*) "opened it up and" (*jump*) "there it was—the codicil!" (*jump*).

Kelly gasped, "What terms?" (*jump*).

But Roberts' attention had been distracted by that very jump of Kelly's and the simultaneous jump of Morgan. As another boom swept upon them and her own legs rose with the rest she was conscious of the fine athletic rhythm and precision of their performance.

"You know, I don't know," she said, with a jump, "why they don't use" (*jump*) "this in the A.A.U. track meets."

"What," demanded Kelly through clenched teeth, and jumping badly, her white-faced thoughts on something else, "were the terms!"

"Fifty thousand to Trumbo," Roberts replied, her blond legs clearing the passing hurdle with grace and *élan*, "one hundred thousand to" (*another clearance*) "Zolicopher, and all the" (*a wide hurdle this, first the teeth then close-following a higher boom*) "rest, residuary or what you" (*jump*) "call it, to Zenobia!"

"Oh, no, no," said Kelly, and her foot caught a boom.

Roberts snatched her up as she fell, swung her over the next hurdle and jumped beside her, grinning.

"And," Roberts announced joyfully, "here's the pay-off!" (*jump*) "He makes Bossy her executor" (*jump, and again she had to steady Kelly*) "until she's thirty!" (*Kelly sagged on this jump*) "And he leaves Bossy" (*she swung Kelly over the hurdle*) "a cool fifty thousand dollars!"

The spider, as suddenly as it had become alive, became dead wood and steel. The three young female persons jumped once more in rhythm after it was motionless.

"Now," Roberts demanded with the proper pride of a bearer of glad tidings, "ain't that something!"

"It certainly is," Kelly agreed, white-faced and swaying, "it's practically a warrant for Bill's arrest for murder."

Morgan, who had completely foamed out of her New Look at the top, collapsed upon her bustle.

7

*The Imminent Arrest of an Advocate. Two
Cousins and a Codicil. Fraud, Collusion! Trial
Before Jury. Taps on a Window Pane. The Anger of
an Advocate and the Surprise of a State's Attorney.*

Now that it had become obvious to all in the green parlor
that his arrest for murder was only a matter of time, perhaps a very few minutes of time, Wm Sultan was, secretly,
delighted at the expressions of suffering concern which he
saw upon the faces of his staff. He did not misinterpret it.
He was not so fatuously ridiculous, he hoped, as to imagine
that such a dry stick as himself could inspire the romantic
sentiments of such a singularly attractive young person
of the opposite—ah—gender as, for instance, Kelly. But,
as an employer, his pulse did quicken at his secretary's
white-faced anxiety for him as it reflected so favorably
upon his labor relationships. He coughed complacently.

And his sympathy went out to that other member of his
personnel who had so unwittingly and with such enthusiasm been the messenger of his misfortune. He found it as
an employer very gratifying to see that Roberts, that receptionist who to his very face bearded him with the flip-
pant appellation of "Bossy" now, in her remorse, looked as

if she had been run over by a truck—or Kelly and Morgan. He coughed sympathetically.

And last but not least, in that resilient sweater of long-wearing wool far from least, was his file clerk. The green color of that most excellently knitted wool matched, incidentally, Morgan's green eyes; and in those eyes there was a crystal tear. He recalled that the late Horace Seneca Sultan, who had admitted that his understanding of women was virtually if not practically complete, had once advised him, "That whenever you see a tear in a woman's eye, m'boy, kiss it away—with the point of a clean bleached *linen* handkerchief." But, as a suspected and nearly arrested murderer, Wm Sultan felt that such a service would be a little presumptuous of him. He coughed regretfully.

State's Attorney Hastle said, "Well, Mr. Hay?"

Zolicopher Hay put down that codicil which, with Trumbo Gates, he had read again and yet again. He more precisely centered his glasses upon his nose. His lips flattened over his teeth in his habitually petulant expression, and then, oddly enough that expression went away and was replaced by one of firm and considered resolution. In the course of this transformation, and it took more than a few seconds, he had kept his gaze fixed upon the rosebuds in the green carpet. He raised his eyes, by chance to Morgan's green sweater, and with a slight shake of his head, as a man momentarily distracted, met the pouncing eyes of the state's attorney.

"I do not," he said with quiet resolution, "question that this was written by Mr. Attley and expressed exactly his intentions at the time that he wrote it." He deliberately turned his eyes to Zenobia Beal, who sat on the sofa like the cream on the top of a pan of milk. "But," he continued, skimming it, "the terms of this codicil are preposterously unfair. When I began to manage Mr. Attley's affairs he had less than a million and a half. The estate has grown to three. He was aware of that service on my part. The only possible explanation of this codicil was that it was written under such emotional stress that he was in effect out of his mind."

Zolicopher Hay again, if unnecessarily, centered his glasses, drawing his thumb and forefingers down the bows and hard behind his ears.

"Mr. Attley was eighty-six years of age," he resumed. "For the past seven years he has not so much as checked his own bank account. He has," and again the lips flattened, "been living in the past with his bananas."

State's Attorney Hastle could not repress a smile as he reflected *what* a witness this would make in his effect on a jury! Even the final persuasion of honesty that lies in unconscious humor.

"I do not pretend," Zolicopher Hay continued, "that Mr. Attley was personally fond of me. I know that he felt greatly bereft and alone after the death of his daughter last year. I know that there was nothing on this earth that he would have so much desired as a direct descendant. I think that he would have wanted so much to believe in the truth of any 'evidence' of such a descendant that he would have—for a time—accepted anything resembling such evidence without question. But—"

Zolicopher Hay removed his glasses and stared defiantly at the vague world with his short-sighted eyes. "But," he repeated defiantly, "in the absence of any evidence that such a relationship did in fact exist, I am with my cousin going to contest this will on the grounds of fraud."

"Get that—shyster!" Trumbo Gates flung out.

State's Attorney Hastle said quietly, "That will be all for the present, Mr. Gates and Mr. Hay."

The truculent young man, the resolute older man, rose and left the room. Kelly, Morgan and Roberts exchanged a quick, sick glance. It was coming now, they knew.

"When I entered this case," Hastle said quietly, reflec-
tively, and it was more frightening than if he snarled, "and
learned that there was some talk of Mr. Attley changing his
will, that a new heir may have been discovered, it seemed
to me that motives for murdering him were likely to be a
little too common to be of much use. Like when a bank's
robbed, or a chicken coop."

He stood with his back to the room, looking out the
window at a golden maple that in that warm October still
held a glory of leaves.

"And so," he continued, "I went ahead on the basis of,
'Well, let's find who *did* do this—and it won't be much
trouble finding his motive.' Going ahead on that basis I
did uncover a case of circumstantial evidence," he said,
still not turning from the window, "against you, Mr. Sultan, that was, and is, as complete and damning as possible
under the circumstances of the crime. That case is," and
he tapped off the points with his finger upon the windowpane, a drumbeat that was peculiarly nerve-wracking, "that
you had the knowledge and capability to inflict death in
the manner in which it was inflicted. That, having done
so, you dragged the body into the bedroom, but that, the
door of the bedroom already being open, you failed to
notice that the arc of the door would not clear the feet of
the corpse. Thirdly, that that being your first visit to this
house, and having arrived at night, and the moon not yet
up, you threw open the wrong window for the 'escape' of
your fictitious 'murderer.' And to complete the case . . ."

The tapping on the windowpane was suddenly metallic.
Hastle turned, and there was a quarter between his thumb
and forefinger. He bounced it in his hand, returned it to
his pocket.

Kelly closed her eyes. She could see him doing that in
front of a jury. And that, she suddenly realized, was what

Hastle was doing. He was giving a pre-trial of his case before a jury that was prejudiced in favor of the defendant. If he could impress this jury he need have no fear about the other one. And she had only to look at Roberts' and Morgan's faces to see how the case was going. And Zenobia . . . Zenobia looked about ready to confess.

"Ah, yes, yes, yes, yes," said Wm Sultan, in evident agreement of his guilt, "but yesterday there was no demonstrable motive and there was—" he wagged a bony finger towards Hastle's trouser pocket—"on the other side of the coin, if I may coin a phrase!" and, as usual, he gave his quiet little coughing chuckle at his devastating wit, "on the other side of the coin," he repeated, in case anyone had missed it, "there *was* a plausible explanation of my otherwise somewhat implausible story."

When Hastle nodded in agreement to this, to her, astonishing assertion, Kelly began to form a low opinion of her own intelligence.

"But both those situations have been reversed," he said, "by the arrival at your office of this codicil." He had been holding the envelope with its single scribbled page in his left hand since he had taken it from Zolicopher Hay on his departure from the room. "From the start," he said, evidently reading the codicil through the envelope, and Kelly could again see him in front of that other jury, "it's been clear that your motive—"

"Expectation of profit," Wm Sultan suggested helpfully.

"That your expectation of profit," Hastle repeated with dangerous alacrity, "must have as its basis a collusion with Miss Beal. This codicil," and again he looked at it through the envelope, "is the perfect basis of such a collusion. Aside from a little bequest of fifty thousand dollars for having been instrumental in the discovery of his great-granddaughter, you gain control of the fortune for nine years. While Miss Beal is the eventual residuary legatee. But whether she expected to be or was a party to murder I greatly doubt."

Zenobia Beal vigorously shook her head in denial, and had any one of the three members of Wm Sultan's staff had her hands upon it it would have continued to spin all the way around again and again like a top. Murder, at times, seems quite moral.

"This envelope is postmarked yesterday," said Hastle, looking up from it. "Yesterday! From the start," he continued, "I was impressed by the oddity that neither Mr. Hay nor Mr. Gates was told that the letter had actually been written until after Mr. Sedgwick had taken to the village the mail habitually left upon the hall table. They were not to be given any chance to take such a letter and to go in to Mr. Attley and demand a showdown then and there! That's why Miss Beal held it out—and gave it to you—and you posted it when you went to the Cobb's Hill bank yesterday!"

Roberts and Morgan, Kelly saw, could no longer look at anybody, and particularly not at Wm Sultan. Kelly looked at Wm Sultan. She saw him flicking a bony finger at the lobe of his ear, the one that was a mite deaf.

Hastle shook his head, spoke with what seemed a sincere reluctance.

"Mr. Sultan," he said, "I've not failed to make inquiries about you and the firm of Sultan, Sultan & Sultan. Believe it or not, I usually try to satisfy my own conscience as to the guilt of a man before making an arrest, but I'll not pretend that I may not have moved even more cautiously than usual in the present instance. Common decency in the consideration of a man's good name to one side, I've been given a rough idea of what I may expect if I *unjustifiably* bring public disrepute upon what I've been informed in no uncertain terms is one of the oldest, and in its chosen branch of the law, one of the most honored legal names in America. Good heavens, Julius Wm Petronius Sultan on *Codicils* is as standard as Rivers & Reeves on *Conveyances!*"

Kelly saw his face become decisive and, although he was an enemy, strangely likeable.

"As an example of what I may expect if I make a mistake," he said, without animus, "two hours after I made my inquiries through official and presumably secret channels, I received a call from the senior partner of the most quietly powerful legal firm in this state. Goodfleece & Warp."

"Ah, yes, yes, yes, yes," said Wm Sultan, looking at Morgan.

"He had just called me up," Hastle continued, "to let me know that he hoped that I was not making a mistake because it seems that the most powerful newspaper chain in this state happens to be controlled by the trustees of the Peabody Pitkins Estate, and it seems that those trustees happen to be an old firm of estate attorneys the senior partner of which seems to have been an associate of Sultan's since his birth and is one of your fellow members in the Codicil Club, one Waldo Wickerworker."

Roberts slapped her thigh. "Good old Bull's Meat!" she cried.

"For men," sniffled Morgan, blinking a tear.

Hastle was not distracted.

"But I'm not making a mistake!" he said, advancing from the window with his short, fighter's steps. "Because the 'other side of the coin' no longer exists! It no longer exists because this codicil—" he shot it forward in his hand like a blow—"removes any possible motive from either Mr. Hay or Mr. Gates! It leaves only one man with the motive and the opportunity!"

He had been crouched forward like a weaving boxer. He slowly straightened. He stood in an impressive, official dignity.

"William Sultan," he said, "I arrest—"

Wm Sultan coughed. It was initially a violent cough that drowned out words but ended on a note like that of an uncle to a favorite but erring nephew whom he would save from the embarrassment of committing further folly in public.

"Amusingly enough," he said, "if you'll flip that alleged piece of silver again I think you'll find that 'the other side of the coin is face up.' Heads, you know," he explained, delighted with his pun, "face up!"

White-faced now in anger, Hastle started to speak, but Wm Sultan rose. He rose like a series of articulated angles with an abruptness that caused the two state police within the room to take a half step forward and then he walked to the window with an aloof composure that kept them standing where they were. He opened the window. He put his head out the window. He took a deep breath of the autumnal and manural air, he took one and closed the window. There was an expression in his eyes which his wide-eyed staff had never seen before and which they did not understand, but which the two state police instinctively understood because they put their hands on their revolvers. His staff did not understand why each quiet word he spoke sounded as if he were slapping Hastle in the face.

"Up to a point," Wm Sultan said, "virtuous obtuseness is tolerably amusing. But if the reflection of your halo upon the lenses of your glasses blinds you to the obvious, permit me to remind you of it. As you very well know, my account of what transpired while I awaited Mr. Attley in his study is entirely consistent with the logical and even inevitable course of action of a murderer familiar either by hearsay or experience with my previous condition of servitude."

He profoundly hoped that his staff could not deduce from this his indecorous military experience, and his hope was justified.

"Your explanation of the postmark upon the cover containing the codicil," he continued, "a holograph codicil, not requiring witnesses, entirely legal and I assure you quite incontestable, is if not inane at least untenable before the claims of a tenant who removed that cover from the table in the hall, who examined the contents, who determined upon murder, who committed murder, who then yesterday found himself under unbearable suspicion, and to protect his life mailed the codicil."

Hastle, who had unconsciously been backing away from him, came to a stop.

"And disinherited himself!" he countered.

"Since you're a public official," said Wm Sultan, "I've assumed that you knew that a convicted murderer or accessory cannot inherit from his victim. Consequently, if Miss Beal should be convicted she would inherit nothing regardless of the provisions of this codicil. Obviously, the reason the real murderer has surrendered this codicil is in the expectation that it will lead to such a conviction. Therefore, since I must spell it out to you, far from disinheriting himself he has not endangered his financial interests at all!"

"A very pretty theory," Hastle said furiously. "But try to prove it!"

"Since Miss Beal knew what Zacharia Attley had written," Wm Sultan said, "do you want to tell a jury that she would have to open the envelope to learn what had been written? Or, since she would tell me, that I would?" He paused to give the questions time to sink in and be absorbed. Hastle's face set in that expressionless expression of the courtroom fighter whose instinct tells him that he is going to take one on the chin. "You've asked me to prove my theory," Wm Sultan said. "If you'd take the trouble to look at your exhibit, Mr. State's Attorney, as I have, you'd find it already proven!" Hastle looked at the envelope.

"Turn it over!" Hastle turned it over. "As you can see," said Wm Sultan, "it's been steamed open!"

"My God . . ." said Hastle, seeing.

Kelly looked at Morgan and Morgan looked at Roberts and Roberts looked at Kelly; and for the first time since the silo they smiled—with thinned tight lips. Very tight.

8

*A Departure Under the Stars. An Assignation in a
Parlor. A Barrister in a Bedroom. Feminine Instinct.
An Appointment in a Graveyard. Strange Instructions.
Roberts! A Piece of Black Thread. A Tiptoe in a Hallway.*

Under the stars, at Cobb's Mill, on the station platform,
three young female persons were walking in circles when
the rails began to hum with an approaching train. It was a
low hum at first, a nervous vibration more felt than heard
above the gritty crunching of the packed gravel under the
soles of their shoes.

"Mr. Sultan won't like this," said Morgan, as her arc
crossed that of Kelly.

"Mr. Sultan won't like being hung for murder," prophe-
sied Kelly, swinging away, and the tension of her voice was
like that of the now audible expectation of the rails of the
rushing wheels of the coming train.

"So he won't like this, so what can he do about it,"
pronounced, not questioned, Roberts, crossing their or-
bits, and there was something steadying in her athlete's
simple concern with physical facts and definite acts. So it
was only a station platform and not a crucial separation;
so that humming, quickening drumbeat in the air was only
the vibration of so many tons of metal hurtling on its

restricted path through the night, and not some disquiet-
ing portent of events rushing towards an unknown destination in an obscure future.

"He's going to think it awful funny," Morgan's obstinate
muttering came from the backswing of her earthbound or-
bit, "that we didn't discover that we didn't have enough
money for more than *one* ticket until we got here, but that
we *did* discover it just in time to have Mr. Sedgwick wait
to take Roberts and me back to the farm."

"So he thinks it's funny, so let him laugh," said Roberts, generously.

The waiting rails were brushed with quicksilver, antici-
pating by yet more than two hours the rising of the belated moon, and in the brightening gleam of the locomotive
headlight the three who had been pacing in separate if in-
terlocking circles swung together in conjunction. Kelly's
fingers closed painfully on an arm of each of the others,
and there was a little jerking motion to her hands, as if she
would shake them, but they did not say anything about it
because there was, also, something pleading in the clasp
of her fingers.

"Now keep an eye on things until I get back!" she admonished.

"Right!" Roberts affirmed, with a reassuring nod.

"Particularly on *her!*"

"Very right," said Morgan, nodding vigorously.

"And if anything starts happening," Kelly warned, and
her face was momentarily as pale as death in the rushing
light, then hollow with dark shadows in the comparative
dimness of the reflected light from the coach windows,
"make sure you're in the middle of it!" Her fingers dug
into their arms. "We want all the biased witnesses we can
get!"

"Right!"

"*Very* right."

Kelly had to raise her voice above the *whishing* of the airbrakes. "And don't let him send you back to town before I get back here!"

"No."

"Never!"

Kelly reluctantly released their arms and the three moved together towards the entrance to one of the coaches.

"If the building super doesn't go back on his promise over the phone," she said, "I'll be able to get in the offices tonight, pick up the Attley files, and catch the milk train out of Grand Central."

Roberts shook her head. "There can't be one," she stated flatly, confident of her knowledge of the facts of life. "Milk trains run *into* the city, not *out* of it. There's lots of old goats in Li'l Old, but cows, no."

"All right then," cried Kelly, "the *anti*-milk train!" She swung a petite foot and its accompanying leg to the revealingly high step of the coach. "But goats' milk, cows' milk or milk of magnesia!" she promised, "I'll be on it!"

Under the stars, at Cobb's Mill, on the station platform, two young female persons stood watching a receding red light, listening to a diminishing hum. Then there was no light and there was silence. They drew closer together but did not look at each other. The silence was blasted by a car horn from the parking field.

II

Although it had been a phenomenally warm October, Zenobia Beal raised cornflower-blue eyes that were as if they had been nipped by frost, or pinched by worry, around the edges.

"I must see you alone, Mr. Sultan, if I may," she whispered.

Wm Sultan said, simply, "You may."

"Later," she whispered.

Wm Sultan concurred with a simple nod as Zolicopher
Hay returned to the green parlor after a short hunting
trip in which he had bagged another copy of *The American Banker.* It should, perhaps, have been more interesting
had he bagged another American banker and sat perus-
ing *his* lines instead of those of the publication, but, and
Wm Sultan laughed, and to his own embarrassment aloud,
that was a consummation scarcely to be expected since he
should have had no *interest* in it.

For that untoward laugh in a house of death and mutu-
ally nominated murderers, Wm Sultan was justly rebuked
by a rustle from *The American Banker* and, in this at least
agreeing, a concurring one from, in the hands of Miss
Zenobia Beal, the *Rural New Yorker.* As a representative
of the Law, this rebuke from Finance and Agriculture was
one to which the hyperthyroid ethical sense of the only
representative, on earth, of Sultan, Sultan & Sultan was
just sensitive, and he again buried his not inconsiderable
nose in the *Law Review.*

Zolicopher Hay turned a page, but never a new one,
of *The American Banker;* the lately deceased dairyman's
daughter turned an agrarian page of the *Rural New Yorker;* and Wm Sultan turned a purported page of the alleged
Law Review. From that judicial if not judicious journal he
raised first his eyes, and secondly his nose, when his ears
picked up the melodious murmur of two young female
voices in the hall. Morgan and Roberts stood in the doorway, each nudging the other to begin the explanation of
their surprising return.

Wm Sultan, ever conscious of his labor relationships,
smiled upon these personable representatives of his personnel.

"Ah!" he said sympathetically, "when you reached the
depot you discovered that between the three of you you
had money enough only for the purchase of a single ticket

to New York upon the train. Fortunately," he added, with an understanding nod, "you discovered it just in time to tell Mr. Sedgwick to wait for you in the car to return you here after Kelly departed upon her—heh! heh—iron horse! Spurred on, no doubt," he could not resist it, "by her sense of duty!" He then expressed his astonishment at this primary *contretemps* and secondary fortuitous circumstance by yawning, as usual, under the cover of the *Law Review*. "If your host and or hostess—" he left it there with judicial impartiality.

"Certainly," said Zolicopher Hay, and, taking another look at Roberts' lean blondness and, in spirit, but the flesh is heavy, discarding from himself forty pounds and even twenty years, he repeated, losing interest in the short lines of *The American Banker,* "but CERTAINLY!"

"Certainly," said Zenobia Beal from between lips pursed as those of one who has just sampled some cream after a thunderstorm.

"Certainly," Wm Sultan affirmed, "a most pleasant *surprise.*"

Roberts swallowed. "I think," she said, "I'll go to bed."

"I think," said Morgan earnestly, "I'd better keep my eye—eyes open a little while longer." And she sat upon a chair facing, determinedly, Zenobia Beal.

Zenobia Beal, with a bashful benevolence so becoming to her bucolic beauty, extended a periodical from a stack beside her on the green plush sofa, a sprawling stack which forced the terminal of her nether extremities to repose somewhat closely to Wm Sultan.

"Perhaps," she presumed, "you'd like to look at this."

Morgan, after a moment, turned a page of *Modest Sweaters and How to Knit Them;* Zolicopher Hay returned one wandering eye to *The American Banker;* Zenobia Beal turned to "The Rural Parson" in the *Rural New Yorker,* and it was a pity that her thoughts were not upon the simple beauty of the words she read; and Wm Sultan turned, as quietly as turns a goldfish in a bowl, a drier page of the *Law Review* . . .

The telephone, thank heaven! rang. This interruption, welcomed like a rich, unmarried, childless and *in extremis* uncle, was answered in the hall by Zolicopher Hay. His voice carried from the hall into the green parlor.

He said, "Hello? . . . Oh . . . Not freely . . . What? . . . But . . . Oh . . . Very well . . . Yes." And through the open doorway those who had been looking at *Modest Sweaters and How to Knit Them,* the *Rural New Yorker* and the *Law Review,* saw him glance at his watch. "Very well," he concluded, and returned to the doorway of the room but not to his chair or *The American Banker.* "I think," Zolicopher Hay said, in the doorway, "if you'll excuse me, I'll go to bed." He went upstairs.

Wm Sultan put down the *Law Review.* "I think," he said, "if you'll excuse me, I'll go to bed."

Zenobia Beal put down the *Rural New Yorker.* "Me too," she said.

Morgan put down *Modest Sweaters and How to Knit Them,* not reluctantly but in the unshaken opinion that they must be nice to have if you have nothing else, and, true to her promise to Kelly, kept an eye upon the two who preceded her upstairs.

III

Wm Sultan sat in a chair in the privacy of his bedroom and, safe from observant eyes, his expression was deeply worried. He did not like to jump to conclusions on inconclusive evidence, and from his posture in the chair, sitting on the small of his back with one long leg crossed over the other knee, the pendulant foot beating a rapid tattoo on the air, then circling doubtfully, then hanging heavily in reflection, he appeared to be in no danger of doing so. But that was, he felt, about the only thing of which he was not in danger.

The evidence was inconclusive, certainly, but he was far from favorably impressed by the postmarked fact that the codicil had been mailed the day after the murder of Zacharia Attley. The earlier circumstances of the crime, the almost conclusive case of circumstantial evidence which had been constructed against himself, had not convinced him of any premeditated plan against himself. It was evident, *per se*, that someone had planned to murder Zacharia Attley before that late client could give into his hands a certain letter allegedly written by one Unice Pease some forty-three years before; but it had seemed to him that it was entirely consistent with the evidence that his own involvement could have been nothing more premeditated than the inspiration of the moment, the murderer simply taking full advantage of the, from the murderer's point of view, fortunate circumstances. Indeed, he still did not see how it was possible that the murderer could have foreseen the exact situation that would exist at the short time at his disposal for the disposal of Zacharia Attley. Neither Zolicopher Hay nor the impetuous Trumbo could have had any time to spare; there had been only the period between the time when Zenobia Beal had announced his arrival to her allegedly great-grandfather and the time when he, Wm Sultan, had stumbled over his corpse in the bedroom doorway. Much had had to be inspirational because much had had to be left to chance.

But the mailing of the codicil on the day following the murder was neither impetuous nor by chance. The murderer had had time to find out what would be and to analyze what was the exact situation existing with the codicil presumably lost, and to estimate quite accurately what situation would result from mailing the codicil and having it received with its belated postmark. In full possession of such knowledge the murderer had deliberately mailed the codicil with the obvious calculation that it would be to his advantage.

And, in the considered opinion of Wm Sultan, it simply did not, at the present, make sense. The codicil had served only to bring the case into a precise but precarious balance between four people, like a four-sided pyramid stood upon its point, a situation giving the murderer no evident advantage or permanent security. That was what worried Wm Sultan. He was most reluctant to jump to a conclusion on inconclusive evidence, but even by crawling in a circle he could reach no conclusion other than that, since the belated mailing of the codicil gave the murderer no evident advantage in the present, it must be intended to give advantage in the future. Or, to go a step further, and Wm Sultan's well-shod foot swung rapidly, in a set of circumstances different from those at present existing. Or, to take the final step and stand full and square upon the conclusion, that the belated mailing of the codicil was a masked move in a preconceived plan that contemplated another move in the future which would alter the present existing circumstances; and that in those altered circumstances someone, to use the vernacular, a privilege which Wm Sultan frequently allowed himself when alone, someone would find himself in the soup and the murderer would be sitting pretty. And since, and inasmuch as, when the murderer had conceived his plan he had been aware of the existence of a cast-iron case of circumstantial evidence against one Wm Sultan, Esq., Wm Sultan had a sort of steamy feeling.

He ran his finger around his collar and, involuntarily, his toes curled inside his shoes; which reminded him that if he were to be seen in the hall after having been in his room for some minutes it would seem more natural if he had made some move towards the assumption of informal apparel, and he changed his shoes for a pair of house slippers.

He did so reluctantly, convinced of the impropriety of a clandestine appointment with a young female person. The appointment was, *of course,* of an impersonal nature, and the young female was clearly in a distressed condition, which last consideration had made refusal of her request quite impossible. He had first observed her distress in an indecisive manner in which she had repeatedly looked at him when she had come downstairs from her room shortly before dinner; and those indecisive glances had continued until she had taken advantage of Zolicopher Hay's momentary departure from the parlor to request a private and secret interview. He did not falsely ascribe the slightest boldness to that request of Zenobia Beal because she could not possibly have foreseen that his file clerk would return after her departure for New York and sociably remain with them in the parlor with the clear, and sociable, intention of remaining as long as they did. But he had observed that Zenobia Beal had observed that he had left his *Law Review* upon the sofa, even as he had observed that she had observed that he had observed that she had left there her *Rural New Yorker;* it was strange, he reflected, how feminine instinct instructed even an innocent country girl to go about such things.

Wm Sultan straightened his tie in the mirror and was given the reflection that he needed something more than house slippers to present a completely convincing picture of the house guest who has forgotten a book in the parlor. He put on a wine silk dressing gown, although of course not going so far in dishabille as to remove his suit coat, and feeling quite devilish went downstairs to the parlor.

He found Zenobia Beal, in tomato red mules and a spinach green housecoat, holding the *Rural New Yorker.* When she saw that it was indeed he who had entered she

took a folded sheet of paper from the pocket of her housecoat.

"I don't care what it says," she said, "but I want you to
read it!"

Unfolding the sheet of paper Wm Sultan read, in a vigorous handwriting:

> Dear Zenobia
> I must see you privately and we can straighten
> out the acknowledgment of your claim—meet
> me at 11:30 tonight at the family cemetery—
> and make sure Mr. Sultan doesn't suspect.
>
> Trumbo

"Ah, yes," said Wm Sultan, and then after a moment
added, "yes, yes, yes. And when did he give you this?" he
asked, returning it.

Zenobia Beal shook her head. "He must have left it
in my room," she explained, "while we were still in here
with Mr. Hastle. I found it there when I went up before
dinner."

Wm Sultan was looking at his wristwatch. "A little over
an hour to go," he mused. "Suppose you meet me outside
at eleven sharp and we'll look into this together."

Zenobia Beal's eyes were wide. "You mean I really
should go?"

Wm Sultan smiled reassuringly, and with an air of play-
fulness that avoided discourtesy but was unquestionably
insistent, waved his hand towards the door of the room.
He did not want to make a raw recruit, so to speak, nervous by explaining too far in advance the plan of campaign
and the possibilities which might be encountered.

"But it sounds so strange . . ." Zenobia Beal said dissat-
isfied. She halted obstinately shortly within the doorway
of the room, and read, "Meet me at 11:30 tonight at the

family cemetery—and make sure Mr. Sultan doesn't suspect. It—"

She broke off when she saw Wm Sultan's finger at his lips. He had heard behind her a creak on the stair, and while there are few things that stairs in old houses do better of their own volition than creak in the night, he felt, he thought, he believed that in the present instance, and all things considered, he knew of another explanation. He picked up an abandoned pamphlet on a chair, handed it to Zenobia Beal and signaled for her to enter the hall.

Morgan stood, one foot in the air. And while this in itself might not be thought an unusual position for anyone walking downstairs, it is less usual for that foot to be pointed like a classical ballet dancer's, and for it to be approaching the step below like that of a timid and tender bather testing the temperature of water which is suspected of being quite capable of imparting a quick and deadly chill. Morgan saw Zenobia Beal standing looking up at her, and she came down on the foot so heavily that the jar numbed her heel.

"Ha, ha, ha!" she laughed airily. "I forgot that interesting little booklet you gave me!" And, slightly limping, she tripped down two steps further before Zenobia Beal came up and met her.

Zenobia Beal was also smiling. "I noticed that you did," she said, "and I thought you might want it again."

Morgan looked with loathing at the copy of *Modest Sweaters and How to Knit Them* that was held out to her, and she looked with longing at the door to the parlor; and she tried to think of some further excuse, but she had committed herself, and she was caught, and she took the damned flat-chested pamphlet and stomped back upstairs to her room and slammed the door.

Wm Sultan, slightly red in the face, and with moist eyes, permitted himself a dry cough or two before returning upstairs with the *Law Review*.

IV

"Roberts!"

"Ummmmm."

"Roberts!"

"Ummmm?"

"Roberts!"

"Clock hasn' gone off yeh . . ."

"Roberts!"

"Iss early . . ."

"Roberts!"

"Di'n geh sleep three clock—lemmelone."

"Roberts!"

"Phone office be late."

"Roberts!"

"Terrible headache. Stop shaking me."

"Roberts!"

"My God, I'm a guest!" The shock of it awakened Roberts and she sat up straight. She pointed at the dark window. "Don't tell me I got to get up in the middle of the night and milk the chickens!"

"Roberts. Listen to me."

"You listen to me. I couldn't get to sleep until three o'clock in the morning and I have a terrible headache and—"

"Look, you big lug! You were asleep before ten o'clock because it's only ten thirty now!"

"Only a half hour sleep all night!" gasped Roberts. "My God, no wonder I feel awful!" she ducked under the covers again.

Morgan picked out the largest spherical undulation beneath the light bedcovers suitable to that warm October, and brought the flat of her hand against it, swingingly. Roberts sat up. Roberts threw, back the covers. Roberts stood up, her hand upon a certain spherical contour, and she could locate it exactly because she habitually slept raw. She began to come around the end of the bed towards Morgan who had, diplomatically, gone to the other side of the bed.

"Roberts—listen to me—I've discovered a plot!"

"You'll look good under it," said Roberts, her hand still upon that spherical contour, and still continuing around the bed.

"That's just it!" Morgan whispered, tremulous in excitement. "She's meeting someone in the family graveyard at eleven thirty and Mr. Sultan mustn't know!"

Roberts came to a stop. Roberts removed her hand from a red spot the size of a hand upon her long blondness and clasped her forehead with the hand and shook her head and turned around and got back into bed and pulled the covers around her neck and said, "I guess you can't help it. All right, get it off your chest so I can get back to sleep."

"The family graveyard," Morgan repeated, her green eyes as luminous as that Will o' the Wisp that particularly delights to dance among old tombstones and new—dug—graves—in—the middle—of the night . . . —"at eleven thirty!"

Roberts nodded and Roberts yawned. "The time," she said gently, "of the funeral tomorrow morning. Also the place. There's a family graveyard out behind the orchard. The orchard is those trees in lines you see on the side of the hill. Now go pick an apple or something and let me sleep."

"'And make sure Mr. Sultan doesn't suspect!'" Morgan whispered significantly, leaning over the bed. "That's what I heard her say to someone in the parlor! If you had any imagination," she protested, "you wouldn't try to laugh that off!"

Roberts rubbed her eyes. "Where'd you hear all this?"

"Coming down the stairs. They were talking in the parlor."

"Who?"

"Zenobia and I couldn't get a chance to find out who he was. But that's what I heard her say."

"What else did you hear?"

"I didn't hear anything else. There was just kind of a murmur of voices and then those words."

Roberts turned over contentedly. "Only words you were able to hear—" she yawned—"you weren't hearing them very clearly. You misunderstood—or imagined—why meet anybody—graveyard—nearly midnight—silly—"

Morgan decided to retire with disdainful dignity because she was far from certain herself but that that might have been just what had happened. She paused momentarily at the end of the hall between the door to her bedroom and that to the bedroom of Zenobia Beal, and then, on a thought, she went to the open door at the head of the stairs of that old-fashioned room known and used as a sewing room.

She found a spool of black thread. She wrapped some around her fingers. She made a loop in one end. She returned to the hall to her former position between her bedroom and that of Zenobia Beal. She took two silent steps and slipped the loop over the doorknob of that other dear girl's door. She entered her own room but kept the door ajar until she threaded the other end of the thread through the keyhole. She then closed the door.

She drew the thread taut and tied it to one of the posts of her four-poster bed; to be precise above a carved pineapple and below a cluster of carved—they may have been leaves but, considering the house, they were probably bananas.

She undressed and donned a white nightgown that had been advertised as being of angelic cut; it was certainly cut. There then arose one of those problems which are so unexpected and so baffling. Her intention had been, as a matter of course, to tie the thread around her toe. In all the books she had ever read that was the way it was done. But those works, and it is to be feared that they must have been fictional, had not, not a one of them, mentioned what was to be done about the bedcovers or with the toe. One couldn't, Morgan learned by experimentation, just leave a toe out of the bedcovers by itself.

Her toe was attached, firmly, to a foot and the foot to a leg and the leg to the rest of her. She was, she reflected, habitually a hunch-up sleeper, and should she leave a leg out in the cold, or to be factual about that warm October, out in the cool, once she was asleep her leg would curl up, pulling its foot with it and the foot its toe—

She almost screamed as the thread gave a jerk that nearly severed that troublesome toe from her foot. Almost instantly she was at the keyhole of her door. She saw Zenobia Beal standing in the doorway of her bedroom looking cautiously down the hall. Then Zenobia stepped into the hall on tiptoe, reclosed her door, and was out of sight.

9

*Under the Tree. False Reassurances. A Change
of Guard. Horrible Cry of a Cat. A Guardian Angel—
Watches—Goes Astray in the Night. An Outdoor Girl.
A Barrister in a Pagan Grove. An Assault.*

When Wm Sultan returned to his room he removed his
dressing gown, which left him completely dressed, and
changed back from his house slippers to his shoes. He enjoyed a few dry chuckles over a few arid books reviewed
with attic wit in the *Law Review*. Since cigarettes, when
lit, glow in the dark he enjoyed a final one in his room
before going downstairs. He switched on the lights ahead
of him and switched them off behind him on his way to
the front porch where, presently, Zenobia Beal joined him
in the dark.

He could recall the general direction from the porch of
a tree which he had observed on the lawn that had, around
its trunk, a circular bench. He conducted, in silence, his
clinging companion to that arboreal seat, and arranged
that they should sit on the side of the tree facing away
from the house. Voices carry more ahead than backward,
and while the tree was far enough from the house to insure
that softly modulated voices would not be overheard Wm

Sultan was not the man to ignore an added and convenient precaution.

He did not wait for his fair companion, who still clung to him in girlish timidity, to speak. Contrary to the theories of some psychiatrists, it had been his own observed experience that to give voice to fear was to give a quality of reality, a substantial body, so to speak, to what otherwise might remain mere vague phantoms in the imagination. He preferred, in short, that Zenobia Beal should suffer a complex in the future instead of panic in the present.

"Very amusing, isn't it!" he said softly and with a little soft chuckle. "Like playing hide-and-go-seek again, or run-sheep-run! Should be ashamed of myself. Not at all necessary, of course, but can't resist it!" He chuckled soundlessly, but since she was clinging to his arm he knew that she could feel his shoulder shake and realize that he was chuckling, particularly since her head was against his shoulder.

"I've been so worried," she whispered.

"Don't whisper," he said casually, "just speak in a low tone." He chuckled again. "Childish trick to play on Mr. Gates," he said. "But then he deserves it for having written a childish note. A graveyard—Mr. Gates is indeed very young. To meet in a graveyard—" he chuckled again.

"But it's just halfway between his house and this," Zenobia Beal explained. "If you're walking."

"Ah, yes, yes, yes, yes," Wm Sultan quickly adopted this reassuring explanation. "Very natural place to meet then, since on the road—"

On the road the single light of a motorcycle came to a stop and the sound of its motor stopped with it. A second light appeared beside it and went back down the road the sound of its motor diminishing. The first light went out. There had been a change of guard.

"Perfectly natural," Wm Sultan resumed. "Very likely Mr. Gates does not agree with Mr. Hay's expressed intention of contesting the codicil. Very wise of him. Very likely wants to make some financial arrangement with you. But he should not," he concluded firmly and he hoped convincingly, "have sought to impose upon your inexperience by depriving you of—ah—friendly advice."

"I know I can trust you," murmured Zenobia Beal. "That's why I showed the note to you although he wrote that I shouldn't."

Wm Sultan regretted that he could not give a modest cough, but the carrying quality of a cough made that impossible. He was, however, satisfied that the emotion in her voice was not one of alarm, and that he could get down to business.

"How will you go to the dedicated ground?" he asked.

"The graveyard? Why, I'll go through the orchard in back of the barn and past the spring house and through the wood lot and then the spruces Mr. Attley planted around the graveyard when he put all the beautiful new tombstones in when he came here and there I'll be."

"Excellent *précis* of the terrain," Wm Sultan complimented her. "That," he added, "is the way you will *not* go. Now, is there some vehicular adit to the cemetery?"

"Vehic—oh, yes, there's a road down to the main road where it curves around the hill."

"Screened?"

"Bluestone," affirmed Zenobia Beal proudly.

"Ah yes," said Wm Sultan. "But is it, ah, well, *planted* with anything?"

"Oh *yes!* Rhododendron with spruce trees in back. Mr. Attley always said that when the Banana Pioneers came to lay him away he wanted them to—"

"And," Wm Sultan interrupted gently, his thoughts on time, "you can reach the road without going through the orchard?"

"Yes, but—"

"I see," he continued, looking at the wrist of the hand that clung to his lapel in innocent trust, "that you're wearing a wristwatch with a luminous dial. You will wait here fifteen minutes. You will then, avoiding the orchard, go to the road giving access to the—ah—graveyard. You will not enter upon the road. You will follow the screen of verdure to the point where the road debouches upon the—ah—graveyard. You will remain hidden at that point until I appear . . ." he broke off, looking at the eastern sky. "It appears," he resumed, somewhat testily as he was seriously annoyed by his negligence in not consulting an almanac, "that the moon will presently arise. Moonlight, however," he continued, "gives dangerous leeway to the imagination in making an identification, and you will not make your presence known until—"

Zenobia Beal climbed halfway up his frame as a tomcat, a mean, stinking tomcat with ragged ears and yellow spots, gave a pugnacious and lascivious yowl in her ear.

"Until," Wm Sultan gently lowered her to the ground, "I thus identify myself. You will then make your precise location known by reaching over your head and swaying a branch of spruce." He saw no advisability of explaining that it was designed to induce any possible pot-shotter to shoot too high. "I will then join you," he continued, "and advise you on the final arrangements for your private, so far as he will know, informal little chat with Mr. Gates."

And with a little comforting squeeze to the clinging fingers which he detached from his lapels, he casually walked off into the darkness.

II

There are those who can rise to an emergency, and Roberts rose magnificently. From a sound sleep she rose straight up in bed and stood there dripping from the glass of cold water which Morgan had thrown upon her after, thoughtfully, drawing back the bedcovers. Morgan wasted no time on false apologies to one who had been proven in error, nor did she waste any time on preliminaries.

"She's gone!" she said. "Sneaked out of the house. And Kelly," she added darkly, "told us to keep an eye on her!"

Roberts walked off the bed.

"O.K.," she said crisply, taking, as usual, action in her stride, "scram down and keep an eye on her until I can get something on and then I'll take over."

Morgan, in her angelic nightgown, went down the dark stairs like a falling one. She schlossed to a stop in her bare feet on the waxed entrance hall, oozed up to the front door and eased it open without a creak. She listened. She heard nothing. She slithered through the door to the front porch. She saw nothing. She heard nothing. She slipped down the porch to its steps to the driveway. She saw nothing and she heard nothing. She began to have a panicky feeling that she was failing Kelly, that she was failing Roberts, that she was failing Sultan, Sultan & Sultan. Morgan, she resolved, couldn't do that to Morgan.

Where was Zenobia Beal whom, not two minutes before, she had heard, from the head of the stairs, close the front door? On her way to, Morgan swallowed, the graveyard. And where was Roberts? Dressing. And if anyone was to keep, or get, an eye on Zenobia Beal, whom was it up to? Morgan's lips grew thin and Morgan took a deep breath.

And where was This Graveyard? "Behind the orchard." And what was an orchard? "Trees in lines?" And where had she seen trees in lines? Behind the barn. With quick and resolute steps and tender and wincing feet, an angelic figure set out for the barn. Presently she found it although she did not recall that it had had before such a strong

smell of oil and gasoline. Nevertheless she went around it
to the back of it, which must be behind the front of it, and
continued, over a stone fence, through a plowed, and odor-
iferous field. But it was nice and soft on the feet, it was
so nice and so soft on the feet. She came to another stone
barricade, stormed it, stood triumphantly on top, her life
blood from a scratched toe paying the price of victory, and
looked for Trees in Lines to conquer. Before her she could
see some clouds in the low sky, and there must be a big city
over that way somewhere because the clouds were all lit up;
that she could see. But the trees must be a little further on.

She was on the point, the very movement, of leaping
from the uncomfortably cold stone beneath the cringing
soles of her feet when she was held up, swaying, by one
of those thoughts which distinguishes genius from medio-
crity. For it to have occurred to an Outdoor Girl that
trees, as flora, are distinguished by their height, and that
if there were trees within the immediate vicinity before
her their tops should show against those low and luminous
clouds, such a reflection should have been no more than
the mirror of that repetitive experience which is termed
environment; but for this thought, this perception, to
strike a maiden of Manhattan was, conservatively, genius.

And with this first awakening to the potentialities of
celestial navigation the vivid imagination of the not backward angel, grasped the thing entire; and with hands on
hips, although the angelic cut sleeves gave in that posture
the impression of folded wings, and with outthrust head,
Morgan turned in a full circle studying, if you please, the
intermittently visible horizon of the stars. To her right
rear she gave scant attention because there below the stars
glowed the upstairs lights of at least two bedrooms, one
of them hers, but to her left the stars were blotted out by
some intervening physical body, as of a hill, which had
fuzzy edges, as of trees.

Again Morgan was arrested upon the point of leaping from her vantage point. She was arrested by the yowl of a cat from the direction of the house. She did not know how, but she knew that it was a mean old tomcat with ragged ears and yellow spots. She shivered, because even a warm October night in New England is a little cool for mortal angels, and with clenched teeth took to the air, briefly, before coming down on her knees in her first step towards that fuzzy protuberance that was then somewhat further from her than it had been in a direct line from the house.

III

Roberts was no sissy, but with that unfailing care of the constitution so typical of athletes and unusual in congressmen, she did take the time to towel herself with a pillow case before donning clothing. A wool dress was the quickest thing and that, with golf shoes, was what she quickly slipped and laced on before departing from her room and the house. The farmstead, including the tenant house and the barn, were some distance to the rear of the owner's manor, and since from what Morgan had earlier told her and to which she now gave some credence, the most likely of Zenobia Beal's destinations appeared to be a graveyard that was somewhere behind the orchard that was behind the barn, Roberts went out the back door.

An Outdoor Girl, despite her city residence an Outdoor Girl who could ski, shoot, ride, swim or sail, in an outfit by Abercrombie (she had a rich uncle) and in a fashion to make many a He-Man look like a tomboy, she was instantly cognizant of two facts. The first was that the moon would soon be up, and the second was that until it was up it would be as silly a waste of time trying to find Morgan as—

Her thoughts momentarily froze as she heard a mean, yellow-spotted tomcat give a yowl of rage and, or because of, frustrated love around somewhere on the front lawn.

—as, she finished her thought, it would be for anything except another tom or she cat to try to find that
cat. Ho-Kay, tombstones, here I come! And with a single
orientating glance at the stars Roberts set off for the barn
with no more deviation from the plumb line than that of a
well-aimed rifle bullet. At the barn, with the silos standing clear and sharp like watchtowers against the stars, she
turned for a good, long look at the house, as that mariner
who fixes his location by a lighthouse. She would soon
be among trees with only small patches of sky visible and
affording to the navigator infinite opportunities for shocking inaccuracy, but she should once in a while be able to
catch a glimpse of the lights and angle of the bedroom
windows and having one good fix easily determine if she
had veered to port or starboard.

The barn was, astern, slightly off the port beam of the
house. First were the lights of Morgan's bedroom and then,
for'ard, those of the cabin of the surviving partner of Sultan, Sultan & Sultan. She moved ten paces to the right
and noted that the ports were of themselves not visible but
only the shafts of light, must be a little mist, smoke or,
since this was ashore, dust in the air. Roberts returned to
her former position, counting the paces and checking the
angles of the windows with her eye, and then moved ten
paces to her left, true left, raising an arm, planting the left
foot in line with the arm, dropping the arm and pacing
forward. She stared at the relative width of the foreshort-
ened windows, closed her eyes, memorizing, took another
look for verification, returned ten paces to her right, again
faced the house, did an about-face that was worth an admission to our military academy in this day of atomic
warfare, and marched around the barn to a point where
the space between the silos appeared equal to that of her
former position, turned her back on them, and, within

fifty yards, entered under trees that may or may not have
been in line but indubitably smelled of apples.

She had not the slightest suspicion that anyone was
following her.

IV

Wm Sultan reluctantly left his fair companion by the
tree. He knew that she was reluctant to see him leave, although, considering the night, she could not see him far.
He felt what he told himself was a grandfatherly tender-
ness towards that female orphan so recently deprived of a
great-grandfather. There was no question in his mind but
that the tender trust which she so innocently gave him
was of the same—ah—impersonal nature, however much
against nature such impersonality might be.

Putting her out of his mind, for the nonce, he reviewed
the task before him while he walked into it with a casual
but rapid gait. Since murder had once been committed,
the proposed appointment seemed a little too obviously an
assignation for assassination. And yet, and notwithstand-
ing, the opportunity was too obvious to be ignored, if
a little too obvious to be taken completely seriously. It
should be quite enough, he felt, if Zenobia Beal were de-
toured from her usual, natural or expected route to the—
ah—graveyard. With that simple provision against any
ambuscade against her on the way, he could make a re-
connaissance of the field to discover if Mr. Gates had yet
arrived, and, if so, pinning down his position. He could
then secrete himself in a position that would "cover" Zenobia Beal and have her call Mr. Gates to her. That part was
essential. In the event of any untoward indication, or false
move, Mr. Gates would, later, wake up to regret it. In the
advent of an amicable proposition, that person who by the
terms of the codicil stood in the relation of a guardian to

Zenobia Beal would be able to assay the proposition and guard her inexperience from any commitment detrimental to her interests.

Wm Sultan nodded his head judicially, and avoiding the barn set off at a tangent that he estimated would save him a hundred paces in bisecting the orchard. At one point, off to his right, he heard some brief sound that at first struck him as resembling what might be expected from some un-inhibited female who had stubbed her toe, but the implausibility of the corollary of the impression—that any female would be stumbling around at night in those plowed fields, or, to entertain pure fantasy, that if so stumbling she should be in an unshod condition—was such that he instantly dismissed it other than as a prime example of the nightmare proclivity of the nocturnal imagination.

With secret shame that even the disciplined mind was capable of such fancied dissipation, Wm Sultan entered the orchard. He entered it at a bad time. At, to be exact, the moment that the rising moon tipped as in bloom the gnarled branches of the apple trees. In the orchard grass there was fallen fruit, unseen but scented, and its strangely stirring fermented twang hung in the air like some inciting incense in a pagan temple. The fatal apple of Eden, Wm Sultan mused, had not been plucked from a tree but breathed as it lay brownly returning its cider to the earth, breathed as it lay breathing its acrid, atavistic urge into the air. He had a wish that Kelly were with him . . . that he might, of course, dictate to his secretary a note upon . . . He sighed and walked rapidly on.

All things considered, particularly that of being alone, he was as pleased as not when he emerged upon the further extent of that pagan grove, clearly unsuited to a Christian country, and saw before him the spring house, numerous rows of cordwood, and, beyond, the woodlot that . . .

A female figure stepped into the moonlight ahead of him and stepped out of sight behind a comer of the spring house. It was only a passing glance in dappled moonlight, but in that glimpse his hawk-like eye had discerned that it was a female figure by the fact that it wore a skirt, and his logical mind, since there was no other member of her sex involved in that night's affairs, had as instantly known her identity.

He did not, even in that moment of surprise, blame Zenobia Beal for having violated his instructions. It had, indeed, been in the back of his mind that he had been so anxious to reassure her possible alarm about an appointment in a graveyard that he had, perhaps, failed in impressing upon her that she should, for her safety, precisely follow his instructions. But a simple regard for her safety dictated that she be halted.

A tattered-eared, yellow-spotted tomcat rent the quiet night with a yowl; and Wm Sultan hastened around the corner of the springhouse to join that endangered daughter of the soil who would be awaiting him. From the far corner of the stone house a pin-wheel of blackness sped at him through the air; there was a flash as of black light inside his head, and instant unconsciousness.

10

*Breathless Adventure. Fourteen Blankets. A Graveyard.
Subversive Sabotage. A Light in a Window. The
Angel and the Gravediggers. Shivering Stone. A Pillar
of Salt. Murder! A File Clerk in an Occupied Grave.*

Morgan was not breathing enough. She discovered this when she hopped over a clod in a fashion that would have done credit to an experienced sister of the soil and landed with her toe against one of those stones which give to New England its peculiar, its very peculiar character. She discovered that she did not have enough breath to make a comment adequate either in length or volume.

Like most persons unaccustomed to athletic exertion she had always been under the erroneous impression that breathing was something that took care of itself; and as with all persons the tension of excitement, like a tight band around the chest, had further restricted her inadequate inhalation of the atmosphere. To these two common causes of oxygen deficiency had been added a third that was more personal. Had Morgan been a Girl Scout and built a campfire the smoke from the two sticks would have risen in a straight, unbending column; but instead of standing in a straight, unbending column she had been

leaping from stone fences and hopping clods with ga-
zelle-like grace and alacrity, and as a result of this passage
of her body through the ambient atmosphere, that seemed
to howl around inside her nightgown like an arctic bliz-
zard, she was definitely prejudiced against admitting the
frigid stuff right inside her in her lungs.

It was only when, after expanding her last gasp of carefully warmed air in comment upon the ancestry of the
stone which had stubbed her toe, and as a result of this extravagance found herself becoming a little faint and reel-
ing on wabbling knees, that, reluctantly and bitterly, she
filled her lungs and let them shiver with the rest of her.

It was this pause that tested her courage. If like a fool
she had rushed in where her angelic nightgown should
normally have feared to tread, she now had time to reflect
that poor old Morgan was being given the works, the dirty
end of the stick, a raw—or to make some very small allow-
ance for the nightgown—a virtually raw deal. When she
thought of poor old Morgan she could have wept.

There was that poor, brave girl out in a howling bliz-
zard with bleeding feet like one of Washington's Heroes at
Valley Forge surrounded by screaming wildcats and what
was ahead of her? a *graveyard!*

She did weep; and, weeping, stumbled on. When they
found her frozen mangled body in the morning they'd be
sorry! Then they'd appreciate her!

She went partly through and partly over a stone fence,
only dislodging the top layer of rocks with the more tender portions of her kneecaps, and found herself in high
orchard grass that was like a million little snakes wiggling
around her shaking shinbones. She stepped upon something cold, wet, squashy and as slippery as the skins of
that fruit with which the late Zacharia Attley had had
a pioneering association, and poor old Morgan plunged

forward in a nosedive, quite literally, her nose burying itself in another rotten apple.

It was not, however, a poor old Morgan who got grimly to her feet, wiping her nose with a complete and circular motion as if it were a doorknob, and breathing both in and out the heady fumes of cider. It was a Morgan to whom the moon-tipped branches of the trees of the orchard appeared to be blood-red.

Fortunately, she was no longer cold. Indeed, she seemed to have skipped even the transitionary state of warmth and felt, as she ejected a soft and soured apple seed from between her teeth, burning hot. She took a breath like a furnace and went full-steam ahead.

There was clear sky overhead, not branches, and in a dark shadow that was a depression on the terrain there was, she found when it icily lathed her feet, a small and shallow brook. Off to her left something like a small house loomed in the moonlight and what, vaguely, looked like long stacks of something, the whole meriting no more than a glance over her shoulder before she plunged into more trees, like an avengeful angel after an heretical driad. But she stopped short when she came to the temple-like colonnade of triple columns of blue spruce, more like the dead souls of trees than trees in the moonlight, as aloof as death, as cold as death, as solemn as death, as silent as—

Morgan clenched her teeth just in time, and then cautiously inserting her finger pushed her heart to the back of her mouth and swallowed it again as her ears recovered from the wildcat yowl of a yellow-spotted tom off some place behind her. She was no longer unduly warm. In the time that she had stood looking, sickly, at the spires of the blue ice, or spruce, and in an instant of auditory reception, her habiliments had shrunken from fourteen blankets to a film of gauze; and her courage from that of a fire-snorting

dragon to that, infinitely greater, of a sniffling but determined rabbit. The rabbit, and Morgan, entered the triple
columns of the patiently waiting blue spruce; as indeed
the great advantage of the spruce over the sprightly is that
the spruce has so much more time.

Now, Morgan tried to swallow, *tombstones*.

But not, Morgan saw instantly, tombstones. When the
Attleys and the Atwaters and the Atkins and the Afteralls
had set aside upon a hillside this, their God's Acre, it had
been in the necessity of an early and unorganized community and in a humility of homage. But when, by the bene-
fice of bananas, Zacharia Attley had, some two centuries
later, sought to disguise the poverty of his ancestors, who
had yet, oddly enough, been men without either bananas
or their antithetic refrigerators, who had been simply men,
not advertising men, he had removed those pitiful head-
stones of those to whom memory had been more than marble and had replaced them by something that would impress
those who came to bury, if not to praise, Zacharia Attley.

They had been replaced by monoliths of granite, or
if Attleys, marble, upon which reclined, sat, kneeled and
stood youths and maidens, cherubs, angels and seraphim,
and, in impersonation of the first Attley a Pilgrim (*not an
immigrant Puritan*) Father, with a top hat and blunderbuss,
before which combination it was readily believed that the
Indian fell, if nothing else than in sheer astonishment.

And around and about this enclosure in which eter-
nally, but unfortunately immovably, frolicked these sculptured attitudes of life and hope of a better future, rose the
pagodas of the cynical and vegetable spruce. The rabbit
entered the graveyard. A mere nothing, of course, to the
courageous reader, but to her it seemed like a good deal.
Indeed, as her teeth dissolved in her mouth, she felt that
it was a hell of a lot. In fact, she couldn't offhand think of
a hero in history who compared with Morgan; including

that pirate who had been her great-great-great paternal grandparent.

Swallowing her liquid dentures, for her exertions had left her in need of nourishment, she slipped from marble maiden to granite youth, so typical of the New England temperament; she peeked over a cherubim's shoulder and under an angel's wing; she looked longingly at the Pilgrim Father's blunderbuss, wishing it were stealable and the powder dry, and was at last compelled to conclude that her earth-bound viewpoint was too low for a spying-out of flesh and fabric among the marble crowd.

Before her was a monolith of marble with, for an invitation, nothing on top. Morgan dug her frigid digits into the stone, hoisted a heel, hooked it over a corner, and elevated her cold and unwilling flesh upon the comfort of the comparatively warm block of veined Sienna.

She straightened her legs, wincing at the loudness of the sound of the breaking ice in the joints of her knees and thighs, and stood looking into the blunderbuss of the Pilgrim Father. Seeing the expression in his face, Morgan quickly raised her hands, but before, in perverted humor, she could whisper, "Don't shoot, Mister!" she heard the sound of other, and presumably human, voices.

II

From the onomatopoetic *clug!* which Roberts heard after hurling the billet of wood, she shrewdly surmised that it had found its mark upon a cranium. She felt the quiet but substantial pride of one who has broken a difficult clay pigeon at a trap-shoot. And, even upon reflection, she had to admit in simple justice to herself that it had been a nice shot to make. For one thing, she had not been expecting the pigeon. Indeed, when she had heard its wild mating cry, or yowl, her first thought had been simply, "Well, now I've been followed by everything."

It had not been until she had heard the fluttering of
its wings, or to be literal the pattering of its running feet,
that all had become clear to her. With the rapidity of a
double play, she had realized first of all that while it was
not beyond the physical capacities of a tomcat to travel so
far so fast, it was beyond the wayward curiosity of any cat
to have done so in the straight line necessary for this one
to have kept pace with her from the house; and her second
realization had been that its footsteps were a mite heavy
for those of a cat.

Her physical reactions had been equally certain and
prompt. She had plucked a billet from a cord of stovewood
and nicely leading the footsteps approaching the far corner
of the springhouse had let it sail end-over-end at a height
and speed calculated to have its arrival at the far corner
of the springhouse coincide in altitude and time with that
of the head of the two-legged tom who had yowled at her.
She had not waited to observe the outcome of her timing
any more than a pivoting second baseman needs to look
to learn if the first baseman has caught his peg; if he has
caught it, it will be heard.

He caught it, and Roberts heard. The reassuring *clug!*
was followed by that sound, so difficult to describe but
so readily recognized, of a body falling inertly upon the
earth. A sound not loud but, again, one that under the
circumstances was most reassuring. And the deep silence
which then ensued indicated clearly that the play had been
successful, that the runner was "out."

Pausing only to pick up a heavy stone, Roberts did not
loiter there to learn his identity and perhaps make his
acquaintance at the unpredictable instant of his revival
but slipped *back* into the orchard, her instinct identical to
that of the quarterback, if we may change games, who feels
that play has gotten out of hand and calls time until he
can receive some new instructions from the coach. Roberts

not only felt that the game had gotten out of hand, she no longer had the slightest idea what game she was supposed to be playing.

"Keep An Eye-a On Zenobi-a" had sounded as simple as it was catchy; but there had been *nothing* said about clunking other and unknown characters with billets of cordwood, or, Roberts reflected, hefting the reassuring weight of the rock in her hand, with anything else for the matter of that. *It was time for a talk with coach.*

She understood just enough of what had happened to know that she did not get the general idea at all. If she still found it difficult to admit that the yowls she had heard could have issued from anything except a veritable and yellow-spotted tom, she did nevertheless accept the fact that they had issued from a two-legged one and therefore, unless human eccentricity in the country had reached a point not yet reported in the city press, had been some sort of prearranged signal or call of identification. O.K. The character had caught a glimpse of her at the spring-house, had mistaken her for Zenobia, had yowled to let Zenobia know who it was and had confidently come trotting up just in time to be a clay pigeon. But what was she supposed to do? Just go on prowling around conking everything that yowled, barked, brayed, or mooed? In a farming country, she felt that that could become serious. *It was time for a talk with coach.*

Roberts walked back through the orchard not sneakingly but hastily. The reassuring weight of the rock in her hand far outbalanced any apprehension that someone might jump out from a tree trunk and say, "Boo!" Her old-fashioned motto was, "Let the booer beware." Her self-confidence, however, needed bolstering when she saw the light in Morgan's window. She knew, unfortunately, Morgan. She could see Morgan sitting up in bed with wide green eyes like some little, well, not so little, see-all

know-all angel while her imagination made child's play
of her, Roberts', keeping an eye-a on Zenobi-a. She knew
that, unfortunately, to Morgan's imagination all things
were possible and all failures clear proof of subversive sabotage. Roberts could see Morgan hunched forward in the
bed, her green eyes narrow and glittering, when she, Roberts, reported having failed to lay a single eye upon Zenobia, much less keeping one there. She could hear Morgan
hint, not delicately, that she was in the pay of That Trumbo or Zolicopher Hay.

Roberts sighed as she rounded the barn on the home
stretch to the house. She'd do anything they asked her to
just so long as she knew what she was supposed to do, but
she felt that coach better learn about that unknown player
who had been tagged out at the springhouse. She was glad
to see that the light was still on in Mr. Sultan's room, it
was time for a talk with Bossy, time to tell him about that
clay pigeon she had picked off at the springhouse.

III

In that quick and vivid imagination in which Morgan so
often saw herself as the heroine of spectacular if improba-
ble scenes, she now could see herself on top of the mono-
lithic pedestal. It was only justice that that imaginative
faculty which had so often been the source of calamity
should now come to her succor; that she should see herself as if from that lower and more shadowed area from
which were approaching the voices, that she should see
the monolith brushed on its top by moonlight and herself
above in the full soft spotlight of its radiance; for to see
that was to see that any movement of that illuminated
figure could not fail to arrest the attention of the most
casual eye. Her arms, raised in jesting surrender to the
stone blunderbuss, remained raised, and the white trailing

sleeves of that angelically cut nightgown, innocent only in heaven, gave wings to that angelic figure that would throughout the ages remain there poised for flight.

Below her, Morgan saw a black pit and a softly glistening mound of earth; beyond this she saw two masculine figures approaching before she decided that it might be wiser to close her marble lids over her glistening eyes.

"There," announced a voice, "she be." It was a deep voice, as from a cask, with a fine aged-in-the-wood quality.

"There," agreed another voice, "she be." It was a lighter voice, as from a keg, with a twang like hard cider.

"And *she* better be there, Peevey," said the first voice, but much closer. *"She* better be."

"She better be," repeated the second voice, but with less bass and heart in the implied, if vague, threat.

"I thought you had her," said the first voice in deep suspicion. "I could," it continued, going to one side of the pit and the mound, "sworn I saw you pick her up."

"I thought you had her," said Mr. Peevey in a blustery quaver, going to the other side of the pit and the mound. "I did, too, George!"

George expectorated into the pit. "And all the way to home," he mused darkly, "I was thinking it was about time you pulled her out for a drink."

"I," said Mr. Peevey, and their voices came together in front of the pedestal as they rejoined after having surrounded the pit, "was thinking the same thing about you. I was, too, George!"

"She better not be hid out," rumbled George. "She better be where I sat her."

"And she is!" Mr. Peevey cried, bending to one side of the monolith. He straightened with a gallon jug in his hand. "Here she is," he said, displaying her, and there was now a quiet firmness in his voice. "Like I promised you, George," he added.

George bowed his large head and presently he gave a bellows sigh from his barrel chest.

"I'm sorry, Peevey," he said, "that I mistrusted you had a mind to hold out on me." He shook his head as the jug was held out to him. "No," he said, "you can carry it."

"Carry, hell!" and there was a spirited twang in Mr. Peevey's voice, followed by the *plunk!* of a drawn cork. "There ain't going to be any more slip-ups or misunderstandings. I told you we'd throw away the cork once we was done with *her*—" and the cork arched through the air like a silver fish diving into the black depths of the pit— "and right here and now we're going to drink her dry! Better'n sittin' in a car seat anyhow. Better'n sittin' to home. Licker's always better without women around, somehow."

George rolled an eye at the pit. "We could," he offered uneasily, "sit on the chain across the road."

He was answered by a gurgle in the course of which he leaned wearily against the marble block of the pedestal and somewhat later, for comfort, hooked an arm over a corner of the pedestal. Finally, the gurgling stopped.

"Since you don't want any," said Mr. Peevey in breathless explanation of his discourtesy in drinking first.

"*Well,* now . . ." said George and extended his hand. He raised the jug to his nose and breathed deeply. "A quart *and* a pint?" he asked, and despite his basso profundo it was the voice of the child who asks to be told about Santa Claus again.

Mr. Peevey hooked an elbow over the opposite corner of the pedestal and relit that pipe which had, earlier, gone as cold as his heart on discovering that the jug was not with them. By the unhurried gurgle which came to his ears, as of a contented brook, he knew that he was not pressed for time in making his reply.

"Near kills me," he said, his pipe aglow, "when I think I was a growed man with a grandchild afore I learned what a

difference that pint makes. Allus afore," he resumed after
pushing down a sulphurous eruption in the bowl with his
thumb, "like all the other dumb damn people around here,
I *only* softened a jug by putting in *one* quart of applejack
afore fillin' her up with hard cider. But that *other* pint—!"
He reached out his hand because the gurgling had stopped.

George sighed, and the long hot blast was very comforting to Morgan's marble toes.

"Peevey," he said with another sigh, and Morgan curled
up her toes to thaw out their under sides, "Peevey," he
repeated, but being a man of basically unreliable character did not sigh again, "Peevey . . ." he said a third time,
feelingly, and let it go at that.

A gurgling stopped and George pushed his hand along
the edge of the pedestal.

"I know," said Peevey, surrendering the jug, "how 'tis.
You could sworn you seen me take it away with us afore."
He tried, just for a change, blowing into his pipe instead
of sucking on it, and it made pretty little eruptions of
sparks in the bowl; the longer a man lived the more he
learned about enjoying life, although there was a trick or
two he'd misremembered somehow. "That's how memory
is," he concluded philosophically, reaching for the jug on
the instant of silence from the jug.

George pushed his elbow down the side of the top of the
pedestal and propped his head against his hand at the moment that Morgan had reached the utter end of endurance.
If she tried to hold her arms up and out in front of her one
second more she would either fall on her face or be strick-
en with petrification. With a smooth, unhurried movement
she put her hands on her icy hips, and had folded wings.

"It's a fact," George confessed, and in his subterranean
voice it seemed a profound one? "It's a fact, Peevey," he
repeated his confession, and it would have cost him fifty
to a city psychiatrist, "it's a fact," he confessed.

Mr. Peevey nodded understandingly. "Memory," he said, weighing the bottle, "almost gone?"

"For a fact," said George, raising his head from his hand, but then only to jerk his thumb upward instead of looking up, "I don't remember this stachoo."

Mr. Peevey lowered the bottle and looked up.

"I," he twanged, "remember it. Particular," he specified, "them hands on the hips. Jes' like my old woman would be if we was havin' this li'l drink to home."

Beginning with the toe on which he was breathing, George looked at the toe and then the ankle and then the calf of the leg and then up and up and out and up again and then abruptly bowed and emphatically wagged his head.

"These artist fellers," he said in deep disgust. "Whoever saw a woman as looked like that?"

Mr. Peevey sighed spiritedly. "Well," he said, "a man can hope, can't he?"

"Not," said George, in true New England spirit, "extravagantly." He reached.

"Well," Mr. Peevey conceded, deftly withdrawing the jug, "there may be more than strictly necessary, but I'm damned if I'd complain!"

In reaching, and again vainly, for the bottle, George's hand brushed Morgan's leg. He shivered.

"My God," he said, "stone's cold, ain't it?"

"What," asked Mr. Peevey, "do you expect? Steam-heated stachoos?"

"Well, make good business for plumbers."

"My cousin," said Mr. Peevey thoughtfully, "he's a plumber."

"Better tell him about it." Reaching, he missed again.

"Well . . ." Mr. Peevey tipped the jug . . . "No. He's never thrown any business my way."

"Don't tell him then."

"Won't."

"Serves," said George, with another vain try, "him right."

"Sure does," agreed Mr. Peevey. "Been waiting a long time to get back at him, too."

George saw the jug sidling up Mr. Peevey's arm. Since there was no way to stop it short of mayhem he said, in honest envy, "That pint!" But, to his natural surprise, he saw that the jug had miraculously stopped.

"It's somethin'," Mr. Peevey agreed with a complacent smirk. "I just saw a shiver go over this stachoo."

"You never did have no head for licker."

"Good as yourn!" cried Mr. Peevey indignantly. "Drunk more, that's all."

"Then," said George complacently, "give me the jug."

Thus neatly out-maneuvered, Mr. Peevey surrendered the jug and angrily knocked the dottle from his pipe on Morgan's toe. She kicked involuntarily, instantly, and instantly froze as Mr. Peevey's pipe went through the air and into the pit below. Mr. Peevey's eyes slowly, and with a terrible reluctance, went to that marble foot that now stood in the air between his head and that of George; and the eyes of George slowly, and with a terrible reluctance, went to *that* that now stood between his head and that of Mr. Peevey.

Slowly, but with that horrible determination of men who must know the worst, their eyes moved to the ankle, to the calf of the leg . . . and in that ultimate crisis Morgan remembered that she was an angel.

"Peace on earth," she announced in a clear, sweet tone, "good will towards men!"

Mr. Peevey cleared the pit at a single bound, and if the greater initial inertia of George's greater weight made him second in the crossing of that Rubicon the greater momentum of his greater mass soon made it a dead heat.

"Don't look back," came back Mr. Peevey's voice in a cry of warning, "or you'll turn to a pillar of salt!"

Morgan's errant foot wabbled back to the pedestal and she sank, like a broken icicle, to the posture of a runner on the mark. Moving behind a Pilgrim Mother she had seen a substantial figure that could be only that of Zenobia Beal. Then she heard someone running at right angles to the direction in which Mr. Peevey and George were running, and it was a man and he stopped short on the other side of the pit, his head wagging from side to side as if unable to make up his mind whether to look after the running men or at her; and as usual in those cases she won. He looked at her and he was Mr. Zolicopher Hay.

As he opened his mouth to speak bright orange flashes came from the stone blunderbuss that was pointed at her, and as a runner who hears the signal gun Morgan started running and it was only incidental that it was straight out into the air and with her eyes tight closed. First her feet and then her posterior came into contact with a slope of soft earth and then she was brought to a stunning stop at the bottom of a dark pit rimmed with moonlight.

Into that moonlight lurched Zolicopher Hay and leaped upon her. She fought like a demon and presently and wildly found herself on top and at approximately the same instant realized that he was dead. Something hit the back of her neck and she looked up with a frozen scream of horror at the moonlit slope of fresh-dug earth above the grave. Something brighter than the moist earth was slowly sliding down the slope, something that metallicly reflected and amplified the pale moon's light, and then it fell and the automatic lay even colder than her flesh against her hand. She seized it, and began to claw her way out of the occupied grave.

11

The Yowl of a Barrister. The Aim of a Receptionist.
The Canonization of a File Clerk. The Case of the
Devil's Advocates. The Peril of a Misplaced
Milkmaid. The Accusation of a State's Attorney.

Wm Sultan said, with dignity, "I yowled."

"Ah," said State's Attorney Hastle. He raised weary eyes from the fading brightness of the electric light on the desk of the late Zolicopher Hay and looked at the windows pale with the dawn. "Perhaps," he said, "you'd be kind enough to—?"

"Certainly," said Wm Sultan and, courteously, yowled.

State's Attorney Hastle gave a start and reached, subconsciously, for his shoe although it was still on his foot. Then, checking that movement, he had, as the last notes ripped the atmosphere, a strange impulse to make a rumbling noise in the back of his throat and to rub his back against something.

"Not bad," he conceded. "And then you ran forward to join, as you supposed, Miss Beal?" Wm Sultan inclined his head. "And you say that you did recognize your assailant?"

Wm Sultan again inclined his head. "I was satisfied as to her identity in my own mind," he said. "In the fraction of a second before it went blank," he added precisely.

"On a glimpse of her," Hastle said monotonously, "in the moonlight, as she was turning the far corner of the springhouse, and although you had mistaken another glimpse of her for Miss Beal only a few seconds before,"

"I consider it," Wm Sultan said, and as if that ended the matter, "quite likely that there had been on that first glimpse a subconscious recognition which the conscious mind brushed aside under its conviction that the only female who could be abroad was Miss Beal, but on the second glimpse the impression was sufficiently reinforced to overcome the erroneous preconception. My receptionist," he said, "has a certain lithesomeness in action that is rather distinctive."

"And," said Hastle, his eyes still on the window pale with the dawn, and stacking his flat words one on top of the other like breakfast pancakes, "you woke up hearing pistol shots?"

"Two," Wm Sultan said precisely. "But with the impression that they had been preceded by others."

Hastle poured a little sweetening on the pancakes. "And," he said, "although unarmed, you made your way towards the sound of the pistol shots?"

"After," Wm Sultan corrected, "bathing my face in the brook that flows from the springhouse."

"Ah yes. You were alarmed by the shots, fearing that something might have happened to Miss Beal or your receptionist, and so you stopped to wash your face and comb your hair."

"Precisely," said Wm Sultan. "The stimulus of icy water is excellent for dispelling the groggy, woozey or slap-happy aftereffects of a blow which has induced unconsciousness. There is little to be gained," he pronounced pedantically, "in staggering upon a field of action in a semi-comatose condition."

Hastle nodded thoughtfully, smacking his lips. "And you were standing by the grave," he said, "when you were picked up in the light of the officer's motorcycle."

Wm Sultan inclined his head. Hastle stared at its covering of sandy hair.

"That's not much of a bump," he commented casually.

"My head," said Wm Sultan, raising it, "is notoriously hard."

Hastle let it go. There it was, like a hair in the syrup, and you might not like it but there was nothing you could do about it.

"And you had no idea that Mr. Hay was in the grave?" he asked.

"I had," said Wm Sultan, "no idea that the corpse of the late Mr. Hay was concealed by the darkness in the excavation."

"In fact," Hastle polished it off, "you had no idea that Mr. Hay was even out of the house?"

"I had," Wm Sultan agreed, "none."

Hastle sat back in his chair, making a brushing motion with his hand on the desk top as if pushing aside an empty plate.

"Thank you, Mr. Sultan," he said.

"Not at all," said Wm Sultan, rising. "Please consider me entirely at your service."

"I will," said Hastle.

II

"I've done a bit of shooting," said Roberts.

"Ah!" said State's Attorney Hastle.

"And played softball."

"Ah."

"And tennis."

"Hum."

"Lacrosse."

"Oooh."

"Socker—hockey—basketball—and swordfish spearing," Roberts concluded. She gave her wide, fine smile. "But who can't talk a good game of golf? You still pay off on the score. Let's dry up this nineteenth hole and go outside. I'll wait around the corner and you run towards the corner. Four gets you five I can hit you four out of five before you can take a second step around the corner—with anything you want!" she added generously. "Clods—bricks—bullets—"

"I'll take your word for it," cut in State's Attorney Hastle.

Roberts shook her head doubtfully. "I don't know as you should," she said. "I think you'd feel better if—"

"I doubt it," cut in Hastle again, shuddering. "But," he said, "as I get the picture, you timed his approaching steps—let fly—and beat it."

"Right."

"You never actually saw the—" and thinking of Wm Sultan he thought of the right word—"ah, missile strike the, ah, target?"

"No, Bossy," said Roberts, looking at the pearling dawn.

"*What?*"

Roberts started. "Sorry," she said, "something you said . . ." Then Roberts got it and inside her head, so to speak, she shook her head. *So he's got you going, too,* she thought. *Ba-bee! You got to hand it to grandpappy, he's sure got something. He creeps up on you. Like brandy Alexanders.*

Hastle cleared his throat like an angry housewife sweeping a hall with an old-fashioned broom, in a series of dusty explosions.

"So you could not," he said, "testify under oath that the billet of stovewood did in fact hit him?"

"I didn't see it," said Roberts, "but I heard it."

"You heard it hit *something.*"

"*Clug!*" said Roberts.

"We have been over the scene," Hastle reminded her. "On that side of the springhouse there is a passage approximately four feet wide between a cord of stovewood and the stone wall of the springhouse. Could you testify under oath that the sound you heard could not have been that of the billet you had flung striking either the wall or the stack of wood?"

Roberts looked at him level and hard. "If you think I'm that inaccurate," she said, "come outside."

Hastle moistened his lips. "Or," he said, "one of the projecting roof beams of the overhanging eaves?"

Roberts was honest and Roberts looked away from him. Because of the weight of the missile and the expected height of the target she had given it a fairly high trajectory.

Hastle smiled and sat back in his chair.

"Thank you," he said. "That will be all just now."

III

"Like," said Morgan, drawing up her foot with its band-aided toe, "one of Washington's soldiers at Valley Forge!"

"Ah," said State's Attorney Hastle. "A true labor of love."

"We all," Morgan nodded vigorously, and her red curls catching the first rays of the rising sun glowed like the vigorously stirred embers of a fire, "*all*" she repeated emphatically, "love Mr. Sultan!"

"Ah!" said Hastle.

"Like—" and her green eyes searched for it—"like—" they narrowed, then suddenly widened in perception—"like a dear, young grandfather!"

"Ah-hah-ha-hum!" commented State's Attorney Hastle.

"*And,*" said Morgan, leaning over the desk, "I saw her sneaking around behind a Pilgrim Mother with a Child in her arms and a Hoe in her hands and a Pumpkin at her feet!"

Hastle nodded patiently. "You showed me the memorial statue," he reminded her. *"Another Wellborn Attley, 1652-1683.'* With a child in her arms," he repeated, "and a hoe in her hands, and a pumpkin at her feet. A pumpkin at her feet—practically on the ground."

A true employee of Sultan, Sultan & Sultan, Morgan looked pained. *"Virtually* on the ground," she said.

"At any rate," said Hastle, in his turn leaning over the desk, "the effectiveness of the memorial group largely lies, does it not, in the fact that it rests upon a pedestal that rises only a few inches above the earth and gives the impression of the pumpkin growing there right on the ground!"

Morgan nodded and wagged a finger at him. "Just," she said, "like the *Pilgrim Father* with the big-mouth shotgun."

"Just," Hastle agreed, "exactly! And there are," he coaxed, "a great many monuments and figures, aren't there?"

Morgan wagged a finger at him. "I don't know," she said confidentially, "when anything's ever made me so homesick! It was just like being on the platform of the IRT at Times Square at the rush hour!"

Hastle nodded sympathetically. "And you're not very tall," he said.

Morgan's green eyes narrowed. "I've never had any complaints before," she said.

"Of *course* not!" declared Hastle. "I was only thinking that your view must have been greatly restricted?"

"It isn't the size of the total," Morgan persisted grimly, "that most men are interested in."

"Neither," said Hastle, removing his glasses and wiping them and then putting them on again, "am," he said, "I." He sighed, but reluctantly, bringing himself back to official business. "The only thing I've been wondering," he said as casually as a, general recommending war, "is how you were able to see so much when you were surrounded by non-transparent objects."

If on her earlier questioning Morgan had side-stepped this point of view as one which her discouraged experience with the world had told her would appear out of focus to those with weak imaginations, she knew when the time had come to stop dodging and to walk right up on the pedestal.

"I was an angel," she explained simply.

State's Attorney Hastle had in his time dealt with a variety of witnesses, he had in his time met many interesting people, he had in his time heard most stories; but this, this, was a First. Since he had absolutely no idea what to think, much less to say, he, with rare presence of mind, did not say it. And not only did he not speak, he did not think. He was, in a vague sort of way, thankful that there were no candles on the desk. That should have presented a problem, and, frankly, he did not feel up to the particular problem that this would be.

"I," kindly explained St. Morgan of the Files, perceiving his perplexity, "climbed up on the pedestal and was a marble angel."

Like the rising sun slowly came the dawn of reasoning perception to the mind of the state's attorney, illuminating the obscure, revealing the cryptic.

"Valley Forge," he said, cryptic in his own turn, and chuckled somewhat. And then, as all became quite clear, he laughed outright. "And that," he said, "is why no one saw you!"

"Yes," said Morgan.

Laughing, State's Attorney Hastle said, "That, I hope, will be all!"

IV

"Not a soul a-stirrin'!" said Mr. Peevey.

"Ah," said State's Attorney Hastle.

"Not," rumbled George, "a soul."

"Kind of late, wasn't it?" asked the state's attorney.

"Why?" asked Mr. Peevey.

Hastle started to speak, stopped, shook his head. "Damned if I know," he admitted.

"That," said Mr. Peevey, philosophically, by which is meant the usual serene superiority of a thinker admiring his own notions, "is the way it is. Man and boy," he continued, making something impressive out of that not too unusual development, "man and boy," he repeated impressively, "for forty year, I've been a-diggin' out where you lay 'em in. I've dug dry," he reflected, "and I've dug wet. I've dug hot, and I've dug cold. I've dug summer, and I've dug winter, I've dug spring, and I've dug fall."

He looked at an ashtray on the desk contemplatively, and then with a judicious but reluctant shake of his head went to a window and opened it and disinfected a flower bed with that nicotine solution so injurious to aphids. He returned to his chair at the desk.

"I've dug morn," he resumed, "and I've dug noon. But the only respectful—and profitable—time to dig's at night. Ain't right the kinfolks of the deceased should see you a-sweatin' and a-cussin' to git down the hole." Mr. Peevey crossed his legs and his swinging foot thumped against the desk in accent to his words.

"A grave," he pronounced, "should be like an Act of God—there it weren't, and there she be! And asides," he rubbed his hands, "you can't count on it as regular occupation. Not around here leastwise where folks dies mainly in bunches in February. Where—" he demanded, leaning forward and slapping the desk with his hand—"is my competition? Where's Buckins? Where's Kent? Where's Dewey?"

He shook his head with the commiseration of a crocodile. *"Day-diggers,"* he said significantly. "Buckins," he amplified, "became an eleven-month loafer a-waitin' for Februaries. Kent, he couldn't keep it up no more, not from workin' in the livin' daylight and a-thinkin' of death all day—only time to think of death's at night! And Dewey? You know what happened to Dewey!"

Hastle nodded sadly.

"Got," said Mr. Peevey, not letting it slip, "so's he could talk about it less and less until the older he grew the less he could talk at all until at last—how many years it been now since he's passed the time of day?"

Hastle shook his head and then nodded emphatically.

"Absolutely right!" he said. "Only time I'll ever dig a grave's at night! Let's just consider that settled. Now boys, we found a cork in the grave, and a pipe, and alongside the mound a gallon jug that from the smell of the earth around it must have had something in when it was thrown away. Now you know me, hell, I'm just Old Hastle you boys took mercy on and gave a job to—ha! ha!—when he sure needed one, and can take it away from him any time he gets so uppity he thinks he can step on your toes without—ha! ha!—getting' kicked in the seat of the pants! Ha, ha!— But, hell, boys, just how did all that happen?"

"Why," said Mr. Peevey, giving George a silencing look, "it's pin-money to me, that's how. Only pin-money. Like my old woman's egg-money. Come along a deceased and I goes and buys a quart *and* a pint and pours her into a gal and fills her up—this time of year, and it's the best one!—with a little hard cider, and sticks a cork in, steps on it, and finds a friend, and don't pulls her out until *she's* six by seven by two and a half! But, then, raisin' her up and lookin' down at *her,* you get some mighty amusin' thoughts. Now that cork, it was from the jug; that pipe, hell, you could smell it buried *eight* feet deep, been promi-sin' my old woman seven years now I'd throw it away some day; and that jug—gawmighty, Hastle, there was only *two* of us! We'd just simple plain had plenty when we gave her a toss and walked away."

Hastle nodded. "Officer Gurney says you were going down the state highway about sixty when he stopped you and took you back."

Mr. Peevey grinned. "We'd had a couple," he reminded the state's attorney. His face sobered. "Yes," he said, "and George and I had heard the shots as we walked down the cemetery road to the car—and whatn'ell would you expect anybody to do under those circumstances?"

State's Attorney Hastle again nodded and again under-standingly.

"And you didn't see anyone at all while you were in the graveyard?" he asked.

"Not a soul a-stirrin'!" said Mr. Peevey.

"Not," rumbled George, "a soul."

"I take it," said the state's attorney, "that you boys took your sip right alongside the hole?"

"A-leanin' on a block of marble," affirmed Mr. Peevey

"Alongside the hole," said George, his basso-profundo making it deep, deep, deep.

"I've seen the very stone," Hastle said encouragingly, his voice taking on a twang in compliment to Mr. Peevey's and a bass-viol note in compliment to that of George. His brows puckered as one who cannot quite remember. "Any-thing on it?" he asked.

Mr. Peevey did not even need to look at George nor George at Mr. Peevey. Born and bred in a rural community where a slip of the tongue, like the slip of a plow from the straight line of a furrow, may and will be remembered—and not uncommented upon—from a male's adolescence to his senility, neither had to exchange signals to know that there was on a drunken aberration, fancy or hallucination which neither would ever be such a complete fool as to admit to any human, living or dead.

"On it?" said Mr. Peevey, and shook his head. "Bare's a baby's bottom, far's I remember." He looked in innocent inquiry at George.

George furrowed his heavy brows.

"Barer," he said.

"Ah," said State's Attorney Hastle. "No," he offered with a chuckle, "angels?"

Mr. Peevey also chuckled. "Not more'n six or eight," he said.

George rumbled subterraneously. "Ten," he said. "I counted ten balanced one on t'other like acrobats!"

V

"Like Run-sheep-run," said Zenobia Beal, "or Hide-and-go-seek!"

"Ah," said State's Attorney Hastle. "Then," he continued, "you weren't taking Mr. Sultan's precautions seriously? And that's why you didn't wait where he'd told you to wait?"

"Of course," said Zenobia Beal.

"And?" asked Hastle.

"And those two—you know them, Mr. Peevey and George —they were feeling warm and I didn't want them to know I was there—knowing how they talk, like who doesn't around here! it's enough to make a body move to the city where people never talk about those they know—but after they started down towards the state road together I slipped over towards where they had been and then came those terrible, horrible, *wicked* shots!" She put her face in her hands. "Aimed right at me! Like you saw," she reminded him.

Hastle nodded. "The baby in her arms," he affirmed, "has an elbow knocked off and the handle of the hoe is knocked through." He considered the scene. "Plumb through," he pronounced.

"And poor, dear Zolicopher!"

Hastle nodded.

Zenobia Beal's voice was a whisper of remembered horror: "He suddenly stepped out from behind one of the monuments, and just as I started to speak to him then came those terrible, horrible, wicked shots—and I saw him stagger—and then I looked at where I'd seen those wicked flames—it was so *close!*—and then they flashed at me and I heard them strike beside me and I jumped behind the statue and then I ran like mad back—" she looked at the room pitifully—"home."

Hastle nodded. "Did you," he asked with a smile, "see any angels in the graveyard?"

"Of course," said Zenobia Beal, in covert criticism of his obtuseness since he had been there to see for himself, "it's full of them!"

"Ah," said the state's attorney, "but did you see any of them *move?*"

"Mr. Hastle," Zenobia Beal said, deeply hurt, "maybe such things were seen by Mr. Peevey or George but *I* hadn't been drinking!"

Hastle nodded absently, his eyes on a sheet of note-paper on the desk.

"Mr. Hay," he said, "hadn't informed you that he was going to go out of the house?"

"Oh, no, sir!"

"And so your presence there was due solely to this note from Trumbo which you had found in your room?"

"Yes, sir."

"And you had it with you?"

"Oh, yes, sir!"

"Thank you," said State's Attorney Hastle in dismissal.

VI

"I was at home all evening," said Trumbo Gates.

"Ah!" said State's Attorney Hastle.

"After," Trumbo said with a quick, hard smile, "I once got home."

"Ah," said Hastle.

"Sure," said Trumbo Gates. "You ought to know. Shouldn't you? One of your little boys burnt a lot of gasoline following me around all evening!"

"Umm," said the state's attorney. "And," he took off his glasses and put them on the desk and leaned his elbows on the desk and massaged his face with his hands, "suppose you tell me again about your date with Mr. Hay."

"There's little to tell," said Trumbo, "as I've told you." His young, dark and violent face turned towards the young, bright and immeasurably peaceful day that shone through the window. "I don't," he said "like this—lawyer. Yes, I'll admit it, you know as well as I do that Willy's been shooting off his head all over town and a party-line telephone about what this—lawyer—did to me at the station the other night." His face turned from the window. "All I'm telling you, Hastle, is this: I can't let myself be around that man—or there's one killing you wouldn't have any trouble in solving."

Hastle nodded. "I'm not blind," he said.

"All right then," Trumbo said. "That's been the way things were. Now there was something Zolly wanted to talk over with me, I don't know as it makes any sense yet and so it's none of your business, but he brought it up this afternoon when you were here—" he looked again at the window, the white peace of the dawn accentuating the dark passion of his face—"or yesterday afternoon now," he corrected himself, "and I told him I was damned well going to drive a good ways off from Cobb's Mill and try to forget the whole lousy business for a few hours. He said it could keep, so we arranged he'd walk over to my house at eleven o'clock and thirty minutes." He smiled thinly. "Zolly was kind of exact about time."

Hastle nodded, rubbed his eyes again. "Walk?" he asked through his fingers.

Trumbo's dark lips bared his white teeth. "With a motor-cycle cop in front of this place and one in front of mine," he said, "the state road didn't seem so good."

Hastle nodded.

"Zolly was hell on time," Trumbo said again. "So, since I was going out to have a couple he insisted I give him a buzz about ten to let him know if I'd for sure be home and reasonably sober. So I did, and everything was still all right with him then, and I sat around and waited with a bottle until I heard the shooting."

Hastle nodded, caught himself, and stopped. There would not be much mechanical, bored agreement in what was to come.

He said, as if trying to remember, "Your house is on the same side of the road as this one, isn't it?"

Trumbo Gates nodded, his white teeth again showing in his dark face.

"And I could have gone out my back door," he said, "without being seen by your little leather puttees boy on the road, and I could have gone up to the cemetery and met Zolly halfway and bumped him off. In fact, since you haven't mentioned it at all, I imagine he was shot with that Luger I brought back from overseas, wasn't he? Gave it to him as a souvenir—far as I know he always kept it in the bottom drawer to your right there."

State's Attorney Hastle obediently opened the drawer, not for the first time, since he had questioned the house-hold help, and not to his surprise did not find the auto-matic. He shook his head and looked up from the drawer.

"Yes, Trumbo," he said, and without warning his voice was suddenly as deadly as a gun, "and one of the oldest mistakes a murderer makes is trying to act too innocent, so innocent he tells things against himself. *I* agree with you. You could have gone out the back door and up to the graveyard and waited to kill Mr. Hay and Miss Beal together."

Trumbo Gates threw back his chair. "Zenobia!" he said, standing over the desk. "And how would I know she'd be there?"

"By," said Hastle quietly, turning a sheet of paper around so that the other man could read it, "this." He smiled thinly. "You look surprised," he said, "and imagine my surprise. I've been wondering what else you could do except look surprised. Of course, if you'd killed her, you'd have been able to recover the note, as no doubt you planned. But it's hell to try to be a successful murderer, Trumbo, when you're a poor shot!"

Trumbo's fist struck the desk with crashing violence.

"Damn you!" he cried. "I never wrote this!"

State's Attorney Hastle rose wearily.

"So it isn't your handwriting?" he said wearily. "Oh, why be a fool?"

He found himself pulled over the desk by hands on his shoulders. He looked into a face convulsed with rage.

"Yes!" Trumbo Gates cried in his face. "Yes, it's my handwriting! *But I never wrote it!*"

12

*An Emotionally Disturbed Barrister and a
Shocked Secretary. Helpless Victim! Female
Fury. Strange Actions of a Secretary. Inspired
Allurement of a File Clerk. The Secret of the Silo.*

It was by mid-morning of that fair and warm October day
very quiet at Fairview Farm. The road on which it faced
did not have an automobile route number and was lightly
traveled even in the summer, and not at all on this October
morning, the authorities detouring all traffic to another
road that ran behind the Attley holdings, behind the hill
to the north. In creating this island of peaceful seclusion
in a countryside that was, as more than one newspaper
would describe it, "seething" with excitement and curiosity, State's Attorney Hastle was moved only by the high
motive of upholding the dignity of the law. He was not, by
his public statement, quote:

"He was not going to permit any three-ring circus with
the members of the bereaved household exhibited like
freaks in a sideshow!" unquote.

In this high motive he had the full support and co-op-
eration of the governor of the state . . . and incidentally
of that most politically influential chain of newspapers

controlled by the Peabody-Pitkins Trustees, and in particular that dialectic dietitian, Waldo ("Bull's Meat") Wickerworker.

That Trustee's fellow member of the Codicil Club sat
in his chamber receiving his secretary. The extreme formality of his manner was proper not only to the gravity of
the occasion but it also, Wm Sultan felt, might help her,
like a ritual, to accept with dignity a somewhat shocking
situation. At least he was of the opinion that she would be
somewhat shocked when she learned that he was as good
as convicted for the murder of Zacharia Attley and Zolicopher Hay. He felt, himself, somewhat shocked by it.

He had been writing at the desk provided in the guest
chamber that had been assigned to his occupancy, when
Kelly had entered the open door. Her color, or absence
of color, and her expression, or her rigid absence of any
expression, had told their own story of her experience in
stepping off the train into the arms of the police, in having
her briefcase of the late Zacharia Attley's papers and sun-
dry letters relative to the case impounded by court order,
of learning that his scheduled funeral had been postponed
because of another murder and, *ipso facto,* another corpse;
it had told of groups of staring people, of a nerve-wracking waiting until a telephoning back and forth and hither
and yon had gained her a permission for, and a polite police conveyance to, Fairview Farm, where awaited her the
still Surviving Partner of Sultan, Sultan & Sultan.

Since he had been informed of her imminent arrival,
in the ordinary course of things Wm Sultan should have
in advance, as a matter of course, drawn another chair
within a discreet distance of his own so that his anticipated employee would not be kept standing for perhaps
several seconds after her arrival; but as it was in his mind
that, although she knew it not, this interview was to be
in the nature of a farewell, and since in that circumstance

he trusted her own strength more than his own, the idea seeming to have discovered in him an unsuspected weakness of character, a strange, angry reluctance to accept the facts of life that was a weakness excusable in children and young female persons but shameful to a man. In its essence, since he was disconcerted by this shameful weakness and mistrustful of its good behavior, he had decided that it might be just as well if he had something to do, like moving a chair, when she first entered the room. That way, he had cleverly figured, he would not have to look at her . . . Only because, of course, *she* might be upset and it's always embarrassing to have someone, even anyone, look at you when you are upset.

By this careful calculation he had upon her arrival gone to the furtherest corner of the room and had picked up a chair and had carried it in front of his face and had set it down at a discreet distance from his own chair at the desk, and then had walked the three discreet paces to his own chair and had sat down and with a graven and gravely courteous smile, suitable to the mortality of the season, and had looked at an interesting point two inches over the top of her head and had begun telling her the facts of life, and death, as they had transpired in the course of her absence.

He concluded, and not in ill manners but in that quintessence of good manners which is quite willing to appear boorish if it contributes to the ease of another person, he did not look at her on his conclusion but turned his eye back to the desk and added two or three lines to the paper that he had been writing on her entrance. He continued to move the pen, thoughtfully, if not to write with it, until she spoke.

"You say," Kelly said tightly, "that they've sent for a handwriting expert?"

"Ah, yes, yes, yes, yes—" Wm Sultan put down his pen and faced her, his self-control expressing itself in a look of frigid disinterest—"yes! That is to say, Ah, no, no, no, no, no!" he corrected himself when he thought about it. "Handwriting experts," he explained, "are, like all mystics, gentlemen of unquestioned probity whose interpretations *only* are subject to the highest bidder. But," he coughed, "there is a group of amalgamated technicians who make documentary analyses, and since their report is based upon physical proof instead of forensic opinion they are consulted by clients throughout the world when there is some desire to know the actual facts instead of favorable fancies." He coughed again, and it was a modest one. "At my suggestion," he coughed modestly, "Mr. Hastle—a very cleverly cautious young man, I might add—" even if Kelly winced that the gentleman in question was five years older than the speaker—"consented to call in the 'Bureau of Documentary Certification,' in our city."

Kelly faced it, her chin up. "I don't know why," she admitted, "but I can see you think it'll be proven that Trumbo did *not* write it."

"If he had," Wm Sultan said, "it passes belief that he could be so inane as to deny it."

"But—forgery—" Kelly said, raising her fingers to her temples—"*forgery!* Good heavens, it takes skill, craftsmanship, like engraving or etching or—"

"*Tracing,*" said Wm Sultan. "The exact words of the note proposing the assignation," he continued, "were: 'Dear Zenobia—I must see you privately and we can straighten out the acknowledgment of your claim—meet me at 11:30 tonight at the family cemetery—and make sure that Mr. Sultan doesn't suspect. Trumbo.'" He had accented certain words and seeing her widening eyes he nodded in affirmation. "Rather reminiscent, isn't it?" he agreed.

"But it doesn't make sense!" Kelly cried distractedly. "What's the necessity? Why should—"

Wm Sultan, determinedly looking two inches above her, well-remembered however, head, said gently, "You've had so little time to consider this that, perhaps, you haven't had a chance to reflect that, with this note a forgery that forgery has an essential and similar corollary."

Kelly looked at him with honest blankness, unwilling to admit that which in fact she did not perceive.

"No," she said stubbornly. "No matter which way you take it, it's still completely contradictory!"

Wm Sultan coughed as only an author, insisting upon conveying the honor of a first glimpse of his brainchild, can cough. It was a cough that was that cough in which modesty and pride are intermingled as indistinguishably as the sexes on Broadway.

"While the household and your fellow members of the staff have been sleeping," he said, "I've whiled away the time by writing out a little précis of the case—a mere nothing telling who did it and how—that you might, ah, find amusing to peruse." He thrust it into her hands.

Kelly read and, reading, felt the greatest amazement and the most deadly fear she had ever known. The pages fell like snowflakes from her numbed fingers into her lap, that extension of stretched fabric between and over her paralyzed thighs. Paralyzed or not, she rose upon them and crossed that area of discretion which he had placed between their chairs.

"But—" she said—"but, Bill!" and with complete indiscretion she reached out a hand and embedded its fingers in the bones of his shoulder. "But there must be something you can do! You must show this to Mr. Hastle!"

Wm Sultan smiled gently. "I have never," he admitted, "practiced criminal law, but I find it incredible," he said stoutly, "that it should ever accept logic in preference to evidence, properly admitted in accord with the laws thereof."

Kelly, being feminine, did not appreciate this beautiful logic which was to result in his innocent conviction for murder. Women are so unreasonable!

"*Thereof,*" she said turning away from him, "and *whereas!*" She turned back to him. "Then what *are* you going to do?" she cried.

Wm Sultan crossed one dark worsted knee over the other and looked at his reflection on the toe of one black boot. The tip of a bony finger absently explored the knot of a black and gray striped tie.

"It's quite a simple thing, really," he said to his reflection on the toe of his boot. "An apparatus, or gadget, of some sort that X-rays or violet-rays or some sort of rays the deposit of ink left by the point of the pen. I really don't know whether Hastle sent operatives into New York to have it done there the first thing this morning, or whether—but in either case I'm quite certain that by noon it will be demonstrable that Trumbo did not write the note of assignation. I have," and Wm Sultan pointed the mirror toe of his boot at the précis which had fallen from Kelly's lap to the floor, "essayed to outline the means by which, so to speak, heh! heh! the links of the chains by which I am to hang have been forged."

"Bill—!" Kelly said.

Wm Sultan was careful not to look at her. "But," he said, inserting his dangling foot into a beam of morning sunlight and catching a dazzling gleam, "there is absolutely no iota of admissible proof of my contentions. Truly," he said, and that white morning's sun seemed the essence of truth, "there must have been in existence for some time conclusive evidence of the identity of the perpetrator of the foul deed, or deeds," he amended, looking out the window, and away from Kelly, with frozen calm. "But that evidence has, of course," he admitted calmly, "long since been destroyed."

Kelly stood staring at the précis on the floor. Kelly continued to stand staring at the précis on the floor.

Wm Sultan coughed. "I have—ah—been giving some thought," he said, "to the—ah—future circumstances of the—ah—former staff of our offices. I appreciate," he said, scowling at a scuff on the bottom of the heel of his boot, "that it's a serious imposition upon young working women of good character to receive a recommendation from an—ah—convicted murderer. And I've been thinking that as some slight recompense for that injury—if it meets with your approval?—that perhaps a severance pay of—ah—shall we say?—a sum equal to the average annual wage of the staff, prorated of course according to the individual variations from the average, projected, shall we say? five years into the—"

Wm Sultan never finished that projection because one side of his jaw went so far to the other side under the impulse of a slap that speech was quite impossible.

He saw, through vibrating eyes, Kelly pick up the précis from the floor and he saw Kelly walk from the room and he saw Kelly slam the door, but his ears were still ringing too much for him to hear it.

II

Long and blond, Roberts followed her petite and brunette companion, she followed her because had she hung back she would have left a forearm in the other's grasp. She followed her through the deserted kitchen, the domestic staff having since early morning barricaded themselves in the third floor behind a supply of cider ample to withstand any reasonably protracted homicidal siege, and Roberts followed her out the back door and around to the side of the house.

"Boost me in that window," Kelly commanded.

"Look, Kelly—" began Roberts.

"Boost me in that window," Kelly said, very quietly.

"Sure, sure!" said Roberts. "Sure," she added, opening the window. "Sure!" she said, boosting Kelly into the window.

"Thanks," said Kelly, standing inside the window.

"Sure!" said Roberts, breathing freely only when Kelly went out of sight from the window.

Kelly looked at the green carpet of the bedroom, and the white chalk-marks had not yet been carpet-swept or vacuumed away. She looked at the other window to the room, the wrong window through which Wm Sultan's "murderer" had escaped. She resolutely swung open the door of the bedroom, and tried not to look when, opening, it swung over the chalk lines that marked what had been the position of Zacharia Attley's legs. She stood, for a moment, staring at the brown study, and trying to keep her eyes from that small white circle on the rug which marked where had been found a certain quarter-dollar. She did not, however, look at the pictorial representations of bananas on the walls.

Instead, she quickly weaved her way between the herd of great brown chairs and put her hand upon the doorknob of the first set of doors to the adjoining office. That was what made it so awkward; that Zacharia Attley, for undisturbed repose in his study, and probably a study of bananas, had had double doors installed between his studious sanctum and that residential office where occasionally there might be the rustle of a paper or the click of a typewriter key. If anyone were in the office . . .

But, so far as Kelly either knew or could surmise from what she had seen, there was only one state police officer at Fairview manor and he was sitting in the hall ostensibly to answer the telephone, which was ringing, approximately, every four minutes. It was reasonably deducible that State's Attorney Hastle, before taking a spot of shut-eye in the ten-room-and-one-bath hostelry of the Cobb's Mill

Inn & Restaurant Bar, had reached the sensible conclusion that, from the murderer's point of view, things had reached the irreducible minimum. Mr. Trumbo Gates had retired to his bachelor cottage, Zacharia Attley not having been altogether a fool, on the Attley property for a little long-interrupted sleep; while in the manor house there remained only Zenobia Beal and Mr. Wm Sultan. Under those circumstances the least of State's Attorney Hastle's worries would seem to be that anyone should attempt to bump anyone else off: there comes the point where one from two leaves only one.

Kelly opened one set of doors and just as resolutely opened the second set and entered the residential office of the late Zolicopher Hay. She went to the desk and searched among the multitude of papers that encumbered it. She found what she sought. Without waste of time she also found an envelope and another sheet of paper, and still without waste of time she tore the flap of the envelope into four pieces and she took a pen from the desk and she went to a window through which stood that bright and innocent morning sun; and with cold chills running up and down her back, despite the warmth of the room, she pasted the two sheets of paper on the windowpane and traced upon the outermost what the refulgent rays of the autumn sun revealed was written upon the one beneath.

The telephone rang outside in the hall, and the officer answered it; and Kelly removed what she had pasted on the window, and she reclosed the double doors to the study, and she climbed out from the bedroom window into Roberts' arms; and Roberts reclosed the window, and Roberts followed her forearm that was caught as in a trap by the fingers of Kelly.

And Kelly said, "We can be hung for this, but . . ."

"O.K.!" said Roberts, when Kelly concluded. "Consider it done."

III

"Get in the front seat," said Kelly, "and drive to This Trumbo's. And," she added, curling up on the floor in back, "if you so much as glance back here may *somebody* have mercy on your soul!"

Morgan backed the car out of the garage and turned it with only one simple and practical question.

"Will the cops shoot?" she asked.

"No," said Kelly, from the floor. "Tell the guard at the road that you're going to Mr. Gates' house and he won't stop you. Turn into This Trumbo's driveway when you get there and the guard on the road there won't stop you. Get it?" she called, and was startled as the brakes of the car squealed to a stop.

"I've got to go see Mr. Gates for a minute," she heard Morgan say as if suddenly struck by a terrible reluctance. She then heard her add, like a kid called away from dinner, "But I'll be right back!"

A masculine voice said, as if swallowing, "I'll be here until four o'clock."

"Oh," she heard Morgan cry, "how nice!" and the car lurched in a turn and sped away. "Kelly," came back a small voice, "I think there's something I better tell you before—"

"Before," Kelly snapped from the floor, "we get to This Trumbo's, you might learn what you're supposed to do! Park this bus so one side's turned away from the road where the state cop's on guard. *And get Trumbo to take you upstairs!*"

"But Kelly," Morgan protested as the car slowed for another turn, "how?"

"I," said Kelly, "am a dirty name. *Etchings,* you dope!" she hissed as the car came to a stop.

Clear and cool Morgan called, "Yoo-hoo! Trumbo! Have you got any etchings?"

"I," said Kelly to herself, "am a dirty . . ."

"Well!" called a masculine voice, and from kind of high up in the air, it seemed. *"Well! . . . I'll be right down!"* it added.

"Oh, don't bother!" called Morgan, flinging open the car door. "I'll be right up!"

"Well . . ." said Trumbo Gates from his bedroom window in a tone of awe, and perhaps suspicion.

Morgan laughed. "Can't make a millionaire walk downstairs!" she called, entering the house.

"Well," Kelly heard Trumbo Gates say complacently if cynically. *"Well!"* she heard him repeat in complete satisfaction and acceptance of this new state of his affairs; and not for the first time Kelly wondered at the genius of Morgan.

She quietly opened the rear door of the car on the side facing the house and, bending low, scurried in the front door which Morgan, and again she wondered at the genius of Morgan, had left open. In the hallway Kelly looked back. On the road the motorcycle officer was staring at the road and slowly but with resolute envy, the honest sort that will not deny its own existence, he was shaking his head. It was perfectly clear that he had no intention of looking at the bedroom windows in the sensible fear that he might see something to make him more envious.

Upstairs, Kelly heard Morgan's voice:

"Oh! But those aren't *etchings! That* one's a woodcut, and *that* one's an engraving, and *that* one's . . ."

Kelly looked into a dining room with presumably a kitchen behind; she went to the opposite side of the hall and entered a living room, crossed it to a study-office-den or what-have-you, behind, a room with two books, one glass-topped desk, one radio-phonograph, twenty-four or -five feet of record albums, one either 8 or 16 mm.— and frankly she did not give a hoot which—film projector

facing a screen over a cold fireplace in which lay the black-
gray death of paper and of wood . . .

In the car again, Kelly calmly reached a hand over the
back of the front seat and honked the horn.

"The horn!" she heard Morgan stage-whisper in pretty
dismay from in back of the bedroom window. "Oh, I must
go down, someone must be there!" There was a pause and
then there was the sound of footsteps and then Morgan
called up worriedly from beside the car, "I can't understand it. But—" another stage whisper—"the cop on the
corner's getting ideas!"

"The hell with him," came Trumbo's voice, and it was the
voice of one of those men who is a perfect grouch until he
has had his breakfast, and, in this particular instance, had
had it attractively served and then snatched away from him.

"I'm sorry!" sobbed Morgan and threw the car into
gear. "You know," she said, after the car had turned into
the driveway of Fairview Farm, "if you hadn't honked—I
was *almost* prepared to make *almost* any sacrifice, Kelly!"

"Don't talk to me!" cried Kelly, the words torn from
her by the thoughts that were screaming inside of her; but
that was a very serious error.

IV

Tenderly fondling his cheek, as he felt not without justice that its former tingling had been an accolade to his
labor-relationships, Wm Sultan stepped out of the house
for a breath of air and, perhaps, a sight of that employee
who had so emphatically impressed her loyal partisanship
upon him. He stepped out the kitchen door as, towards
the front of the house, he heard an automotive engine
receding towards the public thoroughfare, and somewhat
piqued by this departure of a conveyance from the placidity of Fairview Farm, which placidity he well understood
was like that of the prison of a goldfish bowl, he started to

turn the corner of the house to see who might be departing
when he had his further arm violently grasped and found
himself spun around to face his agitated receptionist.

"Bossy!" Roberts cried. "Come with me!" and started at
a dead run for the barn.

Under these departing circumstances, making a quiet
and considerate discussion so difficult, Wm Sultan replied
by following her at a dignified pace for three steps, and
then indulgently breaking into a dog-trot for four more
before in simple masculine pride he felt called upon to put
on a slight burst of blinding speed to overtake her; with a
result that after the very slightly blinding burst of speed
he just began to run like the devil to keep her from getting
out of sight. He saw her enter that doorway at the barn
on the other side of which on a previous occasion he had
had such an interesting discussion of silage with Zenobia
Beal; and on now entering it he found Roberts pointing
dramatically up the ladder of one of the silos, though not
the one from which he had previously seen the silage fall.

"UP!" cried Roberts. "Morgan has fallen *in!*"

An odd lot of memories went through Wm Sultan's
mind as he soared to the top of the silo. He recalled on
the night before having met in the upstairs hallway, as she
had sneaked in from the back stairs, a bedraggled, carrot-
topped angel who had held one hand behind her back and
very little before . . . He recalled green eyes glittering at
him over a stack of yellowed letters, and he recalled a hand
sweeping those letters from a desk to the floor below . . .
And, from an utterly deplorable series of events earlier
that summer he recalled . . .

And, from his youth, Wm Sultan recalled a former silo
of his acquaintance. Quite different from this, an affair
of decayed wood, bursting at the seams, so to speak. This
recollection was, somehow, mixed up in his mind with a
recollection of a long-wool sweater that seemed to have

something to do with the urgent cries that came, in Roberts' voice, from below his feet:

"Morgan! . . . Up! . . . Morgan! . . ."

"*Up* Morgan!" he repeated to himself, taking the rungs of the ladder with the alacrity of a monkey with a blowtorch on its tail. "Up *Morgan!* Down *Modest Sweaters and How to Knit Them!*"

But there was no sense of humor in the heart of the last of the Sultans, and as he climbed, he had to shake his head to knock some water out of his eyes. Silos, he reflected, were notoriously damp . . .And, to judge by the height to which extended the doors, this one had not been tapped yet . . . Then how could Morgan have fallen far? . . . Unless . . . He turned his eyes from the automatic silage unloader that hung from the top of the silo like a tarantula over the top of its hole, and peered down into the silo. Close against one side of the silo, in its deepest shadow, was that thing which so few years before he had seen so often and so horribly, that inert thing that looked like a flung bundle of clothes . . .

But why in heaven had they put the doors so high above—

"Morgan!" Roberts' voice called at his heels. "Morgan!"

Wm Sultan swung himself over the door to the inside of the silo, hung a fraction of a second, let loose and dropped another ten feet—at a rough, round figure. The sawdust in which he landed brought back very clearly that recollection of a summer in his youth: new silage, untapped and bedded down against spoilage . . .

He was, during this time, picking himself up and flinging himself to that bundle of clothes— Oh, no, no, no, *no!*—which he had seen from above. He fell to his knees beside it and found that it was a bundle of clothes. He looked up, *up,* at Roberts, and he found that Roberts was not there.

13

The Houdini Gambit. The Rabbit in the Air. The Head
of the Bureau of Documentary Certification. A Window
Shade and What It Reveals. An Innocent Country Girl.
A Licentious Lawyer and His Jealous Gun Moll.

The Associated Press representative was, as usual, weary. It had been precisely twenty-seven years and three months and nineteen days before that he had first become weary with the routine publicity tricks of prosecuting attorneys. As chess players give names to the routine moves of certain gambits, *King's, Queen's, Cunningham's,* so in weary familiarity he knew Hastle's moves in the present case as the *Houdini.* It was the one where the prosecutor acts very mysterious and tells the press nothing and then with the air of a conjurer completing a trick pulls the culprit out of a hat.

Consequently, when State's Attorney Hastle announced that he was making an arrest the AP man excitedly stifled a yawn and said, "Goody, goody, and when do we see the big white rabbit?" He continued to yawn when he was informed that orders had already been issued to bring the still unnamed white rabbit to the courthouse. But when, a half hour later, he was informed that the state's attorney had just sneaked out a back door of the courthouse and had been driven away at an illegal speed, the AP man brightened up and enjoyed his best laugh in two days. Even a wearisomely old trick can become quite amusing if something goes wrong with it.

What had gone wrong, although this was not known to the AP man, was that the white rabbit had taken a walk into the thin air right out of the state's attorney's hat.

II

When Roberts came to the bottom of the silo she dusted her hands, quietly and slowly opened the door to the barn, saw nothing but female Holsteins, went quickly to the far end of the barn, slipped out a door there, and, unobserved, went around in back of the barn and, still unobserved, entered the orchard. She came out of the orchard just in time to see a car drive into the old carriage house, and presently Morgan walk out of the front of it and Kelly sneak out of a door in the rear. Roberts cast a glance at the top of the nearer silo and shook her head. Bossy had certainly not been taken for his walk in the woods any too soon. She circled thumb and finger and saw Kelly's sigh of relief. Kelly also circled a thumb and finger and Roberts sighed with relief.

"Have time to tell Morgan?" she asked as Kelly joined her.

"*When?*" Kelly asked, and replied, tartly.

"Cheese it, the cops!" said Roberts softly. Two state policemen had come into view beyond the garage, were walking towards the barn. Roberts started walking, pulling Kelly along with her. "Laugh," she said. "I've just tried to but can't."

Kelly laughed.

It was heard. "Hey you!" came a hail from the state policemen, and they stopped in innocent surprise and awaited interrogation with the clear, steady gaze of those who have prepared their stories in advance. One of the men was a lieutenant of state police. Lt. Kipps was a big man with a hard eye and a flat voice. When he came up to the two who awaited him one look at those innocent expressions and into those honest eyes warned him that something was wrong somewhere.

"Where," he asked, "is Mr. Sultan?"

Roberts shook her head. "I haven't seen him for a while."

The police lieutenant gave Roberts a hard look, a hard look that told her she was being given a hard look.

"You were seen entering the barn with him," he said flatly.

Roberts nodded. "Took a look at the cows," she said, "and after recovering from the excitement went outside again and saw Kelly in the orchard." Kelly nodded. "She wanted to come back," Roberts continued—

"But Mr. Sultan felt like more of a walk—" Kelly chimed in.

"And so," Roberts concluded, "we came this way and he went thataway."

The police lieutenant nodded. "Bert . . ."

Bert nodded and started into the orchard.

"Just tell him I want to see him."

"Yes, sir."

Roberts smiled at a windcloud in the clear blue sky and dropped her eyes from the cloud to the top of a silo and then looked into Kelly's smiling eyes. *Yes, sir, Bossy hadn't been taken for his walk into thin air any too soon.*

III

The door opened, and it was the first thing that happened in an hour, and State's Attorney Hastle strode into the green parlor. He looked at the sofa where, side by side, still and tense, sat the members of the staff of the fugitive; he looked at the chair in the corner where shrank Zenobia

Beal; he looked at the other solitary chair where scowled
Trumbo Gates. He turned to Lt. Kipps of the State Police
and another man who had followed him into the room.

"Mr. Lane," he said, introducing a scholarly-appear-
ing little man with large tufted eyebrows, "is the head of
the Bureau of Documentary Certification in New York City.
For your information," and his eyes held the three on the
sofa, "it was Mr. Sultan himself who suggested the Bureau. Early this morning," he continued more generally, "a
representative of my office flew to New York by chartered
plane. Some two hours ago I received a telephonic report
and ordered that Mr. Sultan be . . . But now that Mr. Lane
is here there's no need to await the apprehension of the
fugitive before settling other matters. Mr. Lane, would
you please explain to these people just what you found?"

Mr. Lane had opened a briefcase. He removed a sheet of
paper and said, "This was submitted to us for determination of the authenticity of the handwriting. It reads, 'Dear
Zenobia I must see you privately and we can straighten
out the acknowledgment of your claim meet me at 11:30
tonight at the family cemetery and make sure Mr. Sultan
doesn't suspect Trumbo.' The texture of the paper—" he
held it up to the light of a window—"is very thin and a
superficial examination suggests tracing which," he continued, without taking a breath, and detaching a long cyl-
inder from the outside of the briefcase, "an enlargement of
a violet-ray negative supports by physical evidence."

With a deft gesture he unrolled it like a window shade
on the laps of the three who sat on the sofa, and Zenobia
Beal and Trumbo Gates rose from their respective chairs
and stood behind the sofa. The penstrokes of the handwriting were nearly as wide as a pen, but thin in texture as
if made of black chiffon. A glass wand that had once been
an Old Fashioned cocktail stirrer pointed at a dense black
dot in the center of the curve of the opening "D."

"In free-handwriting," that breathless voice went on that had held so many juries breathless, "the pen does not halt, hesitate or go back in the middle of a stroke. The pen that wrote this did so halt." The wand tapped a dozen other arcs and loops that showed other such dark indentations or, in more than one case, narrow dark ruts side by side within the pale width of the penway. "But in tracing," the voice did not pause, "it is not possible to follow the large loop or curve without hesitancy or back-tracking. These records of the varying pressures of the pen, of back-tracking and hesitancy left by the variable depths of the deposit and penetration of the ink are the physical record of such a tracing."

The window shade was rolled up.

"Well," said Trumbo Gates. "Well, well, well!"

Zenobia Beal put her hand to her mouth. "But—then—who?" she whimpered.

Hastle smiled, and Trumbo Gates smiled, and Lt. Kipps smiled, everyone smiled except the three who sat on the sofa and, perhaps, Mr. Lane, who was busily engaged in untying another window shade from his briefcase. He again rolled it out on the laps of the three on the sofa. They sat as still as if it were a cobra.

"There was also submitted to me," Mr. Lane said breathlessly, "these two pages in the purported holograph of one Zacharia Attley comprising a codicil to a will. You will observe," and the glass wand pointed like fate, "the identical stigmata of tracing which you saw before."

The window shade was whisked up like those on a city street when a fire engine has been heard outside. Mr. Lane refastened it to his briefcase.

"But I didn't!" suddenly cried Zenobia Beal. "It must have been that *wicked* man!"

State's Attorney Hastle took a turn up and down the room and then began speaking as he took another. "From the start," he said, "Mr. Sultan's guilt was obvious. It also appeared obvious that his motive must lie in a collusion with you. And yet," he said, raising his chin and his eyes as a man who is determined not only to see but to believe in the better things of life, "and *yet,* I could not believe that one of our own sweet country girls, raised in the pure atmosphere of—the country—could be guilty of such sly, calculating and heinous intentions against one who had been the benefactor of her grandfather, her grandmother, her father and her mother."

"No," Kelly interrupted firmly, "I don't believe any man could be such an ass. But then, of course," she remembered, "he's a politician."

Hastle gave one quick glance at the couch, and in that glance was something that suggested that he was very far from an ass, but, oddly, that glance was directed at Morgan and not at Kelly.

"The solution to the enigma," he continued, taking another turn up and down in front of them, "is found in the following simple convincing chain of events. An attorney of an old, a very old, and an honorable, a most honorable firm, trades upon that very fact to enable him, literally, to get away with murder. An innocent country girl calls at his office with facsimiles of what, in his legal training, he well knows are untenable pretensions to a great inheritance. But he concludes they may at least confuse, if not deceive, a lonely senile old man for a few hours—and that will be enough."

Morgan's face was slowly becoming the color of her hair.

"Now," Hastle continued, "it *does* so confuse the victim, supported, as it is, by the transparent honesty of the simple country girl whom he has known since her birth! And he writes a letter to his attorney asking him to call at his earliest convenience to give his advice, and then, as

the importunance of the affair impresses him more he calls
that attorney on the telephone—just as that attorney had
foreseen!—and requests his immediate presence. And the
attorney does come here, and murders him, and seizes and
destroys the trifling evidence, and then the next day mails
another letter to himself in the envelope in which he had
received the first!"

"Addressed to New York, and received here," said Kelly.

"No," said Hastle, "received in New York by a member
of his office staff who brought it to him here the next day!"
And now he looked full at Morgan. Morgan was breathing,
hard, even though Kelly and Roberts had, now, virtually
stopped breathing.

"He mailed a letter," Hastle continued, "which he had
prepared in advance by *tracing* from the handwritten notes
which Zacharia Attley had brought to him a year ago on
the occasion of having drawn his last will and testament!"

He flung out a finger at Zenobia Beal. "You've stated
there were such notes!"

"Yes, sir," she quavered.

"And though you told Mr. Gates and Mr. Hay about
them did either of them ever see or have their hands on
them?"

"No, sir. I burnt them."

"The preliminary drafts!" Hastle affirmed, and faced
the couch. "And this second enclosure which the attorney
mailed in the envelope was a 'codicil' to the will granting
him complete control of the fortune for nine years and a
little bonus of fifty thousand dollars! But—with his legal
mind he knew full well that to prosecute him for murder
was impossible when that prosecution, to prove necessity
or motive, should have to prove that documents which had
been destroyed had not in fact been authentic, and that a
man who was dead had in fact changed his mind about a
codicil which he had written to his will! Only now, with

that codicil a proven forgery, a tracery which only he could have made, that proof does exist!"

"Oh, the *beast!*" cried Zenobia Beal.

Roberts started to rise, but Kelly pulled her down. Morgan took a deep breath and opened her mouth to speak.

"What did your cousin," Hastle pointed a shaking finger at Trumbo Gates, "what did your murdered cousin, Zolicopher Hay, tell you yesterday afternoon?"

"That he wanted to have it examined for forgery."

"And what did you tell him?"

"I thought he was nuts and said so."

"Why?"

"I recognized the handwriting. He wanted to talk it over more, but I was fed up with the whole mess and wanted to get somewhere else and have a few drinks, so I told him I'd be at home about eleven-thirty and the rest of it."

"And whom did he suspect?"

"I told you I thought it was nuts," Trumbo evaded, and then said, "Zenobia."

"Exactly!" cried Hastle. "Then he had no reason to fear mentioning it to Mr. Sultan?" He did not need to wait for a reply. "*There* it is!" he cried. "*There* it is," he repeated in quiet and chilling conviction. "Mr. Hay *did* so mention his suspicions to Mr. Sultan and told him of his appointment later with—" he had to look over his shoulder because he was facing the sofa—"you. And now what could that lawyer do? What except murder the man who had this fatal determination and, for good measure, have you blamed for it!"

Then Hastle looked at Zenobia Beal. "I assure you," he said kindly, "you were never in any danger. A couple of shots were placed *near* you to make it look as if Trumbo had tried to dispose of all rivals to the estate, but you were the last person on earth that Mr. Sultan would have harmed since in case of your death he would have lost control of the estate!"

"Oh, the *beast,*" said Zenobia Beal again, and then sprang backward as Morgan, breathing heavily, rose from the sofa.

"So she's so innocent!" Morgan said. "Where's the gun? That's what I'd like to know, where's the Murder Weapon?"

Hastle looked at Lt. Kipps, and Lt. Kipps opened the door and said, "Bert."

A state policeman entered.

"Did you, some two hours ago, make a search of the house for the murder weapon?" Hastle asked.

"Yes, sir."

"Did you find a Luger automatic?"

"Yes, sir."

"Had it been recently fired?"

"Yes, sir."

"How many bullets were missing from the magazine?"

"Four, sir."

"Where did you find it?"

"Under the mattress of the bed in the room occupied by Miss Zenobia Beal, sir."

Zenobia Beal screamed.

"Yeah!" said Morgan.

"While the members of this household were having coffee *earlier* this morning," asked Hastle, "did you make a search of the house for this identical murder weapon?"

"Yes, sir."

"Did you find it?"

"Yes, sir."

"Where?"

"Under the mattress in the bedroom occupied by—"

But his words were cut off as Morgan cried, "Ooops!" and clasped her hand over her mouth.

"Oh my God," said Kelly.

If she'd only told us she was going to frame her, thought Roberts despairingly.

Hastle nodded, but he was a nice man, married twenty years, three children, one married, and he did not smile or feel like smiling.

"That," he nodded, "is the missing link. A girl in love with her boss." Roberts caught Kelly's arm as Kelly started to rise. "The messenger who brought Zacharia Attley's original letter. The girl who saw her lover and another girl—" he looked at Zenobia Beal—"leave the house together last night and who, in jealousy, followed them. Who saw the murder and saw who committed it. *The only person on earth to whom the murderer would entrust the still loaded murder weapon!*" Hastle shook his head. "No doubt," he concluded sadly, "she had been ordered to plant it on the premises of Mr. Gates, and that's why she called on him today, but her womanly jealousy overruled her instructions and she tried to ruin her rival!"

Morgan sat down again.

Hastle again nodded, "Above any question or question of a question," he said, "this gun business proves the complete innocence of Zenobia Beal and the complete guilt of that licentious and unscrupulous lawyer who made his file clerk his gun moll!"

14

*An Incredible Discovery. In the Center
of a Hurricane. Fatal Proof. A More Startling
Discovery. Sultan's Harem United Again.*

Kelly said, "I'm deeply shocked. Aside from the fact that it's going to make it hard to get another job when one's last reference is from a murderer. He was really," she concluded, "very inconsiderate."

Hastle was not in the least fooled. With her white, tense face and her stricken eyes Kelly could, just then, have fooled anyone under the age of two and a half. *The dirty dog,* was Hastle's thought. *The trifling, licentious* and *dirty dog.* A fine young woman, this, and completely convinced by his presentment of the case! She was handing him something.

"I think you ought to see this," she said, "just to learn how plausible he was. He gave it to me when I met him in the orchard, and practically accused him—" her voice broke.

Hastle said, "Certainly," and taking the two sheets of note paper sat down in a chair and read them. He heard her say, stubbornly:

"Mr. Lane, perhaps I'm stupid, but if both of these things, the note and the codicil, were traced, they had to be traced from *something,* didn't they?"

"Yes," Mr. Lane said in a breathless sort of sympathy, "that's what I meant by saying that a superficial examination of the note indicated tracery." He put it in her hands. "As you can see," he continued, "the sequence or occurrence of the size of the words is abnormal—I mean," he pointed out, "that there's no regular graduation of the size from the beginning to the end of a line—but that without rhyme or reason one word will be appreciably larger or smaller than those on either side of it—or a phrase will so begin—"

"Oh, Good Lord!" Kelly cried. "I know where he copied this from! Last evening he—Mr. Gates—brought in a written account of the funeral arrangements—"

Trumbo Gates jumped from his chair. "Yes!" he cried. "That's it! Why I didn't think of it before—'Cemetery'—'Dear Zenobia'—'11:30!'"

Hastle looked up from the précis. "Where?" he asked.

"We were in the office!"

Lt. Kipps looked at Bert and Bert left the green parlor. He directly returned with a sheet of paper. Hastle again looked up from Wm Sultan's précis and indicated Trumbo Gates.

"For identification, Mr. Gates," he said.

Trumbo Gates glanced at the sheet of paper. "That's it," he affirmed.

Hastle indicated Mr. Lane and returned his attention to the précis. Mr. Lane took the report on funeral arrangements and the assignation note to Zenobia to the window. He turned from the window.

"Yes," he said, "there's not a doubt the note was copied from this."

Hastle was shaking his head and smiling, and, shaking his head and smiling, he looked around for some place to throw the précis and, finding none, put it in his pocket. He deliberately stopped smiling when he looked at Kelly.

"Yes," he said, with a grave nod, "a very brilliant deduction, as one might expect, and very carefully incapable of any evidential proof—or disproof!" He looked at Mr. Lane. "That's it, then," he said. "Mr. Hay, incapable of suspecting such an old and honorable name, told Mr. Sultan of his suspicions that Miss Beal might have forged the codicil—and of his intended meeting with Mr. Gates. And while no one knew better than Mr. Sultan that she was innocent no one knew better that once it was proven a forgery he was a lost man. So he forged the assignation note to Miss Beal, and left it in her room, in order to have Mr. Gates blamed for the crime."

Kelly was not listening to him; her entire attention was concentrated upon Mr. Lane, whose entire attention appeared to be concentrated upon that sheet of paper bearing the report on the funeral arrangements.

A breathless voice said, "Mr. Hastle, may I see you privately for a moment?"

And when State's Attorney Hastle and Mr. Lane left the room Kelly began, very faintly, to breathe again. She was very pleased that Mr. Lane had discovered for himself that that report was, incredibly, a tracery itself; for since she had made it herself from the original in the office across the hall that morning she felt that it was ever so much better that she had not been compelled to be active in its discovery.

II

A general alarm occasions a hurricane of police activity; and as with that agitation of the natural elements the most peaceful spot is in its center, so the most undisturbed spot within the area of the siren-shrieking hurricane of the general alarm was the interior of the No. 2 Silo at Fairview Farm.

The air was quite still. It was also silent. And the as usual ambient atmosphere was infused with only that twilight light that is permitted to penetrate into an ensilage container at even midday. The thieving rays of the sun, were they permitted to enter directly, like they had a key to the joint, would swipe some of the carotene content; therefore they are kept out and the carotene in. Just like Wm Sultan.

He could appreciate, dimly, a bad practical joke, and as far as practical jokes went he could and would admit that this one was not more moronic than the mean average. To be lured to the top of the silo by the false and surprisingly painful intelligence that an accident had befallen one's file clerk, to be induced to hang by one's hands and then drop into the interior of that silo by a pitiful, a heart-rending bundle of clothes below, to find that that bundle of clothes was in verity only a bundle of clothes, and then to discover that one's inducer into the enterprise had abandoned one, that the ensuing and continuing silence gave clear notice that she was not busy at opening one of the lower doors, and they could be opened only from without, to find, in short, that one's most generous and gentlemanly sentiments had been given the works, *that* was, he realized, the idiot's delight of a practical joke.

A man of patient temper, as he frequently reminded himself, he realized what had happened to him for at least ten seconds before he became murderously angry. But, as he well knew, the purpose of a practical joke is to make the victim angry, trusting to *his* decency not to give you your just deserts, and Wm Sultan was doubly distilled damned if he were going to give Roberts the satisfaction of discovering that he was in the least dismayed, disturbed or discommoded. He sat down on the bundle of clothes and smoked cigarettes. It was not until an hour and a half had gone by, and he had smoked his last cigarette, and the air which had not been refreshing to begin with was becoming stifling, that his outraged pride cooled down enough for him to forget it for a minute and find another explanation for his situation.

When, sensibly, it occurred to Wm Sultan that his staff wanted him out of the way for a while, that in short his situation was neither practical nor a joke, his blood ran cold because if he could not flatter himself that he knew his staff, past experience *had* given him some faint inkling of their potentialities. Wm Sultan rose and, before he took off his coat, spent some five seconds in an appraisal of the situation. The inside of the silo was as smooth as the inside of an egg, and the only exit was not far from twenty feet above his head.

He took off his shirt and tied the cuff of one sleeve to that of one cuff of his coat. He took off his trousers and tied the cuff of one leg to that of the other sleeve of his shirt. He took off his undershirt and he took off his shoes. He rolled his shoes in his undershirt, knotted it into a compact bundle with one end of a jersey sweater that had been part of the bundle of clothes, knotted the other end of the sweater to a cuff of his trousers. There was a useless skirt in the bundle of clothes because it was of heavy wool and with a knot in either end there was little length left between, but there were useful stockings which, after removing the straw, he tied in tandem to the free cuff of his coatsleeve.

With the shoes as the weight he began swinging the cumbersome clothesline around his head; and yet it was on only the twenty-seventh attempt that the shoes went through the aperture and only his hold on the nylons prevented the tail of the kite from following. He walked to one side and pulled and jerked until the knob of shoes was caught in the angle between the bottom edge of the opening and the side of the silo.

Hand over hand, Wm Sultan went up his clothesline quite quickly, straddled the partition, dropped his clothes down the tube that gave access to the silo, quickly followed them. At the bottom he untied knots and redressed.

III

They sat in silence while outside in the hall voices murmured and outside the house cars departed and cars returned. It was an eternity in tension and less than a half hour in actual time before State's Attorney Hastle marched back into the green parlor followed by Mr. Lane and Lt. Kipps.

Hastle said, "Before Mr. Sultan's disappearance he gave into the hands of his secretary these sheets of paper." He took them from his pocket, unfolded them. "I am," he said, "going to read certain excerpts from them." He adjusted his glasses and read aloud:

"*Since Mr. Gates denies having written the note addressed to Miss Beal and found by her in her room, I have no doubt but that it will be found to be in fact a forgery. To be more specific, a tracery made from a report on the funeral arrangements written by Mr. Gates. The inevitable corollary of this is that the codicil will also be found to be a tracing . . .*

"*But since the late Zacharia Attley did himself tell me over the telephone that he had in fact written and given to be posted to me a codicil in favor of his newly discovered great-granddaughter, Miss Zenobia Beal, it was in fact written . . . and taken by the murderer from the table in the hall . . .*

"*But the situation of the murderer on the day following the crime was one of extreme danger because the absence of the codicil, as I pointed out, meant that neither Miss Beal, nor as an accomplice myself, could have had any motive in committing the crime . . .*

"Silence!" Hastle suddenly thundered. "I'll have no interruptions!" He resumed reading:

"*This problem was brilliantly solved by, and as far as I know it is an accomplishment unique in the history of*

forgery, the turning of an authentic document into a forg-
ery simply by tracing it! . . . By this masterpiece of trickery,
motive is given to Miss Beal and myself and made even more
deadly when the 'forgery' is later 'discovered!' . . .

"Because while I do not question that the note received
by Miss Beal is a tracery of Mr. Gates' handwriting, we have
here the brilliant opposite of the trick with the codicil, we
have a self-forgery achieved by him tracing his own handwriting!"

Trumbo Gates was standing quite still, and that immo-
bility in that violent man was startling.

State's Attorney Hastle continued reading: *"At the time*
of making his written report on the funeral arrangements
he could not know the exact situation which would be in
existence the following evening and therefore could not have
traced the note to Miss Beal at that time. The various hours
mentioned in the report—10:30—11:30—12:30—were to
give him a later choice, and he had only to trace the report
in full and later trace the note from that copy."

Hastle refolded the pages and put them in his pocket.

"All right," Trumbo Gates said. "Fall for that line if you
want to. But try to prove it. Try!"

Hastle said, "Mr. Lane, will you tell us something about
the report on the funeral arrangements which Mr. Gates
identified as the one he gave to Mr. Hay?"

Mr. Lane raised the thin sheet of paper to the light of
the window. "It is," he whispered, "an obvious, a patent
tracing."

Trumbo Gates struck his fist on the back of a chair and
the chair fell over.

"It can't be!" he cried. "It's impossible!"

"Not impossible," snapped Hastle, "just careless! You
happened to get the copies mixed up, Mr. Gates, and gave
the wrong one to Mr. Hay!"

"Prove it! Try! Try!"

Hastle looked at Lt. Kipps. With a pair of tweezers Lt. Kipps was taking charred scraps of paper from an envelope and putting them on the table.

"And what," Hastle asked, "were you able to determine from those scraps of paper, Mr. Lane?"

"That they once composed the original from which this tracing was made."

"And where did you find them, Lieutenant?"

"In the fireplace of the living room of the residence of Trumbo Gates."

"You lie, damn you!" Trumbo Gates cried, almost inarticulate with rage. "You've framed me! There weren't any scraps left when—"

Roberts screamed. Wm Sultan was standing in the doorway.

Whether, to Trumbo Gates, it was the unendurable sight of that attorney who had been his Nemesis or a belated recognition of the confession which had been in his own last words, it was unquestionably the distraction occasioned by the appearance of that erstwhile fugitive from a silo, like a white rabbit out of a black hat, that gave Trumbo Gates the opportunity to escape from the room by going through a side window, carrying the glass with him.

On the driveway a police car roared to life and went down the driveway at a speed that made what would happen to it when it tried to turn into the stone-walled road a foregone conclusion.

IV

Wm Sultan's staff sat stiffly on the sofa tightly holding hands; and Wm Sultan benignantly stood beside the chair of Zenobia Beal.

"I shall submit the forged codicil," he assured her, "as a *true copy* of the original!" And at Hastle's startled look and then comprehending expression he experienced that sublimely smug satisfaction peculiar to a man of the law who anticipates making a spot of unique legal history. There was, he had to admit it to himself, no doubt about it: Sultans were hell on codicils! He was on the point of flicking an imaginary speck of dust from the cuff of his coat when he saw that there were, in fact, grains of sawdust in the corrugation of the wrinkles, and he gave Roberts a hard look.

"I think you're wonderful, Mr. Sultan!" said Zenobia Beal.

Hastle gave her a hard look. "We do change our opinions, don't we?" he said, and made friends for life of Kelly and of Morgan and of Roberts. "For my part," Hastle continued, "I'm free to admit that when I first read this—" he again had the précis in his hand—"I did so with a very skeptical eye. Oh, not as to the mechanics of the murder of Mr. Attley," he continued. "I'd seen that it was possible that Trumbo had hastened back to the house, waited until Miss Beal had gone into the front hall to tell you that Mr. Attley would see you, had then stepped into his bedroom and struck him down without a word, removed the documents which he knew to be in his dressing-gown pocket, placed the body in such a position that it looked as if it had been dragged in from the study and opened both windows. Then, when he was set, had blown the fuse with a quarter, had opened the door in the dark, moving the legs out of the way and then replacing them, holding you back in the meantime by having, just as you thought, cocked a revolver. And, believe me, Mr. Sultan, I'd foreseen that he could have rolled the quarter into the study! And it had even occurred to me, that if he had opened two windows in advance, and then went out one of them and closed it after him, that when you later entered the room and found one window open you would assume you had heard that window raised. But there wasn't any *proof!*"

Witt Sultan coughed modestly. "I had the advantage of you," he said, "in knowing that I was innocent. Consequently after Mr. Hay had been murdered and Mr. Gates denied having written the note to Miss Beal—once the thought of forgery entered my head—everything became rather obvious. It even seemed a little unlikely that the possibilities of these various tracings would occur to anyone unless he had had some past experience in forging. Then, of course," and his cough made a mere nothing of it, "I recalled having noticed the name of the Bureau of Documentary Certification in Mr. Hay's personal address book."

Wm Sultan looked at Mr. Lane and Mr. Lane looked at Wm Sultan. "It seemed obvious," Wm Sultan continued, "that Mr. Hay must have consulted you about some suspected forgery. I then recalled that Mr. Gates was employed in the Cobb's Mill Bank. I also recalled that Mr. Hay had stated that Mr. Attley had not for some years— seven, I believe?—even checked his personal bank account. The opportunities open to Mr. Gates for repeated forgeries appeared striking."

Wm Sultan smiled kindly at Zenobia Beal, who was looking up at him in wide-eyed admiration.

"I then further recalled," he continued, "the extraordinary authority which Mr. Hay appeared to exercise over that violent young man. Now, Mr. Lane," he suggested, "since both the principals are dead, and have no near relatives—?"

Mr. Lane nodded. "Under the circumstances," he whispered, "I don't feel it would be a breach of a client's confidence. Mr. Hay consulted me six months ago about several checks signed with the name of Zacharia Attley. They were tracings. In some instances they had been drawn in favor of and in others indorsed by Trumbo Gates."

Wm Sultan nodded. "That was my conclusion from the evidence, and it made obvious Mr. Gates' motive for the murder of his cousin. Mr. Gates could not profit from his earlier crime until he could prove the codicil a tracing, but the moment that was discovered his cousin would know only too well who was guilty." Wm Sultan shook his head sadly. "A violently ruthless young man," he concluded, "unfeeling, merciless, and with that quick brilliance of mind that so often goes with a violent temperament."

"A wicked beast," said Zenobia Beal.

Hastle's eyes narrowed. "By the way, lieutenant," he said, "there will be no charges against this—" he indicated Morgan—"young woman for having tried to protect Mr. Sultan by planting the murder weapon on Miss Beal." He smiled at Zenobia Beal. "That's all right with you, isn't it," he asked, "now that you no longer think Mr. Sultan is a wicked murderer?"

Wm Sultan took it, he took it like a man. He looked straight into his file clerk's green and glittering eyes until he happened to remember the exhibits on the table and turned to look at them, and incidentally his back on Zenobia Beal, and after sternly blinking his eyes three times he looked at the charred bits of paper.

"Brilliant—yes," said Hastle. "But they always slip up! Giving the tracing instead of the original of that report on the funeral arrangements to Mr. Hay, and then being so unbelievably careless as not completely to destroy his other copy after tracing the note to Miss Beal!"

"He hardly seemed able to believe it himself," Lt. Kipps agreed.

"Incredible," Wm Sultan agreed. "The reason I felt that I was lost was that it was incredible to me that there could be any evidence remain—" his voice trailed off as an icy chill went down his spine.

He stood feeling like an icicle as he looked down at that report on funeral arrangements which Trumbo Gates had given to Zolicopher Hay. He recalled Zolicopher Hay's fingers pleating nervously at the sheet of paper . . . but the one on the table before him had not the mark of a single crease. He saw it then, he saw it all, completely.

He was shocked to the depth of his legal and ethical being that evidence once destroyed had been recreated again and planted upon a murderer. Murderer though Trumbo was, if he had been there he would never have permitted . . . and then Wm Sultan understood that Kelly and Roberts had understood that too. So they had protected him against himself in the silo while they went about . . . Never intending that he should ever know.

"Something wrong, Mr. Sultan?" It was Hastle's voice.

No, and Hastle must not know, no one must ever know that anyone other than Trumbo had forged the links of evidence.

"No," said Wm Sultan, turning, "just a little weak, that's all." He looked at Morgan again, and he looked into Roberts' blue eyes, and he looked into the depths of the dark eyes of Kelly. "Move over," he said, "and let grandpappy sit down."

Hastle laughed as he looked at Wm Sultan and Wm Sultan's grinning staff.

"By the way, counselor," he asked, "what are you going to do with that fifty thousand?"

"I am," said Wm Sultan, "going to set some very worthy and very capable young people up in a picture-framing business."

COACHWHIP PUBLICATIONS
ALSO AVAILABLE

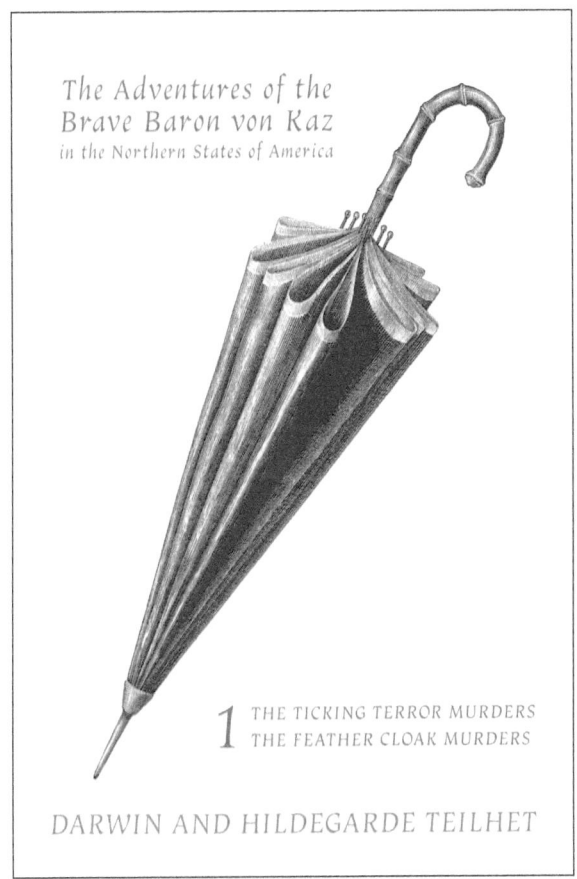

The Adventures of the
Brave Baron von Kaz
in the Northern States of America

1 THE TICKING TERROR MURDERS
THE FEATHER CLOAK MURDERS

DARWIN AND HILDEGARDE TEILHET

COACHWHIP PUBLICATIONS
ALSO AVAILABLE

*Death Has
Seven Faces*

HUGH AUSTIN

COACHWHIPBOOKS.COM (PRINT)
COACHWHIP.COM (EPUB)

COACHWHIP PUBLICATIONS
ALSO AVAILABLE

SCHOLAR TURNS DETECTIVE
IN TWO SOPHISTICATED MYSTERIES

MURDER IN THE ZOO
MURDER IN CHURCH

Babette Hughes

COACHWHIPBOOKS.COM (PRINT)
COACHWHIP.COM (EPUB)

A DIRGE FOR HER

VIRGINIA RATH

COACHWHIP PUBLICATIONS
ALSO AVAILABLE

BLOOD ON HER SHOE

MEDORA FIELD

COACHWHIPBOOKS.COM (PRINT)
COACHWHIP.COM (EPUB)

MURDER

À LA RICHELIEU

THE ADELAIDE ADAMS MYSTERIES

ANITA BLACKMON

COACHWHIP PUBLICATIONS
ALSO AVAILABLE

DEAD
WEIGHT

ADDISON
SIMMONS

COACHWHIPBOOKS.COM (PRINT)
COACHWHIP.COM (EPUB)

COACHWHIP PUBLICATIONS
ALSO AVAILABLE

COACHWHIPBOOKS.COM (PRINT)
COACHWHIP.COM (EPUB)

SALLY WOOD

MURDER
OF A
NOVELIST

DEATH
IN LORD
BYRON'S
ROOM

www.ingramcontent.com/pod-product-compliance
Lightning Source LLC
Chambersburg PA
CBHW020505020726
47493CB00001B/183